...THERE WAS A MUFFLED SNAP and then the sound of the apartment door's eerie squeak. Mary Alice's knees buckled, and she pressed against the wall to keep from falling down into the tub. A band of light swept under the door. She heard steps in the bedroom and something else. Whistling. Raspy, absent-minded whistling.

The bathroom door opened. Through the opaque curtain she couldn't see anything. She concentrated on the soap film she felt beneath her fingers. The whistling continued, but became tuneless. She could almost feel the intruder's heat. The flashlight beam seemed to pass over the bathroom floor tile by tile searching for something. She stopped breathing and remembered the shower ruse in the movie hadn't worked.

The cold tiles chilled her back and her legs ached as she forced her muscles to remain immobilized. The blood pounding in her ears made her think of swimming underwater. Closing her eyes, she imagined she was skimming over the sandy bottom of her favorite cove with ten feet of lake water above her. She wanted to scream...

CANA RISING
A MARY ALICE TATE SOUTHERN MYSTERY
DINAH SWAN

"...Swan's well-drawn characters carry the story, and make this an engaging mystery..."

~Suzanne Tyrpak
Author of *Vestal Virgin - Suspense in Ancient Rome*

"A wonderful, utterly charming mystery as southern as sweet tea and in the great tradition of Sue Grafton. Impossible to put down."

~Blake Crouch
Author of the bestselling thriller *Pines*
and the new series from Fox, *Wayward Pines*

Books by Dinah Swan

Mary Alice Tate Southern Mysteries
Cana Rising
Now Playing in Cana

Women's Fiction
Hacienda Blues
Romantic Fever

CANA RISING:

A MARY ALICE TATE SOUTHERN MYSTERY

Dinah Swan

by

Dinah Swan

CANA RISING
copyright © 2013 by Dinah Swan

Cover Design: Jeroen ten Berge
Book formatting and layout: TERyvisions

ISBN-13: 978-1482328059
ISBN-10: 1482328054

Cana Rising is dedicated to the author's mama,
Patricia Tarr Leavitt

PROLOGUE

"SHEREE, YOU'RE A STOOGE AND a druggie," Scott Bridges said. "You can't just boogie. You want to go to jail?" He eased his gun belt onto the dresser where it coiled next to her pink hairbrush.

"I done my part," Sheree said. "You got two arrests. I'm scared." She looked at her bare feet and the nail polish in bad need of a touchup. She knew he'd be hard to convince, but she also knew her days as a drug informant were dwindling. Pretty soon some dealer was going to put it together, and she'd get nailed. She felt her breath coming fast and fought to stay calm.

"I'm protecting you, baby." He pulled her onto her bed.

"Scott, this part ain't working either." She avoided his eyes by staring at the Cana Police Department badge on his chest.

"It's working for me," he said in his playful bad-boy voice. He leaned back, relaxed and in control.

"I appreciate what you done for me but—"

He sat up. "You appreciate what I done? Do you remember where I found you?"

"Yes, but I don't do that no more and—" She was drowning. She felt like a child arguing with a sadistic stepfather who enjoyed setting her up and trapping her in her own words.

"Lap dances at The Pink Pony?" His voice heated up. "Selling meth in the bathroom to support your own habit? What else?"

"Scott, Georgia Horn says I got a right to an attorney—"

"That bitch runs a women's shelter, not the police department. You talk to a lawyer, our deal is off and you go to jail. You listening?" He grasped her jaw and twisted her face toward him.

"Scott, this ain't TV. It's scaring the shit out of me." She started to cry, and the squiggly mewings she heard herself make frightened her even more.

"I can take care of you." He released her and shifted into his good cop voice. "Sheree, look at me. Tell you what, a month more, or just until the deal I'm working on is done, and I'll get the DA to cancel the informant contract. You can go away. I'll help you." He relaxed back on the bed.

"You swear?" She got control of the tears. She didn't trust him.

"Swear." He ran a finger down her bare arm.

"Scott—"

"Cross my heart, hope to die." He drew an **X** over his heart and raised his right hand.

She sat on the edge of her bed and finished off the fifth of Southern Comfort she'd been sharing with him. The blackout drapes made the room dark, but the clock said four p.m. It was going to be a long night.

"What do you want to do?" she asked. She looked at him sprawled on her bed and tried to remember why she had ever thought he was fascinating. Somehow Scott's games made her feel more used than any of the things she'd done to get drugs.

He sat up close to her and tapped each button on her blouse.

"Well, Miss Delio, ma'am, looks like I'm going to have to strip search you."

She acted her part without enthusiasm; he didn't seem to notice. Afterward, she listened again to his secret drug bust plan. It was coming to a head quick and big fat heads were going to roll, he said.

Later in the blackness of her bedroom Sheree couldn't see Scott lying beside her, but she could feel his heat. She hoped he'd leave the apartment before she sobered up. As she sank into the hazy layers of drunken sleep, she sensed a shadow slide through the dark like hawk wings over the night desert. The compressor of the AC window unit cut in, grinding up the sultry air. Before she passed out, she felt Scott kick her lightly and jostle the bed as he turned.

CHAPTER 1

MARY ALICE TATE KNEW HOW to put on a party. She'd been in training most of her life. But it had taken courage to throw this one. She realized she was the target of gossip: Why had she divorced her successful doctor husband and come back home to Mississippi? Why did she live alone at her late father's lake retreat? Why was she spending all her time with Georgia Horn at Cana's Women's Center?

In fact, the party was a fund raiser for the center. No doubt it seemed odd to some that her reintroduction to Cana society should coincide with the event. But, she reassured herself, at the party everybody would see she was fine. It would be as though she never left Cana. Thirty-five wasn't too old to start over. She was a lot wiser now.

I'm not some loser divorcee skulking back home to live with my mama.

She inspected the softly lighted living room one last time. Heavy wood paneling colored the room like honey. A gigantic stacked stone fireplace dominated one wall. Antique Turkish carpets, some nearly threadbare, covered the oak floors. Leather and muted fabrics upholstered a hodgepodge of sofas and chairs. A wall of glass exposed the panorama of lake and woods outside. She wiped off a wet dog nose mark from a glass door.

"Come on, Boon. Help me check the food." The yellow lab followed her into the kitchen.

She peeked in the refrigerator at the trays of hors d'oeuvres: baby artichoke hearts with prosciutto, miniature crab cakes, crudités, shrimp kebabs, and mini spring rolls. The counters were laden with cheese straws, rumaki, antipasto, brie with cranberry marmalade and a spiral cut smoked ham. A copper chafing dish held spicy Italian sausage bites; a silver one warmed Swedish meatballs. Sneaking a taste of pâté, she danced to a Kenny Chesney tune on the radio. She hoisted a tall service bucket of punch from the kitchen counter, turned toward her Grandmother's sterling punch bowl and collided with Boon.

The bucket popped into the air while her feet scrambled but found no purchase. Boon shied away as the bucket hit the floor and spilled its load.

From her position sprawled on the kitchen floor, Mary Alice watched eight gallons of the famous Tate family champagne punch sluice across the tile floor like a wave over Panama City Beach. Boon watched intently, perhaps waiting to see if the liquid that covered half of the kitchen floor was palatable.

The punch tide leveled out and washed back toward Mary Alice, surrounding and then soaking her. "Boon, don't move." The canine padded through the foamy punch making doggy tracks on the dry half of the kitchen floor. "Oh shit."

Fifty guests were due in half an hour. As she poked her finger in the rip in the knee of her new DKNY slacks, the door between the garage and kitchen opened and in stepped a statuesque, attractive woman wearing a garnet silk summer dress. Behind her stood another woman holding a large, white box.

"Mary Alice." Elizabeth Tate stepped gingerly through the flood toward her daughter. "What have you done?" She snapped off the radio.

"Mama."

"Maria, get my cell phone from the car," Elizabeth said. "Call Mr. Treadwell at Star Liquor and tell him to send out six cases of champagne. Put it on my bill."

Maria set down the box, turned, and without a word went back out the way she entered. Boon followed her.

Mary Alice worked her mouth like a goldfish. How had her mother known it was champagne punch?

"Tell him I said to shake it," Elizabeth called. She scowled at the departing dog.

"Mama," Mary Alice protested, her voice sounded whiney. Thirty seconds with her mother, and Mary Alice was a ten year old.

"I'll get Maria going cleaning up this mess," Elizabeth said. "You go change. Put on a dress."

"Mama, I have more champagne." She got up from the floor and felt liquid running down her legs and into her shoes. The opening bars of *You Make Me Feel So Young* tinkled from the living room. She wanted to tell her mother to butt out. She wanted to quote Tennessee Williams and tell her mother to get on her broom and ride up, up over Blue Mountain the way Tom had finally told his mother, Amanda to do. She felt her hand clutch a heavy silver cold meat serving fork.

"Who's banging on that piano?" Elizabeth turned an ear toward the music, striking a dramatic pose like Norma Desmond in *Sunset Boulevard*.

"I hired Parker Fisher."

"He still does parties?"

Maria entered with a sponge mop and bucket. She gave Mary Alice a blank stare and looked to her boss for orders.

"Thanks, Maria," Elizabeth said. "Nobody will come in the kitchen for awhile. We should have enough time."

Mary Alice stood gaping as her mother, the most southern of all southern belles, grand dame of Cana, Mississippi society, swooshed off her fringed, chartreuse silk stole and launched into action.

"Go on, Mary Alice, before anybody gets here." She fluttered her right hand in a four-fingered point toward the door.

Mary Alice slunk out. As the swinging kitchen door fanned back and forth, she heard her mother's voice rhythmically loud-soft, loud-soft. "Maria, put those awful shrimp-thingies in the fridge. All we need is to poison everybody in Cana who matters."

Zombie-walking up the stairs to her room, Mary Alice remembered that less than an hour ago she'd been putting the finishing touches on her party after nearly ten years in Dallas with ex-husband, Dr. Cham Mauldin III. She had stood on the deck that overhung the lake, looking back at the retreat her Daddy had built and left to her. She had smiled thinking how pretty the Tikis and twinkle lights around the deck would look after dark. That was an hour ago.

Now a "Revenge on Mama" movie was starting in her head. Mary Alice had begun to fantasize intricate payback scenarios in junior high. In one, she poisoned her mother because she wouldn't permit one of Mary Alice's girlfriends to spend the night. Elizabeth said the girl would steal things. In high school the scenarios became increasingly elaborate—hang, draw and quarter Mother, burn Mama at the stake or sear her with mustard gas. Tonight she wanted to throw her off any one of the Tallahatchie River Bridges.

In her bedroom, Mary Alice shucked her designer slacks ensemble and wiped the perspiration from under her arms. Lifting a halter-top, white linen sheath over her head, she shook herself to settle it on her body. After three tries, she fastened the heavy gold mesh necklace her mother had given her for Christmas. It choked a little and the clasp scratched.

She looked in the mirror, thankful that a brush and fluff of her dark hair was sufficient. Her Daddy said she had his eyes, big and brown like Hallmark card bunny rabbit's. She knew she had her mother's Miss America smile and the teeth that supported it—white and perfect. She wasn't a true beauty, but somehow the sum of the parts added up to quite attractive, really cute, a doll. At thirty-five, she could still turn heads, but if the blush wasn't quite off the rose, the handwriting was on the wall.

By the time she found the right pair of low-heeled sandals, she could hear her mother greeting the first wave of guests that included the publisher of the Tupelo *Daily Journal* and after him a state legislator and his wife. She heard more cars on the pea gravel drive, but paused on the stairs to look out the huge window.

She watched Clay Sykes on the pier gently push the last of the floating candles out onto the water. They wobbled drunkenly and then drew away as though pulled by the rising full moon. Clay Sykes had worked as a caretaker for Mary Alice's father. After her father died, Clay stayed. That was five years ago.

She let her gaze skate across the lake to the clump of tall pines on the shoreline that marked the secret Indian cave only she and her Daddy knew about.

Daddy, I wish you were here.

"Zachary Towree, you scamp," Mary Alice heard Elizabeth say. Her voice resonated, *making Mary Alice think of a splash of vinegar on a fresh wound.*

She snapped out of her reverie and looked at her watch. It was just after eight.

"You didn't come to my garden party last month. I have a good mind not to let you in."

Mary Alice exhaled and started down the stairs. Zach would make her feel better.

"Miz Tate, I apologize again," Zach said. "I had to be down in Jackson. I heard it was a great party."

Pausing on the bottom step, Mary Alice watched Zach's right hand linger in her mother's. Her mother had always flirted with her boyfriends, at least the ones she knew about and approved. It had irritated Mary Alice when boyfriends described her mama as "cool" or called her a "babe." Mary Alice knew they didn't really know her mama.

"I hope you do run for governor," Elizabeth said. "We could use a man from North Mississippi in office."

"If I win."

"Of course, you'll win." Elizabeth glided though a series of feminine glances paired with fluttery fingers.

Mary Alice silently filled in the rest of her mother's answer: and my daughter will become the first lady, and I'll get to redecorate the governor's mansion and visit my grandchildren. That is, if Mary Alice doesn't mess everything up.

As Mary Alice approached, she felt Zach's gaze slide over her bare shoulders and down her body.

Elizabeth saw it too as she turned to shake hands with Leonard Bass, a bank president and a board member. Mary Alice had heard that he'd lost a fortune on a land deal, but he was making a fuss now, encouraging his wife to up the amount of their donation check.

"Hello, beautiful," Zach said, keeping his eyes on Mary Alice.

Mary Alice felt like Cherries Jubilee waiting to be ignited. When Zach wasn't busy looking like a successful political candidate, he had a smoldering, sexy quality. She wondered why he had never married.

"How's our District Attorney? Jail all locked up tight?" Mary Alice asked, taking his arm. He made her forget all about her mama.

He smiled at her as though she was his. "How'd you like to get out of here?" He walked her a few steps toward the door.

She leaned against him and smelled the subtle cologne, the Bourbon and something she couldn't name. Something masculine like sweat that hadn't yet soured. She snatched another whiff. "It's my party, you idiot. I can't leave." He made her feel like a sultry movie heroine in her slinky dress. Her nipples rose, pushing against the linen. She saw that he noticed.

"Too bad. I tell you what..." He pulled her closer and whispered in her ear.

She giggled and felt a flush crawl up her neck. "I'm not doing that." She could imagine being discovered in a compromising position in the back of his huge SUV.

"Let me know if you change your mind. While you're deciding, I'm getting us a couple of drinks." He flexed his eyebrows like Groucho Marx and headed for the bar, but only made it a few yards before he was waylaid by a banker, a lawyer and a golf pro.

Mary Alice smiled. The party was warming up nicely, and her mama wasn't in sight. She'd gotten off to a bumpy start, but now everything was working. The Women's Center volunteer at the door was scribbling receipts for donations as fast as she could.

Mary Alice looked around the room. Leaving Dallas had been a good idea. In Cana, there were good people who would help her put her life back together. Some might gossip, hungry for the details of her divorce, but all that would be old news in a few more months. She sauntered through the packed living room into the dining room.

"Is that Georgia Horn talking to Dr. Reynolds?" Elizabeth asked.

Mary Alice jumped, sending a cheese ball skittering to the floor. She glanced through the open door into the living room.

"You know it is, Mama," Mary Alice said, retrieving the cheese wrapped green olive nibble. "Want me to ask her to go help Maria in the kitchen?"

"Don't be a smarty pants. My objection to her has nothing to do with her race." Elizabeth grinned and waved to a couple across the room.

"You don't like Georgia Horn because you didn't pick her to run the Women's Center," Mary Alice said.

However, Mary Alice knew that the main reason why her mother didn't care for Georgia Horn was that Georgia had paired Mary Alice with Sheree Delio, a Women's Center client, and Mary Alice had taken the former drug addict under her wing.

"I started that center." Her jaw tightened and the cords in her neck flared.

"See what I mean?" Mary Alice said.

Like Mr. Hyde switching back into Dr. Jekyll, Elizabeth smiled. "It's a party. Your table looks lovely. I adore the centerpiece."

"Thanks, Mama."

"But I cannot understand why you want to live out here all alone when there's plenty of room in our house in town. There are eight bedrooms and a carriage house. I'd never know if you were home or not." Elizabeth kicked at the fringe of the carpet.

"I like it out here, Mama." She eyed the miniscule scar along her mother's hairline, evidence of a second facelift. She'd rather stick a darning needle in her eyeball than go live with her mother.

"Like your father. He escaped out here and now you—" Elizabeth put her hand over her mouth and turned her head away.

"Mama, I need some space. It's been hard for me since—"

"It's so isolated. A serial killer could—"

"Mrs. Tate, I aim to protect little Mary Alice here from any and all killers, serial or not." Zach handed Mary Alice a glass of white wine and put his hand on her mother's shoulder. "I'm the District Attorney. I can do things like that."

"Zach Towree, I've known you since you were tiny, and you could always charm the scales off a snake."

"Did I tell you what a good color that deep cherry red is on you?" he asked. "You should wear it more often."

Mary Alice agreed. It was the color of blood. However, she enjoyed watching Zach work her mother. Elizabeth Tate occupied the top of Cana's social registry, but still she purred at any man's flattery.

Lord, Mama wants me to marry him.

"Mary Alice Tate." She recognized the heightened speech of Cana's Little Theatre Director, Chase Minor. Beloved by most, Chase was fifty, gay and outrageously flamboyant. Zach turned and joined the group behind him, as Chase approached.

"I have one word for you: *Foxes*." He paused dramatically, hooded eyes cast down, head turned. "You are Birdie. Tortured wife of Oscar, sneaking liquor, betrayed by her whole goddamn family." Chase paused to ease his salmon silk tie. "Lillian Hellman's *The Little Foxes* is the quintessential southern tragedy and you—"

"Chase, you know I don't act anymore." The last role she wanted was Birdie. She had lived Birdie.

"We begin Thursday. You must come." He took her hand in both of his. "We've missed you. The Theatre has missed you. Your audience has missed you." He sounded like Maggie Smith.

Mary Alice felt tempted. She had always loved the adrenalin rush of being on stage, in the moment, where anything could, and often did, happen.

Chase gingerly selected a cigarette from an antique, silver case, but delayed lighting it. She remembered she had given the case to him ten years ago after a production of *Crimes of the Heart*. She'd played Babe. Babe hadn't divorced her abusive husband; she'd shot him.

"Chase, I don't have time to be in a play. I'm working with Georgia Horn at the Women's Center. I can make a donation." Mary Alice ran the numbers in her head to think how much she could contribute. Since she moved from her mother's home in town out to the lake house, she had expenses. Neither Dr. Cham Mauldin III nor the Texas court had offered her alimony. What she inherited from her father when he had died five years ago was tucked into a barely adequate trust, now her only source of income. At least she wasn't dependent on her mother. But everyone knew, Tate women didn't work. Rich husbands supported them.

The pianist changed to a jazzy version of *You with the Stars in Your Eyes*.

"I put a script on your desk," Chase said.

"Thanks, Chase."

"Chase, will you excuse us?" Zach asked. "Mary Alice promised to dance with me."

Chase looked annoyed. "Of course. Read that script and phone me, Mary Alice," he called.

"I promised to dance with you?" Mary Alice asked. He led her outside onto the broad, redwood deck. The air, cool for early September, felt refreshing.

"I thought you needed saving." He took her wine glass from her and set it on the deck's railing. Moonlight reflected on the tranquil surface of the lake occasionally broken up by one of the floating candles. Voices drifted around them, but they were alone. Zach took Mary Alice in his arms. They moved together, dancing, settling into the rhythm of passion. She closed her eyes and felt her body press his.

Maybe she should leave with him. It was her mama's party now anyway.

The pianist segued to *Bewitched, Bothered and Bewildered.* Someone inside sang, "I'm wild again, beguiled again, a simpering, whimpering child again."

Zach's embrace felt solid and made Mary Alice want to dive to the center of it where protection waited like simmering soup, just-out-of-the-dryer blankets or a crackling mesquite fire.

As she lifted her face to kiss him, she saw Georgia Horn standing directly behind Zach.

"Sorry to interrupt." Georgia didn't sound sorry. "Could I talk to you for a minute?"

Zach broke the embrace and turned to Georgia.

"Not you, counselor. I need Mary Alice," Georgia said. "She'll be right back."

Mary Alice doubted that was true by the way Georgia was gripping her arm. As they wormed through the crowded great room, Mary Alice heard snatches of overlapping conversations.

"Coach says they're ready, but y'all remember last year."

"It's been in the Tate family for at least three generations."

"Hell no. Last time I got a case of the crabs."

"You think they're real?"

Georgia pulled Mary Alice into what had been her father's study and closed the door."

"What's going on?" Mary Alice asked.

Georgia pointed to a wingback chair by the fireplace. In it sat huddled a disheveled blonde, Sheree Delio. She looked like a frightened kitten.

"Sheree? What's going on?"

"I'll be outside the door." Georgia left the room.

As Mary Alice approached the woman, she broke into sobs. Mary Alice couldn't understand what she was saying.

"Sheree, get control, honey. You're safe here. Calm down. What happened?"

Sheree raised her tear-stained gamine face. "I didn't do it."

"Do what?" Mary Alice asked. She stroked Sheree's head. Mary Alice felt fear grip her insides. Considering Sheree's past, all manner of horrible things could have happened.

"I just woke up, and he was dead. He ain't breathing or nothing. They're gonna say I did it."

"Whoa. Slow down. Who's dead?" Mary Alice felt dizzy.

"Scott, Scott Bridges."

Mary Alice couldn't put together what Sheree meant. She knew that Sheree had a deal as a drug informant in exchange for clemency on a drug charge of her own, and that Scott Bridges was her police contact. Mary Alice also knew that Sheree and Scott were having sex. Mary Alice believed Sheree was being coerced.

Sheree dissolved into racking sobs. Mary Alice squeezed into the big chair beside her and held her. Sheree felt like an injured humming bird. Maternal feelings flooded Mary Alice. She knew how vulnerable Sheree was. Over the last five months Mary Alice had heard the details of Sheree's life growing up with an abusive father and then a stepfather, about her drug addiction and about working in a strip joint to support her habit. That she was pretty was about all Sheree Delio had going for her. That was until Mary Alice came along.

She remembered how delighted she'd been watching Sheree flower as she turned her life around with Mary Alice's guidance. Sheree had completed drug rehab. Mary Alice got her a job, a bank account, a car, but what she really obtained for Sheree was self-esteem. Sheree had started reading, talking about junior college and planning a future. Mary Alice couldn't have been prouder.

"You done so much for me," Sheree said. "I'm sorry I let you down."

Mary Alice felt all her work to help Sheree was disappearing like rain water down a storm sewer. "Unless you killed him, you didn't do anything," Mary Alice said. In her heart, Mary Alice knew Sheree was too much like her to kill anyone. Though light years apart socially, they'd clicked like soul mates, sharing intimate secrets, a taste for excitement and a fondness for junk food.

"Tell me everything that happened," Mary Alice said.

In the middle of Sheree's recounting of Scott's visit and their tumble into bed, Mary Alice became aware that something didn't quite fit. "Wait. You didn't call the police?"

Sheree shook her head, her huge eyes filled with dread.

"Oh honey," Mary Alice said. "We have to call the police. Right now. I'm going to get Georgia to do that. You stay here."

Mary Alice felt the pâté she tasted earlier turning to bilge in her stomach. It wasn't fair. She flashed on before and after images of Sheree who'd come so far. But now it looked like Sheree Delio would be joining the ladies in the Central Mississippi Correctional Facility, where make-overs didn't count.

Georgia made the call to the sheriff and waited with Mary Alice and Sheree. "I told them to come to the side door, that there were guests here," Georgia said.

Mary Alice stayed beside Sheree, holding her. "It'll be all right."

"Are they going to arrest me?" Sheree asked.

"Probably so," Georgia said. She sat on the desk.

Mary Alice's hope that Sheree would be secreted away to the county jail without alerting the party guests was shattered by the distant wail of a siren. It was joined by another; the two entwined screams shrieked like voices from hell.

Before it was over, a half dozen sheriff's deputies and Cana police occupied the house. Handcuffed, Sheree was led out the front door like a Salem witch on the way to the gallows. The stunned crowd of guests parted to let Sheree pass. Mary Alice's mother turned a peculiar shade of white and for once appeared to be speechless. When the cops and the accused had departed, the guests milled as if they had been waiting for an overdue train that had finally arrived. They abandoned their drinks and left in bunches. Some looked dazed; others appeared energized by the story of a policeman found murdered. Threads of gossip were spun and woven into a tapestry of half-truths; the air felt thick with their lint. Mary Alice retreated to the study feeling like someone dear to her had just been kidnapped and the ransom would be steep. Through the study door, Mary Alice saw her mother smiling, shrugging and making the best of things, but Mary Alice knew what was coming.

CHAPTER 2

S HEREE DELIO COULDN'T HAVE MURDERED anyone.

At 3 AM, Mary Alice gave up on sleep. Frazzled by Sheree's ugly public arrest, Mary Alice couldn't remember much about the end of the party. She could still see the chilling picture of Sheree, looking like a doll that had been left out in the rain, walking through the gauntlet of Cana's finest. She supposed her mama had taken care of wrapping up the party. Elizabeth hadn't missed the opportunity to lecture Mary Alice.

"DEAR GOD IN HEAVEN, WHY did that girl come out here?" Elizabeth had demanded to know.

"I'm her friend. She needed help," Mary Alice said. She knew nothing less than a complete renunciation of Sheree would appease her mother.

"Friend? Oh please," Elizabeth said. "That girl is trouble with a capital T."

"Mama, she didn't kill that cop," Mary Alice said. She didn't think her mother was listening to her.

"Trash is what she is. After all you've done to help her. I've never been so embarrassed in my life. Policemen leading killers out of my house. Grand finish to an evening, don't you think? I'm surprised people didn't ask for their donations back."

It's not your house.

Mary Alice wished she could find some way to shut her mother up. Choking her seemed like a possibility. She imagined her hands tightening around her mother's surgically enhanced neck. But Mary Alice didn't think she'd have the strength to finish the job. Anxiety has sapped her, and apprehension was busy untwisting her last intact mental fibers. She could tell by the way the police had treated Sheree that being accused of murdering a cop was particularly heinous, and they'd make sure Sheree felt the full force of their wrath.

"I don't care whether she did it or not; she shouldn't have come over here," Elizabeth said. "The gall." She charged back and forth in a dance of ire and then strode outside onto the deck.

Mary Alice followed imagining that she could run very fast, hit her mother and tumble her into the lake. Mary Alice was a strong swimmer with terrific lung capacity. She could hold her down for over a minute.

"Mama, I'm sorry. I had no idea she'd come here. She's in jail now. There's nothing we can do about the party."

"Did you see Shannon Richardson's face? I thought she'd hemorrhage." She fanned her face with her hand. "Damn, double damn."

"We raised a lot of money for the center," Mary Alice said and immediately wished she hadn't.

"We're going to need it," Elizabeth said. "After this show, I doubt the Women's Center will be at the top of anybody's giving list."

"Georgia asked the cops to come to the side door," Mary Alice said. "Nobody would have known anything if they had. It was completely unnecessary to bust in here guns blazing."

"A suspected cop killer on the loose?" Elizabeth scoffed. "What did you expect? Why didn't you tell her to turn herself in at the police station? Georgia could have driven her down there."

"Sheree was in no condition to do that." Mary Alice wondered how her mother could feel no compassion for Sheree. But then she remembered that the party, the Women's Center, all of it was all about Elizabeth Tate and her place in the world. White trash, Sheree Delio didn't fit into that world.

"I guess we'll just have to blame it on the drugs she uses," Elizabeth said. "People will understand that. I'm exhausted."

WITH SHEREE'S HISTORY OF DRUG abuse, Mary Alice knew others would be quick to find Sheree guilty of murdering Scott Bridges. Georgia had agreed their first step was to try to come up with bail, but the Women's Center didn't have that kind of money.

Mary Alice sat up in bed. Mystery author, Sue Grafton wouldn't let her private investigator character toss and turn. Kinsey Millhone would take a run on the beach, shower, brush her teeth and then get in her Volkswagen bug and do something. But what?

Mary Alice's knowledge of criminal investigation came from cop or lawyer TV shows and from reading Sue Grafton,

Elizabeth George and Janet Evanovich. She identified most with Grafton's Kinsey Millhone.

Kinsey would talk to somebody. Ask a lot of questions.

Mary Alice got out of bed, pulled on her ancient, stretched-out bathing suit and left Boon snoring on the foot of the bed. Without turning on a light, she padded out on to the redwood deck and paused in the velvet darkness. The humid air moistened her skin. She listened to the din of the cicadas, crickets and frogs, knowing what they didn't seem to know. Winter was coming.

At pre-dawn, the chilly lake stung, but felt like bath water by mid-lake. Mary Alice stroked evenly through the water and in spite of the blackness, headed straight for her destination. Her father said she had natural sonar, like a dolphin. When she reached the far shore, she dove deep and by touch found the gap in the rock wall. With breath to spare, she swam underwater through the opening and surfaced inside the cave. She pulled up onto the wide rock ledge and felt her way to the Indian arrow heads that lay in a circle where James Tate had arranged them years ago. Mary Alice suspected her father had put the arrow heads in their special cave to teach her about Indians and to create a little magic for her. She touched each lightly as she always did. She could almost feel her father sitting on the rocky ledge beside her. She concentrated on the silence that finally produced the memory of his voice.

"Not only the Indians used these caves," her Daddy had told her, his voice echoing in the vault. "Traders off the Natchez Trace used to cache their goods here. There's no better hiding spot than a cave. But sometimes they trap people. A cave can kill."

Now, as in the past, the secret cave never failed to forge a link between Mary Alice and her Daddy. It felt mystical; her father almost materialized.

"Daddy, Daddy," she whispered. The loss of him hurt still. Her throat tightened. She sat until the coldness inside matched the chill cave air, and then she slipped off the ledge into the water and dove for the underwater opening. Swimming steadily across the lake under a starless gray sky, she thought about her father's warning that she was never to go inside a cave alone or ever bring a friend to one.

But she had entered the forbidden caves. She switched to the breast stroke and remembered the first time. She had never told her father. She had not been able to resist the thrill. The caves offered danger; they broke taboos. The banned caves were far more exhilarating than sports competitions or acting in plays. Even the challenge of an Outward Bound camp in Utah when she was fifteen paled in comparison to the scary, pitch black of the caves her Daddy said could kill her. She realized that the caves had been her first foray into the forbidden.

She reached the dock, pulled up out of the water and dried herself as she ran up the stairs to her room.

In twenty minutes she had slipped into a sky-blue cropped top and not-quite-a-mini skirt. She pulled her thick dark hair into a pony tail and found some pink lipstick, achieving a retro look. When she pulled out of the garage at 4:30 AM, driving her father's old 1995 BMW, she wasn't sure exactly what Kinsey Millhone would do, but she knew where Mary Alice Tate was headed. She could sense her inner excitement, like a vibrating electrical grid.

"I can't let you see the prisoner. Now you know that Mary Alice," Otis Turner said. He had been napping in the run down Cana jail on a sofa mottled brown from years of coffee stains. The smell of pine floor cleaner wafted as Otis shuffled about the office tucking in his uniform shirt. His pants zipper was half way down.

"Otis, Sheree Delio is from Cana. I'm Mary Alice Tate, and I went to high school with you. I'm not some New York lawyer." Mary Alice pulled a box of sanitary napkins from a bag. "I want to give her some feminine supplies I happen to know she needs."

Otis' shoulders rose stiffly in an attempt to stifle his discomfort at having a box of Kotex thrust under his nose. "The matron can give them, this, to her when she comes on."

"And in the meantime? Think about it, Otis."

Otis looked like he didn't want to think about menstrual blood in the jail or anywhere else. "Only her lawyer, which she don't have yet, and the police can talk to her," he said.

"I've been working with Sheree through the women's center for months. Since I got back in town. I'm like her case worker. Otis, you can sit right with us and hear everything I say. I'm not going to try to spring her."

Otis laughed. "Mary Alice, it ain't like on TV with little interview rooms and like that. It's a small town lock up."

Mary Alice took this as a weakening. "Has she been arraigned or whatever you call it?"

"No, but Mary Alice the evidence is pretty overwhelming."

"Otis, Sheree didn't kill Scott Bridges." She moved in closer, close enough for him to smell her.

"Maybe not but they found him dead in her bed and she ran off." Otis slapped his own face. "I ain't supposed to discuss the case."

"How do they know he was murdered?"

"Mary Alice, please don't make this hard for me. They got to do tests, autopsy, but the coroner thinks it was murder," Otis said. "There's evidence."

Mary Alice thought the cops wanted to blame someone. Anyone.

"Look, Otis, if she hasn't been formally charged yet, maybe all the rules about lawyers and police aren't in place yet."

"Well I—"

"Just ten minutes." She gave her pony tail a toss. "Please."

"Ten?"

She could tell the Kotex box and the fact that Otis had always had a crush on Mary Alice were taking their toll. "I swear I won't tell anybody."

He flapped his arms. "Mary Alice."

"My lips are sealed." She mimed zipping her lips, locking them and throwing away the key. The clock behind the jailer said five till five.

"She's the only one in the jail right now." He shifted his weight. "You got five minutes." He moved from around the counter to a door with a one-way mirror panel and extracted a bunch of keys from his uniform pocket. When he saw himself in the mirror, he ran his hand through his hair and pawed at his stubble.

Mary Alice lightly touched his hairy arm. "Thanks, Otis. I'm worried sick about her. I won't mess this up for you, I promise." She meant her words. She liked Otis, but she also knew that successful detectives didn't always play by the rules.

The keys jangled as he unlocked the door. Mary Alice followed Otis inside. The room was ringed with a dark brown wainscot, topped by expanses of rheumy beige. The space held one small jail cell and a larger one that Mary Alice suspected was the drunk tank. She crossed her arms. The temperature couldn't have been more than 60 degrees.

Sheree Delio sat huddled on the bottom bunk in the smaller cell. She didn't look up until Mary Alice pulled a chair close to the bars.

"Sheree, I only got a minute. Talk to me." She fought the urge scream. It was too, too horrible.

The young woman raised her chin, her once pretty face now a mask of misery and exhaustion.

"I brought you some pads," Mary Alice said a little too loud, hoping Sheree would go along with the ruse.

"Wait," Otis said grabbing the Kotex box. "I got to go through that box first. I'll be right back." He scurried back to the front office to check in private the box of maxi pads. The door snap-locked behind him. Ka-chunk.

"Sheree, are you okay?" She tried to sound in control and hoped Sheree couldn't hear the hysteria bubbling just out of range.

"Mary Alice." Sheree sounded like a little girl.

Mary Alice thought her heart would break. "You have to tell me everything. You were so upset and the sheriff got there so fast—"

"I knew they'd blame me."

"Why?"

"The empty triptan cartridges. I just knew."

"Cartridges?"

"My migraine medicine comes in pre-loaded cartridges."

Mary Alice recalled once seeing Sheree inject herself with a plastic tube looking device. "Migraine medicine would kill him?" Mary Alice asked. Her head spun. She hadn't expected anything like this.

"He was dead in my bed, and they think I had reason to kill him. For somebody like me, that's all they need."

"Wait. They have to prove—"

"Mary Alice, I appreciate what you're trying to do, but you best just forget about me. A cop's dead, and they got to pin it on somebody. I'm a white trash, drug-using stripper."

"Scott Bridges was forcing you to have sex with him! I can testify."

Sheree leaned forward and put her head in her hands.

"You can't give up, Sheree. Georgia and I are going get you out of here." Mary Alice felt her stomach tighten.

"Why you so sure I didn't do it?"

"Because I know you. Now talk to me." Mary Alice wanted to say, because we've come so far together; we belong to one another. She reached through the bars and touched Sheree's hand. Sheree curled her fingers around Mary Alice's.

Keys jangled in the door lock.

"There's one thing, but I can't talk in here," Sheree whispered.

The door opened, and Otis entered with the box of pads. "Okay, that's five minutes."

"Otis, that's not even two minutes," Mary Alice said. She needed lots more information from Sheree.

"Next shift will be here in a minute. You got to go on, Mary Alice." He pleaded more than ordered.

Mary Alice rose and scooted her chair away from the bars. "Sheree, you dig deep and get some strength 'cause we're going to fight this. I know you didn't kill that cop."

Sheree looked down.

"Sheree."

"Mary Alice, please come on," Otis said.

Otis ushered Mary Alice out the side door of the jail. Early light crept over the crepe myrtles that bordered the parking lot. The pink hem of the sky matched the blooms.

"Good to have you back in Cana, Mary Alice. I don't think I've talked to you since your Daddy's funeral. I was so sorry he passed on."

"Thanks, Otis. I appreciate your letting me see Sheree." Mary Alice was having difficulty breathing. Sheree looked awful. "She needs to have her migraine medicine," she said more to herself than to Otis.

"They know. I'll remind them." He looked away.

She nodded and released her grip on her bare arms. "It's freezing in there, Otis."

"AC don't work worth a hoot," he said. "Too hot or too cold. Your tax dollars at work."

"Can't she have a sweater or at least another blanket?"

"I'll ask." He sounded about as hopeful as if he were going to request a catered lunch of shrimp and grits served on Lenox and accompanied by a vintage Pinot Grigio.

Mary Alice shivered and rubbed her arms.

"Maybe I'll see you over at Mickey's some time," he said. He stared at a bubble in the asphalt and tucked his hands in his pants pockets.

Mary Alice imagined what her mother's reaction would be if she found out her daughter had tipped a brew in a sleazy bar with Otis Turner, jailer.

"Yeah. Maybe so." She squinted at the September sky. "Thanks, Otis."

On the way to the Women's Center in downtown Cana, Mary Alice stopped at McDonald's for coffee in hopes that caffeine would ameliorate the effects of getting up at 3 AM. She made herself order a biscuit. She knew from past experience that low blood sugar resulted in bad decisions.

"You're Mary Alice Mauldin, aren't you?" the woman behind the counter said.

"Tate," Mary Alice said, buying time while she tried to place the familiar face. "It's back to Tate." Then she remembered. "Paula Ray, right?"

"Dubose. Ray, then Moncrief and now Dubose. You staying here now?"

"I'm living out at my Daddy's lake house. How you been?"

"Good. Took this job to get away from screaming kids. Not really."

"Kids? You have children?" Mary Alice asked.

"Four."

Mary Alice nodded. Wow. Paula Ray Moncrief Dubose had four children. There was no way she could catch up. Some other thought tried to wiggle loose in her brain, but Paula handed her the coffee and the thought evaporated.

"Thanks, Paula."

Mary Alice drove slowly to the Center, talking aloud to herself. "Sheree's just knocked out by all this; she doesn't mean what she says. She needs help. Georgia will know what to do. And Zach. Hell, he's the DA, but he's fair. He'll help me. Lord, what would Daddy do? If they find her guilty of first degree murder, she'll get life." The biscuit on the seat beside her turned into a hockey puck.

A pickup truck with three children in the truck bed turned in front of her.

Tears slid down her face. It wasn't fair. Sheree had been doing so well. Had a job, a car, a place to live. Mary Alice pictured Scott Bridges intimidating Sheree.

That bastard Bridges used her. I wouldn't blame her if she had killed him.

The children silently sucked on popsicles and watched Mary Alice cry.

Who the hell gave children popsicles for breakfast? She wanted to pull up alongside the truck and yell at the adults in the cab—or better, take the kids home with her and feed them oatmeal with chopped apple and raisins.

Then the loose thought birthed at the McDonald's counter floated up. She'd missed her last menstrual period. Certain the miss was due to stress, she'd ignored it. She'd missed periods before. She made a mental note to check the calendar to see when her next one was due. It was no big deal. Yet.

She turned into the Women's Center parking lot and slid the nose of the car under a huge Magnolia. She repaired her face in the visor mirror. Bail. She'd have to see about bail. *And a lawyer. How much does a good lawyer cost?*

CHAPTER 3

MARY ALICE THUMBED THROUGH A Carol Wright Gift Catalog while she waited for Georgia, who was holed up with a client in the inner sanctum of the Women's Center. Mary Alice had about decided to order a dozen Squirrel Chaser Pouches for the house and an Ionic Cleaning Brush for Boon when Georgia called her in. The client discreetly had left by another door directly into the parking lot.

"I called down to the police department," Georgia said. "They won't tell me anything." She sat down behind her desk.

"I talked to her," Mary Alice said, sitting in the only available chair. She explained how Otis Turner had let her in the jail. "She told me I'd best just forget about her. You should have heard her voice." Tears welled as she recalled the jail interview. "No fight in her at all."

"Pretty common response." Georgia sorted papers on her desk as she talked.

"She's reverted." Mary Alice wiped her eyes on her fingers and then tapped them together to evaporate the tears. The thought of Sheree turning back into her pre-Mary Alice condition made Mary Alice feel she was coming down with the flu.

"Sheree doesn't think much of herself so she doubts that we do." Georgia pushed a paper into the shredder. It whined like a small air plane. "And she thinks she's let you down."

"We need a plan." She wished Georgia would leave the papers alone and listen.

"I can't do anything this morning. You saw the waiting room."

"But Sheree—" Mary Alice heard the desperation in her voice.

"Until she's arraigned, bail set and a lawyer appointed, there isn't much we can do anyway. The system moves like cold glue."

"We have to do something."

"We don't even know if they'll keep her here. Slow down Mary Alice."

"Where would they take her?" Panic leached into her voice.

"Wherever they have space and there's less publicity. She's accused of killing a police officer."

"I hadn't even thought about her moving." She wondered what other vast territories of knowledge she lacked and if she could learn the twists of the law fast enough to help Sheree.

"Look, I have to find help for all those folks in the waiting room," Georgia said. "You want to gather up some food for Gloria Edwards' family? That would help me a lot."

Mary Alice shrugged and nodded. When she had first met Georgia Horn right after she'd come on the Women's Center board, Georgia had asked Mary Alice if she would collect some food for a family down on its luck. If Mary Alice had said no, she wouldn't be working with Georgia now. It was Georgia's test of character. Mary Alice had gone to her mama's pantry which was where she planned to go again.

"Come back this afternoon." Georgia said. "But drop off that food soon as you can."

"Okay."

"We'll know more soon. They can't hold her forever just because she hated him and he died in her bed."

Mary Alice exited through the crowded waiting room filled with black, brown and white faces, mostly women, each needing something. Even the most anxious face didn't come close to looking as desperate as Sheree Delio had that morning in jail. But looking at them, Mary Alice could see that while Sheree was her number one priority, Sheree could not be Georgia's number one.

I'm all she's got.

She took a deep breath and squared her shoulders.

Less than two miles from the Women's Center sat Linnley, the ancestral home of the Tate family. Mary Alice drove up the cedar lined circular drive toward the cloud white Greek revival antebellum mansion. Linnley, delicately designed and expertly crafted, had survived the War Between the States. It was on every registry and was *the* house to see during Cana's spring pilgrimage. Linnley made people passionate about a white porch rocker in which to sit and sip a mint julep. Linnley made rebel-hating liberals calm down and find their manners. Mary Alice had always disliked having to tell people she actually lived in Linnley.

She drove around back and parked near the pool house. As she walked from the car, her eye ran up the grassy terrace to bank upon bank of azaleas shaded magenta to rose pink. The contrast between the ethereal lightness of Linnley and the heavy energy of the Women's Center was as jarring as the music she heard on entering. She remembered that on Saturdays her mama's personal trainer came for an hour.

She followed the noise to what had been her playroom. Elizabeth Tate had converted it to an exercise room after Mary Alice married and moved to Dallas. She paused at the door to watch a young woman stretching her mother into an impossible position. Elizabeth, wet with sweat, groaned.

"Mama, you mind if I cull some canned goods from the pantry for the Women's Center?" Mary Alice shouted.

Elizabeth Tate righted herself. "That's enough, Bonnie. Gods, will it ever cool off?"

"Want me to turn down the AC, Mrs. Tate?" Elizabeth's personal trainer asked as she turned off the music.

"Leave the temp alone. It's the humidity," Elizabeth said, drying her face and neck on a fresh terry hand towel. "What time is it?"

"Just after nine," Bonnie said. She began tidying up the gym. Mary Alice waited.

Elizabeth looked up at her daughter. "Ask Alberta what you can take. Last time you took all my Trappey's brand. Don't take them. You okay this morning?"

Mary Alice shrugged. "Sheree's in jail. I'm not happy about that."

"I heard about that," Bonnie said. On all fours, she tightly rolled up Elizabeth's yoga mat. "They say she murdered a cop."

"You heard?" Mary Alice asked. "How?"

"Police scanner. My husband keeps it on all the time. The static relaxes him."

"What'd they say about Sheree?" Mary Alice asked.

Elizabeth paused in dabbing at the sweat between her breasts to listen.

"She killed a cop with some kind of drug," Bonnie said.

"Scott Bridges," Mary Alice said. She couldn't believe Bonnie knew all about it.

"Bonaparte?" Bonnie asked.

"No, Bridges."

"No, that's what the other cops call Scott Bridges," Bonnie said. "Bonaparte was Napoleon's last name."

"Really?" Elizabeth said. She caught her daughter's eye in the mirror and smiled. "And was he like Napoleon?"

"He was short. My husband said he has, well had, that attitude all short guys have. Warren won't hire a man to work for him unless he's at least as tall as the pole lamp in his office. He says—"

"Bonnie, do you think you can come again Tuesday morning?" Elizabeth smiled signaling the end to the conversation.

"Yes, Ma'am. You betcha." Bonnie gave them a cutesy wave with both hands and backed out of the room.

"I'm going to shower," Elizabeth said. "Have coffee with me before you leave."

"I can't. Georgia needs the food now," Mary Alice said. After her mother's response to Sheree's arrest, Mary Alice had trouble seeing herself sipping coffee with her mama. Mary Alice couldn't bear to hear again how dreadful Sheree was and how put upon Elizabeth was. No, Elizabeth might end up with a pot of hot coffee in her lap.

"Georgia needs. Georgia needs," Elizabeth mimicked. "You take my food, but you can't take time for coffee with your mother."

"I'll come back later."

"I rue the day I ever suggested you serve on the Women's Center Board."

"Be back for lunch." She smiled and held it until it sickened and died.

"Never mind; I have a luncheon engagement." Elizabeth, in high dudgeon, exited, but then returned. "And another thing, you better stay away from that tart, if you want to reassume your rightful place in Cana society."

"What happened to innocent until proven guilty?" She felt her anger seep like leaking battery acid.

"I'll tell you what happened. Birds of a feather flock together. You're not her social case worker or parole officer. You have no official reason to be associated with her. She's like those orphaned kittens and stray dogs you used to bring home. You always have to save something. You can't rescue her. She'll get a fair trial. Leave it to the lawyers."

Mary Alice struggled to resist throwing a towel at her mother. "A court appointed lawyer and a murder charge for a woman with her record. Hmmmm. Does that sound fair?"

"Sheree Delio sold drugs, took drugs, prostituted herself, and who know what all else," Elizabeth said. "What did she expect? And then you helped her and what did she do? If she's innocent, she's a damn fool."

"She's not a stray cat, Mama." Mary Alice didn't know how to tell her mother that Sheree had rescued her just as much as she had rescued Sheree.

"Mary Alice, I'm begging you to stay away from her for your own good. I'll send her some money if you'll promise me you won't contact her."

"The Women's Center is going to help her."

"It already did. You did, and I did. I own the apartment where she murdered a policeman. She got a special low rent because of you." She pulled her towel tightly around her neck. "I have to get in the shower before I catch a cold. Mary Alice, please think about what I say. About the repercussions. You can't have it both ways."

"I beg your pardon?" Mary Alice said. She picked up a band of yellow stretchy-rubber that her mother used in her workout, and repeatedly yanked it taut.

"You are stubborn like your father. Do as you please. You always have, but I can tell you that if you muck about with trash like that—" She shifted her voice from panicky to reasonable. "You'll never see it coming, darling. You'll wake up and realize the cotillion is over and you never got your invitation." She turned and silently left the room.

The elastic yellow band slipped from Mary Alice's hand and snapped her wrist, making a welt. She let the pain distract her from the thought of winding the band around her mother's moist neck. She knew her mother was right about Mary Alice's stubbornness, but she believed sticking by Sheree was the right thing to do. Her father had said, "don't be a quitter" and she'd always taken his advice.

Mary Alice went to the kitchen to collect two paste board boxes of beans, okra, peas, corn, greens, flour, grits and a can of Crisco. She grabbed a package of Pepperidge Farm cookies for herself. She fought to deflect her mother's negativity, but still it spawned doubt.

She'd be stupid to risk becoming *persona non grata* over helping a woman who maybe couldn't be helped, at least by her. What a mess.

Damn. I hope Mama's wrong.

And another idea had begun to creep into her consciousness: detective work felt something like the danger of climbing into a subterranean cave or driving too fast or dating a boy her mother didn't like. Adrenalin chewed at the edge of her awareness.

On her way out, Mary Alice opened her mother's key cabinet, found the master for the Magnolia Arms apartments, and tucked it into her purse. She knew Janet Evanovich's Stephanie Plum borrowed keys to get into places she needed to see. In more than one book, she'd broken into houses. Stephanie Plum wasn't a cop, yet she took action. Mary Alice knew she had to help Sheree and do it quick.

Mary Alice backed the BMW around and drove down the driveway between perfectly groomed borders and hedges. Her mood became lighter the farther she drove. She rolled down the window and turned on the radio. As she headed to the Women's Center to drop off the food for the Edwards family, a vague plan took shape.

She needed to see the crime scene. Private investigators always wanted to see the crime scene. No one who believed Sheree was innocent had seen it. People often found only what they were looking for. It was up to Mary Alice. And it wasn't breaking in if she had a key. Besides, her family owned the apartment complex. And no one would ever know. She felt an inner vibration that matched the car's.

CHAPTER 4

At her father's oversized cherry desk, Mary Alice opened the Pepperidge Farm cookies she'd nabbed from her mother's pantry and extracted the first paper cup full. Then from the lower right desk drawer she lifted out her father's .45 pistol. She ran her fingers over the gun's cold metal contours. They felt unfamiliar, but good. She set the gun on the desk and took out a sheet of paper. At the top she printed "Crime Scene" and beneath it wrote:

1. *Clothing, dark to avoid detection and non-descript to avoid description. With Pockets. Running shoes.*
2. *Flashlight, check batteries.*
3. *Plastic baggies.*
4. *Apartment key.*
5. *Latex gloves.*
6. *Cell phone.*
7. *Unrecognizable car and/or car hiding place.*
8. *Weapon.*

She looked at the pistol as she munched a cookie. She knew her Daddy's shotgun sat in a cupboard in the utility room and wrote, *Shot in Cup.* Beside "Weapon" she printed in caps, LEARN TO SHOOT GUN. At the bottom of the page she scrawled, *Look for anything unusual, anything the police missed.*

When she had lifted the key to Sheree's apartment from her mother, Mary Alice had only a hazy notion of what she might do. Now examining the crime scene felt imperative. She might find something the police, who didn't know Sheree, overlooked. And what was the downside? If somehow she got caught, which wasn't likely, she could say she was going to help her mother redo the apartment and wanted to check it out. It was lame, but the Cana Police weren't going to arrest her over it. And there was another benefit to sneaking into Sheree's apartment. It was exciting.

Someone knocked on one of the sliding glass doors. She crumpled the list and shoved it in her jeans pocket. When she entered the living room, she saw Clay Sykes back-lighted by the bright morning sun.

"Come on in," she said, wiping cookie crumbs on her jeans.

Clay Sykes stepped into the living room, holding up a plastic bag full of spent candles. "I fished these out of the lake." He shifted his weight back and forth. "From your party?"

"Thanks, Clay. What do I owe you?" She wondered why he hadn't just put them in the garbage.

"Nothing. You let me fish in it. It's only right I clean up."

"Thanks. I appreciate how you help keep the place up. I know Daddy would, too."

A long pause followed. He turned to go and then turned back. "You planning to shoot that gun?"

"Gun?" She turned and saw the pistol on the desk in easy view through the door. "Mama's worried about me all alone out here. I thought if I told her I had a gun she—"

"You know how to shoot it?"

"Point and pull. Right?"

"I could show you," he said.

Clay showed so little emotion that he was impossible to read. "Thanks, Clay. Maybe so."

He nodded and left the way he came, loping across the deck toward his ten-year-old pickup.

Mary Alice heard it rumble away. There was something about Clay she couldn't quite put her finger on. Maybe it was that it was hard to tell how old he was. He'd been the caretaker for Mary Alice's father for over a decade. She suspected he was infatuated with her, but in a different way than Otis Turner was. She labeled him odd and left it at that.

AT NINE THAT NIGHT, MARY Alice drove to the Magnolia Arms Apartments and hid the car two blocks away in what had been her great grandfather's carriage house. She scurried through the dark, excited by her mission and fantasizing about Charlie's Angels. Long ago one of them had attended Ole Miss; was it Kate Jackson?

She hid in shadows across the street and watched. The New Orleans styled building of twenty units though older, had architectural details that newer complexes lacked. Her eye traced the wood louvered shutters, some with broken slats, and the rusting wrought iron trim. Mary Alice thought it looked like a place Ann Rice might want to rent to write another vampire novel. An iron gate, frozen open, yawned like a spiky mouth.

On tiptoe, she shot across the street, through the gate and into the brick courtyard nestled between two giant magnolia trees. A stumble on a broken paver sent her lurching into one of the trees. She froze. No one came out. When she'd driven by in the afternoon, the place looked faded but elegant. But now the huge magnolia branches seemed to clutch at her, and the windows in the façade looked like sinister eyes daring her to approach. Grasping the key in the pocket of her black stretch running pants, she felt its jagged teeth against her palm.

Yellow tape still marked Sheree's door, but the stairs were clear of warnings and there were no police or sheriff's cars in view. An orange cat sat on the balcony watching her. Quietly, she squeezed past the magnolia's branches and climbed the stairs. Weary air conditioners wheezed. She stood in the shadow of the apartment's door, 1-B, the key trembling in her gloved hand. She worried about getting in and getting caught. She liked the feeling.

She turned the key in the lock, and the door opened with a horror movie squeak. Over her shoulder, she saw the orange cat head for the open door. She slipped in past the yellow warning tape and shut the door in the cat's face. The stale air hit her. She fished for the flashlight. It wasn't in her pants' cargo pocket. *Damn. Detectives don't lose their flashlights.* She furiously patted all the pants pockets as though she were swatting horse flies.

As her eyes adjusted to the dark, she made out the kitchen and the door to Sheree's bedroom. Feeling again for the light, she found it in her jacket pocket. The evening was too warm for a jacket, but it matched the pants and provided extra pockets. Sweat trickled down her back and soaked her arm pits. She knew mistakes born of bad planning and inattention meant trouble. Getting caught wouldn't help Sheree.

She edged into the bedroom. Blackout drapes covered the single window; the room was pitch black. The tiny flashlight beam shot out and hit the stripped bed. Nothing suggested Scott Bridges had died there two nights ago. She surprised herself with a flood of sadness for the young cop whose life had ended. She wondered if he had been aware he was dying. He'd probably never seen the attack coming.

A wave of claustrophobia slid over her like a shroud, and she frantically panned the beam across the walls and furniture stopping on the closet door.

Which TV detective always checked victim's pockets?

She opened the small closet door and was sliding her hand into a coat pocket when scraping sounds outside made her douse the light and freeze. She felt like a quart of ice water had just been poured down her back.

Footsteps, deliberately quiet ones. She listened without breathing. The magnolia branches rubbed the stair railing. Someone was outside Sheree's door. In five steps, Mary Alice made it into the tiny bathroom. Shaking, she closed the door, stepped into the bath tub, and pulled the thick plastic curtain closed. She remembered a woman in a movie had done this to hide from a kidnapper, but Mary Alice couldn't remember if it had worked.

Her blood pulsed in her ears while her mouth went to dust.

There was a muffled snap and then the sound of the apartment door's eerie squeak. Mary Alice's knees buckled, and she pressed against the wall to keep from falling down into the tub. A band of light swept under the door. She heard steps in the bedroom and something else. Whistling. Raspy, absent-minded whistling.

The bathroom door opened. Through the opaque curtain she couldn't see anything. She concentrated on the soap film she felt beneath her fingers. The whistling continued, but became tuneless. She could almost feel the intruder's heat. The flashlight beam seemed to pass over the bathroom floor tile by tile searching for something. She stopped breathing and remembered the shower ruse in the movie hadn't worked.

The cold tiles chilled her back and her legs ached as she forced her muscles to remain immobilized. The blood pounding in her ears made her think of swimming underwater. Closing her eyes, she imagined she was skimming over the sandy bottom of her favorite cove with ten feet of lake water above her. She wanted to scream.

The light moved closer and closer to the tub, its spill illuminating the shower curtain. Mary Alice visualized the pretty rocks on the lake bottom.

Meow. The sound came from the living room. The light snapped off. In the dark she heard footsteps leave the bathroom. Then a snarl and hiss from a cat cut the silence and filled the room with screaming and hissing.

The quiet returned after the sound of the outside door closing and footsteps running on stairs. She waited five minutes before moving from the tub and only moved then because she had to throw up. Kneeling beside the toilet, she retched until dry heaves took over and wracked her body. When she sat back on the cold tile floor, her hand pressed something hard wedged beside the toilet. It felt like a coin or a plumbing gizmo. A washer? She felt sure it was what they'd been looking for. Using the plastic Ziploc baggie, she carefully nudged the object into the bag and tucked it into her jacket pocket.

Sweat poured down her limp body. She wanted to press herself against the cool floor tiles.

But what if he came back? Was it a he? She wasn't sure, but knew she was already thinking the person was male. Kinsey Millhone wouldn't do that, she knew.

She struggled to her feet. Should she flush? The noise a toilet would make in adjoining apartments had to be weighed against leaving evidence. Could authorities identify you from your vomit? Flushing won.

She crawled through the bedroom and into the living room. When she opened the front door, the orange cat streaked past her and darted outside. It ran down steps and into the dark. Her heart banged in her chest, as she followed the animal down. It had probably saved her life.

Safe back in her car, Mary Alice felt like Jell-O and repeatedly leaned out the window to pull the night air into her lungs. Her mouth felt like she'd sucked on dog fur soaked in Cod Liver Oil.

As her panic subsided, she sank back into the worn leather seat and felt the same sensation she had when she first defied her father and entered one of the forbidden caves. Every fiber pulsed with sensitivity. She rubbed her arms and permitted herself a slow moan, and then another. It was almost as good as good sex.

After a minute, Sheree Delio was back in her head.

Sheree didn't do it. I knew she didn't. The real killer came back for something.

She pulled the baggie from her pocket and shined the flashlight on a metal button—the kind that are on blazers. It was pewter and embossed with a coat of arms. Was this what he wanted? Had she just removed key evidence from a crime scene?

She stuck the bagged button in the glove box and saw the mini Chocolate Moon Pie. She extracted it and tore the wrapper with her teeth. Gently, she bit through the cookie into the marshmallow, holding the bite in her mouth as she circled her tongue in the goo. The vomit taste disappeared. Crumbs settled on her chest. She cranked the car and pulled out onto the street. The combination of spent adrenalin and sugar produced a powerful high. Drunk with exhilaration, she wanted to drive too fast, dance too close or drink too much. She turned on the radio and boosted the volume. What had the intruder been whistling? She tried to hum it, but the thread was gone.

CHAPTER 5

TWENTY-FOUR HOURS AFTER HER CRIME scene caper, Mary Alice was comfortably back into her southern-lady-being-courted-by-a-southern-gentleman role. She nestled into the buttery soft leather sofa watching Zach pour her a cognac. She had been to Zach's house before, but this was the first time he'd cooked for her.

She admired how he had adapted the house his mother had left him into a masculine domain without the clichés of bachelor pads. A glass case filled with antique firearms replaced Mrs. Towree's Limoges and Waterford collections. The fussy oriental rugs were gone and in their place were smaller, bold Dhurries and a large red Kazakit rug that set off the hardwood floors. Pastel colors had changed to deep yellow and bronze and his mother's elaborate window treatments were replaced with simple lambrequins and sheers. The place was spotless.

"I think the first time I was here I came to sell your mama some chocolate candy for a senior class fundraiser," Mary Alice said.

Zach sat across from her, comfortable in the muted plaid wingback. "She buy any?"

"All I had with me. I waited in the foyer while she got her purse." Mary Alice sipped her drink. "I love what you've done." She was aware that she preferred her lake house's worn and comfortable disarray, but that Zach's house would be the choice of most women. But after all she didn't have to choose.

In the background Tony Bennett sang "—but I get a kick out of you."

Mary Alice liked that Zach enjoyed big band music. Her father had, too.

"Thanks," he said. "I'm glad you like it. Back then, I never would have expected I'd be living here. I didn't even want to practice law then."

"What did you want to do?" Mary Alice asked. Zach's history interested her, but at the same time she realized her questions were those that southern ladies asked men to draw them out and make them feel important. Her entire upbring-ing had taught her what to say just as it had taught her mama and her mama's mama.

"Sounds silly, but for a long time I wanted to buy a big sail-boat and sail the world. Live on it."

"No, it sounds simple," she smiled at him, pleased that he was confiding in her. "Maybe you still can when you retire." She tried to imagine living on a sailboat. Where did all your shoes go?

"I've lost my taste for it." He rose and walked to the air conditioner thermostat and touched the button. "Okay if I turn this down a tad?"

Mary Alice resisted pulling her white silk jacket around her. "Whatever suits you."

He loosened his tie and sat down beside her on the sofa instead of in his chair.

"Dreams change," she said, thinking of her storybook marriage to a doctor. "How come yours did?"

"Daddy died; Mama needed me. There wasn't anybody else. We decided I should do something practical like law. I got into politics to break the boredom."

"You almost got married once, didn't you?" A month ago, she wouldn't have asked him this question. Their relationship obviously had moved to a new level of intimacy.

"Nearly. It wouldn't have worked out."

"Marriage is tricky. It isn't what you think it'll be," Mary Alice said. She hoped he'd ask her about her divorce from Cham, who Zach had known well. She wanted to confide in him, to share something intimate with him. She wanted to tell him how Cham had intimidated her, squashed her spirit and nearly driven her crazy.

"I'm not against marriage," he said. "Don't get me wrong. In fact all my political advisors say if I want to run for governor I need a wife."

"Is that a requirement? Like citizenship?" She curled her feet beneath her, letting her skirt slide just above her knees.

"Not required. More like an immunization. The state needs a first lady, and of course if you're single there are those who think you're gay. Most Mississippians don't want a queer head of state."

"We've had gay governors. Or one at least."

"Deep in the closet behind the wooly coats nobody wears anymore."

Mary Alice sipped her cognac. "So you'd get married to get elected governor?"

"No, no. Don't get me wrong. I'd love to have a partner to share my life with. I was so busy with law school, building a practice, elections, Mama's illness and her death. I couldn't imagine a family too. But now I think I was wrong. A family would have given me more than it took away."

The talk of marriage excited Mary Alice. In the grip of the Cinderella myth, she felt his every sentence was a veiled promise of a proposal. They'd only been dating a few months, but she'd known Zach Towree all her life. What she had not known was how vulnerable he could be. She wanted to hold his hand and tell him everything would be all right. But by the time she put her snifter on the mahogany coffee table and turned to him, he'd changed the subject.

"Did you really like the lamb?" he asked. "It's a new recipe."

"I loved it," she said. She hoped he hadn't felt uncomfortable confiding in her. Why did men have such a hard time opening up?

"I never prepared it that way before. Got the animal from over in Tula." He nudged her glass onto a coaster.

"The lamb?"

"If you eat meat, I think you ought to know where it comes from."

"Yes, but—" She admitted his way seemed more honest. And more brutal.

"Not to mention local meat is more apt to be free of chemicals and antibiotics. Of course, I prefer a deer or elk I shot myself."

Was there a man in Mississippi who didn't shoot animals, Mary Alice wondered? She'd steeled herself to this practice in order to have male friends. Killing for food was one thing, but doing it for sport or enjoyment, quite another.

"The entire dinner was wonderful. I had no idea you cooked. I mean really cooked."

Zach slid closer to her and put an arm around her. "I want you to know all about me, Mary Alice." He picked up her hand and held it as though he were going to do something with it but hadn't decided what yet. Maybe take fingerprints.

"Tell me about being a District Attorney." She leaned into him. He smelled clean and citrusy.

"I wanted something to get my name out, so I ran and won. But I don't plan to be a prosecutor forever."

Mary Alice remembered her mother telling her how Zach had annihilated his competition. Mary Alice liked strong men who knew what they wanted and went after it. Gutsy men tended to be exhilarating.

"Can I ask you a question about a case? Say no if you can't talk about it." As soon as the words were out, Mary Alice realized Zach's answer would take them away from not toward intimacy. But she had to ask about Sheree.

"A case I have?"

"Sheree Delio. I'm real worried about her."

"You should be. She killed a cop."

"No, Zach. I know her. She couldn't have and—"

"Wait. Back up. What do you mean?"

"I told you that Georgia asked me to help Sheree when she got out of rehab. Your office dropped the charges in exchange for community service and her work as an informant with the drug task force."

"Not exactly dropped. We could always reopen a case like hers. Of course now drug charges are the least of her worries." He released her hand and reached for his brandy.

"Zach, I think somebody else killed Scott Bridges and—"

"Why?"

"Because he's dead and Sheree didn't do it. She's rotting in jail because the bail is so high; she has no legal help and no kin. I can't even get into see her." She thought about the button now hidden in her lingerie drawer, but of course couldn't tell Zach about it. More and more it seemed that taking the button was an act of colossal stupidity. The button might have freed Sheree, and Mary Alice had been unable to find a way to get it into the police's hands.

"An attorney's been appointed for her."

"Bobby Lee Buchanan. Need I say more?"

"Mary Alice, I'll tell you what I can, but I can only tell you things that the public has a right to know anyway. It's my job to prosecute her. The evidence is substantial."

"Zach, I got to know her pretty well. She turned her life around completely. She quit drugs—took drug tests every week—got a job, cooperated with your office." She paused. "Did you know Scott was taking advantage of her?"

"Advantage?"

"Forcing her to have sex with him." Mary Alice wanted to shock Zach and say "Scott was fucking Sheree" because that's how Mary Alice felt about it. But she opted for the less vulgar expression. She didn't think Zach liked women to use the F-word.

"I didn't know," Zach said.

"He was using her. Had her scared to death that if she didn't sleep with him he'd put her back in jail."

Actually, Sheree had told Mary Alice that at first she was attracted to Scott, but later when she tried to end the sexual part, he had become a problem. "I'm going to kill myself or kill him, if things don't change," Sheree had said. "I can't stand it anymore." Mary Alice had understood exactly why Scott Bridges, at first, had been so appealing to Sheree. Mary Alice shared Sheree's attraction to risky men.

As with the button, Mary Alice didn't tell Zach what Sheree had said.

Zach patted her knee. "I appreciate your loyalty. You helped her. Naturally you bought into her recovery. I admire that, Mary Alice. But Scott Bridges was found in her bed dead of a lethal dose of a drug."

"Her migraine medicine?"

"Yes. It's called triptan," he said. "He'd been injected with at least ten doses. They found the empty cartridges and the needle marks. That much would have caused a man like him to have a heart attack."

"A man like him?"

"Bridges' medical records show he'd had a heart attack. He was also a smoker."

"If he'd had a heart attack, why wasn't this just another one? Why is it murder?" She forced herself to speak calmly, but her voice sounded like a snake's hiss.

"Because people with heart disease can't use triptan," he said. "It constricts the blood vessels. Even a few doses in a heart patient could be fatal."

"And you think she knew about his heart and killed him with her medicine."

"And hoped the police would think it was another heart attack," Zach said.

"Then why would she run?"

"Maybe she wasn't as tough as she thought."

"When will you know for sure? The cause of death?" she asked. The idea that Sheree could act as Zach described seemed so preposterous to Mary Alice she refused to argue the point further.

"Tomorrow. Bridges was police; they'll rush the autopsy."

Mary Alice wanted to be alone to sort out what Zach was telling her. She tried to picture Sheree zapping injections in a sleeping Scott Bridges, she but couldn't.

"Maybe she was high on meth, and they had a fight," Zach said. "That's off the record, of course. You yourself just said she didn't like the arrangement with Bridges and—"

A sick feeling crept over Mary Alice. "Zach, I didn't mean she'd kill him over that." *God Almighty, I just gave the DA a motive.* "Sheree wouldn't hurt anybody. She was too scared, too beaten down." Mary Alice felt like she was drowning. "Even if she had gone back on drugs which I doubt, she wouldn't kill Scott like that."

"How would she do it?"

"She wouldn't."

"Somebody did."

"Did they test her for drugs after they locked her up?" she asked.

"I doubt it. She was at your house. Did she seem high?"

"No, but a test would have cleared her of the suspicion she was using again," she said. "You just now said she might have been on meth."

"A drug test isn't standard with arrest. And even so, the presence or absence of illegal drugs in her body wouldn't convict or free her." Zach turned on the sofa to face her.

"But—"

"Mary Alice, I'm sorry to have to be on the other side of this from you. But I'm the DA. Folks here elected me to do this. Like I said, I can discuss things in the public domain, but that's it. You understand?"

"Zach, I'm sorry. I should have never mentioned it. Of course, you have to do your job."

"If she's your friend, I know you feel helpless. She doesn't have much going for her."

"She never did. Sheree's a psychology text book of abuse, neglect and trauma. But in spite of it, she was turning her life around." Tears filled her eyes, and she let them tumble over. She felt that in a way, Sheree's failure was her failure. Then she felt Zach take her in his arms.

"I want us to stay close friends through this. I don't want to lose you because I'm the DA. This too shall pass. In a couple of years, I plan to be doing something else, and by then I want to know you lots better." He kissed her.

"I'm sorry I ruined our evening."

"Didn't ruin it for me. We'll stop talking about it." He rose and pulled her up. "What would you say to some of my famous Crème Brûlée right about now?"

She tried to smile. He took that as a yes.

"And I want to revisit the topic of a trip down to Florida with you," he said. "I can use a former client's beach house anytime in the month of September. It's some fancy place, I'll tell you. You'd love it."

They walked into the vast gourmet kitchen. Nothing was antebellum about the kitchen. The cabinets were furniture quality, the appliances, industrial grade. Italian tile graced the walls and the floor was hard wood inlaid with tile in the work areas. Heavy, creamy crown molding coupled the twelve foot ceiling to the walls. Mary Alice perched on a bar stool while Zach torched the crème brûlée sugar topping. She pressed her fingers to the cold granite counter top and half-listened to the description of the Florida house. As a southern beauty queen she'd learned to tune out and smile.

She regretted mentioning Sheree. Zach couldn't be of much help. And worse, whatever bridges to intimacy they had been building, were now blown to hell. He was making fattening desserts while his head was in Florida's sand and surf.

"—and two swimming pools," he said.

The heady odor of melting sugar brought her around.

"I'll have to ask my mama if I can go."

Zach smiled and snapped off the mini torch.

IN BED THAT NIGHT, MARY Alice berated herself again for discussing Sheree with Zach. She feared she'd messed up things with Zach and sealed Sheree's death warrant all in one evening's conversation. She couldn't believe she'd told Zach that Scott Bridges forced Sheree to have sex and that she was afraid of him. Did Mary Alice think that the DA was going to help her because he wanted to take her to bed? And what was she going to do with the coat button she found in Sheree's bathroom? Take it down to the police station and tell them she found the missing clue? She'd say, "Y'all check out the prints and you'll have your killer." She should never have removed evidence. She should have left and come back in the morning, pretending to help her mother with the apartment's renovation. Then she could have "discovered" the button and called the police.

While Mary Alice kicked herself, a thought was born of her guilt. She owed Sheree. Mary Alice had screwed up. While she was getting off on playing Charlie's Angels, and not even playing that well, she had compromised Sheree's case. The button was the single clue of the entire case, and she had rendered it useless. Maybe worse, instead of painting Sheree as a victim, Mary Alice had described her as a woman with a motive. With Scott Bridges dead it didn't much matter if he had been abusing Sheree. The DA wouldn't have any trouble establishing that under the right conditions, Sheree Delio could kill Scott Bridges.

I screwed this up, but I'm going to fix it. I owe her.

She decided then to get Sheree out of jail—to post bail herself. She could get Sheree into a fighting mode. She'd transformed her once. What was one more make-over?

Boon jumped up on the bed, circled once and flopped down in the middle. Mary Alice draped her arm over his furry back and gradually dropped off to sleep.

She dreamed of diving to the bottom of the lake following an elusive button. Scott Bridges' body floated up as she descended into the dark.

CHAPTER 6

"I ALREADY TALKED TO THE BANK. I'm paying Sheree's bail bond," Mary Alice told Georgia. It was early Monday before the Women's Center opened and the time when Georgia took a two mile walk through town. Mary Alice tagged along wishing she'd worn something cooler. Her cream colored Capri length pants and matching Chinese styled top were fully lined and already she could feel sweat gathering, pasting the lining to her back.

"No." Georgia clapped her hands together. "No." She turned into Cana's city park, her strides long and quick.

"Why not?" Mary Alice asked. "We gotta get her out of there if—"

"Mary Alice, I know all the nuances of jail and bail, and I'm working on it. Do not use your money to bail her out."

"Stop a minute and talk to me," Mary Alice said. She felt a trickle of sweat worm down her spine.

Georgia turned and headed for the shade of a live oak tree.

"Why don't you want me to bail her out?" Mary Alice asked. "The center doesn't have ten thousand dollars."

"Because there's not only Sheree to consider here and her bond will cost twenty thousand."

"Not any more. Her lawyer asked for it to be lowered, and the DA didn't fight it."

"I don't suppose you had anything to do with sweetening up the DA." Georgia corralled a hank of Spanish moss tickling her head.

"No. I would have, but I didn't know that was even possible." Mary Alice couldn't believe the argument she and Georgia were having. Couldn't Georgia see that Mary Alice was right?

"That's part of what I'm talking about. You got a huge heart, but you don't know diddly squat about what you're doing." Georgia flopped on a park bench whose plaque stated that it had been placed by the United Daughters of the Confederacy.

"Why shouldn't I bail her out?" Mary Alice sat beside Georgia and smoothed her slacks to keep the linen from wrinkling. "She's too demoralized to think in there."

Nearby, a three-tiered, marble fountain splashed into a pool. Three young children walking its rim threatened to fall in. Two women, absorbed in conversation, ignored the youngsters.

"Reason one is that I'm working with a legal organization in Birmingham that helps indigent women," Georgia said. "It'll provide counsel if they take her case. They think it's better she's in jail so she doesn't get stupid and run off or go get some drugs and get in more trouble."

"If they take her. Are they waiting for the autopsy?"

"Maybe," Georgia said. "But I think they accept the cause of death as heart attack due to a drug overdose."

"Georgia, you didn't see her. She needs to get out."

"The other reason is you, Mary Alice." Georgia's face tightened down as her eyes held Mary Alice. It was what Mary Alice called Georgia's Voodoo look.

"Me personally?"

"She's not your little fix-it project. You're losing perspective on this. We have lots of women to help. Women we have a chance to save."

"Sheree has a chance. But if she goes to jail for murder, that's it for her."

"And will that be it for you, too?" Georgia asked.

"How do you mean?"

"Psychology 101. You're working out your problems through hers."

"You mean my divorce?" Mary Alice asked.

"I mean your marriage. Why do you think I put you two together? You were both hurting in the same way. I knew you'd understand her. I didn't know how far you'd go."

"My marriage?"

"What'd you tell me about it?"

A child fell into the knee deep water and one of the women ran to the pool and jerked him out. He let loose an ear-piercing scream. An agonizing pause preceded his next wail. The woman swatted his backside, and he shrieked as though he were being burned alive.

Mary Alice thought back to the first time she had really talked to Georgia. Right after she had come on the Women's Center board, they'd stayed after a director's meeting and ended up on Georgia's back porch with a bottle of wine. Mary Alice had needed to spill her guts to someone, and Georgia had been willing to listen.

"I told you about the time Cham slapped me." She didn't like where Georgia was taking the conversation. She looked at her lap at the creases that were hardening in the linen slacks. "He didn't hit me very hard."

"What you told me about was ten years of mental abuse. The one slap was what made you finally leave." Georgia's voice, a breathy flute, pulled Mary Alice in.

"Somehow I triggered the meanness in him. I think he sensed I hated him and that I was scared of him."

"Why you heartless bitch. Imagine triggering stuff in that kind doctor. Can you hear yourself even now? You're just like Sheree. Guilty."

"She's not guilty."

"Maybe not of murder, but like you, she feels guilty."

Mary Alice wanted to leave. She looked around for the screaming child, but couldn't see him or his mother.

"Guilty?" Mary Alice repeated.

"At fault? In the wrong? Culpable?" Georgia said. "You remember telling me how he got you all worked up for a trip to Aspen and then canceled because you told him his shirt looked stupid?"

Mary Alice heard her voice turn child-like, and she felt tears pushing up. "I didn't say it was stupid."

"What did you say?" Georgia asked.

"I asked him if he planned on wearing a particular shirt on the plane. He didn't say a word. Just went in his study and closed the door. But I knew. When it came time to leave, he was still in the study. It was a silly shirt with golf clubs printed all over. I shouldn't have cared what he wore."

"You don't think he overreacted a little?"

"Yes. Now I do. But this isn't about me."

"I think you still blame yourself just like Sheree blames herself for all the shit that's come down on her. What I think about your ex is that the bastard deliberately put on his stupid shirt knowing you'd say something." Her voice became a whisper. "Your pain makes you empathetic, but it also blinds you. This is about you."

"I have to do something." She wanted to tell Georgia about the button she'd found and her vow to help Sheree because of it. But she knew Georgia would understand how messing up the investigation made Mary Alice vulnerable. Georgia would say that Mary Alice was helping Sheree out of guilt.

"Hold off on bail for a few more days. Help me with another client."

Mary Alice looked at the ground like a child unfairly punished. "Sheree told me she had something to tell me but couldn't talk in the jail."

"She needs to tell her lawyer what she knows."

"She trusts me."

"Until Friday," Georgia said. "Four days."

Mary Alice nodded. "Who do you need help with?"

"Girl named Millie Cole. I know her mama. Millie's been trading sex for crack with a couple of low-life dope boys in the projects."

"How do you find out stuff like that?"

"Listening to the people who come in my office." Georgia looked at her watch. "I have to get to that office."

Mary Alice walked beside her, keeping pace. They passed the children who were now poking sticks into an ant hill. A woman sat alone on a nearby bench in a fog of cigarette smoke. The boy who had fallen in the pool squinched up his eyes and stuck out his tongue at Georgia and Mary Alice.

"I'll call with Millie's phone number," Georgia said.

"How old is she?"

"Seventeen." Mary Alice shivered and wondered if she'd ever acquire the toughness Georgia seemed to have.

As they crossed the street, three cars politely paused for them. From the park they could hear a child screaming.

"Fire ants," Georgia said, smiling. "It was a fire ant hill. Probably all the justice I'll see this week."

Mary Alice stifled a laugh and wondered if Georgia had always been so unencumbered by bullshit. Mary Alice hoped Georgia's directness would rub off on her.

"Millie needs a psychotherapist," Mary Alice said.

"I know, but ours is off this week, so you'll have to do."

"What do I say?" Mary Alice asked.

"Millie needs someone to talk to, to give her attention. You're good at that, Mary Alice. Help her build some self esteem. I'm not forgetting about Sheree Delio. If we lose her that's bad, but I can't afford to lose you, too."

The group of Hispanic women waiting outside the Women's Center parted and Georgia unlocked the door. Mary Alice put on her sunglasses, took a deep breath and walked back to her car.

AN HOUR LATER IN A back booth at McDonald's, Mary Alice drank coffee and thought about what Georgia had said. Georgia Horn with her major in Psych from Alcorn State had analyzed Mary Alice in a fraction of the time it had taken her Dallas therapist. Mary Alice knew she wasn't over the wounds inflicted by her husband, but she didn't think Georgia was right about everything.

Why wait to bail out Sheree? Mary Alice knew Sheree wouldn't talk to Bobby Lee Buchanan, her court appointed lawyer. Mary Alice prayed that whatever Sheree said she wanted to tell Mary Alice would help. They were desperate for clues.

She sipped her cold coffee, pushed a napkin around in the wet on the table and wondered what Kinsey Millhone would do. This case wasn't shaping up like a typical mystery novel. Usually by page seventy the detective had at least one lead. Mary Alice had zero, except for the one she ruined—the button from Sheree's bathroom. Kinsey would talk to everyone connected to the case. She'd just walk up like she had a right to know and start asking questions. Kinsey would interview Scott Bridges' pals and even better, the ones who called him Bonaparte. Kinsey would talk to the apartment manager where Sheree lived. And what about people who knew Sheree? The dealers and thugs might know something. Kinsey had a cop buddy who slipped her vital information. Mary Alice thought about Otis Turner. Kinsey Millhone used whatever and whoever she had.

Mary Alice considered that she was a Tate and that had always counted for something in Cana. Her mama frequently played that card. Who did she know that knew somebody who would help?

She looked at her watch and when she looked up, Paula Dubose was approaching. Her brown uniform, greasy from her shift, bagged and did nothing for her rotund body.

"You're becoming a regular," Paula said. "I saw your mother in here yesterday."

"My mama?"

"Yeah. She comes through the drive-through after golf. Gets fries."

"My mama?" Elizabeth Tate ate McDonalds' French fries? It was almost easier to imagine her at Mickey's swilling beer and shooting pool.

"She don't know me, but I know her. It's her." She eased her plump feet into a pair of hot pink wedgies.

Mary Alice smiled. Elizabeth Tate professed to hate all fast food because it was trans fat, chemical laden garbage. People who ate it were either lazy or stupid or both. They deserved the health problems that resulted and they were certainly inferior to Elizabeth Tate.

"Next time she comes, super-size her for me."

Mary Alice drove out of the parking lot and waited for a red light. *Mama's sneaking fries; Sheree's in jail; what's next?* When she looked across the street she got her answer. Climbing into a new white Lexus was her ex-husband, Dr. Cham Mauldin III.

CHAPTER 7

MARY ALICE HID AT HOME the next day, Tuesday, to avoid running into her ex. He had family in Cana. Was probably just visiting. But in her head a voice nagged that his appearance had something to do with her. However, when he didn't call or visit by Wednesday noon, she relaxed and shifted all of her worrying energy back to Sheree. The autopsy's assay for triptan in Scott Bridges' body had clearly indicated he died of a myocardial infarction due to a massive dose of the drug. He'd been murdered.

At one o'clock Georgia called to update her on the Birmingham lawyers.

"Why can't they decide?" Mary Alice relaxed her grip on the phone. "Sorry, I didn't mean to yell."

"I'd have thought you'd be happy they're interested in Sheree's case at all."

"I am. I'm just upset."

"They want to talk to you," Georgia said.

"Me? Why?"

"Probably checking to see what kind of support she has," Georgia said. "You need to do this. We want Irene Bardwell to represent her. She's the best."

"When?" Mary Alice propped her feet up on the coffee table and ran her gaze up and down the pre-bleached striations in her designer jeans.

"They'll be here Friday. Ten o'clock."

"Not till then? A week in jail? I need to get her out."

"Stop. You wait until Friday like we said. Mary Alice, this is top notch representation that is almost free. Sheree needs this more than she needs to be out of jail."

"Georgia, I'm her friend." Mary Alice didn't want to tell lawyers about Sheree's past.

"Well, you can tell them that," Georgia said. "And you are more than just a friend. As a Cana Women's Center Board member you have legal authority and responsibility."

Mary Alice wanted to question Georgia about this legal authority, but Georgia charged ahead.

"Did you talk to Millie Cole yet?" Georgia asked.

"No. I may as well tell you. I'm hiding out. I saw Cham in town Monday."

"He messing with you?" Georgia sounded maternal, along the line of a mama bobcat.

"No, laying low is a precaution. He's got a huge medical practice in Dallas. He can't stay in Cana long." Mary Alice heard footsteps outside and a knock.

"Good. Don't forget Millie."

"Hey, I gotta go. Clay's here. He's going to show me how to shoot Daddy's gun."

"Any particular reason a sweet southern belle like you needs to know how to fire weapons?"

"Daddy's .45 isn't weapons plural, and yes, I think it'll make mama feel better about my being out here alone," Mary Alice said. "Or at least get her off my back."

"I have to meet with the city council at four, but after that, I'm driving out there to pay you a call. I can tell when you're not giving me the whole truth."

"I'm not lying." Mary Alice waved at Clay, who waited outside on the deck. He wore the same clothes he had on when he cleaned up after the party, but he looked like he'd shaved.

"Come ahead. Bring a bottle of wine. And, just so you know, there is a long and proud tradition of Tate women who wield arms." After she hung up, she almost regretted inviting Georgia, who had a way of pulling out secrets Mary Alice didn't even know she had. Georgia, however, revealed little about herself. Mary Alice vowed not to tell Georgia about going in Sheree's apartment and finding the button.

She shoved her feet into her new L. L. Bean canvas hiking boots and grabbed the gun. "Hey, Clay."

After the usual patter of greeting, Clay took the gun and slipped it into a canvas bag. "I thought we'd go across the lake. Target practice. I know a good place." He headed for the small boat tied to the dock, and Mary Alice followed.

They didn't talk on the ride, and when they passed a fishing egret, Clay pointed it out with the briefest of nods. She was never on the lake without thinking of her father, who lived in every ripple and reed. She suppressed the longing for him. He'd died suddenly of a heart attack when she was in Dallas. There had been no good-bye.

At an inlet, he cut the motor and coasted ashore. As the waves washing the shore made squashy sounds, he helped her out of the boat.

"Look at this," she said. Tin cans sat on every available log and stump.

Before he let her load the gun, he gave her a safety lecture.

"Okay, Clay. I got it. Don't point it at anybody; don't keep it loaded. I understand it's dangerous."

"It's supposed to be. Remember guns change everything. You can't take one out and wave it around and expect an intruder to just get scared and leave you alone. You need to be prepared to shoot."

"Stop them in their tracks."

"Better if you don't kill them," he said.

"Shoot their legs out from under them. Right?"

He didn't comment.

She wondered what she would have done if she had had a loaded gun at Sheree's apartment when she'd been hiding in the bath tub. She thought of Kinsey Millhone who had blown away a killer when he found her hiding in a trash can.

Clay showed her how to load the gun and how to hold it. "There'll be some recoil. Try holding it with both hands."

She put on the ear protectors and squeezed off two shots which went wild into the brush, shattering only the peace.

"Aim like this," he said.

When he moved in to demonstrate, she smelled an earthy masculine aroma.

"Try those cans over there." He spoke right into her ear so she could hear through the ear protectors.

She fired and hit two cans out of five. "This is fun." Then she hit four out of five.

"Sure you ain't done this before?" he asked.

"Call me Annie Oakley."

"She a good shot?"

"She's a character in a musical comedy. But based on a real woman. Never missed."

"Try a few more of those cans. Over yonder." He pointed to a row of soup cans on a rotten log fifteen yards away.

"Draw, you mangy varmints," she called and blasted away. Through the smoke she saw that none had survived. Clay reset more cans, and Mary Alice knocked them down until the ammo got low.

She smiled at Clay as if she had just shot all the ducks in the shooting gallery and won the biggest teddy bear. She sensed the familiar buzz, the hormone high that accompanied potential risk—like sneaking into a movie theatre. At thirteen, she'd done that with Julio Rodriguez and then, high in the balcony, she'd let him French kiss her.

"Okay. We did it. Ready to go?" Clay asked. He didn't look so excited about her obvious skill. "Unload it. I'll clean it for you when we get back, if you want."

On the boat ride back across the lake, Clay asked, "What happened to Annie Oakley?"

"She decided she wanted a husband more than sharp shooting prizes so she started missing. Ego restored, Frank Butler proposed. The end."

Clay didn't say anything for awhile. "She couldn't have both, huh?"

"No. It's a very realistic play." Mary Alice glanced behind her at Clay and realized that although she had known him for years, she didn't know him at all.

When she turned and looked at the approaching dock, her stomach hardened like old dough. Standing on the edge of the deck was Dr. Cham Mauldin, III.

Even in his tailored suit she could tell he'd put on weight. He held a plastic go-cup that she assumed contained bourbon.

A soft fold of tummy hid his belt. She squinted and tried to see him as the groom he'd been ten years ago, but she couldn't do it.

Before she could deliver a curt, but non-inflammatory greeting, Cham pointed at Clay.

"Sykes, you been out for a spin on the lake with my wife?" Cham asked. His voice, rife with innuendo and shaped by liquor, overplayed his southern accent. He loosened his tie.

Clay kept the boat back, away from the dock.

"What you want, Mauldin?" Clay asked.

Mary Alice hadn't ever heard anyone use a challenging tone with her powerful doctor husband. Ex-husband.

"Wouldn't be neighborly to be in Cana and not visit my wife, would it?" He smiled like a psycho-killer, and Mary Alice felt her stomach flip-flop.

Mary Alice knew his tricks. If she argued that she was no longer his wife, he'd twist things somehow and make her sorry she'd said anything. If she sarcastically agreed that she and Clay had been sporting together on the lake, he'd probably jump in, capsize the boat, drown Clay and assault her. She could almost smell the odor of bully.

"Go on, Cham. I have nothing to say to you," Mary Alice said.

"Don't start your game shit, Mary Alice," Cham said. He'd had more than one drink. "You get up here right now."

"Clay, back us off a few yards," Mary Alice said.

The motor whined as the boat pulled ten yards back.

"You'll run out of gas," Cham said. "I can wait." He ceremoniously sat on a low Adirondack chair and propped his feet on the deck railing.

Mary Alice fought the sensation that she was sinking into a vat of wet concrete which would slowly fill her mouth and nostrils. Why was Cham such a threat? They were divorced. Her anxiety forced the answer.

After their divorce, she'd returned to Dallas to get a final load of possessions. At Cham's request she'd agreed to meet him; it seemed so civilized. They'd had a drink, then two and Cham somehow turned into to his former self. He was courteous, charming and self-effacing. They'd gone to the house, now his house, and somehow ended up in bed. He was gone when she awoke. It was stupid, but not such a big deal. It happened to formerly married couples all the time. She came back to Cana, told no one and pretended the night never happened.

But a few days later, Cham started calling her, asking then demanding she come back to him. The calls stopped when she threatened to call the police. That was two weeks ago.

He couldn't know I've missed a period.

Her breath came faster, almost in rhythm with the pulsing motor. The idea that Cham had come to claim his unborn child, if there was an unborn child, petrified her and her fear spawned paranoia. He was a rich, influential doctor. He'd force a DNA test to prove paternity and then he'd get custody. He'd steal her baby.

Mary Alice snatched the canvas bag from the bottom of the boat and freed the gun. She pulled the pin on the Beretta and inserted the shells like she'd been doing it all her life. Chewing her lip, she aimed at the colored glass floats that she'd set out on the deck railing for last weekend's party.

"Don't capsize us," Clay said, his hand on the throttle, ready to adjust the boat.

When Cham looked at her aiming the .45 he turned white. He struggled to get out of the low slung chair, but a loose board in the arm caught his sleeve, and he flopped like a caught mackerel.

The blast exploded not only two glass floats, but a few feet of the railing. Fragments sailed into the air like fireworks.

Cham fell out of the chair. On his knees he scrambled behind it. "You fucking, crazy bitch—"

Mary Alice fired again to cover his epithets. More glass broke, this time closer to him. Then she sat in the boat, cradling the gun and looking at the man she had once promised to love and honor.

She clearly remembered their wedding in the garden at Linnley, the most elaborate Cana had seen. And she could recall the honeymoon in Maui where they couldn't get enough of each other. He had been charming, witty and if not humble, he was fun. Most important, he'd been exciting, even daring. And now he hid behind a chair amidst broken glass, frothing and swearing—not charming, not witty, and not fun.

"You've got one minute to be off my property," Mary Alice said in a low, even tone.

Screaming curses, the doctor scampered across the deck to his white Lexus and roared away.

Clay took the gun from Mary Alice and stuffed it in the bag. He motored the skiff to the dock and helped Mary Alice out. She was shaking, but there were no tears.

"I'm sorry, Clay. I didn't know he'd come out here—"

"You okay?" Clay asked.

"I will be in a minute. Think he'll call the sheriff and say I tried to kill him?"

"You got a witness says you didn't and bullies are usually cowards. He'd rather keep it quiet his ex-wife made him piss his pants."

"He pissed his pants?"

Clay pointed at the circle of wet on the wood chair.

She smiled. "I didn't mean to get him mad at you."

"You didn't. Your ex and I go back a ways."

She could tell by Clay's expression that Cham had some how cheated or humiliated Clay.

Clay shrugged. "It was years ago." He handed her the canvas bag with the shells and the gun. "If you're okay, I'll be going."

"Thanks." She was glad he hadn't mentioned cleaning the gun. She didn't want to get too far from it. When Clay was out of sight May Alice pulled off her boots and dove into the beer colored water. She swam furiously, her clothing slowing her, screaming into the water. Calmer after ten minutes, she side-stroked back and forth a few yards from the dock.

If Sheree felt like I did a few minutes ago, maybe she did kill Scott Bridges.

Mary Alice turned over and back stroked, keeping an eye on the gun on the deck.

Had Cham really come back to claim her, show everyone that he was in control and that wives did not leave Dr. Mauldin? She reconsidered the pregnancy theory and decided it was crazy. She wasn't pregnant. She'd missed one menstrual period. She'd get a test kit at the drug store just to be sure. She floated and tasted the mineral flavored lake water on her lips. *Is he going to come back?*

She pulled herself up onto the deck and felt the late summer breeze prickle her skin.

Sitting on the deck, trying to explain her behavior to herself, she heard a car coming up the drive. By the time the car came to a stop near the back door, she had reloaded the Beretta. Mary Alice thought she might aim to hit him this time. Georgia Horn got out of the car.

Georgia picked her way among the glass and wood fragments and looked at Mary Alice whose wet hair made her look like a deranged marmot. "This have anything to do with Sheree Delio?"

"Only very indirectly," Mary Alice said. Her voice trembled.

"Looks like somebody shot up the place."

"Annie Oakley."

"And?"

"I got Clay to teach me how to shoot Daddy's .45 because I went over to Sheree's apartment and thought about carrying a gun. I didn't, but someone came in while I was there and I found a button on the floor I think they were looking for and if the cat hadn't meowed they would have found me in the bathtub and maybe killed me even though I didn't find the button until after they left and I was vomiting into the toilet. I don't plan to carry the gun around, but its good insurance, don't you think?"

Georgia lifted her chin in a half nod and said nothing.

"Cham came over and acted all threatening so I fired the gun, not at him, not right at him, but he peed his pants and ran off. Maybe Sheree really did kill Scott. I think what you said the other day is right. I'm possessed by this. I'm not helping." Mary Alice felt sobs shake her before she felt tears. Once she started crying, she couldn't stop.

Georgia sat beside her on the dock and held her, hushing and rocking her.

CHAPTER 8

As dusk lengthened the shadows on the lake, Georgia and Mary Alice walked up to the house. Mary Alice took a hot shower and changed clothes. Georgia poked around in the kitchen.

"Okay if I fry up these chicken breasts?" Georgia asked, as Mary Alice came in the kitchen.

"You don't have to cook," Mary Alice said. She wore shorts and a New York Giants tee shirt. With her hair wet and slicked back, she looked slightly drowned and entirely miserable.

"We have to eat," Georgia said. "Why don't you peel these potatoes? I make good cream potatoes."

"Okay." Mary Alice found the peeler in a drawer and began flicking potato skins into the sink.

Georgia brought her a glass of white wine.

"Thanks."

"You're welcome."

"Thanks for coming out to save me," Mary Alice said. "I'm sorry I flipped out." Bits of potato skins coated the sink. "You're right. I need to let go of Sheree." Although she felt drained, the idea of abandoning Sheree released a wave of panic inside her. She leaned against the counter.

"If you remember, I was coming out anyway." Georgia dipped the chicken into an egg batter and dropped the pieces one at a time into a bag of seasoned flour.

"You thought I was lying about something," Mary Alice said.

"Omitting something—you went to Sheree's apartment last Saturday night." Georgia clutched the bag tightly and shook it.

"That was stupid. I don't know what got into me. You want to see the button I found?"

"Not particularly." Georgia wiped the flour from her hands. "It's useless as evidence, and you don't know it belonged to the killer. It could have been wedged beside that toilet for years."

"It was something, at least," Mary Alice said. "I messed up, Georgia. I have to make it up to her."

Georgia took a sip of wine. "When we talked in the park a couple of days ago I tried to tell you something, but I didn't say it right."

"You said I was losing perspective and getting too emotionally involved to help Sheree; that I was trying to fix my problems by fixing hers." She filled a three-quart pot with water. "I can see that now."

"Hold on." Georgia tested the temperature of the grease in the frying pan by tossing in a few drops of water. They spit. "I want to tell you a story." She eased the chicken into the waiting fat.

Mary Alice turned on a flame under the pot of water and went back to skinning the potatoes.

"I grew up here in Cana. Neither of my parents was educated, but we weren't real poor. Papa mowed yards in summer and swept floors in winter. My mother worked as a maid until 1966 when Project Head Start opened up here. She got a job there the year I was born and was running it the year I graduated from Alcorn State." She rinsed her hands under the tap.

"I took my little psychology degree to Atlanta and got a job in social services working with the underprivileged, undereducated and underpaid. I liked it. I had real cases. But I also had real responsibility."

Mary Alice eased the potatoes into the warming water and sat on a bar stool. She sipped the cold, tart wine.

"I was assigned to the case of an eight-year-old boy who had been removed from his home because the county found his mother unfit to care for him," Georgia said. "He wasn't showing up at school regularly and there were other problems. I hated what was happening to them, and so I worked the case hard to see what could be done."

Using long handled tongs, she carefully turned over each chicken breast. "The more I worked with it, the surer I became that the boy's mother was fit to raise him. She was on welfare, but not on drugs. And she loved her son. I got the case reevaluated, and based on my recommendation the boy went home to his mama."

Mary Alice turned down the burner under the potatoes and put a lid on the pot. "And you learned not to get emotionally involved with your cases," she said.

"I'm not finished. A few weeks later the boy shows up in the emergency room beaten to within an inch of his life. I felt terrible—as though it was my fault. I'd put him in a dangerous environment."

"What'd you do?" Mary Alice sat very still watching Georgia fry the chicken, dodging the popping grease.

"I almost quit a job I loved. No matter who beat the child, he probably wouldn't have been beaten if he had been in foster care instead of with his mama where I put him. My superiors were scrambling to blame me, and I couldn't really disagree with them, none of which helped the boy or his mother. So I had to make some decisions about what mattered to me. In this particular case, all I had was a gut feeling about a mama and her son."

Mary Alice wasn't sure of Georgia's point. Was this a parable about letting go and moving on?

"But I trusted my gut. I fought to keep the police investigation open. Turned out the boy's injuries had nothing to do with his mama or his home environment. I stayed the course of what my heart told me. I'm sure I made some mistakes, but it turned out better for everybody because I didn't give up."

"Oh. That's not where I thought you were going with this," Mary Alice said. "You think I should keep trying to help Sheree?"

"If your gut tells you to." She poked the chicken, careful not to break the delicate crusts she'd built.

"I'm not making things worse?" Mary Alice asked.

"You have credibility here in Cana. Most people will think you're a fool to mess with Sheree, but they can't just dismiss you. And it seems to me your instincts are good."

"But what about my losing perspective?" Mary Alice asked. "You said—"

"What? I can't be wrong one time?" Georgia asked. "You need to work smarter, be less driven. But if I were Sheree, I'd want you in my corner."

Mary Alice felt relief like rain after a long drought. She realized that as bad as her fear of losing Sheree had been, her fear of losing her own confidence was even more intense. She'd needed Georgia's approval. Now she had it. She knew Georgia believed Sheree was going to do jail time, but it seemed Georgia had faith in Mary Alice. She watched Georgia serve their plates, barely unable to articulate her gratitude.

"Thanks," Mary Alice said.

AFTER DINNER, THEY SAT IN the living room, each occupying a sofa. One soft lamp burned, turning the room to honey.

"So why you think your ex tripped your fuse like that?" Georgia asked. "He can't force you to go back to him."

Mary Alice smiled at Georgia's directness. Few southern women, black or white came to the point quickly. "I'm not sure." She didn't intend to tell her how a one time sexual encounter had created fears of being pregnant or how that fear had mutated into paranoia. Besides, she didn't feel pregnant.

"If you had any idea, what would it be?" Georgia asked.

"He scared me. Triggered all the old fears. Is there any more wine in that bottle?"

Georgia passed her the bottle.

"I can't fathom how Cham and I got to this place," Mary Alice said, filling her glass. "Maybe if we'd had children things would have worked out."

"Why didn't y'all have kids?" Georgia asked.

Mary Alice gulped her wine to cover her anxiety. Georgia asked about past children, but Mary Alice heard present children. She wanted to tell Georgia the whole story, but it embarrassed her, and she knew Georgia would have them down at Parker Drugs in a flash buying a pregnancy test kit. Georgia would supervise the test and counsel Mary Alice on her options if the result were positive. And there was another reason she hadn't told Georgia. Mary Alice suspected the whole pregnancy thing was partly wishful thinking. It was too complicated. She'd buy the kit tomorrow and end speculation.

"We tried," Mary Alice said. "I just never got pregnant."

Georgia didn't say anything else, and Mary Alice was relieved not to replay that part of her past. Cham had let Mary Alice know that the problem lay with her. He was a doctor; he knew.

The two women listened to the sounds of the night filtering through the screens—millions of creatures struggling to eat and reproduce before they died.

Georgia broke the stillness. "After y'all divorced, did you ever think about going somewhere else besides Cana?"

"No. Not once."

"It can't have been easy to come back," Georgia said. "I think you had the biggest wedding Cotashona County ever saw. Big hoopla, big come down."

"Some people were probably disappointed in me, but even with the embarrassment, I was glad to get home. In Cana, I'm part of something and not just because I'm a Tate. In Dallas I never fit anywhere. As Cham's wife I met hundreds of very nice people, but they weren't my people. Maybe it's just nostalgia, but I love the movie theatre where I kissed Bobby Earl Pitts when we were eleven, I love Ebel's Dry cleaners where they know my name, ditto for Dotty's Café and Parker Drugs. I love that we have towns named Shuqualak, Hot Coffee, Rolling Fork. I missed the music of Mississippi voices. There's nothing better than walking past the long bench on the square where all the old men sit at noon. Hearing them talk and joke."

"You should get a job with Mississippi Tourism," Georgia laughed.

"Wouldn't you miss Cana? Didn't you when you lived in Atlanta?"

"Not the same way you did."

"I know people talk about me," Mary Alice said. She knew some delighted in the apparent fall of a Tate. But she also knew that in time the gossip would die unless she did something to fuel it.

"How'd your mama take your coming back?"

"Schizophrenia. One day, head high, don't anybody say anything about my daughter and the next day, pulling my hair and telling me what a fool I was and how I'd never find a husband as good as Cham."

Georgia laughed and stretched out on the sofa.

Of course now that I'm dating Zach, mama's thrilled."

"How y'all getting along?"

"It'll be easier when Sheree's case is decided," Mary Alice said.

"I'm sure it will."

"What about you?" Mary Alice asked. A cool breeze sneaked in off the lake, soft as a baby's sigh.

"What about me?"

"Men. Any men in your life?" Georgia had dodged this question before. "And don't give me that when-would-I-ever-have-time-for-a-man crap."

"It's the truth."

"You told me there was a guy in Atlanta."

"There was."

Mary Alice waited. Even if Georgia didn't confide in her about a failed relationship, it felt good to talk like this with her. Since college, Mary Alice couldn't remember any close girlfriends, ones she could trust with secrets. She wondered if Georgia was tight with anybody.

"Remember the story I just told you about recommending a child be returned to his mother and then him getting beat up?" Georgia asked.

"Yes."

"My superior, who of course had approved my decision, got worried he'd get sued or fired."

"And?"

"He was my boyfriend."

"Your boyfriend was your boss?" Mary Alice sat up and looked at Georgia.

Georgia nodded and shrugged. "He hung me out to dry quicker than anybody and then when it turned out I was right, he acted like he was only putting a professional distance between us while the heat was on. My trust of the other gender is a bit low," Georgia said. She narrowed her eyes and returned Mary Alice's gaze.

They sat in silence. A night bird cried in the woods beyond the lake.

"Georgia?" Mary Alice said.

"Uh-huh."

"How'd you have the courage to stand up and fight? You know, in Atlanta?"

"I'd like to tell you it was because I was raised in the church—and by parents who had a strong moral code. But I don't think so."

Mary Alice waited for more.

"It was a crisis of conscience. I thought I was going to lose everything anyway so I took a chance and asked myself what would I do if fear wasn't controlling me and all my decisions? When I stopped being so scared, lots of ideas popped up."

"You're tougher than I am."

"I don't know about that, Miss Oakley," Georgia said. "I have to tell you that even though I don't approve of guns, I wish I'd been a fly on the wall this afternoon." Her deep contralto laugh jiggled the air.

Mary Alice joined her, letting the sounds soothe her. Hearing Georgia's story made Mary Alice hungry for a deeper intimacy. "You told me you thought I wasn't giving you the whole truth. Remember?" Mary Alice asked. "Now I think you're not telling me everything."

"About what?"

"Is there anybody you open up to?" She felt the room turn brittle as parchment.

"Don't get paranoid. I just want to know you."

"You know me," Georgia said.

"Is it because I'm white and you're black?" Mary Alice asked.

"No," Georgia said in a low voice. "It's because you're nosy and impertinent." She laughed. "Good things take time. Hey, you got any ice cream in the freezer?" Georgia asked.

"Cherry Garcia and Jamoca Almond." She gave up on pushing Georgia. She hadn't known her a year yet. Relationships took time. "And some Klondikes, Heathbars and frozen Snickers. And other stuff."

At ten o'clock, Georgia left. Mary Alice locked the doors and killed the lights. In bed with Boon snoring softly beside her, she wondered if Georgia had been trying to tell her something or if she had been trying to find out something. She kicked back the sheet and lay naked in the moist night air.

She hoped her prying hadn't offended Georgia. Courting Georgia's friendship wasn't some trip into another exciting world that would satisfy Mary Alice's passion for new thrills. Mary Alice hoped that knowing Georgia Horn might arrest the desire for risky stimulation by replacing it with something more meaningful.

Georgia will reveal herself, or not, in her own sweet time.

But Georgia had said Mary Alice was brave to come back to Cana. Georgia thought Mary Alice was helping Sheree. Mary Alice hadn't expected that.

As the night symphony lulled her to sleep, she lapsed into a dream. She was acting in an old-fashioned melodrama directed by Chase Minor. Georgia was in it too. Both of them wore crinolines and picture hats. Georgia was singing a song about how men were no damn good.

CHAPTER 9

THURSDAY NIGHT, MARY ALICE WAITED for thirty minutes at Denny's. When Georgia's teenaged client, Millie Cole didn't show, Mary Alice drove over to the Cana Little Theatre auditions. The night had cooled enough for her to roll down the car windows. The breeze blew her hair. Dumping her emotional burden on Georgia had felt good yesterday, but today the anxiety had returned. As she pulled into the theatre parking lot, the oldies station played a Neil Young tune. Neil was searching for a heart of gold, and he said he was growing old. She understood.

Housed in a converted storefront just off the square, the 150-seat theatre looked like a Christmas store or a bordello. Everything was red plush. Mary Alice had always thought it felt like a giant womb.

The theatre people, Chase Minor called them Thespians, were delightfully zany. She depended on them to dispel the residual unease she carried from Cham's visit and her worries about Sheree. She paused in the tiny lobby to chat with Theatre Cana regulars and saw several new faces.

"Mary Alice," Chase squealed when he saw her coming down the aisle. "Goody, goody. You can read first."

"Chase, I'm so sorry, but I cannot audition."

His enthusiasm snuffed by her rejection, he retreated into a snit.

"I'll do props or sell tickets," she promised him.

"Anybody can sell the damn tickets." He stalked away and announced that auditions were commencing.

A thirtyish woman Mary Alice didn't know read the part of Birdie from Lillian Hellman's *The Little Foxes*. "There are people who eat the earth and eat all the people on it like in the Bible with the locusts. And other people who stand around and watch them eat it."

Hearing the playwright's words, Mary Alice agreed with Birdie that it wasn't right to just watch them do it. She thought of Sheree who shared a lot with mistreated Birdie even though distanced in time and social station. Mary Alice had vowed not to stand around and watch them eat Sheree, but preventing Sheree's annihilation was another thing entirely.

Chase smiled broadly and thanked the woman for her reading. He had his Birdie.

"Mary Alice," a tall, slightly-faded beauty said. "I'm sorry we missed your party. We were in Orlando. The twins had a Wendy-Peter Pan birthday party."

Mary Alice recognized Evelyn Alexander, whom she'd known all her life. Evelyn had been a Chi Omega at Ole Miss and had never quite given it up. Mary Alice suspected her mother wished Mary Alice had turned out like Evelyn.

"Evelyn Alexander. I missed y'all." Of course, Evelyn must have heard about Sheree's arrest at the party, but her good manners prevented any comment on the unpleasantness. "Are you trying out?" Mary Alice asked.

"Burt is. He wants to be the old man, Horace. He dies a dramatic death on the staircase, and Burt's been practicing all week. Our housekeeper nearly had a coronary when she saw him sprawled out on the front staircase. If Chase won't let him read that scene, I don't know what Burt's going to do."

"Burt's a wonderful actor." Burt Alexander had to be a wonderful actor. Mary Alice knew of two affairs he'd had, and she was pretty sure Evelyn was still in the dark.

"While I'm thinking of it, come over Sunday after church." Evelyn said. "We're having a small gathering for just a few old friends. It's unforgivable, the short notice, but can you?" Evelyn looked as though her personal happiness depended on a yes from Mary Alice. Elaborate last-minute brunches and cocktail parties were common at the Alexander's. The good feeling Mary Alice called "in the Bosom of Cana" swamped her.

"I think I'm free. It'd be wonderful to see—"

"Quiet in the house please," Chase's assistant barked. "We're trying to audition." He tapped his pen on his clipboard.

Evelyn whispered, "Are you going to the Weeds' party next Saturday?"

"I forgot. It's at the river house, isn't it."

"They've got two hundred folks coming; it better not be at the condo."

"Isn't there an Ole Miss football game Saturday?" Mary Alice asked.

"Ladies," the assistant hissed. "Shush."

"Sorry," they said in unison.

95

Another young woman was reading Birdie from the same scene. "Everybody knew that's what he married me for. Everybody but me. Stupid, stupid me." She didn't read as well as the first Birdie, but she sounded like she had personal insight into the character. It occurred to Mary Alice for the ga-zillionth time that Cham had married her for reasons other than love and that she married him because he was fast-tracking to doctor-world. But she knew she thought she'd loved him.

Why did people always marry and then seem to screw it up? Mary Alice's Daddy had explained they didn't love themselves so had no chance of loving another. Would she repeat the same pattern if she married Zach?

Mary Alice wanted to tell Birdie to swallow her pride, leave that bastard husband and go back to her own people. Mary Alice always knew what other women should do.

Mary Alice left auditions early promising to help with props. She drove around town thinking about being back in Cana. She'd missed being well-known to so many people. People who knew her family, her grandparents, who saw her in dance recitals and school plays. People who autographed her cast when she broke her arm and who took in the stray animals she brought them. In Cana, she existed; she was part of a chain that went back in time and was forged with trust and respect.

She wasn't sure Georgia had understood how important Mary Alice's ties to Cana were. But Georgia had understood about Cham.

The thought of her ex-husband made her shiver. *Shoot. I forgot to by the test kit.*

She passed strip mall shops: pizza, eye doctor, cheap shoes, bank and a dry cleaners and entered the historic town square. The court house, built in 1841 and somehow spared by General

Sherman, occupied the center of the square and was said to be more attractive even than the court house in New Albany. The copper-domed cupola looked down on pricy shops, restaurants, three banks and a dozen law offices. Since she was a child, the names had changed, but not the feeling. A few blocks off the square, she passed Mickey's Bar and Grill and turned into the nearly full parking lot.

As she pushed open the door, a couple came out. The man stepped aside and held the door for her. Mary Alice thanked him. He gave her a nod and a "yes ma'am."

You don't get manners like that in Dallas. Or anywhere else.

She paused inside the door, recalling her first visit to Mickey's when she was barely sixteen. She and three friends, made-up and dressed to look older, kept to the shadows and inveigled drinks from older men. She had loved the smoke, the jukebox tunes, the sexual tension that charged the air, and she'd envied the waitresses who got to banter with the regulars and priss around Mickey's in tight jeans and low cut tops. The girls got thrown out, but as soon as Mary Alice got her driver's license, she led her friends to bars on the coast where nobody knew them and IDs were only sporadically checked.

Through the cigarette smoke haze she saw Otis Turner, alone, anchoring one end of the bar. She approached. "Otis Turner." Mary Alice smiled a Miss America contestant smile into his face. She felt like an undercover detective setting the stage for an interrogation. Her pulse picked up.

His mouth dropped open. "Hey. What are you doing here?" He jumped off the bar stool.

She felt a twinge. She liked Otis and didn't want to use him. He seemed so pleased she'd joined him. But she needed information more than she needed integrity.

"Just left auditions for the play." She shrugged as though stopping at Mickey's were *de rigueur* for theatre folk after auditions. She reasoned to herself that sometimes the ends justified the means. Sheree had no one to help her except Mary Alice, and Mary Alice had screwed up the only piece of evidence that might have helped Sheree.

"Waymon," he called to the bartender. "What'll you have?" They settled at the bar next to each other.

"Vodka tonic with a twist."

She navigated through pleasantries about her mother, Otis' brother's soybean crop, the price of gasoline, and why she was not going to act in the play, hoping he would mention Sheree. When he didn't, she thanked him again for letting her in the jail to talk to Sheree.

"Mary Alice, I know you're worried about Sheree." He downed the rest of his beer and gave a nod to the bartender when he delivered Mary Alice's vodka.

"I know. Y'all are treating her great, and I shouldn't worry," she said.

"She killed a cop. They're not treating her so great," he said, looking straight ahead at his reflection in the bar mirror.

She looked at him in the mirror and then swung around on the bar stool to face him. "What's going on?" The smoke in the bar felt like icy sludge choking her senses. If they were hurting Sheree—

"Nothing illegal, but she hasn't confessed and that's pissing off the whole department."

"Because she didn't do it."

"Somebody did. You know." He flipped over the cardboard Budweiser coaster and flipped it back.

"I'm posting her bail tomorrow." She lifted her drink and drained half of it. She knew that even if he wanted to, it would be impossible for Otis to keep his job and to report that somebody was mistreating Sheree. Mary Alice had to get Sheree out before something bad happened.

Otis' beer arrived. "She won't even talk to her lawyer."

"What would you do if you had Bobby Ray Buchanan between you and jail?" she asked. She didn't mention Irene Bardwell taking over Sheree's case.

He shook his head. "Where you going to take her?" he asked. "After she's out."

"I thought she could stay at the battered women's shelter." She thought of Sheree as battered. Battered by life.

Otis straightened up on the bar stool and turned a quarter turn toward her. "She got any family at all?"

"No. She doesn't have anyone."

"That's not true."

"What?"

"She's got you, Mary Alice."

A sharp stab hit her gut. She took Otis' words as affirmation and wanted to hug him.

"And I'm scrabbling like a caught crab in a basket. Otis, I know about flower arrangements, which fork to use, bread and butter letters. I don't know about criminal defense." She pressed her cold glass against her cheek.

"Get her out and get her a real lawyer." He almost whispered.

"But Otis, somebody did kill Scott Bridges and nobody's looking for him."

Otis shrugged. He didn't seem to want to cross Mary Alice, but she knew he didn't agree that Sheree was innocent. She wished she could tell him about the person who came to

Sheree's apartment and the button. "Otis, somebody needs to look for the real killer. That's what will free Sheree."

"You don't go look for something you got."

"But Sheree didn't—isn't it possible somebody's framing her?"

Otis gulped his beer. "You could hire a private investigator."

"Maybe Kinsey Millhone."

"I don't know her, but there's a bunch in Jackson and Memphis too." He dug a cigarette pack out of his shirt pocket and laid it on the bar.

"I couldn't afford Kinsey." She allowed the silence to stretch between them, giving Otis time to think. It was going to take all the available cash she had to make bail. Hiring a PI wasn't going to happen.

"I'll tell you a weird thing about all this is Scott's wife, Katherine," Otis said. "She wasn't at his funeral."

"She'd have to be upset her husband was found dead in another woman's bed."

"That's true, but still." Otis wiped the beer from his lips. "People usually care about keeping up appearances. I mean, he is dead."

"Maybe she couldn't face it," she said.

"There's another thing," he said. "Sheree's lawyer got her bail lowered, and Katherine Bridges didn't say nothing. The victim's family usually raises hell about any breaks for the defendant."

Mary Alice shook her head. The movement made her look at her reflection in the bar mirror. She looked tired. "You know Scott Bridges? Did you like him?"

"He was a prick," Otis said. "Sorry. He was a jerk. Always bragging. Nobody liked him or wanted to work with him."

"Why?"

"Everything had to be his way, and he took all the credit."

"Were they jealous?"

"Just because nobody liked him doesn't mean he wasn't good at what he did. He made that drug task force. In a month, we had more arrests than we'd had in two years. Even after they cut resources. I'm sorry he's dead, but I don't miss him."

"Y'all called him Napoleon?

"Couple of guys started calling him Bonaparte. He was fixed on hisself and of course, was just a little peanut."

"What did he brag about? Women?"

"He was always talking about girlfriends, but mostly it was a bust that was about to happen all because of his great detective work."

Mary Alice imagined Scott Bridges strutting around the station boasting about the women who were wild about him and the dealers who were terrified of him. He must not have known about Waterloo.

"But Otis, maybe one of the dealers Scott busted killed him."

"They're in jail."

"Did anyone check? Maybe there's somebody y'all didn't get."

"Mary Alice, he died of a massive dose of a drug for migraines. Sheree used it and had some. They found the spent cartridges with her fingerprints. She had means, opportunity and she had motive."

"What motive?"

"Let's just say he was making her do things she didn't want to do."

"Informing?" she said. "Did everyone know about that?"

Otis paused a second. "Yes, and sex. Scott let everyone know she was giving up more than information."

Mary Alice rubbed the back of her neck. So everybody knew Sheree wanted to get away from Scott—from the informant deal and probably from him personally. Everybody believed Sheree was guilty.

"Mary Alice, don't you do nothing now." Concern coated his voice. "Bail her out and leave it to the lawyer. You could get hurt."

"Don't worry, Otis. I'm—" For the first time it occurred to her that she could be in danger if she was right about somebody framing Sheree. That somebody wanted Sheree to take the blame and wouldn't tolerate interference. She finished the last of the vodka and tonic.

"Good to see you, Otis." She wanted to tell him, "if there's anything you can tell me that'd help her, call me. I need somebody inside, Otis. Somebody who'll hear gossip, tips, clues." But Otis worked for the Cana police; he couldn't take her side. She slid off the bar stool. "I'll get her out and leave it to the lawyers." She answered his wave in the bar mirror with one of her own.

I can't trust anybody.

As she drove home, the rural quiet was penetrated by the car radio advertising Toyotas and legal services. She parked beside the house, turned off the car's engine and sat listening to the insect chorus ricocheting among the trees. Joining Boon on the deck, she collapsed into a chair and scratched the lab's damp fur. The lake rippled the moon's reflection into a free form of melted gold. Boon sighed and rolled over onto Mary Alice's feet.

The splintered breach in the railing looked like a bombed bridge. Beneath the gap, Clay had neatly stacked the lumber he would use for repairs.

She saw Cham on the deck as he had been yesterday. When was the last time she had said "I love you" to Cham?

She could remember just after they were married, waking early and watching him sleep. She had loved to trace the arch of his cheekbone to his closed eye and back again over the ruffle of eyelashes. She had stifled the desire to stroke the blond hair on his brow. It might have waked him.

She couldn't isolate the day it all started to turn like a big slow B-52 changing course. Maybe it was the night he said her neckline was too low for her, that she looked ridiculous. She had tried to laugh it off. She had failed. Certainly the turn-about was well underway by the time he humiliated her in front a dozen doctors and their wives with a fabricated story of how her ancestors held slaves before the civil war and sold out to Yankees after it.

She forced Cham from her mind by looking at the empty chair beside her, and thought of all the times she and her father had sat outside watching lightning bugs wink beside the dark water.

"Daddy would know what to do," she told the dog. She wished a ghost Daddy would materialize.

Even after a few bourbons, her father could patiently guide her though her options. What to do when a boy broke her heart, when her mama wouldn't speak to her for a week or when she failed algebra. She could hear him repeat, "Don't project your fears into the future. Take care of today. Pull your chair over here close to me."

"The Birmingham lawyer is going to help us or not help us," she told Boon. "All I can do is be myself. Tomorrow I'll bail her out, and she can help herself."

She let her thoughts drift. What had Otis said about Scott Bridges' wife? She didn't come to the funeral. Why? Had the DA's office even talked to her? And did it matter that she didn't protest lowering Sheree's bail? Did she even know?

Mary Alice felt a churning, like gears that spin and slip. She remembered something about six degrees of separation. Anything you needed to know was no more that six people away—someone you knew who knew someone else who knew someone and so on. She knew a lot of people. Deeply inhaling the soupy Mississippi air, she fixed on the waning moon.

I need to talk to Katherine Bridges.

CHAPTER 10

MARY ALICE'S FRIDAY MORNING INTERVIEW at the Women's Center with two attorneys from Birmingham lasted barely fifteen minutes. Professional and inscrutable, they asked her a few questions about her background; they seemed to know all about Sheree. They promised that on Monday they'd let Georgia know who would be taking Sheree's case.

"I've arranged for the money at E-Z Bailbonding," Mary Alice said, sinking into a chair opposite Georgia's desk. She kicked off the heels she had worn to complement the navy blue outfit. The Vera Wang jacket fit as though it was tailored for her; the slacks made her legs look long. She hoped the ensemble said responsible, capable, but then wondered if her sartorial message should have been, help me, help me.

Georgia sipped her coffee straight from a thermos. "Police office called. They'll release Sheree after lunch."

"They want a few more hours to torment her?"

"Why don't you let me go get her?" Georgia asked.

"Alone?"

"Yes. They won't mess with me. It might be easier for Sheree. Newspaper might be there. Look better if I'm the one taking her out."

Mary Alice nodded. "Tell her I'll come see her tonight." She picked up a flyer for an auction and fanned herself. The barometric pressure had taken a swan dive and the air conditioner couldn't keep up.

"You get her stuff?"

"Mama's having her old apartment all but gutted. She sent her things over to the shelter-house. I don't think anybody ever died in one of mama's properties before. She's talking about having that psychic who lives out on the highway come and do something."

"Like what?"

"Make sure Scott Bridges' ghost isn't there, I guess. But she's afraid somebody at the Episcopal Church will find out."

Georgia laughed and tilted back in her chair as far as she dared. The chair had been donated to the center and had been known to dump its occupant on the floor if pushed too far. "Don't expect much from Sheree at first," Georgia said.

"I know. Hope is the only thing that's going to get her back to normal," Mary Alice said. She felt the beginning of a headache coming on. Nothing was easy. The adrenalin rush she'd felt a few days ago had fizzled. She wasn't getting anywhere, and the hunt for clues was more depressing than exciting.

"You going to tell Sheree about the button you found?"

"Yes. That's its only use. Like you said, it won't hold up as evidence of anything, but she might see some meaning in it."

"Or it could be something she dropped and the cops missed."

"If it was insignificant, why was someone looking for it in the dark?"

"Maybe they were looking for something else. Or maybe he was going to leave something."

"No. He or she was looking inch by inch. For something."

"Okay, Nancy Drew, you going to tell her about the mystery visitor too?" Georgia asked.

"I think so. It might make her remember something." Mary Alice had a vague feeling that because Sheree had been present when Scott was murdered, she knew what had happened even if she didn't consciously know. Maybe a hypnotist could make Sheree recall what happened that night. Mary Alice rubbed the back of her neck.

"I'll let her know about the lawyer," Georgia said.

"Hardly a choice."

"It's still Sheree's decision. We need to remember that."

Even Georgia was annoying Mary Alice. The headache ratcheted up a notch. She changed the subject.

"Georgia, you know anything about Scott Bridges?"

"He got appointed to run the Drug Task Force because the police chief didn't think there were any illegal drugs in Cana. Scott changed the chief's mind in a week. I told them a year ago about drugs in the projects—how the pickups worked, which houses. They didn't do squat. But Scott Bridges got cops placed in nearby buildings with binoculars so they could see the comings and goings. He videotaped everything. The projects are clean now."

"Otis said his wife didn't attend his funeral."

"You talking to Deputy Turner again?"

"And anybody else who knows anything. Nobody else is doing anything."

"Why can't you get your boyfriend to check things out?"

"And say what? Oh Zach honey, I think maybe Scott's wife killed him when she found out he was doing Sheree. Could you check it out?"

"I was kidding, Mary Alice."

"You don't like Zach Towree, do you?"

"Why you say that?" Georgia asked.

"Because you're stalling for time right now by asking that."

"We've had our differences. He's a good ole boy, you know." The sound of the front door opening stopped her. Georgia went to the door of her office and looked into the waiting room. "I'll be with you in a minute."

Mary Alice had a clear image of the Cana good ole boys. They weren't the rich, racist planters and bankers of generations back, but they still held tremendous power. They weren't all racist, but they were all men, their women exerting influence indirectly.

"I'm going to find a cop Scott Bridges worked with," Mary Alice said. "He might know something." She felt reluctant to leave.

"But he ain't going to want to tell you," Georgia said. "Nailing Sheree is what they all want."

Mary Alice had to work to control her voice. All anybody ever said was no, this or that won't work. Nobody had any good ideas, but they shot hers down. "I still want to talk to a cop. You have any idea who'd be good?"

"Tom Jaworski," Georgia said. "He probably won't talk to you, but if he does, it means he's curious about what happened and why."

"How do you know him?"

"I know them all," Georgia said. She looked at the office door signaling she had to talk to the client in the waiting room. "Tom's clean as far as I know. Smart too."

Mary Alice got up and stuffed her feet back into her shoes. Their pinch made her think of Chinese foot binding. "Call me on my cell phone if there's trouble with the bail."

"You okay?" Georgia asked. "I mean from Wednesday?"

"You mean Cham?" She walked to the door.

Georgia nodded.

"No further contact," she said. "I witnessed him peeing his pants. He probably has a hit out on me."

Mary Alice left by the side door and headed for Parker Drugs. There she encountered six people she knew and realized she wasn't going to purchase a pregnancy test kit. She bought a Hershey bar. Outside the weather had turned muggy. The air seemed saturated with rain that wouldn't or couldn't fall.

Back in the car, she struggled to crank the BMW. It seemed that every third trip it gave her trouble. Rhum-a-rhum-a-rhum.

Please start. I can't afford to buy another car.

It coughed to life and in five minutes she was through town, heading north to a seventies subdivision of ranch houses. The phone book had provided the Bridges' address. Boon rode shotgun.

"Katherine Bridges finds her husband in bed with Sheree and kills him," Mary Alice told the dog. "She couldn't take it any more. But to maintain the appearance of innocence, she'd come to his funeral. Wouldn't she?"

Boon slapped the upholstery with his tail.

"And why would she kill him with Sheree's migraine medicine? She'd bring a knife or a gun. Unless she saw the drug there and decided she could use it instead of her weapon and pin it on Sheree. Why would she even know the stuff would kill a person? Unless she has migraines too. And of course she'd know her husband had a weak heart, would be susceptible."

The dog stuck his nose out the open window as though clues rode on the wind.

Without a badge, Mary Alice knew she wasn't going to get anything out of Katherine Bridges, but she wanted to see Scott Bridges' house. Private investigators looked at things like that. Clues were everywhere if you knew what you were looking at. And doing something, anything, felt better than stewing. Her headache had receded.

"This is not like breaking into a crime scene," she assured the dog. "I'm just going to ring the bell. Maybe she's back home and will talk to me. I'm not being stupid."

Boon pulled his head in and gave her a worried look that said he wanted to stay in the car.

"What? You don't think I should do this?" she asked the dog.

He curled up on the seat, put his head down and covered his nose with his tail.

She slowed and turned into the subdivision. The letter W sagged on the Woodlawn Pointe sign. The Bridges' house, number 103 sat in a stand of trees. Thick pine straw blanketed the yard. A concrete bird bath lay on its side. She turned into the driveway. No cars, no lights. Leaving the engine running, she went to the front door and rang the bell. She could hear the bong, bong, but no footsteps. She rang again and tried to look in the smudged window beside the door. The place felt empty, eerie.

She looked around and then walked to the back of the house. All the windows were covered. In the sliding glass patio door's track, she saw a dowel. As she tried to peer through the sheer draperies, she wondered if the door weren't locked, would she go inside. A crow landed on a branch overhead and screeched, startling her. She stumbled, tripped on a flower pot, fell and landed on the aggregate patio. Her palms stung.

Quickly, she got up and walked to the car, making up stories she'd tell anyone who had seen her. But there was no one but Boon.

She pulled back onto the main highway from Woodlawn Pointe and accelerated to fifty.

"It's logical she'd go away considering the circumstances of her husband's murder," she told Boon. "That's not surprising. But if she left before the funeral, maybe she's running away from something or someone."

But what did surprise Mary Alice were the flashing red and blue lights of a Cana Police black and white vehicle moving up on her rear bumper.

She pulled over onto the shoulder and fumbled in the glove box for her license and registration. A melted Moon Pie fell on the floor.

A tall uniformed officer sauntered to her car.

"Afternoon Ma'am."

The slope of the road's shoulder tilted the car so much that the officer towered over her. He bent and loomed in the window. Mary Alice looked up at him. A purple birth mark covered part of his neck, and though he was young, his hairline told her he'd be bald on top in a couple of years. "Is that you Kenny? Kenny Bates?"

"I'm Officer Kenny Bates." A wad of tobacco pushed out his left cheek; he spoke out of the right side of his mouth.

Mary Alice smiled as though a lost brother had materialized. All the Bates boys, who looked like they'd have relatives named Muley, Vern and Junior, were known to be mean, terrorizing bullies. Kenny, the youngest of five, held the honor of being the worst. "I haven't seen you since high school."

"You remember me from school?" School was *scoo*. His tough cop tone changed. She watched him waver between the domains of official and personal. Kenny liked talking about himself.

"Your brother, Wayne, was in my class. You were one back, weren't you?"

"Two back from Wayne."

She could see him trying to work out in his mind what to do. She knew she hadn't been speeding.

"Why'd you stop me, Kenny?" She said it as though she were asking him if he'd like another serving of homemade banana cream pudding.

"Miz, uh ah, Mary Alice, you were trespassing."

"Trespassing? When?" She gripped her license, aware he hadn't asked for it. They were watching Scott Bridges house, maybe looking for the real killer.

"Back there in Woodlawn. The Bridges' house."

"Gosh Kenny. I'm so sorry. It wasn't posted. I just rang the bell. I didn't touch a thing."

"Mind if I ask you why you were there?" The menacing timbre returned, congealing his words like drying syrup.

"I wanted to see Katherine Bridges."

"Why?"

"Kenny, that's not anybody's business. And she wasn't home." She tried to sound as if her business were personal and possibly of a female nature. "Have I committed a crime?"

"No, ma'am. The police are curious about anybody at Scott Bridges' house seeing as how, well, you know."

"Good, I'm glad the police are interested. I promise I won't go back." Mary Alice forced herself to look calm by trying to think of the capital of North Dakota.

"We'd appreciate it." Kenny smiled, revealing a row of soft, yellow-brown teeth. Between slits, milky blue eyes observed her. "You drive careful for me now. You hear?" He spit a stream of brown juice near her front tire.

"Thanks, Kenny. You do the same for me." *You patronizing asshole.*

He lumbered back to his cruiser, did a u-turn over a double yellow line and sped away.

She tried to put her license back in her wallet and realized her hands were shaking. He had never asked for it. Were the police interested in Katherine Bridges or someone else? Kenny Bates' creepy score was a ten plus. How had she gotten into this?

She felt an urge to race home, shower with Givenchy bath gel and then do something normal like read her horoscope or high-end mail order catalogs. Instead she drove to the District Attorney's office.

"I'll just be a little while," she told Boon, who hated waiting in the car. "You got shade and water. Take a nap in the back seat."

She crossed through the greenbelt known as Faulkner's Corner with its bench dedicated to the memory of the irascible writer from over in Oxford and cut between two brick buildings. In the tight passage she squeezed past Arnold Bell who for a moment held her against the bricks with his rotund belly while he chatted amicably and looked at her chest. Out on the square she heard a child screaming and a patient mother explaining, "Thomas Ray, you cannot have any more pralines this morning." The store windows reflected her silhouette, dark against the bright reflected sky. The odor of chocolate wafting from the candy store seamlessly rode into the smell of mildew from the used book store, housed in the oldest building on the square. When she crossed the street to get to the courthouse in the center of the square, Cana's only taxi waited for her to pass.

She found her way through the court house maze to Zach's office. His door stood ajar.

"Why, Ms. Tate, what a pleasure," Zach said, standing as Mary Alice entered. "You had lunch yet?" As he came toward her and embraced her, the Kenny Bates anxiety melted like a pat of butter on grits.

"No, I didn't come for lunch."

"But you gotta eat." He took his suit jacket from its hook behind a rattan screen and slipped it on.

"I don't want to disturb you. I know how busy you are."

"I was going to make one of the clerks go eat with me at Dotty's. Friday's blue plate special is catfish." He headed to the door and opened it, waiting.

"Well, okay. Thank you. I love Dotty's catfish. I grew up on it."

"Me too."

They walked the block from the court house to the restaurant famous for its Mississippi farm raised catfish, slaw, hush puppies and peach cobbler. Even though it was only one o'clock, Mary Alice could feel the thank-God-it's-Friday mood in the street. Zach held the door for her; the café's greasy breath enveloped them.

Between them, they knew everybody in Dotty's Cafe and passed among the diners greeting and exchanging pleasantries. The men good-naturedly teased Zach for being on a date with a pretty girl while on the government's time clock. Mary Alice couldn't stop smiling. It all felt so homey, so safe, so American or at least so southern. Maybe some watery-blooded Yankee girl could resist it, but not Mary Alice.

After they were seated in a booth by a window she said, "You notice how they treat us like we're a couple?"

"Darlin', we're an item."

"What are they saying?"

"Don't ask me," he said. "You forget how things are in a small town?" He drank his huge glass of sweet tea that the waitress had brought without request.

She smiled and shrugged. It was good to be reminded of how people talked in a town of less than twenty thousand. And if the town was talking about her and Zach, it had forgotten about her and her ex.

Zach ordered the special for both of them from Dotty, the owner, who never wrote an order down and never made a mistake with the bill.

Mary Alice waited until the catfish arrived to mention the police. "Zach, Kenny Bates stopped me a little while ago for absolutely nothing."

"The county sheriff's office fired his big brother last year, but now the city has Kenny on the force. Lord help us." He took a bite and chewed. "Why'd he say he stopped you?"

"For trespassing."

"Were you?"

"I drove out to Scott and Katherine Bridges' house. I just pulled in the driveway and rang the bell and left when nobody answered. How can that be illegal?"

"It's not, and it's not trespassing." He snapped a hush puppy in half.

"He never even asked to see my license. By law, don't they have to run your license if they stop you?" she asked.

"Since he knew you, I guess he didn't want to bother. That can take a while."

"It was almost scary and certainly creepy," she said.

She thought of her ex-husband's recent visit, about which she hadn't told Zach.

"Why were you visiting Katherine Bridges?" he asked.

"Just stabbing in the dark trying to help Sheree. Zach, what I want to know is, are y'all investigating Scott Bridges' wife? Is she a suspect too?"

Zach reached over and wiped a speck of tartar sauce from Mary Alice's chin.

"She suddenly disappeared," he said. "I'd like to know why."

"She's run away?"

"She's not home and didn't answer our calls." He rattled the chipped ice in his glass. "That's all I can say."

"But she had motive too," Mary Alice said. "He humiliated her—even told people he was sleeping with Sheree. That's motive."

"If Scott had died in her bed, Katherine Bridges would be a suspect. Right now we'd just like to keep tabs on her," Zach said. He waved at the woman with a pitcher of iced tea.

"Can I get y'all anything else?" Dotty asked, refilling his glass. Her country accent revealed her South Georgia roots.

Zach took a sip. "Best damn sweet tea in Mississippi. How much sugar y'all put in a gallon?"

Dotty puckered her mouth and pooched out her lips. "I reckon it's at least a pound. I'll check with Nettie Mae. But you have to dissolve the sugar in boiling water. That's the secret."

"Everything was so good, Miss Dotty," Mary Alice said thinking that she just consumed about 5,000 calories.

"Glad you liked it, hon. Nothing else today?" she asked. "Got some peach cobbler left and chess pie and—"

"Thanks, Dotty. Just the check," Zach said.

"Tell Martin at the counter you had two specials." Dotty said. She scooped up their plates and was gone.

"Sheree's getting out of jail today, and I want to help her all I can," Mary Alice said. She felt a need for Zach's support and wasn't getting it.

"I heard." He set a generous tip on the table.

"Zach, it's not against the law for me to ask people about the case, is it? I'm not a policewoman, but could I get into trouble for—for example, for talking to Katherine Bridges, if she'd been home?"

They walked to the cash register where Zach paid for lunch. The restaurant was emptying out. Four older men, two white and two black, sat at the luncheon counter.

"You can talk to anybody. If they don't want to talk to you, and you insist, it's harassment. You're a free citizen, and you can talk to people. Anybody say you can't?"

"No."

"Who you want to talk to?" he asked. He opened the café door, and they stepped out on to the sidewalk. Heavy gray clouds had gathered.

"I know this sounds silly, but anybody who knows Sheree."

"Like on *Law and Order*? Gather facts and filter them. Make connections."

"I guess," she said. She couldn't tell if he was making fun of her.

"Sheree's your friend; help her if you can," Zach said. "Don't expect it to be like a TV show. Hire her a good lawyer and get out of the way."

She nodded.

They stepped aside as a mother with a stroller passed.

"Mary Alice, be careful. You go digging around you might bump into the wrong people. It could be dangerous."

"I understand."

"Promise me you'll be careful," he said.

"Cross my heart and hope to die." She drew an **X** over her heart.

"Don't forget we're going to that artsy fund raiser tomorrow," he said as they walked toward her car.

"I did forget," she said. "And I don't have a dress to wear."

"I never knew a woman who did. Your mama will kill you if you don't show up."

"Queen of Arts, Daddy called her."

"I better run." he said. "Democrats are strategizing about money."

"Isn't it early to be raising money?" she asked. "The election's two years away."

"Never too early for money. But don't worry, when the time comes, the war chest will be full." He touched the side of her face. "I'll pick you up at seven tomorrow night."

"I'll be almost ready."

"Be careful Mary Alice. You're dear to me." He squeezed her shoulders. "I wish you wouldn't go off on your own—"

"Zach, I'll be talking to people I know. I'll be careful."

Driving home she listened to the news on Mississippi Public Radio, but it was all bad. She snapped it off and let the feel of Zach's embrace return. It felt so wonderfully normal to go to lunch at Dotty's with Zach. She'd missed feeling protected.

The trick was to keep a balance. With too much protection, she knew she'd feel smothered. And her desire for excitement always warred with her cozier instincts. Going too far in either direction meant trouble.

The warm feeling blew out the window, and the image of Kenny Bates leering at her took its place. Boon woke from his nap and pushed between the seats to sit up front. He was a good listener.

"I need to talk to that cop who knew Scott. Tom Jaworski," she told the yawning dog. "And to Katherine Bridges. She can't have gone too far." Some internal gyroscope righted itself again. Balancing the intrigue of the good cop and the missing wife with Zach's solicitous behavior felt right, harmonious.

She imagined Katherine and her going through the papers in Scott's desk and finding incriminating evidence pointing to a killer who wasn't partial to drug enforcement. She saw herself meeting with Jaworski. What would he be like?

"I wish I could tell Zach about hiding in Sheree's bathroom and finding that button," she told the dog. "He'd have a shit fit. Have me followed. This is schizophrenic, dating the man who's trying to put away your friend. I have to prove to him that Sheree's not guilty."

Boon nestled in the seat, his head resting on the center console, his eyes liquid brown.

"I have organized parties for a hundred, planned a ga-zillion fund raisers and finessed the most delicate social situations. I hosted an arts talk show on Dallas TV. I ought to be able to dig up dirt in the town I grew up in."

She realized she was speeding and slowed to the limit. Raindrops splattered the windshield, and she flipped on the wipers. Through the smudged dirt she could hardly see.

"I need a flow chart. Who to interview, what they know and when they knew it. I got nothing so far. What am I going to tell Sheree?"

But Boon had dozed off. She pressed the windshield washer button, but nothing happened. The wipers squeaked, begging for more water.

CHAPTER 11

GEORGIA'S CAR WAS PARKED IN the driveway when Mary Alice arrived at the Women's Center's shelter house. Donated by a board member, the place looked like a normal three bedroom, two bath ranch except that it seemed to have absorbed the misery of its unhappy occupants. Mildew stained the roof, the paint had faded, and the shrubbery drooped.

Mary Alice hoisted the bags of food and clothing from her car's trunk and dashed through the light rain to the door. Georgia opened it immediately; Sheree stood behind her, looking tiny in an oversized tee shirt. Her blond hair, still wet from a shower, waved around her face. She looked like one of those big-eyed children in a Margaret Keane painting.

"I brought you some new clothes," Mary Alice said, hugging Sheree. Over Sheree's shoulder she could see half a dozen boxes of Sheree's stuff, all her life's goods.

"Thanks, Mary Alice," Sheree said. Tears ran down her cheeks. "Thank you." Her voice quavered making "you" sound like *who-who-who*.

Mary Alice hugged her again. "You're safe now. Hush. We're going to help you. It's all right." And she meant it. In spite of the run-down house, the rain and Sheree's pitiful life's accumulations, Mary Alice felt hopeful.

"Got some fried chicken," Georgia said, pointing to a Colonel Sanders bucket.

"Crispy?"

"It was an hour ago."

Mary Alice poked through the red and white bucket and selected a thigh. "Did you eat?" Mary Alice asked Sheree.

"Maybe later on," Sheree said, sinking into one of two brown tweed sofas. She pulled her bare feet up under her, and Mary Alice thought that Sheree might disappear into the cushions.

"Sheree, listen to me," Georgia said. She wiped the grease from her fingers on a KFC napkin. "I have to go in a minute, and I want you to think about something."

"What?" she squeaked, barely audible.

"Ask yourself if you've got the guts to fight this. You think a week in jail on a murder charge was bad? You ain't seen nothing."

"Georgia, she's already terrified," Mary Alice said.

Georgia rose from the dinette and sat on the coffee table across from Sheree. "I've been through this kind of thing lots of times. What makes the difference is if you got some fight in you. You might have to testify in court. You need to be mentally and physically strong. If you can't cut it, you'll have to plea bargain and do the time." Georgia forced Sheree to look her in the eye. "But you cannot waste another minute sniveling and feeling all betrayed and hurt. Somebody's framing you for murder and that should make you mad. I want you mad, girl. I'm getting you a good lawyer, and Mary Alice spent her own money for your bail, but you are your own biggest resource. We're with you. I want to know, are you with you?"

Sheree wiped her face on her tee shirt hem. "Think I have a chance?"

"Yes. Will you win? I can't say. But you have to want to win or we're wasting our time." Georgia walked to the front window and looked out at the rain which pelted the lawn and bounced off the parked cars.

Mary Alice wondered how Georgia was able to practice what she called tough love. Maybe her own tough life enabled her. She thought about the boyfriend in Atlanta who had betrayed Georgia. Mary Alice suspected she wouldn't have such stamina in a similar situation. How did people go through hell and come out not only unscathed, but even stronger?

"We'll talk tomorrow," Georgia said. "Get settled. Mary Alice's staying tonight. I'll come by tomorrow." She wrapped a chicken breast in a piece of foil and put it in her bag. "Don't forget the rules. Lock the door behind me." Georgia quickly hugged Sheree and gave Mary Alice one of her wide-eyed expressions that meant it's in the Lord's hands now. At the door she took off her shoes. Mary Alice watched her race through the downpour that was already filling the ditch that bordered the front.

"What are the rules?" Mary Alice asked. She could see Georgia's footprints in the soggy lawn. She closed and locked the door.

"Mostly I'm supposed to let her know everything. Not supposed to leave, do any drugs, you know." She followed Mary Alice into the kitchen.

"Want to try to eat something?" Mary Alice didn't want to start in with questions too fast.

"I'd puke."

"You have to tell your body things are getting back to normal. Part of your strength depends on nutrition. Eat some chicken."

Sheree shook her head as if Mary Alice had suggested puree of possum innards with a side of hog jowls.

"You need something in your stomach."

Sheree watched the rain sliding like fat tears down the kitchen window. Distant thunder growled.

"How about an Oatmeal Cream Pie?" Mary Alice unloaded the brown paper grocery bag. Little Debbie Nutty Bars and Oatmeal Cream Pies headed a line of junk food that marched down the counter, sink to stove. Cheetos, Movie Time Popcorn, Lance's Peanuts, Zapp's Barbeque Chips, Mini Oreo Go Packs, Hostess Ding Dongs, Moon Pies, a jar of Kraft Marshmallow Cream, Brach's Candy Corn, Reese's Cups, Kit Kats, Hershey Bars and Butterfingers.

Sheree walked up and down the counter twice before she picked up the packet of salted peanuts. She removed a cold can of Diet Coke from the refrigerator and sat at the white Formica kitchen table. The Coke hissed with each peanut she forced into the can.

Mary Alice tore open the chips and a Kit Kat. "What about something from the chocolate group to go with that?" she asked.

"Reese's Cup." Sheree tipped up the Coke and drank; a few peanuts worked into her mouth.

"Catch."

Sheree caught the Reese's cup in her left hand. "RC Cola was better than Coke. Do they still make RC?"

Mary Alice shrugged. "Barq's Root Beer was better than A & W. I worry about the future of soda. Canada Dry Ginger Ale's still hanging on, but you can hardly find a Cream Soda."

Sheree and Mary Alice not only shared a love of fattening snacks, neither tolerated anyone judging, commenting, or warning them about such foods. When she found out Sheree had terrible migraine headaches, Mary Alice wondered if Little Debbie and her ilk might be contributing factors, but she never said a word, thinking that food choices were perhaps all that Sheree had firm control of.

"Did you know there's a whole line of Mexican junk food?" Sheree asked. "Same kinds of things, but it's all in Spanish."

"A parallel universe," Mary Alice said. "Best news I've heard in a week."

They sampled each of the four basic food groups—sugar, salt, grease and chocolate— and traded junk-out experiences. A mutual love for mini Bama Pecan Pies and Snowballs had first opened the door to their relationship. Sheree had said she didn't trust anybody who didn't love and regularly eat Bama Pecan Pies.

When the food frenzy petered out, they moved to the living room, carrying their favorites and placing them within easy reach on the coffee table. Mary Alice switched on one of the lamps. Each woman took a sofa.

"Sheree, you said you had something to tell me," Mary Alice said. "Something you couldn't talk about in jail." With tiny controlled strokes, she licked the frosting from a mini Oreo. The sweetness seemed to osmosize directly from her tongue into her bloodstream creating tiny waves of joy. No wonder there were so many obese people in the south, especially in Mississippi. They knew how to mask pain with glucose.

Lightning lit the room like a camera's flash, chased seconds later by thunder's rumble. Sheree waited to speak until it moved on north and east.

"Scott had some big bust he was working on. He said local authorities were covering up shipments of drugs coming through here. Called it a drug depot."

"You believe him?"

"Yes. And he said he was closing in."

"And some important people were going to take a fall?" Mary Alice leaned toward Sheree. What Sheree was talking about was a motive for killing Scott Bridges.

"He was excited about that part." She stuffed a handful of Cheetos into her mouth. "He liked the idea of taking down the high and the mighty. That's what he called them."

"I don't suppose he shared where the depot is or who's covering up."

Talking around the Cheetos, Sheree said, "Here in Cotashona County. Over and over he said the high and the mighty were going to be taken down. Heads were going to roll."

"How many heads?"

"He didn't say exactly. Maybe ten, maybe more."

Mary Alice had an image of mighty rolling heads dumped from an executioner's basket tumbling down Main Street toward the square. The mayor, the aldermen, the tax collector, all of them rolling on hot asphalt in the searing light of day toward the court house clock tower.

"Tell me about last Friday night," Mary Alice said. Gently she pealed the wrapper from a Hostess Ding Dong, her voice matching her touch.

Sheree didn't speak for a minute. "What do you want to know?"

"What time on Friday did Scott come by your apartment?"

"The afternoon. Maybe four."

"When was the time before Friday?"

"Last Monday. He had told me to find out if there were more drugs than usual available. Like, were the dealers fat? He came back on Friday. He said he wasn't staying, but then he did."

"And he made you have sex with him?"

"I'd made up my mind I'd rather go to jail than let him— but then somehow I ended up handcuffed in his little fantasy." She shrugged.

Mary Alice sucked in a breath and hoped Sheree didn't hear.

"Sheree, that wasn't your fault any more than what your stepfather did to you was your fault. Scott Bridges had power over you."

"I know; you told me before. Abused people abuse others," Sheree mimicked Mary Alice.

"He's a short guy with a big ego. He's a cop, but nobody respects him much. Power was important to him."

Sheree sucked the orange Cheetos' powder from her fingers. "Yeah."

"Are you glad you're free of him?"

"Yes, but—"

"What?"

"Scott was always exciting. You get a taste for it."

Mary Alice recognized the truth in what Sheree said. Addiction to drama wasn't unlike an addiction to dope, alcohol or sex. She knew.

There had been the time one summer at the country club when she, barely old enough to drive, had started something with a man, Darnel, who'd come to Cana to work at the bank. The memory popped vividly. The bank arranged for country club privileges during his two month stay. Darnel, who should have known better, bought her cokes and later, *Cuba Libres* by the pool; two weeks later she was in his apartment. She made him tell her about sex with other women; she let him kiss her as much as he wanted. Mary Alice had reveled in her sexual power, maintaining tension just short of the falling off point. The sixties pop lyrics, "Young girl, get out of my mind, my love for you is way out of line, better run, girl," summed up the situation. Gary Puckett and the Union Gap knew Mary Alice. She'd concealed her age with makeup, seduced Darnel and loved every minute of it. Looking back, even as an older teen, she knew she'd been monumentally, colossally stupid and very lucky. But she also recognized her addiction and its power. She still didn't know what drove her to seek thrills, and she doubted Sheree understood her feelings either.

"Why'd you run?" Mary Alice asked.

"I saw my triptan cartridges all over the bed," Sheree said.

"How many?" Mary Alice asked.

"I didn't stay to count. Probably all I had."

"Which was?"

"Ten." She tapped the cellophane wrapper of a Snowball.

"How did you know that's what killed him?"

"I didn't for sure, but I knew he was dead and those little green plastic thingies were on the bed and floor. You can tell when they've been used."

"And you drove to my house?"

"I got scared. I had nowhere else to go."

It occurred to Mary Alice that Sheree hadn't skipped town; she'd come to her friend, Mary Alice. Sheree left the crime scene because she believed Mary Alice would help her. And Mary Alice could help. She knew she could. If it cost her a pound of social status, so be it.

"Turn on that lamp. I want to show you something." In the tight pool of light, Mary Alice held out the baggie with the metal button she'd found in Sheree's bath room.

"What's this?" Sheree started to open the baggie.

"Don't touch it. I found it in your bathroom. The police must have missed it."

"My bathroom? When?"

"Saturday night. I got mama's master key and went in."

"How come?" Sheree inspected the button.

"I needed to do something—take action. I don't know. I found this wedged in a crack beside your toilet."

"Toilet?"

"I was throwing up in it. Maybe this would be a good time to tell you why."

After Mary Alice told the story of hiding in the bath tub from the whistling man, Sheree got up and took a piece of cold chicken from the refrigerator. "You think he was a cop?" she asked.

"Don't know. Tracing that light slowly over the floor like he was searching for a contact lens. Assuming it was a man, it seemed like he was sneaking around just like I was. When the cat meowed, he took off like a bat out of hell."

"But it could have been a woman?"

"All I saw was shadows. Distorted by the flashlight. It could have been a gorilla."

"You think it was the killer?"

"In books and movies, murderers always come back to the scene of the crime."

"You sure he didn't drop this when you were hiding in the bathtub?" Sheree pointed with a chicken wing at the baggie.

"He didn't get near the toilet before he bolted."

"It's not mine." She handed the bagged button to Mary Alice.

"It might have prints on it."

"Can you find out?" Sheree asked.

"I don't know." Mary Alice said. "It's not admissible now anyway. I screwed up when I took it. I was scared, and I panicked. I'm sorry, Sheree. I'm really sorry."

"You and Georgia are the only people in Cana trying to help me," Sheree said. "It still might help us know who to look for. I mean if we found William Gelly's prints on it, that'd say something."

Mary Alice searched Sheree's face. She felt relieved Sheree wasn't angry about the mistake, but thought maybe Sheree didn't realize how important the button could have been to her case. In mystery novels, detectives could find the manufacturer of a button, what coats used them, what stores sold those coats and often, who bought a particular coat.

"You think Sheriff Gelly's behind this? He do something to you in jail?"

"Not directly, but I know he don't like me." She nibbled the chicken wing as if she didn't want to hurt it.

"Why?" Mary Alice felt a familiar chill creep down her shoulders.

"They wouldn't let me have no books or nothing to read in jail. I went to shower, and when I came back my blanket was gone."

"Nobody touched you, did they?"

"No. They turned the AC down to about sixty degrees. Shit like that. Tried to make me crazy. Kept the lights on all night, the radio half-tuned to a gospel station."

"They think you murdered a policeman."

"Mary Alice, I didn't kill Scott, but we'll never find out who did. Even if the sheriff is protecting drug stashes in Cana, you can't prove nothing."

"What if I find the stash?"

"Doesn't necessarily connect to Scott's murder, and it don't pin the blame on somebody else," Sheree said.

"You've been thinking about this a lot."

"I had some time." Without tearing the wrapper, Sheree picked open the Reese's Cup.

"Scott ever talk about his wife?" Mary Alice asked.

"Once I mentioned her, and he blew up. I never said nothing again."

"I wish I could talk to her. She left town, didn't attend the funeral." Mary Alice unscrewed the lid from the jar of marshmallow cream. "You think Katherine Bridges knew about you and her husband and was mad enough to kill him?"

"Maybe. I don't know nothing about her."

"I need to talk to somebody." Mary Alice inhaled the jar's aroma.

"Like who?" Sheree asked.

"Somebody in the drug world."

"Drug world?"

"Don't keep repeating everything I say. You must know a dealer. Dealers are bound to be connected to the scene, to each other." She edged a finger into the white goo, captured a dollop and sucked.

"So?"

"What'd you tell Scott about the action on the street?"

"Same as usual."

"He say anything?"

"That's when he called it a depot. Big loads from Mexico all going someplace else."

"He definitely said from Mexico?"

"Yes. The Mexico part really pissed him off."

Mary Alice pulled apart another Oreo cookie and scraped the wafer of filling onto her tongue like a communion host. She held it in her mouth. People, especially the law, rarely blamed America's voracious appetite for illegal drugs; instead, desperately poor, third-world citizens who made and supplied the products got all the blame. Maybe Scott Bridges had hated both sides.

"Mary Alice, the dope boys I know won't talk to you," Sheree said.

She swallowed. "Think about who will talk to me. I'm not a cop."

"I'd have to go with you," Sheree said.

"No. That's too dangerous. Police might be watching you. There's got to be another way."

Lightning flared and without a lapse, the thunder crashed. The power went off. In the pitch blackness the wind-driven rain tore at the house. Gum tree branches raked the roof and fascia.

"Mary Alice?"

"I'm here. I'll go look for a light."

"Wait. I just thought of something. Just now in the dark. Right before I passed out, you know, the night Scott was killed? I felt something, like somebody was in the room hovering over the bed."

LATER, BEFORE DAWN, MARY ALICE looked at her watch. Four A.M. Still without electricity, the air felt dank. Even after the storm had passed, she'd slept fitfully, wracking her brain for connections. All she had were fragments that led nowhere. The coat button she'd found was a dead end. It's only significance lay in its connection to the intruder. She didn't know what to make of Sheree's assertion that she'd felt somebody in the room. Sheree had admitted being very drunk. But Scott Bridges' knowledge of a warehouse of illegal drugs did provide a motive for his murder.

Mary Alice had risked $10,000 on Sheree's bond. It had been the right thing to do, but she'd naively assumed things would go better once Sheree got out of jail. Sheree was innocent. So far, victory seemed a long way away.

The electricity came back on and with it all the lights in the house that had been on before the blackout. Junk food wrappers littered the coffee table like tornado wreckage. Mary Alice struggled up from the sofa to turn the lights off. A crick in her neck throbbed. She looked at the other sofa where Sheree slept.

Her usual makeup washed away, she looked like a child. Her skin glowed clear and opaque in the lamp light. Cheetos dust caked her delicate finger tips and the corners of her mouth. Mary Alice resisted stroking her hair and pulled the fleece blanket up around Sheree's shoulders.

Then a scary thought popped up. If Scott Bridges died because he was right about a drug depot and a cover up, would somebody suspect that he had told Sheree about it?

If so, Sheree wasn't safe. No one who knew about it was safe including, Mary Alice.

CHAPTER 12

TWELVE HOURS LATER, MARY ALICE was home, in another world dressing for a ball to raise money for the Cana Arts Center. The disparity between her life and Sheree's seemed cruelly apparent. To boost her spirits, Mary Alice slipped the Moon Pie she had brought home from Sheree's out of its cellophane and into her mouth. She always bit off too much and had to work the puffy marshmallow down to a swallowable mass.

"I can't drink champagne at the Arts Gala on an empty stomach," she told Boon who, hoping for a bite, monitored her closely.

"Moon Pies aren't good for dogs," she said. "They aren't good for people, but the good feelings they stimulate outweigh the bad stuff."

Boon whimpered.

"Okay." She fed him a pinch of the pie.

In the sixth grade Mary Alice had been required to write a short essay on her favorite food.

All Moon Pies are baked in Chattanooga. They only look like the moon. They have three kinds of sugar and two kinds of oil, niacin and reduced iron. Also things that are hard to spell which mama says give them a long shelf life. But they don't last very long on the shelves at Jitney Jungle grocery or at my house. Mostly, I like the way a big bite feels in my mouth. It coats all your teeth and doesn't want to get swallowed down. You have to work with it. You can't be a quitter. The longer it stays in your mouth, the sweeter it gets. I hope the Chattanooga Bakery Inc. never quits. Right before I die, I'd like to eat a Vanilla Moon Pie.

She finished off the Moon Pie, washed her hands and returned to her closet. Boon padded in behind her.

"White's too summery for September, black's too—there will be seventy little black dresses there. Look like flies buzzing over the hors d'oeuvres."

Boon rubbed his head on her leg.

She by-passed a mauve Dior cocktail dress her mother had bought for her. It looked like Elizabeth Tate. It made her feel sad to recognize her mother's inability to really see her daughter and to understand what she'd like to wear. But Elizabeth didn't care what her daughter wanted; she cared about what Elizabeth wanted.

Farther back on the rack hung a large zippered cloth bag with a dozen dresses packed inside. She opened it and jerked back as a plume of mothball odor escaped. Inside were bridesmaid dresses she'd worn for girlfriend's weddings.

"I forgot these were here. Lord, there's Patricia Kincaid's and Mandy Lee Harpers'." She pawed past two others she didn't recognize and then an iridescent blue one with an intricate floral detail at the back. She'd worn it in Tracy Bloom's wedding. Tracy died of melanoma five years after her wedding, leaving a devastated husband and a baby daughter. Mary Alice stroked the embroidered flower as though it were her friend's brow. She hadn't thought about Tracy in years. The tissue paper-stuffed dress rustled a soft reprieve.

The last dress in the bag wasn't a bridesmaid's costume.

Green crepe with delicate beading, the ankle length gown said 1930s. "Aunt Margery's dress."

She let her silk kimono float to the closet floor and slid the dress over her naked body. She emerged like a butterfly from its cocoon, pulled up the side zipper and looked in the mirror. The color flattered her, but the bias cut that ran over her body like water created the wow effect.

"Mama will hate it if I wear this."

Boon tossed his head.

She turned profile and saw that the only underwear that was going to work was a pair of panty hose. She also saw that she certainly didn't look pregnant.

"Move over, Boon. I need green shoes."

Aunt Margery, Mary Alice's father's sister had been an artist, and according to Mary Alice's mother, a Bohemian—her word for someone with low morals. Margery usually managed to do exactly as she pleased without regard for the opinion of others. She had died four years ago in Italy in bed with a lover twelve years her junior.

Mary Alice zipped up the bag of memories and closed the closet, grateful that the sexy green dress had saved her from a bout of melancholy over weddings that hadn't turned out the way *Brides Magazine* had promised.

When Zach knocked on the door at seven, Mary Alice called down to him from the bedroom balcony.

"Come in and make yourself a drink. I'll be right down." She straightened the beaded fringe on the hem of her dress and stepped into three inch high heels. The reflection of her great grandmother's pave diamond brooch nestled below her cleavage, winked in the mirror.

Mary Alice paused on the stairs so that Zach could get the full effect. His mouth fell open.

"My God, you look good. Don't move." He came toward her and looked her up and down as though she were a Michelangelo sculpture. "Turn around."

She slowly pivoted. It felt wonderful to be admired. She sensed her aunt sitting on the piano bench smoking a Gauloise and nodding approvingly.

"Quite a dress," he said. "Those are little glass beads."

"Thank you," she said.

"Quite a woman, too."

"Well, Zach, you look pretty swell yourself."

In the car, Mary Alice looked at Zach's profile. Could it be this easy? Cana's most eligible bachelor wanted her. He was good-looking, clever, well to do. And he cooked.

Zach reached over, took her hand and gently squeezed it as if the two shared a juicy secret.

Elizabeth Tate stood in the center of the hotel ballroom beneath the great crystal chandelier as though she were the sun around which planets spun.

"Better say hello to Mama first," Mary Alice said to Zach as they entered the ballroom.

"Is this your grand entrance?" Elizabeth asked. She wore a floor length gown of shimmering burgundy that shouted "one-of-a-kind."

"If we're late, it's entirely my fault," Zach said. "Elizabeth Tate, you look quite lovely tonight."

They traded kisses on cheeks.

Mary Alice saw her mother soften and realized that she had been irritated because her daughter had missed her mother's grand entrance. She wondered what life would be like if her mother weren't so self-absorbed.

"Zachary, would you mind getting Mary Alice and me a glass of champagne? I happen to know they've put out the good stuff early."

Zach smiled. "A pleasure, ma'am. Be right back."

"What are you wearing?" Elizabeth asked. She stepped back and examined Mary Alice as if she were large tropical bug— interesting but hideous.

"Vintage *couture*. Like it better now?"

"Are you wearing a bra? My God, Mary Alice. This is the Arts Gala; Halloween is next month." Mary Alice had heard that exact line before. She tried to imagine her mother before a Grand Inquisitor, pleading for her life. The Grand Inquisitor, a pissed-off Oprah sort, would assail Elizabeth: "You, madam, belittled your child with cruel and unfounded judgments. You killed her." Mary Alice, dead and looking down from heaven, would smile beatifically in agreement.

"Zach said I looked beautiful." She smiled and hoped to God her mother didn't remember the dress had belonged to Aunt Margery.

"He's a man," Elizabeth said. "He didn't get past the cleavage. Is that my diamond brooch?"

"Grandma Tate left it to me. Daddy let you use it until I was old enough to wear it." Mary Alice smiled. "I'll lend it to you anytime."

Elizabeth looked as though she were about to cry. "How could you come to this event that I've worked so hard on looking like a—"

"A what?" Mary Alice knew her mother's exasperation was genuine, but that the tears were crocodile's.

"I think it's vulgar." The corners of Elizabeth's mouth turned down and her lips thickened.

"Elizabeth," a short man in a tux pulled at Elizabeth's elbow. "The band says it doesn't have enough electrical outlets, and I can't find Brad Swainee."

Elizabeth's frown bounced into a toothpaste smile as though a switch had been flipped. "I'll see to it, Tom. Tom you know my daughter, Mary Alice."

"Nice to see you again, Mary Alice. I love your dress," he said. He beamed, all dimples and pearly whites.

Mary Alice considered the possibility that her mother, who thought she knew everything, could be electrocuted.

As Elizabeth charged away, Zach reappeared with two flutes of champagne. Mary Alice downed hers and took the glass intended for her mother.

"Relax darlin'. This is supposed to be fun," Zach said guiding her across the room. "Let's look at the silent auction. There's a Walter Anderson print I want to bid on."

The next hour was a kaleidoscope of greetings: "Darlin', it's so wonderful to see you." "You look terrific, Mary Alice." "Come on out to the farm and ride the horses like you used to do." "Remember that puppy you saved and made Edna Earl carry home? She weighs over a hundred pounds now. The dog, not Edna Earl." "We're counting on you for brunch tomorrow." "I told my husband that if somebody died next Saturday, he was gonna have to get the deputy coroner to go, 'cause he was not leaving our party."

As Mary Alice placed a modest bid on a carved swan, the word, coroner, echoed in her head. Fictional investigators always found out something useful from the coroner.

"Who's the coroner now?" Mary Alice asked. Zach was upping his bid on the Anderson bird print by a hundred dollars.

"That would be Lofton Buress. I believe I saw him when we came in."

Busy second guessing his bid, Zach didn't ask her why she wanted to know. As soon as Zach was absorbed into a group of lawyers, Mary Alice excused herself.

She found Lofton Buress at the bar talking to the bar tender. Lofton had the lugubrious look of many funeral directors. He always had. In junior high, the kids accused him of sleeping with dead bodies. Back then, Mary Alice defended him because he seemed so much like the stray animals she rescued. Lofton became her devoted follower through high school.

He almost tipped over his bourbon and branch when Mary Alice sidled up to him. "Hey there, Lofton."

"I'm fine," he said. "How are you, Mary Alice?"

She smiled at his nervousness and didn't point out that she hadn't yet asked how he was.

"Well, I'm fine," she said. "Mama says you've about taken over your family's business."

"I have. Daddy hardly comes in a'tall any more unless we have several burials at once."

"Three generations in a family business. Rare nowadays." Mary Alice remembered as a child every time she'd pass the funeral home, somebody would say, 'you stab 'em; we slab 'em'."

"May I get you a drink?" he asked.

"No thanks. I exceeded my limit five minutes ago."

He laughed as if she had made a witty remark.

Lofton reminded Mary Alice that lots of southern men retained a boyish sweetness well into adulthood. Mary Alice mused that it probably had something to do with the expectations of their mothers and their good manners, also a result of the mothers. In Dallas, she'd met nice men who seemed competent, kind and gentlemanly, but none whom she'd call sweet. Maybe southern mamas let on to their sons how women longed for sweetness in a hard world.

"And you're the coroner now too," she said. She felt silly flattering Lofton in such an obvious way, but his body language said she was on target. Besides, introductory chit chat was compulsory at a high quality southern social gathering. It'd be rude to get to the point right off the bat.

"I'm deputy coroner now, but I expect I'll get elected if I run."

"It seems funny to me that the coroner is elected in Mississippi."

"People want to have a say in who pronounces a body dead."

"Really?"

"Historically they have. The job is really called Coroner Ranger. Daddy said coroners used to be responsible for the bodies of dead animals. I mean, in addition to dead human beings." He pronounced "beings" as "beans."

Mary Alice gave Lofton her "goodness sakes, my stars" look and shifted the conversation. "Say Lofton, do you know anything about Scott Bridges' death?"

Increasingly she became aware that Lofton Buress was staring at her breasts, which strained against the thin green crepe. She didn't care. Lofton's loyalty had earned him whatever peeps he cared to take and she, after all, had chosen the revealing dress.

"Yes, I do. Very sad," he said. He turned his head to one side and looked down as if he were reassuring the bereaved.

"I've been working with Sheree Delio through the Women's Center, and I just cannot believe she killed him."

"He didn't die of natural causes."

"What happened?" she asked. Good detectives never revealed they already knew anything.

Lofton finished his drink and nodded to the bartender for a refill. "This is strictly unofficial, but he was injected with quite a few doses of a drug for migraine headaches."

"And that would have killed him?"

"Ten times the dose of lots of drugs will kill a person, but in this case, I doubt he needed that much." Lofton lowered his voice. "He had a history of heart trouble, so a major, vascular constriction, that's closing up the blood vessels, would cause an attack."

"A heart attack." Mary Alice said.

"Ironically, he had nitroglyceride tabs on him." Lofton shook his head.

"How long would it take to die?" Mary Alice asked.

"It depends, but he would have had myocardial ischemia, then arrhythmia and then myocardial infarction. Boom. Gone maybe in fifteen minutes. I heard the time of death was about 8 p.m., and he hadn't been dead very long before the police found the body."

Sheree said Scott got to her apartment about four o'clock.

"But Lofton, Sheree Delio barely weighs 100 pounds. How could she have done it?"

"Maybe after he fell asleep or passed out." The bartender delivered another bourbon. Lofton handed him a five and waved him away.

"Couldn't somebody else have done it?" she asked.

"Hey, I'm a coroner, not a cop." He sipped his drink. "It might have taken nerves of steel, but not physical strength. Except one thing was unusual."

"What?" Mary Alice enjoyed watching Lofton shift from undertaker to attorney. He pulled back his shoulders and his voice deepened.

"Well, at least one injection site showed bruising. The murderer must have jabbed the needle pretty hard."

"Needle?"

"Not like a flu shot. The drug comes in one dose cartridges a lot like epinephrine, you know, for people who are allergic to bee stings? Comes in other forms too, but she had the injectable."

"Like a pen."

"Autoinjectable and painless. The needle only penetrates a tad," he said.

"Which means?" Pulling details out of Lofton was getting tedious.

"Maybe the victim woke up. I just thought it was odd. I'm sure it's in the medical examiner's report. Don't you quote me on any of this, Mary Alice. We are off the record here." He leaned back on the bar.

"Lord no. I wouldn't. I'm sure her lawyer has the report." Had Sheree's lawyer even requested the state medical examiner's report?

"A murder in a small town's like a bomb," Lofton said. "In Atlanta, there'd be a little fuss and then on to the next case. But in Cana we're more fragile."

A group of men crowded the bar to order drinks, and Mary Alice excused herself to powder her nose. She almost danced to the rest room. Finally, some information, and even more important, corroboration that her plan to ask lots of questions to lots of people would eventually unearth something useful. She had been unaware of how forthcoming people could be. She felt like calling Tom Jaworski there and then.

Scott arrives at 4. They drink, fool around and pass out by what, 6:30? Someone killed him between 6:30 and maybe 8:30. Where had Katherine Bridges, Sheriff Gelly and Lord knew who else been then? And what did the bruise mean?

The hotel Ladies Room's elegance matched its ballroom. The rose moiré wallpaper interior was punctuated by beveled mirrors and crystal sconces. Cushy rose carpet blended into a rosy granite floor in the lavatory area. Across from the marble sinks with their gold faucets, stood eight private individual stalls that resembled large closets with louvered doors. Mary Alice was about to exit one when she heard two women enter. She froze when she heard Zach's name.

"The democrats love Zach, but they're committed to Bill. Lyman says that if Zach Towree wants the Democratic nomination for governor, he's going to have to come up with a lot of money. That would tip the scales in his favor."

"I don't think his mama left him enough for that," the other woman said.

"But if he can raise the money, I think they'd run him."

"He looks like a governor."

"He looks like a movie star."

The ladies made guttural purrs and entered separate stalls. When their doors snapped shut, Mary Alice tiptoed out of the rest room. She guessed that the woman who mentioned Lyman must have been Mildred Williams, wife of Lyman Williams, leader of the North Mississippi democrats. The Bill she mentioned had to be Bill Eakins, a nice but dull legislator from Grenada who'd paid his dues to the party and now wanted his turn in the mansion.

Mary Alice recalled Zach's comment about talk in small towns, and somehow felt that he knew whatever was being said about him. Zach had presence. He wasn't likely to be flummoxed or even surprised.

Outside the ladies room, Mary Alice took a moment to watch the social pageant unfolding in the ballroom. Beautifully gowned ladies and men in tuxedoes glided into groups that easily regrouped in a continual rondo. Smiles readily lighted up faces and the sounds of Deep South accents spiraled through the room like a jasmine symphony. They were rich comforting tones that she had missed. Texas was not the South. Her eyes misted. How could she have ever left Cana; how could she ever leave it again?

"The band is great," Zach said. He came up behind her and put his arms around her. "Playing forties' tunes. My favorite. Come dance with me."

As they eased through the crowd toward the dance floor, Mary Alice couldn't help but notice the looks people gave them. Mary Alice Tate and Zach Towree were quite a couple. The expressions seemed to approve of them in some deep unconscious way as though the union of two of Cana's best was a good thing for all of them.

The band played *All of Me*, a foxtrot.

"Who taught you to dance?" she asked as he led her through a tricky promenade turn.

"Mama. Didn't your mama teach you?"

"No. I went to Doris Webster's class every Saturday." Under arm turn, rock step and into a basic zigzag.

"Most men don't dance this well even in D-I-X-I-E," she said.

"Mama thought dancing would impress the ladies, and I might need to do that," Zach said.

"She was right." He was handsome, successful, smart, ambitious, unencumbered—not even an ex-wife; he cooked and he danced. What else did she need to know? He wasn't sweet like Lofton Buress or even Otis Turner, but perhaps his mama hadn't had the leisure to teach her boy about sweetness. No,

Zach Towree had a clean hard edge. He was a man who took what he wanted from life.

"You took the part that once was my heart, so why not take all of me?" the vocalist crooned with a voice like melted butter. Mary Alice felt they could have been her words to Zach. The alcohol and the break from the strain of thinking about Sheree made Mary Alice feel reckless.

Why should the men always have to initiate intimacy? It was pretty clear where they were headed. She snuggled closer, and they moved as one.

It was after midnight when they arrived back at Mary Alice's place.

"You want to go skinny dippin'?" she asked. Her fingers wiggled the side zipper of her dress.

Zach took off his jacket. "How cold is it?"

"Who cares?" She kicked off her shoes, slid open the huge glass door and skipped out on to the deck. The waning moon had set; the Milky Way hung above like a star-stuffed net. At the water's edge she stopped.

If she pulled the tight dress over her head, she might get caught like a skunk in a bag. And even if it came off smoothly, there she'd be standing in panty hose—the too tight waistband digging in, the ugly tan panty. Not a pretty sight.

"Last one in is a rotten egg," he said. Stark naked, he walked past her and jumped into the lake. The water convulsed with his weight and for a moment the insect chorus hushed.

The brief glimpse of his body made the hair on her arms stand up.

Spared close examination, she pulled the green dress up, the nylon hose down and jumped in, the ripples from her splash joining his to the far edges of the lake. When she felt a strong arm around her back and then a wet mouth on hers, she flashed on the image of romance fiction book covers where muscled heroes clasped busty beauties to their bare chests. She heard herself sigh.

They stood near the shore in neck deep water. His hands slid over her body as if he were memorizing her. He touched the small of her back, her neck and finally her breasts. He kissed her again.

Over his shoulder, she could see the spot where only four days ago Cham had stood. Champagne and lust eased her mind. She was falling in love with Zach. She wasn't pregnant.

"You're shaking. Let's go in," he said, lifting her into his arms.

LONG AFTER HE HAD HELD her in bed and warmed her with his body, had made love to her and had fallen asleep protectively curled around her, she awoke. Easing from his embrace she sat on the bed looking at his body. Even in the dark, she could discern the pattern of hair on his chest that meandered down his belly to his groin. A used condom rested on the floor.

The sex had been frantic and explosive. Just thinking about it made her shiver and think of wild panthers mating. She knew she'd just experienced the most thrilling sex she'd ever had and while she missed tenderness, she thought it was a fair trade for excitement.

He might turn out to be complicated, but at least this part worked. And then, the darkened room made her think about Sheree Delio a little over a week ago, lying in a dark bedroom while someone killed the man sleeping next to her. What exactly had Lofton Buress said about bruises on Scott's body? If Sheree was going to inject him while he slept, she wouldn't jab him hard enough to cause a bruise. She'd stick him lightly. Sitting beside Zach, Mary Alice tried to picture how it happened. She'd have to stick him ten times if Lofton was right about the autoinjectable cartridges. What if Scott Bridges was bruised because he woke up and the real killer had to overpower him? What did lawyers on TV say? "Offer an alternative scenario as to who else might have killed him." She wished she could wake Zach and discuss it with him.

Quietly, she slipped out of bed and walked out on to the balcony. The scents of juniper and pine mingled with marsh grass. She closed her eyes and felt the soft breeze tickle her naked body. A faint sound outside made her drop to her knees out of sight behind the balcony's solid railing. It was more of a change in the rhythm of the water and land than a distinct noise. She'd been listening to the lake for years and knew it well. She peered through the dark, but saw nothing.

This wasn't the kind of adrenalin rush she liked. Even with Zach twenty feet away, she felt vulnerable. It was no fun when uncontrolled forces stimulated the fight or flight mechanism.

Mary Alice crept back into the bedroom, locked the sliding door and slipped into bed. Pressing close to Zach, she ran her hand down his body, coaxing an erection. He awoke, rolled on top of her and thoughts of intruders in the marsh, pregnancy test kits and Scott Bridges' killer faded like smoke in the wind.

CHAPTER 13

T HEY WERE UP EARLY THE next day. Mary Alice felt like she was in a Hollywood movie's perfect morning-after scene. "It sounds like an impossible balancing act," Mary Alice said. "Conservatives, ultra-right conservatives, liberals, blacks, whites, rich, poor. Appealing to all of them." She looked like a 1930s film star, maybe Veronica Lake, in a slinky silk robe posed by the microwave waiting for the maple syrup to warm. The sun breached the horizon, squeezing its light between the curve of the earth and the clouds.

"Don't forget special interests like tobacco." Zach scanned the sports section of the Sunday Jackson *Clarion Ledger*.

The microwave peeped.

"Trick is to build a broad base and not piss-off those who don't agree with you," he said.

"Moderation. Compromise." She felt a little nervous and hoped she wasn't chattering. They'd done *it*; things were different. She thought Zach felt nervous too. They were discussing Mississippi politics like high school civics students.

"Exactly." He snapped the newspaper and folded it neatly beside his plate.

"Money isn't the main thing for winning a gubernatorial race?" She eased the French toast onto the cobalt blue plate, placed the pitcher of syrup on the table and sat down beside him. Everything looked perfect: crisp linen napkins, orange chrysanthemums, piping plates of food. Probably as good or better than his mama's.

"Money is the main thing in every race," he took a bite. "This tastes great, Mary Alice. I want to eat this every day." He reached for her hand.

She soaked up his approval and thought they'd make a good picture for an advertisement, maybe for butter.

She wanted to ask about his campaign funding, but hesitated since she'd overheard the party chairman's wife in the ladies room say Zach wouldn't have enough money. She wished there was some way she could help him. But, she hoped to keep the mood on romance instead of cash so she didn't mention it. As they ate breakfast, the jumpiness faded, and they shifted easily among conversation, newspaper reading and lingering kisses. Neither mentioned Sheree Delio.

"I have to get going," he said. He stood and slid the chair under the table.

"It's only eight."

"I have to drive to Jackson." He collected his things.

"I wish you could go to the Alexander's brunch with me." Zach spent as much time out of town as in.

"Me too." He caught her in an embrace and kissed her.

He smelled better than a man had a right to.

"Remember you promised you'd be careful," he said. "Don't give that redneck, Kenny Bates any excuse to pull you over."

"Yes sir. I promise." She thought about telling him about the noise she'd heard when she was out on the balcony, but didn't want to alarm him. The solitude and privacy of the lake house was too precious to expose to police drivebys or annoying check ups. The noise was probably nothing to worry about.

"I'll call you," he said.

"You better, or I'll tell my mama you had your way with me and abandoned me." She let the lemon silk robe gap open in the front.

He turned back to her. "It's only eight o'clock?"

She nodded.

AT NOON MARY ALICE PARKED in the Alexander's circular drive and walked around to the back of the house on the raked pea gravel path edged in lariope and sedum. Friday's rain had freshened everything. She still felt high from the morning with Zach. She couldn't stop smiling. A breeze kicked up her skirt.

The party was in full bloom, but she paused to take in the view. The home was distinguished by a double colonnade of cedars off the back marching over the low rolling hills to the Cotashona River. Once there had been a matching arcade of dogwoods in the front, but they were long gone. No one could remember how the Alexander family had hung on to the house after the Civil War. No one asked but not because they weren't curious.

Evelyn and Burt Alexander's brunch was an all white affair. Even though it was after Labor Day, it was still summer and a hot one at that. The furniture, linen, cushions, dishes, flowers and much of the food were white. Evelyn wore a white flowing gauzy dress and white straw picture hat; Burt looked like a swarthy Colonel Sanders. As she worked the crowd, Mary Alice could tell most of the two dozen guests were on their second Gin Fizzes or Bloody Marys.

She heard voices she recognized and joined a foursome of women she'd known all her life.

"If I hear Jenny Campbell say 'high tea' one more time, I'm going to scream. Reminds me of that snooty Hyacinth Bucket on that British sitcom," Miranda Knolls said.

"I always heard high tea was a light meal served at about seven o'clock," Agnes Worthington said. "I don't know if they have low tea over there or not."

"No, no," Miranda said. "It's just tea. Plain tea. There is no high tea. Mary Alice, please tell them Jenny is being snobby calling her tea party, a high tea."

"I don't know, Miranda," Mary Alice said. "Maybe it's like High Mass. Why do we care?"

"Jenny Campbell has become an outrageous anglophile," Agnes said. "She's fallen under the spell of some Brit who works for her husband."

"She's even acquired a phony accent," Patricia Ann Moffat said in her own version of a British accent.

"When is this tea?" Mary Alice asked. She'd never liked Jenny Campbell, but hearing her criticized made Mary Alice feel uncomfortable. Jenny was new-rich having married into a chicken processing fortune.

"Never. Jenny wants to talk about high tea and high society," Miranda said. "She doesn't want to actually pour."

"That reminds me, Patricia Ann, are your girls going to the Thompson twins' party?" Agnes asked.

"Yes. How else are they going to practice what they learned at etiquette camp?"

"Etiquette camp?" repeated Mary Alice.

"Etiquette Boot Camp," Patricia Ann said. "It's wonderful. Not that they don't know their manners, but they teach the more formal aspects of etiquette."

And with that the conversation turned to the fascinating activities of the children.

Mary Alice scanned the garden. She knew well what was coming and that she wasn't going to be part of the conversation. Patricia Ann Moffat had married the same year Mary Alice had. Patricia Ann had two girls. That could have been Mary Alice. She remembered she'd forgotten again to buy a home pregnancy test kit. Her period hadn't started, and she felt a little bloated. But it would come soon. She thought about her morning in bed with Zach.

By having sex with Zach, Mary Alice had decided to end her internal speculation about being pregnant. She couldn't have gone to bed with Zach if she seriously believed she was expecting. It was highly unlikely that the one time with Cham had fostered conception when ten years with him had failed to do so.

"Y'all excuse me. I see Judge Weeds over there, and I need to talk to him." Mary Alice went through a brief separation ritual which involved excessive smiling and gesturing and headed over to the judge.

The retired Judge Weeds peered at the dessert tray.

"How are you finding life back in Cana, Mary Alice?" he asked looking up from the éclairs and tortes. The judge looked like Santa Claus if Santa had a better tailor. Honoring the heat, the judge had shed his jacket revealing a blue long-sleeved shirt of a silky oxford cloth. His blue and gold print necktie coordinated with suspenders that held up honey brown worsted wool trousers that broke gently on his polished deep brown leather shoes.

Where in America did men dress as well as they do in North Mississippi? She looked around the garden at the sartorial splendor—not an ill-groomed man in the bunch.

Apparently putting off the dessert decision, Judge Weeds guided her to a seat under a wisteria-wrapped pergola.

"I'm delighted to be home in Cana, thank you for asking," she said.

"How's your mama?" he asked.

"You know Mama." She smiled broadly to prevent rolling her eyes. "How's Mrs. Weeds?"

"She started writing another novel. I won't see her until Christmas. This one's set in Natchez and damn if she doesn't want to drive down there every other weekend. I don't know how a woman her age can come up with all that juicy, spicy—" He waved his hand. "Stuff."

Mary Alice laughed and then turned to face the judge. "Do you mind if I ask you a question—about legal procedure?"

His smile faded. "How can I help you, Mary Alice?"

"I'm not in trouble. Sheree Delio is."

"I read about that. They say she murdered a policeman."

Mary Alice bet that the judge had more than just read about it. As one of the senior old boys, he'd know what was going on.

"I'm trying to help her, at least until we get her a better lawyer," Mary Alice said.

"Public defender representing her now?" he asked.

"She won't even talk to him any more. Georgia Horn's getting somebody else."

"So what's your question?" he asked with paternal patience.

"I need information. The authorities aren't even looking for the real killer."

"Mary Alice Tate, Private Eye?"

"She didn't do it," she said.

"What kind of information?" He stole a glance at the dessert table.

"I don't even know everything I need to know." She twisted her grandmothers gold locket. "How can I see Scott Bridges' autopsy report?"

"The defendant's lawyer should have filed a motion for it. It's called the discovery process. Everything the prosecutor has, the other side gets to see too. For example, the state medical examiner's report and statements made by the defendant or by witnesses, photos of the scene of the crime."

"But her lawyer would have to file?"

"Yes, it's not automatic. But if he thought he'd be replaced as counsel, he might wait and save himself the trouble." He adjusted his glasses. "Did you bail her out?"

"Yes sir," she said. "I think Scott Bridges was about to expose a huge drug trafficking operation in Cotashona County." She left out that she thought local authorities were in on the deal.

The judge sat up and twisted to face her.

"Why?"

"Scott Bridges was good at what he did; held the record for local drug busts."

"So you deduce someone wanted Scott Bridges dead before he could blow the whistle?" The judge ran his thumbs under his suspenders.

"Yes sir. That's it."

"Just like your Daddy. Mary Alice I need to caution you. While you're sleuthing around, you might run into some bad characters who won't view you as an innocent fact finder. Especially if drugs are concerned." Mary Alice noted that yet another friend was warning her off the case. She wondered if she were being naïve.

"The profits from illegal drugs are phenomenal. A powerful motivator. While I sat on the bench I heard all kind of stories about kickbacks, corruption, deals. But lots were pure fabrication. Like stories about hidden treasure." The judge sat on the edge of his seat and took on the judicial tone for which he had been famous. "During Civil Rights in the early sixties I can't tell you how many times I heard about a stash of guns. Enough semi automatic weapons for every white man in Cotashona County. But there were no guns, thank God. Maybe the question to ask is why such a story gets started."

"One answer would be because there really is a stockpile of millions of dollars worth of illegal drugs stored in a shed in some back pasture," she said.

He barely heard her as he relived the Mississippi battle for civil rights.

Mary Alice knew she'd lost the judge. She gracefully excused herself.

At the buffet table, she helped herself to a slice of frittata, a serving of spoon bread and a pile of artfully carved fruit: kiwi, cantaloupe, honey dew and strawberries. She may have lost the judge, but now she knew about "discovery" and how to get the autopsy report.

She could hear Miranda Knolls in the glass gazebo making fun of Jenny Campbell's British accent. Mary Alice sat in a shady corner of the butterfly garden and ate. She wondered why Jenny wasn't liked. It had to be more than ire over her *nouveau riche* status. Mary Alice hated to think that her own name could be ridiculed in the same way. What would these friends, many of them old friends, do if they decided helping trashy Sheree Delio wasn't cool? What if it turned out Sheree was guilty? Mary Alice didn't feel like dessert and went in search of Evelyn and Burt Alexander.

"Thank you so much for including me. What a lovely party," Mary Alice said.

"You're welcome. I'm so glad I saw you at the auditions," Evelyn said.

"Were you cast?" Mary Alice asked Burt Alexander.

"I was," Burt said, "but that little fairy director has Pinky Shore understudying me. Can you imagine if Pinky had to actually go on?"

"Burt," Evelyn said, slapping her husband's arm.

"I know you'll do a great job, Burt," Mary Alice said. She thought that actually Pinky Shore would make a pretty good Horace in *The Little Foxes*. He wasn't pink and hadn't been since a serious case of pink eye when he was six years old.

"Burt already knows his lines," Evelyn said. "Now don't be a stranger, Mary Alice. You drop by anytime and see me."

"And you come out to the lake soon." Mary Alice skirted by Evelyn avoiding the too-familiar pat that Burt liked to give women.

Mary Alice walked to her car thinking that dropping in on Evelyn unannounced would be like dropping in on a secret weapons plant. Not a good idea.

MARY ALICE LEFT THE ALEXANDER'S estate just after two o'clock and took a Sunday drive on county back roads. She wished Zach were with her. She had an errand in town, but loved looking at the hilly terrain separated by acres and acres of ready-to-pick cotton. The snowy fluff shimmered in the heat; the glare nearly blinded her. She wanted to turn down every road. At the crossroads were two signs: right, Zion Baptist Church and left, White Oaks Cemetery. She turned left.

Her father's grave, marked by an impressive chunk of engraved Georgia granite, lay in the old part of the cemetery. Four generations of Tates and their wives and some children lay side by side under gnarled oaks and paw paw trees. Mary Alice sat on the plot where her mother would someday be interred.

"Daddy, I'm going to tell you everything I know about Sheree's case—about the drugs, the button, Scott's bruise, his wife running off, all of it and then I'm just going to sit still and listen." She hoped a misty ectoplasmic form would congeal nearby and imagined they could concoct a yes/no signal, permitting her Daddy to answer all her questions. She yearned to talk to her father.

Two birds sported in the undergrowth, rustling the dead leaves. She talked and talked until the shadows of the head stones stretched long in the golden light. She stayed until dusk when the kudzu on the distant hills turned dark and dust motes seemed immobilized in the late summer air.

"I have to go, Daddy. You keep thinking about it and let me know. I'm going to go home and feed Boon and then go over to Sheree's. Come along if you want to."

She pulled herself up. Her body felt heavy as if her veins were filled with lead. She always tried to be realistic about death. It was a natural, inevitable process; why resist it? But the cemetery with its granite reminders of mortality, never failed to sadden her.

I want cremation. My children can scatter my ashes in the Mississippi River.

However, the notion of children weakened her resolve on the pregnancy issue. She clutched her belly, adding anxiety to melancholy.

CHAPTER 14

"THIS IS GOOD NEWS," MARY Alice said. She sat at Sheree's kitchen table, a huge slice of lemon meringue pie in front of her. "Irene Bardwell is going to take your case. Today is Wednesday; they'll set a trial date Friday." She tunneled under the meringue to the filling. "Georgia, tell her this is good news." In the three days since Mary Alice's chat with Judge Weeds, zero had happened with Sheree's case. Until today. Mary Alice sensed she was far more excited than Sheree, and it irritated her.

"Irene Bardwell is very good news," Georgia said.

Sheree poked her piece of pie, jiggling the gelatinous lemon goo and said nothing.

"You can have Bobby Ray Buchanan back," Georgia said. She looked at Sheree across the small white kitchen table, her eyebrows raised high.

"I don't mean to sound—I just don't think she'll get me off. She don't even live in Mississippi."

"She has better resources in Birmingham," Georgia said. "She used to work for The Southern Poverty Law Center in Montgomery. Irene Bardwell will be here when she needs to be."

"She's not coming over until Friday?" Mary Alice asked.

"She will be here when she needs to be," Georgia said, over enunciating.

"I need to talk to her before the hearing," Mary Alice said. "I'm calling her."

"Why?" Georgia asked.

"Don't you think I should tell her what I've found out?"

"What have you found out? Who are your suspects?"

"But—"

"Hold it," Georgia said, holding up her right hand. "I appreciate your efforts, Mary Alice, you know I do. But we have a real lawyer now." She pressed the last crumbs of pie crust between the fork tines.

"Friday the judge is going to set a trial date," Mary Alice said. "How long will we have to prepare?" She didn't like talking about Sheree in front of her, but she could tell Sheree felt overwhelmed, confused. In her past, lawyers had simply been guides through the legal morass, not helpers.

"A month, maybe two," Georgia said. "Depends."

"That isn't very long when the real job is proving Sheree is innocent because somebody else is guilty," Mary Alice said.

"Y'all excuse me, please." Sheree rose and headed down the narrow hall toward the bathroom.

"Irene will get as much time as possible," Georgia said, digging in her purse for her car keys. "She's filed for the medical examiner's report, all that kind of stuff."

"I want to see it. All of it," Mary Alice said.

"Pictures of the body?"

"Yes."

"Can you imagine if you were Sheree's lawyer and somebody like you came along and wanted to help out? How would that be for you?" Georgia stood, shaking her keys together like bells.

"If I cared about my client, I'd welcome any help."

"What if your digging around makes the real killer so careful they'll never catch him?" Georgia asked. "Or her?"

"The police, in spite of what they say, are doing nil, zip, nada. Nobody's digging at all. Irene Bardwell's getting a late start, and she doesn't know Cana."

"I have to go," Georgia said. "You're not going to let this go, are you?"

"No. I can't," Mary Alice said. "Every day that goes by means it's less likely the murderer will be found."

"Okay." Georgia drew the word out into three syllables. She called down the hall, "I'm leaving, Sheree. Mary Alice is here."

"Bye, Georgia," Sheree said. "Thanks for the pie." Her thin voice leaked from the cracks around the bathroom door.

At the door, Mary Alice stopped Georgia. "You told me a week ago I should go with my gut and help Sheree."

"You should. Be here for her."

"Moral support isn't going to keep her out of jail," Mary Alice said. She felt aggravated at Georgia. First, Georgia had warned her to back off, then to follow her instincts, as Georgia had done in Atlanta. Now she was saying, back off.

"We have excellent legal help now," Georgia said. "I'm afraid you'll accidentally muddy the waters."

Mary Alice considered the button her earlier sleuthing had produced. Inadmissible evidence now. Maybe Georgia was right.

"I'll limit myself to any opportunities that come along that Irene Bardwell would never know about," Mary Alice said. "How's that?"

"Fine, if I believed you."

"It's not going to hurt for me to talk to that cop. Tom Janowski."

"Jaworski. Tom Jaworski. No, it's not because he's not going to talk to you," Georgia said. "I'm late. I'll call later."

Mary Alice knew that no matter what, she'd call the new lawyer, Irene Bardwell, and she knew she'd try to talk to the cop, Tom Jaworski. Talking was all she could do. Talking produced leads that could be followed.

Look at Stephanie Plum, Janet Evanovich's bail bondswoman character. Plum, hardly the sharpest knife in the drawer and in no way trained to solve crimes or even chase bail skips, talked and talked until she found out what she needed to know.

No one had ever said Mary Alice Tate couldn't talk. And she could listen too.

As soon as the front door closed, the bathroom door opened. Sheree joined Mary Alice in the living room. They sat side by side on the sofa each holding a saggy, plaid pillow.

"I heard what you said," Sheree said.

"You think I'm gonna mess things up?"

"I already told you how I feel. Do what you think's best."

"Did you arrange for me to talk to what's his name, the drug dealer?" Mary Alice asked.

"Larry Don. No. He didn't go for it. Didn't even want to talk to me."

"Why?"

"Paranoid. He sells drugs. That's normal."

Mary Alice felt like she did whenever she played cards. She never won, and worse, rarely even got into the game. Nothing ever opened up for the cards she held.

"But there's somebody else," Sheree said. "He's not big time but—"

"Who?"

"Marshall. Makes meth and sells what he don't use."

"Marshall who?"

Sheree smiled. "Just Marshall. I've bought from him."

"You know anything else about him?" Mary Alice asked.

"Drives a truck, gets a crazy check. What do you need to know?"

"A crazy check?" Mary Alice asked.

"A check from the government; some kind of disability. That's what they're called."

"When can I see him?"

"About seven."

"Tonight?"

"At the Washboard."

Mary Alice felt a tingling mix of excitement and fear. Of course drug dealers would be spontaneous. "Does he know anything?"

"What do you want to know?"

"I don't know." She walked to the window and looked out at the scrabby grass in the front lawn. "Look, if I want to know about baking pies I do research. Get books, go online and most important talk to bakers. Then I can sift all the information together. Maybe something interesting will stand out."

"Like lard?"

"I beg your pardon?"

"You need Morrell lard to make a good crust."

"Lard is lethal."

"That's different research. I thought you wanted a pie."

"I want to understand the current drug scene. Besides what you told me, I'm ignorant as hell."

"Marshall's just out of jail," Sheree said. "He'll know whatever there is to know. But he only does meth."

"It's an illegal drug."

"It's different than coke or crack. I don't think Scott was closing in on a meth ring."

"Because?"

"Mostly it's made by red necks. Little labs in trailers out in the sticks. I never knew anybody who made meth that didn't use it too. Scott was thinking lots bigger. Coke's bigger."

Mary Alice thought about what Sheree had told her about her life—sexual abuse by her stepfather who eventually abandoned her and her paranoid-schizophrenic mother and about the four foster families, one so bad the father went to jail for what he did to Sheree. Mary Alice thought that she'd take drugs too if she'd had Sheree's life.

"How will I recognize this Marshall?" She didn't want to argue about whether or not shipments of Mexican meth were at the core of Scott Bridges' bust.

"I told him you'd be eating an apple." She went to the bowl of fruit on the counter.

"What if I finish before he gets there?"

Sheree handed Mary Alice two apples.

Driving to the laundromat, Mary Alice felt that finally she was doing something that might help. And more important, Sheree seemed to be waking up. She still expected the system to screw her, but she had arranged for the meeting with Marshall. It was a start.

By definition, meetings with sources like Marshall were exciting. Mary Alice wished she'd had more time to prepare. She hadn't even known what to wear much less what questions to ask.

The Washboard Washateria offered no frills, but it was always open and had been on the corner of Jefferson Davis and Dogwood Drive for as long as Mary Alice could remember. She slowly ate the first apple as she perused the shabby bulletin board that offered a hundred acres on which to shoot wild turkeys, free puppies to good homes and a complete Mary Kay beauty makeover by calling Rita Dale Riley. An older Hispanic couple had secured four dryers in the back. Otherwise the place was empty. The excitement of a clandestine meeting was rapidly fading. But as she reread the Mary Kay ad, the drone of the dryers was drowned out by the throbbing pistons of a truck that pulled up within three feet of the door.

"Hey. You Sheree's friend, Mary Lyle?" Lanky and about twenty-five, Marshall wore jeans and an orange tee shirt that advertised car mufflers. *No muff, too tuff* was emblazoned across his chest in fancy script.

"Yes. It's Mary Alice. Thanks for coming." She dropped the apple core into an empty Cheer box that topped the overflowing trash can.

Marshall reminded her of a banty rooster as he snatched an over-stuffed plastic bag from his truck. She hadn't imagined that he'd actually wash his socks and boxers.

"Me and Sheree go way back," he said, his black eyes darting about. "Mary Lyle, I hope she's okay. I sure do." He flung the bag's contents into the mouth of a washer and stuffed what wouldn't fit into another one. Still talking about Sheree, whom he'd known since eighth grade, he fished for quarters in his pockets.

Mary Alice decided not to argue about her name. "Are you going to wash those linty things with your shirts?" she asked.

"Lint? You say lint?" he asked.

"I'm sorry," she said. She thought about her Dallas therapist with whom she'd discussed control issues. She was trying to fix a meth addict's laundry.

"How should I do it?" He yanked the clothes out and began spreading them over several closed washers.

"You bring any detergent?" she asked.

"Tide regular scent okay?" His Adams apple pumped up and down.

She smiled. "Get it. I'll check your pockets."

While Mary Alice took over Marshall's wash, he explained his line of work. Twenty minutes later he was down to ingredients.

"There are only three things you need to make crystal meth. One is pseudoephedrine, two is iodine crystals and three is red phosphorus. Well there's some other shit you need like muriatic acid, methanol, acetone, lye and of course, your hardware—plastic tubing, flask, PVC connectors. The red phosphorus comes from the strike pad on match books." He took a gulp of air.

"Matches?" she asked.

"No. The pad the match is striked on. Spartan brand is best. Can't use those striped or polka dotted strike pads. Got to be smooth light brown. You're going to need a few cases of them. Gets tiring ripping them off, but I can usually do enough in about four hours. They don't have to be Spartans, but the lye better be Red Devil. It's a drain cleaner. I believe Wal-Mart carries it. Shit, now getting the Sudafed is the problem. They put it all behind the counters so you can't buy much at one time. You looking to score by any chance?" he asked.

Marshall couldn't stop talking, and Mary Alice had a good idea why.

"I want to help Sheree. Marshall, she might go to jail forever. I need to know about illegal drugs in Cotashona County. Scott Bridges told Sheree that somebody high up—maybe city council or the sheriff—was protecting a drug warehouse. Scott was getting ready to blow the whistle on them. I think his death had something to do with that."

"Shit. You a lawyer?"

"No."

"A detective?"

"No. Do you know anything?"

"No."

Their conversation traversed the terrain of local drugs until Mary Alice understood why the war on drugs wasn't being won. The information along with the heat from the dryers made her feel as squashed as road kill.

"Your wash is done," she said. "You got any dimes for the dryer?" She rolled a metal basket with a gimpy wheel over to Marshall's washers.

"But a deal like that doesn't surprise me none," Marshall said. "They's some bad cops in Cana. If what the dead cop said's true, I wouldn't be surprised if the Highway Patrol ain't in on it. Makes sense. Doesn't surprise me none. Everybody knows drugs from Mexico come over I-20 or I-10 and north on I-55 headed for Memphis, Atlanta and the East Coast. Stockpiling near here makes sense."

As Marshall explained his theory of drug distribution in the United States, Mary Alice loaded the dryers and inserted the coins he gave her. His talk was continuous, ricocheting wildly from local drug depots to why all drugs should be legalized to why crack cocaine was so popular.

"Marshall, do you know any bad cops. Any names?"

He laughed revealing two rows of white, even teeth. "They're all bad, if you ask me. You ever wonder why somebody becomes a cop?"

"I mean one on the take." She didn't think she could stand a treatise on the dark psychological makeup of law officers according to Marshall-the-Meth-Man. "You know for a fact of any who take bribes?"

"No, I reckon not for a fact." He rubbed his hand over his face.

"You know Tom Jaworski?"

"Actually I do, by word, you know." A dozen times he punched the coin return on the dryer.

"What's he like?"

"I heard about him while I's in jail." Marshall said. "He had a chance to get in on a deal when he worked in Jackson and wouldn't do it. I heard about it in jail." His gaze rotated with the wet clothes in the jumbo dryer. "You learn a lot in jail. The beauty part about jail is that they put us all together and when we come out, we're better equipped than ever to do business. I don't sell on the street, but—"

"Marshall, I can't stay for folding. I gotta go. But I want you to call me if you hear anything. I'm willing to pay you for good information."

"Okay, I can do that." His head moved rhythmically as though he were pointing at ten things with his chin.

"When your tee shirts are still warm, finger-smooth them flat on the folding table. They'll look ironed."

He shook his head up and down. "I could have used you last month. I never fold fitted sheets right."

Before he got started, Mary Alice pushed her name and number into his hand and fled. The BMW cranked the first try.

Driving back home, Mary Alice picked the lint from Marshall's white socks off her black slacks. She'd liked him in spite of his exhausting frenetic energy, but she knew she didn't have time to rescue Marshall. He hadn't been very helpful, but she considered that in the detective business, useful clues tended to reveal themselves later on. Her favorite literary sleuths poked every lead, and only after page 250 or so did the odd tip or isolated clue start to pay dividends. And Marshall knew of Tom Jaworski. The confirmation of Georgia's choice of a good cop seemed to Mary Alice like winning the big slot at the Isle of Capri Casino. Was she finally getting a break?

I can't believe I washed his clothes. Good thing we didn't meet at a motel.

Before the turn off to the lake, Mary Alice became aware that a car seemed to be following her. A chill came over her as if she'd just noticed an adult water moccasin in a row boat with her. The car had maintained the same distance since she left the square. She bypassed her turnoff for the lake and drove out the county road toward a series of hills still visible in the twilight. The car followed. She passed a billboard with a honey-blond Jesus that asked if she were right with the Lord. Beyond the rise of the second hill, she recognized Cooper Pegues' farm and turned into the gravel road, making the house as the pursuing car drove past. She read Cotashona Sheriff's Department on the side. She felt stupid lying to Vivian and Cooper Pegues, telling them she'd seen their mailbox and just had to stop in to say hello, but stupid felt better than scared. They kept her there for twenty minutes asking about her family, if the lake had too many lily pads and if she might want to sell some of her father's guns someday. No one followed her when she left. If it were only a coincidence, she wondered why she felt so frightened.

Once at home, she quickly left the car, ran inside into the kitchen and bolted the door. When she turned, she smelled it—something putrid, something dead in her house.

"Boon. Boon?" she called.

The sickening smell made her head ache. She pulled a dishtowel over her nose and mouth and fished her cell phone from her purse.

"Georgia, please pick up if you're there. I need help, and I don't think I should call the sheriff. Georgia?"

Like a chilly coat from an unheated closet, fear slipped around her shoulders and gripped her abdomen. Her muscles moved in spasmodic jerks, delaying progress and revelation. She shoved the phone in her pocket and staggered into the utility room.

CHAPTER 15

MARY ALICE GRABBED HER FATHER'S shotgun from the utility room. Something was wrong, and the loaded gun in her right hand leveled the playing field. At least she hoped it did.

"Boon," she yelled through the towel over her nose and mouth. Then she heard the scratching and a high whimper. The dog was locked up in the half bath next to the utility room. She edged toward the door and opened it. Boon sprang out and pushed hard against her.

"Baby, are you all right?" She leaned the gun against the wall and ran her hands over his body. Boon seemed fine.

Mary Alice knew there was no chance that she'd accidentally closed the dog up in the bath, but there was no time to worry about that.

She picked up the shotgun, returned to the kitchen and faced the dining room door. Boon stayed pressed to her knee.

When she pushed open the door, the foul smell hit her like a load of concrete riprap.

She flipped on the light switch and started screaming. Boon yelped furiously. Below the dining room chandelier hovered a huge bird, its wingspan over four feet. The sunken, dull eyes told her it was dead. It swung gently, casting ghoulish shadows on the wall. Flight won over fight, and Mary Alice bolted. The dog followed.

Outside, she tried to breathe deeply, but could only achieve harsh pants. She couldn't stop repeating "Oh my God."

Boon kept up a soft growl.

Who had done this? Why?

Her ex-husband who had enjoyed tormenting her came to mind, but the Halloween horror scene in the dining room wasn't Cham's style.

When the cell phone in her pocket rang, she jumped and jerked the trigger of the shotgun. The kick from the blast sent her sprawling on the driveway. The barbeque grill lay dead by the back door.

"Hello? Hello?" she yelled into the phone. Deafened by the explosion, she couldn't hear the caller. "Who is this?"

"It's me, Georgia. What's the matter?"

Mary Alice recognized Georgia's voice. "There's a dead buzzard in the dining room, and I just shot the barbeque grill. Oh my God." She started to laugh hysterically and knew if she couldn't get a hold of herself, some horrible noises were going to replace the laughter.

"Mary Alice, control yourself," Georgia said in her Voodoo-woman voice. "I'm getting in my car right now. I'm on my way. Hear the engine start? I'll be there very soon. I want you to talk to me. Do not hang up. Do you hear?"

Mary Alice gulped, teetering between laughter and tears.

"Breathe deeply," Georgia commanded.

The word clicked, and Mary Alice inhaled slowly.

"After I left you at Sheree's this evening, what happened?" Georgia asked. "Tell me everything you've done."

"I met a guy Sheree knows." Mary Alice's voice quavered. "I hoped he might know something about stockpiles of drugs." She felt like she was suspended in slow motion. She knew she was talking to Georgia, but everything around her took on a surreal appearance. The hairline cracks in the driveway turned into a system of rivers and canyons occasionally blocked by pine needles.

By the time Georgia pulled into the driveway, Mary Alice was up to the part where she eluded the sheriff's car that had followed her from town. Georgia got out of her car and found Mary Alice on the ground near the back door.

"Put the shotgun down, Mary Alice," Georgia said. "It's me, Georgia."

"Oh. Okay," Mary Alice said into the phone.

"And you can hang up the phone."

"I'm okay now," Mary Alice said. With shaking hands she set down the gun and put the phone in her pocket." You smell it yet?"

"Let's call the sheriff," Georgia said. She moved slowly toward Mary Alice. "Someone broke into your house. We need to call the authorities."

"The authorities might be the ones who broke in," Mary Alice said.

"You need to report this. There might be other damage, and your insurance company will need a police report."

"All right." She heard "shell-shocked" in her voice and realized that her resistance had been drained as dry as the tundra.

Georgia made the call to the dispatch number at the Cotashona County Sheriff's Department while Mary Alice sat mutely running her fingers against the grain in Boon's thick coat.

After Georgia hung up, she told Mary Alice, "I want to see this before anybody gets here."

"You do?"

"You don't have to come."

"I'll come," Mary Alice said. "Nobody's here now."

"Good."

Mary Alice led Georgia through the kitchen toward the dining room. "Put this napkin over your nose," she said. She returned the dish towel to her own nose and opened the door to the dining room as though it were Pandora's Box.

Georgia walked around the suspended creature examining it as if it were a sculpture she was considering buying. Rigged with wire to look as if it were flying, the buzzard hung suspended from the huge wrought iron chandelier. "What's that in its beak?"

Mary Alice moved closer to the shiny speck in the bird's mouth. "I can't tell from here." She didn't want to look.

"Wait for the sheriff," Georgia said. She sounded overly-calm, like a kindergarten teacher supervising a bus accident. "You don't want to touch it. Let's wait outside."

"I'm okay, Georgia. You don't have to talk to me like I'm a mental patient."

"Glad to hear it. This stink is giving me a headache. Let's get out of here." She led the way back outside, where they sat on the deck watching the house.

"You can't stay here tonight," Georgia said.

"I'm not running away. That's just what they want."

"But—"

"They want me desperate, so I'll do what they want. That's how they work."

"Well, let's talk about that. You're freaked out. You've been violated," Georgia said.

"I know. And I know Daddy's house may not ever be the same after this for me. But I'm not leaving."

"Even if it's safe, it smells God-awful," Georgia said.

A long pause followed.

"I'll go to Mama's for tonight." Mary Alice turned her chair to face Georgia. "But I'm coming back."

The effort to defy the intruders made her want to "whistle a happy tune." Anna in *The King and I* said it made her brave.

"Why would somebody hang that thing in my house?" She forced back tears. She didn't want the relief of them. She needed the perspective that pain and anger brought.

"Don't you see?" Georgia said. "It has to be something to do with Sheree's case. You've hit a nerve. Bailing out Sheree, helping her get a good lawyer, visiting Katherine Bridges. You got close enough somehow to make someone scared that you're too close."

"Maybe they know I was talking to Marshall," Mary Alice said.

"Who's Marshall?"

"Druggie friend of Sheree's. I thought he might know something. He didn't. He can't even do laundry."

"Lord a mercy," Georgia said.

"Sheree told me Scott Bridges bragged to her about a big drug operation—a warehouse of stuff protected by who he called Cana's high and mighty. Maybe it's not true, but—"

"If it is, it's a motive for his murder." Georgia shook her head and then scratched the top of it. "And you think you can expose people who are protecting a drug operation? Are you crazy?"

Mary Alice wanted to scream at Georgia, Can you try to be positive for once? We don't have much going and maybe that's because we're so ready to be beaten. You of all people should understand that.

But screaming would only disperse her energy and she needed to focus.

"You can walk away from all this, you know," Georgia said. "Sheree will understand. It's gotten personal and dangerous."

Mary Alice looked out across the lake. "What kind of person would do something like this?" she said. "It's so psycho." She considered drug dealers and the sheriff.

"Did you hear me?" Georgia asked. She touched Mary Alice's arm.

Even Katherine Bridges could have done it or had it done.

"Mary Alice."

"I heard, and I can't walk away."

"You think you'll solve this murder and save Sheree?" Georgia rose and looked down the driveway. There was no sign of the sheriff.

"I have no idea," Mary Alice said.

"Then why?"

"I won't abandon Sheree." Mary Alice looked up at Georgia. "I won't quit. I think I can help her—bring attention to her case, keep the pressure on. But I know I can help her by just being there for her. You don't leave people you care about just because there's a crisis."

"What about self-preservation?"

"If I abandon her now, there won't be much of me to preserve."

"That's not a little dramatic?"

"Maybe. But walking out on her won't be good for me. I know that."

Georgia shook her head. "What's next?"

"I want to talk to Tom Jaworski," Mary Alice said. "Marshall says he's okay."

"It won't hurt to try," Georgia said. "It's safer than talking to, what was his name, Marshall?"

"Maybe Scott Bridges told Jaworski something. What if Jaworski thinks he can still do something?"

"You mean finish what Scott Bridges started?" Georgia said. "Take out the drug business?"

"Yes." She ran her hands through her hair. A headache was setting up camp behind her eyebrows.

"Then he better watch his back."

"What does Jaworski look like?"

"Wait," Georgia said. "I hear cars coming."

Sheriff Gelly himself and two deputies responded to Georgia's call. Gelly, built like a 250 pound fire plug, had small, mean, almond-shaped eyes. When he concentrated he puffed air behind his upper lip causing his bristly mustache to flex. The deputies nodded a lot at the Sheriff and rarely met his gaze. Yes, Sheriff this, yes, Sheriff that.

The scene reminded Mary Alice of Sheree's arrest. Testosterone-laden cop power.

After a lengthy search of the house and grounds, Sheriff Gelly interviewed Mary Alice. "You certain you don't know somebody who'd do something like this?" he asked. His thick country accent made his question sound like, "Ya suhtin yeow-don-o sumbuddie ood do summin lak dis?

"No sir," she said. "Maybe I overreacted. It just smelled so terrible." She wanted them all to leave. Hadn't a sheriff's department car just followed her, frightened her? She couldn't put her finger on exactly what, but nothing about Sheriff Gelly felt right.

"This here was in the bird's mouth." The sheriff waved a baggie containing a single brass button. "You recognize it?" He pushed the bag under her nose.

She felt a clutching, gripping in her gut. "Yes," she mumbled. "It's off my DKNY slacks. They're in my bedroom; or they were." Her resolve wilted. Someone had touched her clothing; snipped off a button, a token. She had read serial killers often did that kind of thing.

As she punched Zach's number on her cell phone, she watched a deputy carry the dead buzzard, now bagged, out of the house. The other deputy was dispatched to find the slacks missing a waist button. Zach's phone didn't pick up.

"I'm calling this unlawful entry, vandalism," Gelly said. "That's not what I think it is." He thrust his head forward and glowered. "That might keep the newspaper from trying to make a big deal out of it."

She nodded. "I know Mama will appreciate not spreading this all over town." She envisioned Gelly wiring the buzzard to her chandelier and then coming back to investigate. If Scott Bridges had been right about drugs, wouldn't the sheriff have to be in on the cover up?

The sheriff asked more questions and ended finally by telling her that women shouldn't live alone out in the country.

They were asking for trouble. Mary Alice wanted to push him in the lake.

After the lawmen left, Mary Alice noticed Clay Sykes standing on the deck at the water's edge.

"Hey, Clay," Mary Alice said.

He sauntered over. "You okay?" He nodded to Georgia.

"Yeah. You heard what happened?" Mary Alice said.

"Yeah."

"Go on home, Georgia. It's midnight," Mary Alice said. She went to Georgia and hugged her. "Thank you."

"I'm not leaving until you do," Georgia said.

"All right," Mary Alice said. She sensed Clay wanted to talk to her in private.

The three stood in silence for a moment. Then Georgia turned to walk to her car.

"I'll wait in my car. I'm not pulling out until I see you do the same," Georgia said. The look she gave Clay said, *I got my eye on you.*

"Be right behind you," Mary Alice said.

Clay looked out over the dark lake. When Georgia's car door closed he said, "Whoever it was came by way of the lake."

"You saw someone?"

"No," he said. "But Sunday, I saw tracks between the lake and County Road 140. Be easy to park on the road and carry a raft in. Lake's up now; water's almost to the curve in the road. You know where I mean?"

She did. "On Sunday?" she asked. She remembered the sound on the lake she thought she had heard when she stepped out on the balcony. Zack had been asleep. "But that thing was put in the house tonight, not three days ago."

"There's new tracks over the old ones."

Mary Alice tried to visualize the scene. Clay was too good an outdoors man to be mistaken. "Why make two trips?" she asked, tasting the fear returning, like lips on tarnished metal.

"The first trip sets things up, the second—" He stopped. "I can tell I'm scaring you. I'm sorry. Thought you ought to know."

She sighed and nodded. "Buzzard mean anything to you?" she asked. "It's not part of some secret hunter's lore I wouldn't know about, is it?"

"Buzzards eat the dead."

"I had thought of that," Mary Alice said.

Mary Alice and Boon got in the car; she locked the doors. Clay disappeared into the dark. She was aware that something about Clay Sykes was weird. He showed up at odd times out of nowhere and tonight he seemed to know what had happened. He couldn't be the killer she sought. But then she thought that the real killer wouldn't likely seem like a killer. He'd seem like a nice guy.

She heard Georgia's car start and was glad she had waited. She followed Georgia's red tail lights away from the lake into the dark.

CHAPTER 16

M ARY ALICE AWOKE WITH THE sun streaming in the windows. For a second she didn't know where she was. "Mama's."

The now elegant apartment was a converted store room above the mansion's old carriage house. An antique carriage that appeared in Cana parades was stored below. Mary Alice rode in it when she was homecoming queen.

She'd slept late because she hadn't fallen asleep until nearly 5 AM. The digital clock said 9:10. Boon snored on a hand-hooked rug beside the bed.

High up in the antique canopied bed, she surveyed the room her mother had redecorated last year for perhaps the fifth time in a decade. Floral chintz draperies hung under densely gathered valences and over silky white sheers. The chintz was repeated on the skirts of two round tables which were topped by two more cloths in contrasting colors. The bed comforter, skirt and shams were done in three related prints of blue on gold. One table held a collection of tiny Bilston boxes, the other, dozens of silver framed family pictures. In the group she saw one of her and her father on a horse. She looked deliriously happy. The heart pine floors gleamed orange-brown beneath years of wax. It would have been perfect except for the nearly imperceptible message of "don't break, don't muss and don't touch."

Mary Alice wandered into the tiny bath crowded under the eaves and turned on the shower. While she waited for hot water, she looked at herself in the mirror.

She looked tired. People always said she looked younger than her age. She bet they wouldn't say that anymore. She leaned close to the mirror, inspecting for lines, bumps or other flaws that might need attention.

If this keeps up, I'll need a face lift before I'm forty.

She pulled her thick, dark hair back tight, making her face taut and tried to smile her beauty contest smile. Perfect teeth shone in the mirror, but the light in her eye was dim. She held the pose until steam fogged the glass.

After her shower, she put on the fluffy Turkish terry robe that her mother had thoughtfully placed on a hook on the bathroom door. When she opened the door she saw her mother perched on the gold Italian silk settee.

"I brought some coffee up," Elizabeth said. "Are you all right?" She wore a jade green dress and understated but good gold jewelry.

"Bad news travels fast," Mary Alice said. "Did Sheriff Gelly call you?"

Elizabeth gave her a superior I-know-lots-of-things look.

Mary Alice took her overnight bag back into the bathroom, but left the door ajar. Small town network. Who else was in the chain? It was annoying to be discussed like a missing child.

"Did you call Zach and tell him what happened?" Elizabeth asked.

"He's still in Jackson. I didn't want to wait that long for him to rescue me." She didn't tell her mother that she'd tried Zach last night and gotten no answer.

"I'll send Clancy for your clothes."

"Mama, I'm not staying here."

"Well, you are not going back out there after somebody stuck a dead animal in your dining room."

"As soon as it airs out, I am. Somebody is trying to scare me to keep me from helping Sheree Delio. If I give into that, they win."

"But you win too. You won't be dead," Elizabeth said with a thick staccato laugh. "What is it you lose by moving out of there?"

Mary Alice emerged from the bathroom dressed in jeans, a white shirt with panels of white embroidery down the front. She pushed her feet into her Bjorn clogs. "Because I give them my power and lose part of myself." She knew she could never explain her feelings to her mother. Last night, she'd tried to tell Georgia. She doubted Georgia got it.

"I never heard anything so ridiculous," Elizabeth said. Her face turned red, and her eyes shone like bright marbles. "You're risking your life for that slut."

She felt a hot blast of anger but forced her voice to hide the emotion. "Sheree Delio's not a slut, Mama. Don't call her— you don't know anything about her."

Mary Alice couldn't stop the fantasy movie in her head in which she piled yards and yards of chintz on top of her mother until whatever she said was inaudible.

"I know about her. I saw one of her films," Elizabeth said. She reached out and leveled a tilted lamp shade.

"What are you talking about?"

"When Sidney painted the apartment that I practically gave that ungrateful wretch, he found a hidden video camera. There was a videotape inside, and it wasn't blank."

"What?" She struggled to follow what her mother seemed to be saying.

"A camcorder like grandparents use to film their grandchildren. Those grandparents who are fortunate enough to have grandchildren." Elizabeth stroked the bone china cup as though she could rearrange the delicate pink flowers that edged it. "I happened to be there when Sidney found the thing, or God knows what would have happened to it." She set down the cup and spread her arms like wings across the sofa back. Her long manicured fingernails flexed in and out of the pleated silk upholstery.

"You watched it?" Mary Alice asked. The polished pine floor changed to quicksand, and she expected her mouth to fill with mud any second.

"Enough to know it was pornographic," Elizabeth said. She pinched the button at the throat of her dress.

"Mama, if the camera was hidden, maybe Sheree didn't know about it."

"She looked like she was performing to me. A real pro."

Mary Alice felt sick. What else wasn't Sheree telling her?

"But it's evidence from a crime scene," Mary Alice said. "You can't just take it home." Mary Alice knew there was a possibility that analysis of the movie might reveal more. "How much did you watch?" She was aware that she was arguing about technicalities when her whole being wanted to deny the existence of a videotape with Sheree performing anything her mother could call pornographic.

"A minute was too much. I gave it to Zach."

"Zach? When?" Mary Alice asked, almost shouting.

"Last Friday morning, right after I realized what it was."

Mary Alice sank onto the edge of the bed. "When were you going to tell me this?"

"I told Zach instead of telling you," Elizabeth said. "You shouldn't be messing around with this. It's dangerous, and even if it weren't, it's sleazy."

Mary Alice forced herself not to react to her mother. She breathed deeply and felt the air in her body. She gathered her clothes and looked for Boon's leash.

Zach hadn't mentioned a videotape at lunch Friday. He'd had it almost a week. Why didn't he trust her? But then he wasn't obligated to tell her anything about the case. Zach wasn't, but her mother could have told her about the tape. Her mother knew how important Sheree's case was to Mary Alice. She started to see her mother being attacked by all the fussy embellishments in the room. Like poltergeists, the silver baby spoon collection, the Havilland demitasse group, the antique buttons and the precious Bilston boxes hurled themselves at their mistress.

"You told him what was on the tape?" Mary Alice asked when she felt in control of her emotions.

"Of course. He was going to see it anyway," Elizabeth said. "Are you going to drink this coffee I brought up?"

"Huh? I'll get some later. I have to go." She stuffed her things into an Ikot satchel. She had to force herself to move; she felt as though she had rusted since waking.

"Not back to the lake house." Elizabeth stood as though she could block the way.

"I'm going to the Women's Center first."

"Mary Alice, I beg you not to go back to the lake house. Something awful will happen."

"Keep thinking that, and you'll make it happen."

"Stop it. Your father taught you that ridiculous crap. Elizabeth mimicked her late husband. "Bad things happen because we magnetize the negative and attract it to us."

"I have to go. Come on, Boon." She walked out and down the stairs to her car. Steering clear of Elizabeth, Boon scampered ahead.

Elizabeth followed her daughter out onto the landing. "I'm going to call Brinks and have them install a security system out there," she called down to her daughter.

"Fine, Mama." She waved without turning back.

But Mary Alice didn't drive to the Women's Center. Instead she headed to Sheree's place. She fished a Honey Bun from the glove box and ripped open the cellophane. However, the slimy sugar glaze and uniquely chewy dough wasn't quite enough to distract her. A piece of evidence that she should have been privy to had surfaced and her own mother had given it to the DA. She couldn't recall a time when her mother had supported or sided with her, and Mary Alice's loony fantasies of revenge weren't softening the pain as they used to. She took another, bigger bite.

She slowed the car, aware of feeling disoriented. What if the camera had been running the night of the murder? It was possible. How long did camcorder tapes run? Did they have remote controls?

She tried Zach's cell phone again, but got a message informing callers that he was out of the zone.

I need to see that tape.

As the image of Sheree cavorting naked with Officer Bridges sank in, Mary Alice felt the Honey Bun turn to concrete in her stomach.

CHAPTER 17

"A VIDEO CAMERA?" SHEREE ASKED. SHE looked like a clown with her hair parted into sections, secured with bobby pins. She held a L'Oreal streak kit with both hands the way some people hold a Bible.

"Mama's painter found it," Mary Alice said. They stood in the kitchen by the window. The late morning sun poured into the sink showing up the chipped porcelain.

"I don't know nothing about it." She dropped the kit and scrambled to retrieve it.

"Come on, Sheree. It's your apartment. How could you not know?"

She shrugged and hardened her stance as if she were trying physically to deflect what Mary Alice was telling her—she'd been spied on, violated.

Mama said it was behind a wrought iron filigree plate in a chasing for pipes, high up on the wall and right across from the bed.

"I never looked at that vent thing," she whispered.

"How do you think a camera got in there?"

She shook her head." Scott had a key," Sheree said. "Maybe he—"

"Did he ever talk about wanting to make movies of you two?" She watched a ragged file of ants march from one cupboard to another.

"No."

"Do you know what's on the tape?" Mary Alice asked.

"I can guess," Sheree said. She seemed to shrink. "Your mother watched it?" She placed her fingertips over her mouth.

"Some of it. That's not important."

"But you ain't seen it?"

"No, but Mama said you were in it. She called it pornographic."

"Do you have it?" Sheree asked. With each question her voiced grew more shrill.

"Mama gave it to the District Attorney."

"Oh God." She turned her huge eyes on Mary Alice. "I didn't kill him."

"I know. And there's somebody else knows you didn't kill him." She told Sheree about the buzzard. "If I wasn't a threat, there'd be no reason for anybody to be nervous about my nosing around."

"Mary Alice, please don't get hurt on my account," Sheree said. "If Gelly and them boys are letting drugs through, there's millions of dollars at stake. They ain't going to sit by and let you catch them."

"You think Sheriff Gelly is in on it?" Mary Alice ploughed ahead with her questions not wanting to tell Sheree why she couldn't let go of helping her.

"It'd be hard to imagine it being successful without him."

"A sheriff's car followed me yesterday after I talked to Marshall."

"Then they're watching you. Shit fire, Mary Alice. I hate they put that dead buzzard in your house. Where you gonna stay at?"

"I'm taking some precautions, but I'm staying. It's my home." Mary Alice imagined a newspaper headline, "Woman Found Dead" and the story that reported how Mary Alice Tate foolishly had insisted on staying in a house any sane person would have vacated. But it was her home. Her Daddy had left it to her, she loved it and she vowed not to let fear chase her out of it.

Sheree started to protest, but then didn't. "Was Marshall any help?"

"He talked non-stop for an hour, but not about what I need to know. He thinks all cops are on the take."

"Meth makes you talky. And paranoid."

"Actually, he told me about one cop, Tom Jaworski. You know him?"

Sheree looked down at the hair streak kit and ran her thumb under the box lid. "Not really."

"Sheree, I can't help if you hold out on me."

Mary Alice believed she knew when Sheree was withholding information. She hoped she knew if Sheree was lying.

"He was working undercover vice a couple of years ago and arrested me."

"For?"

"What do you think?" She turned away and studied the ant column.

Mary Alice couldn't remember if Sheree had told her about being arrested for narcotics before the bust that connected her with Scott. She wondered how anyone could make so many bad choices, but given Sheree's background, it was a wonder she wasn't dead.

"What about the video? What'd y'all do the night Scott was killed?"

The color on Sheree's neck and cheeks deepened, and she turned away from the window.

"Sheree, I need to know if the video Mama gave the DA was made the night Scott was killed or some other time."

Sheree turned back to Mary Alice, the strong sunlight making her look about sixteen. "You think we have a movie of the killer?"

"No. Zach would have released you if that was true. But there might be something else on it. At least if Scott's prints are on it that would mean he was making the movie."

"It won't look like I was forced into anything." She tugged at a wisp of hair. "Things went easier if I acted like he wanted me to."

"Yes, but Mama and Sidney can verify that the camera was hidden," Mary Alice said. "If you knew about the camera, there'd be no reason not to set it up on a tripod." They watched two nervous squirrels dig through damp leaves for acorns. Mary Alice thought the squirrels were having better luck with their search.

"I don't see why the camera matters so much," Sheree said.

"Let's assume Scott put it there. He must have used a remote to start and stop it. He could have changed the tape when you weren't home."

"So?" Sheree looked blank.

"Look, they might use the tape to attack your character. It'd be useful to be able to argue that you're a victim, not a porn queen. And maybe there is something else on it. Maybe sounds."

Sheree nodded and sat down at the kitchen table. As though she were setting up an altar, she emptied the contents of the hair streaking kit. Mary Alice remembered that she had first streaked Sheree's hair. It had been right after Sheree got out of drug rehab. They'd been like high school girls experimenting with highlights. Now they were talking about evidence in a murder case.

"What'd he make you do?" Mary Alice asked.

Sheree looked at the floor, mute.

"What'd he make you do?" Mary Alice softened her tone from investigator to confessor.

Sheree started slowly, speaking in a monotone. "He'd ask me if I'd been a good girl." She rotated the bleach bottle around and around. "I'd say yes, and then he'd decide if I was telling the truth or lying."

"What did he decide?"

"Lying." She fell silent.

"What'd he do when you lied?"

"Punishment." She paused then blurted, "He handcuffed me to the bed and did it from the rear. You want to know more?"

"Were you wearing anything?"

"Mary Alice!"

"If I'm going to recognize this particular tape, I need details. High heels? What?" The softness evaporated as an emotional edge pushed in, hard as a February cold front. She felt like a monster, an inquisitor.

"No heels. Scott didn't want me any taller." She paused and took a long breath. "He blindfolded me with my panties and made me beg him to do it again and again." Tears silently crept down her face.

"I'm sorry, Sheree. I need to know. I'm not judging you."

"I know. I know."

Mary Alice hugged Sheree, but stifled the words she wanted to say: *Hush baby, it's okay. I'll make it all okay.*

Mary Alice drove home feeling like she was standing barefoot next to a live trap. Awareness helped, but a trap was still a trap. The videotape wasn't good news, but there was a slight possibility it could contain something useful—something Scott Bridges or whoever made the tape didn't know he was filming. But Zach must have seen the tape. Maybe he had already sent it to a forensic lab.

She turned onto the road that led to the lake house and slowed. How was she going to get the tape? She thought of cop TV shows in which evidence came up missing from the station evidence room. Then she thought about how watching it might be the hardest part. Of all the things Scott Bridges had done to Sheree, secretly making a videotape of her seemed to be the worst. Mary Alice imagined how violated she'd feel if she discovered a hidden camera in her house—a tape of her changing clothes or doing any of a hundred private, intimate actions. She couldn't imagine watching herself.

She pictured Scott Bridges turning on the camera and remembered Georgia telling her how he'd used video for drug busts to clean up the projects. The cop knew about video cameras; probably owned one or more.

When Mary Alice pulled into her driveway at the lake house just before noon, Sheriff Gelly was getting into his car. She parked, got out and slammed the door.

"Can I help you?" Mary Alice asked, southern graciousness noticeably absent.

"I'm done. Just needed to look around in the daylight." He looked at her in a way that made her feel uneasy.

"Did you find anything?" She wasn't going to tell him Clay's theory about the attacker's approach from the lake.

"Nothing was forced. You leave your doors unlocked?"

"Sometimes."

"That's really stupid."

Mary Alice wanted to tell him not to ever call her stupid. Cham used that word.

But she wanted even more for him to leave. "Well, that's me, stupid."

Stupid.

"Don't you smart mouth me, young lady." He took a step toward her, and she could see traces of acne scars on his cheeks and smell the tobacco on his breath. "If you get raped or worse, you'll be crying how we ain't protecting you, how you're a victim."

Mary Alice felt the heat rising inside her like a nuclear explosion. How dare this redneck son of a bitch come on her property and give her a lecture.

"Sheriff, did you call my mama and tell her about what happened out here last night?"

He didn't answer, but his expression told her she was right.

"Is that protocol? Who else did you call?"

Gelly turned away and spat. "I thought she might make it clear to you that you need to go stay in town with her."

"Well that's real fatherly of you, but I'm staying right here." She thought that if he moved an inch closer to her, she'd poke him in the eye.

"We don't have the manpower to protect you out here."

"So you know there'll be more attacks?"

Gelly looked uncomfortable and stroked his mustache.

"What's next? Slash my tires? Set fire to the house? Poison the well?"

"I hope you think it's entertaining next time," he said. "As I recall last night, you were scared to death."

"I just need a man, right?" She glared at him.

"The Brinks Security man will be here after lunch," he said easing toward the car.

"Make him show you some ID before you let him in."

"How the hell do you know that?"

"He will be." Sheriff Gelly heaved himself into his car, cranked it and drove slowly out the driveway.

As she watched him drive away, her fury rose like the dust pluming behind the sheriff's car . She hated to think of Gelly and her mother discussing her. Maybe it was better that she didn't have children. Elizabeth Tate was her only role model for mothering.

They'd be monsters.

As she went inside through the kitchen and locked the door behind her, she heard the phone ring and dashed into the living room.

"Hello?" She sank into an arm chair by the glass door.

"Mary Alice? Thank God. Baby, are you all right?" Zach asked.

"Zach. I tried to call."

"I'm so sorry," he said. "I turned my phone off and forgot about it. Just got back in town."

Mary Alice didn't want to discuss how Zach knew about the buzzard. Sheriff Gelly. Her mama. Likely by now, lots of people knew about the incident.

"I spent the night at Mama's." Relief flooded her voice. She didn't like to admit it, but Sheriff Gelly had frightened her. Sheree was right. Gelly was the kind to be involved in a deal like the one Scott Bridges had tried to expose.

"Why didn't you call dispatch? Somebody could have reached me in an emergency?" he said.

"I knew you were in Jackson. It was over before you could have gotten here."

"I feel terrible."

"I didn't know how else to get you. The office was closed."

"I have to be in court this afternoon, but I'm coming out there right after."

"Okay. That'd be good." She watched the lake turn steel gray as clouds scudded over the sun.

"I don't know who put that thing in your house, but if I find out, they'll wish they hadn't."

"Zach, everybody says I can't stay here, but I am."

"We'll talk about it. But you ought to think what you'd advise a woman in your place to do."

She didn't want to think about that. "Zach, I have to ask you, did you look at the videotape my mama gave you?"

There was a pause. "Yes. And I think you ought to see it too," he said.

"You do?"

"Yes."

"Is that legal?" Something didn't feel right.

"I don't plan to use it. It would only embarrass Scott Bridges' family. The prosecution doesn't need it."

"Why do you think I need to see it?" What had seemed an easily obtained gift was starting to seem like a trick, like bait and switch at the auto parts store.

"It might change your opinion of Sheree Delio. It's pretty graphic; says a lot about her."

So it was a Trojan horse. She stifled her urge to defend Sheree. Better to watch the tape first. "You may be right. I'm so glad you're back in Cana."

"I missed you, too," he said. "I have to go, but I'll be out there as soon as I can."

"Good," she said. She felt relief like a hot lavender scented bath.

"Wait. There's another thing," he said. "The Wootens invited us to their skybox for the Ole Miss— Alabama game on Saturday. After this, you may not be up to it. Maybe in a couple of days—"

"I'm okay. I'm not going to let this change what I do." The tension in her muscles eased, and she relaxed deeper into the chair. *Zach's back. I'm safe.*

"If you're sure. We can always cancel. Ken mentioned it a month ago, and I forgot."

"No, it's fine. I love football weekends. Are they gonna do the Grove before the game?"

"Oh yes," he said. "They always have a tent in the Grove. You sure you want to go, honey?"

"Yes."

"Actually, it'd probably be good for you," he said. "I told them if we could make it, we'd bring some food. You think you could call an Oxford caterer and order something?"

"Sure. How much?"

"Charge it to me. Spend what you need."

"I mean how many are we feeding?" she asked.

"They'll have two tents. Last time there were about forty of us, coming and going. Call CeCe Wooten. She'll know."

"Okay."

"Good. I'm glad we're going," he said. "You need a break from all this craziness."

"I guess. So, I'll see you this evening."

"I'll call before I come. Don't want you shooting me."

"Did Gelly tell you?"

"Said you obliterated the barbeque. Shot the goddamned barbeque pit all to hell, were his words."

"I'm glad you're back."

"I'm here for you, Mary Alice," he said. "Please be careful. Someone has attacked you. Next time they—" He paused. "Forget I said that. Now I'm scaring you. I'm sorry. I'll see you later."

As she hung up, the sun came out and the lake's surface sprang to life with a sparkling invitation. She decided to swim after lunch. This time next month, it would be too cold. This time next month a lot of things would be different.

Mary Alice made a To Do List: call CeCe, call caterer at Laissez le Bon Temps and buy a pregnancy test kit. And then she started making more notes only slightly aware that her command of the Grove ritual was some kind of a test. The pre-home-game festivities in the Grove on the Ole Miss campus were legendary and bore little resemblance to the pre-game tailgating of decades earlier. A successful governor's wife had to be able to Grove with the best of them.

As Sheriff Gelly had predicted, the Brinks Security representative showed up just after lunch. Mary Alice watched a woman named Wendy, install and check the new security system. Petite and sunburned, Wendy wielded the tools on her belt like a magician. After she secured the ladder back on her truck, she typed in Mary Alice's numerical code, 1817, the year Mississippi became a state, and ran Mary Alice through the system's features: zones, bypass, panic button, and on/off.

"But it doesn't work if the phone's cut off?" Mary Alice asked.

"The alarm will sound out here, but the system won't alert our office to call the cops—sheriff in your case 'cause you're in the county." She hoisted a heavy tool bag strap over her shoulder.

"But—"

Wendy cut her off. "The alarm will scare off most intruders." She wiped her nose. "And it's not easy to cut lines. Unless you know the particular installation."

"Thanks." Mary Alice urged her toward the door. She wanted to call Tom Jaworski before Zach arrived. As Mary Alice watched Wendy drive away in her white truck, she thought that Sheriff Gelly wouldn't approve of a woman on a twenty foot ladder stringing wire to install an alarm system.

Mary Alice found Tom Jaworski in the Cana phone book and remembered what Georgia had said about cops uniting against cop killers. She dialed Georgia's home number instead. Mary Alice had already reported in to let Georgia know she was all right, and that Zach had a porno video of Sheree given to him by Elizabeth.

"What now?" Georgia asked.

"I got a new security system."

"Good, I feel much better," Georgia said.

Her tone was mocking, but Mary Alice thought probably Georgia was glad.

"What else?"

"Sheriff Gelly came back for a look-see."

"I think he likes you, Mary Alice."

"I think he'd like me to disappear," Mary Alice said. "But that's not why I called. I'm going to call Tom Jaworski."

"You've been threatening to do that for a week."

"I'm doing it," Mary Alice said. "What do you know about him?"

"They say he's kind of a loner." Mary Alice could hear Georgia eating something. "Worked vice a couple of years, but he rotated. The main thing is that he won't want to talk to you. The official position has got to be that Sheree Delio killed a cop. He isn't going to want to even appear to be helping you."

"What can I do?"

"He hangs out at TJ's."

"Drinks?"

"I've seen him drink."

"You think I ought to ambush him at TJ's?"

"Start off talking about Scott Bridges, not Sheree, and don't go getting your feelings hurt if he swears at you."

"What are you eating?"

"Cookie dough. I gotta go. Oven's ready." Georgia hung up.

Mary Alice closed her eyes. A lot was happening fast and none of it supported Sheree's innocence. But now she was going to get to see the videotape. And Zach was back. He'd protect her. And she had Boon, two loaded guns and a new Brinks burglar alarm. And the list of positives could include Irene Bardwell. Mary Alice had finally reached the lawyer in

Birmingham while the security system was being installed. Mary Alice had emphasized her willingness to help Sheree. Bardwell sounded open, almost friendly.

The videotape today, the autopsy report tomorrow. She'd do like her Daddy had taught her and visualize what she wanted to happen. She closed her eyes and took a deep breath.

I will find evidence that casts doubt on Sheree's guilt. I will find some clue about the drug depot and those covering it up and profiting from it. I will see more clearly than I ever have.

Resting in the flow of the contented feeling reminiscent of afternoons outdoors with her father, Mary Alice linked the emotion to her desire for help.

The phone jangled her from her meditation. She picked up on the third ring.

"Hey, Mary Alice. It's Marshall."

"Marshall?" Laundromat. Meth-man. "Yes. Marshall."

"I was just thinking about what you said about me calling you if I thought of something and I did. I thought of something."

"What, Marshall?" she asked. Her Daddy had been right. All you had to do was energize your want with a feeling. Here was proof.

"I's wondering if you'd like to have a drink? I thought we'd ride over to Clarksdale to the Ground Zero. You ever been there? Morgan Freeman's blues club?"

CHAPTER 18

Zach arrived at sunset with the ingredients for Pasta Puttanesca. In spite of Sheriff Gelly, Mary Alice admitted to herself that it felt good to have a man around. No one was going to break in with dead birds if Zach Towree was present. Mary Alice wore her red off-the-shoulder blouse with skin tight black silk "cigarette" pants and a light spray of Ysatis perfume. The pants, just back from the cleaners, felt snug in the waist.

I'm not pregnant. Cleaners always shrink things.

Zach served the pasta dish with a special red wine, the last of a case bought years ago. "You ever had this?" He held up the bottle of Chianti.

"I don't think so." She pretended to look carefully, but she never remembered any wine.

"I hope you like it." They toasted and sipped.

"Can you sense how the sharp acid taste breaks to a velvety, almost chocolaty finish?" He swirled his wine.

"Ummmmm. Definitely," she said. "And it's so good with this sauce." The sauce was excellent, and she wondered why she felt like a cheerleader.

They ate slowly until the Chianti was gone and the candles were stubs.

"What's this? A security system?" he asked, pointing to at the box of buttons on the wall.

"Mama sent Brinks out," she said. Together they cleared the table.

He examined the key pad. "Looks complicated."

"While the ax murderer is hacking me to pieces, the piercing alarm is supposed to deafen him."

"So then we should look for a deaf killer?"

"Probably mute, too."

"Since you insist on staying here, I'm glad you have it," he said stacking the dishes in the sink. "It's awful isolated out here. I wish you'd reconsider."

For an instant Mary Alice felt a chill like a cool breeze on wet skin. Maybe she wasn't safe.

"Let's leave this mess for now," Zach said. He took her hand in his and led her to the living room where they sank together into the deep, cushy sofa. Wrapped in each other's arms, they watched the last of the sun's afterglow disappear and the lake turn to black glass.

This is too easy, she thought. *We don't even have to talk.* She nestled closer into his secure embrace and returned his kisses, upping the passion with each one. She felt like a romance heroine: willingly taken. But at the edge of the contentment, a memory stirred—her father's words about how she should feel safe and whole without a man, without anyone. Her annoyance grew as the memory pecked like a bird going after carrion on the highway. She was relieved when Zach unzipped the tight silk slacks, plunging her into a sensual vortex removed from troubling thoughts.

They made love right there and afterward, in his embrace, Mary Alice released the pent up tension of the last two weeks. She sobbed uncontrolled on his bare shoulder.

"Go ahead and cry, honey," he said. "Let it out. I'm here. It's going to be all right." He stroked her hair and rocked her. She told herself it was true. Later, he helped her to her bedroom and held her until she fell asleep.

When she awoke in her bed at six the next morning to the sound of the shower, she pulled over the pillow Zach had slept on and inhaled his scent. Problems of dead cops and dead birds faded in the innocent light of the new day. She wanted to lounge in bed for another hour, but realized Zach would want coffee. He had to go to work. She'd set a high standard the last time she made his breakfast. When she heard the shower spray turn off, she grabbed a robe and dashed downstairs.

When Zach emerged minutes later looking more like a successful banker than the Cana, Mississippi DA, she leaned back on the kitchen counter and tried to absorb him. Handsome didn't come close to describing Zach Towree.

"Are you going to court with Sheree Delio?" he asked, measuring a level teaspoon of Splenda into his coffee.

"She wants me to come along."

"Fine, but I want to warn you. I may seem a little distant in court. My attempt to be professional." He sipped the coffee and smiled at her.

"Of course." She hadn't thought of facing Zach in court on the other side of the aisle.

"All that will happen is the judge will set a date to file motions and a trial date," he said. "Be over in ten minutes."

"Good. I have to be at Laissez le Bon Temps at eleven." She refilled his coffee cup and felt guilty that the caterer was on the same list as Sheree's hearing.

"Breakfast?" She opened the refrigerator.

"No thank you," he said and looked at his watch.

"Zach, you said I could see the videotape Mama found," she said. She closed the refrigerator door, delaying her breakfast until he left.

"I'll see that you get it today," he said finishing his coffee. "Steel yourself. But I think you should see it." He took her in a long embrace, kissed her and smelled her hair. "Sorry I have to run."

"I understand. Wheels of justice and all that," she said.

"Eyes open, doors locked," he warned.

"Yes, sir."

She watched him drive away, enjoying the dazed sensation and the lingering scent of him. She hugged herself and wondered if he was thinking of her, wishing he could stay and make love again as they had last Saturday. Five days ago they had crossed the border into the zone of sexual intimacy. The ZSI. She shook herself awake, aware of the undertow of romance, the tug that could make her forget valuable lessons.

After Zach left, Mary Alice washed last night's dinner dishes quickly and put on a swimsuit, a violet bikini. She looked at herself in the mirror, glad she could still wear the miniscule suit. Most women her age didn't try unless they'd had liposuction and tummy tucks. But of course most had birthed babies that tended to ruin figures.

Babies.

No, her body didn't look a bit pregnant. She relaxed her abdominal muscles, pooching out her tummy. She knew that if an embryo were lodged inside, she'd see it through. She turned away from the mirror to avoid encouraging any mommy fantasy to take root.

I'll take the test just to be sure.

On the edge of the dock, Mary Alice gazed across the water. She let her senses absorb the lush southern effulgence that would last for weeks more. In North Mississippi, it was still summer on September 16. She dove off the dock, glad for the shock of the cold, and settled into the rhythm of the crawl. Boon guarded the shore; Brinks guarded the house. The water felt a little cooler than it had in August, but she soon warmed up. Swimming always cleared her head. She felt at home in the water. As a kid, when boys used to tease her and push her under water at the pool, she'd relax and hold her breath. Soon enough they'd be pulling her up, terrified they'd drowned her. She'd laugh at them, and if they dunked her again, she'd sink, knowing they'd always panic before she did.

She wished she'd asked Zach about Katherine Bridges. In spite of dead birds and drug depots, a scorned wife had a motive for murder as hundreds of years of history demonstrated. Where the hell was she?

SHEREE'S HEARING WAS SET FOR 9:30. Before walking over to the courthouse, Sheree, Mary Alice, Georgia and Irene Bardwell met at the Women's Center. Sheree looked like a stewardess for a foreign airline, maybe Ukrainian, in her demure blue suit and navy pumps. Her freshly touched up streaks flattered her ivory skin and at Mary Alice's suggestion, she had toned down her makeup even more. Mary Alice could tell Sheree was as nervous as a new client waiting for a bikini wax.

Irene Bardwell handed Mary Alice a thick manila envelope. "Here's a copy of the state medical examiner's report you asked to see," she said. Irene Bardwell was all business. She exuded intelligence which made up for her choice in attire and hair style. Her ill-fitting suit needed a press and her grayish-teal blouse refused to remain tucked into her skirt. Most dust mops looked better than her hair which seemed to have been cut by two different stylists with communication disorders.

"Mary Alice, you're established here in Cana with a lot of credibility, and you know the lay of the land," Irene Bardwell said. "As long as you don't break laws or put yourself in danger, I welcome your assistance. In fact, already you've unearthed some interesting questions regarding Sheree's deal with the police. You keep me informed," she said.

"I promise, Ms. Bardwell," Mary Alice said in her Girl Scout voice. She knew she should mention the videotape, but something, maybe embarrassment for Sheree, made her wait. She had never really been a Girl Scout. There would be time for that revelation after she'd seen the tape. And besides, she rationalized, the prosecution was obligated by the discovery process to supply the defense with a copy. Irene Bardwell would get the awful tape soon enough. Mary Alice willed herself to ignore the loose thread on Irene's jacket.

Zach was correct. The session in court lasted ten minutes with a trial date set for November 2, forty-seven days away. In court, Zach never once looked at Mary Alice. When it was over, one of the DA's assistants handed her a videotape-size box.

"The DA said to give this to you," the assistant said and walked away.

Mary Alice left the courthouse with Sheree and Georgia, but Irene Bardwell stayed to talk to Zach.

Georgia drove Sheree home while Mary Alice went to select items from Laissez le Bon Temps, the pricey new caterer. The videotape rested safely in the bottom of her purse.

Mary Alice had gone to college with Laissez's owner, Latrice Latcherie, who showed Mary Alice color photographs of her culinary creations. A framed sign bragged that Latrice was one hundred percent Cajun.

"Latrice, this is the first time Zach has asked me to do something like this. It has to be good," Mary Alice said, flipping through the picture book.

Latrice smiled as though the two had a juicy secret. "The Grove will be full of chicken in all forms, gobs of slaw and mountains of chips. We need to set you apart. Something really delicious and different."

"And it has to be able to sit on the table for hours."

"I'll lend you my battery cooling tray."

"Kickoff's at one," Mary Alice added. She felt silly about her nervousness. Why did men and food stimulate feminine wifey stuff? She'd seen female doctors, lawyers and bank presidents turn to fluttery mush over masculine needs for food.

"No mayonnaise, no seafood," Latrice said to herself. "I've got an idea. I'll call you later; let me experiment."

On the way home, Mary Alice called Georgia.

"You home?"

"On the way."

"Irene Bardwell can get a deal with the DA to plea down Sheree's charges to manslaughter," Georgia said. "He's offered ten, seven and three."

"What's that mean?"

"Sentenced to ten years, seven suspended, three served," Georgia said. "Bardwell is recommending Sheree take it. I agree."

"But she's innocent."

"Sheree hasn't made up her mind what she wants to do," Georgia said.

"Why's the prosecution willing to deal?" Mary Alice asked. She slowed as a possum finished its trek across the road.

"Even simple murder can be hard to prove. And—"

"Wait. Simple murder?" Mary Alice asked.

"In Mississippi there's capital murder for which one could get the death penalty. With simple murder, no death penalty. Then there's manslaughter. The maximum sentence for it is twenty years."

"And with manslaughter they're saying she didn't mean to kill him? Like in a car wreck?"

"Crime of passion. But there's another reason the DA wants to deal."

"What?"

"Thanks partly to you, Irene turned up several illegalities with Sheree's informant's deal," Georgia said. "That Scott Bridges was having sex with his informant probably tops the list. I don't have details, but whatever it is, it compromises the prosecution's case."

"I'm calling Sheree right now."

"Mary Alice, a cop's dead. They have to get a conviction," Georgia said.

"Talk to you later."

"Mary Alice, it's her decision. If you get her to stick to her not guilty plea and she gets sent up for life—think about it."

"I am. Talk to you later." She hung up and immediately dialed Sheree.

When no one answered at Sheree's, Mary Alice drove home. *Let her think about it for awhile without me butting in. That's what Daddy would tell me to do.*

But she didn't want to wait. The thought of Sheree in jail for three years made Mary Alice feel like screaming. Jails were dangerous places even when punishment was warranted and Mary Alice knew that Sheree was innocent. Mary Alice pushed on the gas, edging the speedometer ten over the limit.

She suddenly had doubts about Irene Bardwell. Yes, Irene had used the sex with informant information. It had given her leverage with the DA. But the result was Irene recommending Sheree do three years in jail. Zach had been correct when he said real murder cases weren't like on TV.

Mary Alice spent the next two hours watching the infamous videotape. The film was just as Sheree had described the night of the murder. Given the bad girl—big daddy scenario, it looked and sounded like Sheree willingly had played her role. It was chilling. Mary Alice watched it until the screen went dark when Scott turned out the bedroom lamp. She rewound and watched again looking for anything unusual. The third time through, she was interrupted by Boon, who demanded to be fed. She'd forgotten his breakfast and was glad to be distracted from the tape.

"I'm so sorry, Boon. Come on." He followed her to the kitchen where she dished out his dry food laced with one third can of wet food and two vitamin pills. While he scarfed it down, she changed his water.

When she returned to the living room, the action was over but the videotape was still running. Almost nothing was discernable in the darkened bedroom. As Mary Alice approached the TV to stop the tape, she saw a flicker. It wasn't an image, but it was something. Something unusual.

She rewound.

Again it came, and this time it looked like a shoulder and the side of a head as though someone had walked by the camera. Next were blurry, moving images impossible to decipher. She rewound again and again and each viewing convinced her that somebody else had been in the room with Sheree and Scott on the night he was killed.

Hadn't Sheree said that before she passed out, she felt like somebody was hovering over her?

Mary Alice suspected that Zach hadn't watched the tape all the way through.

This tape has to go to a forensic specialist.

She dialed Zach's number at the office. When his secretary told Mary Alice that he'd be out of the office for the rest of the day, Mary Alice called Otis Turner. Otis was a cop, but he was also a long-time acquaintance who had nursed a long-time crush on Mary Alice. She hadn't seen him since the night at Mickey's Bar, but she thought Otis would help if he could do so without anyone knowing. She tried him at home.

"Otis, this is Mary Alice Tate. You got a second?"

"You bet, Miss Mary Alice. Hang on; let me turn down this TV... I'm back."

"Otis, if you have a videotape of a crime, but it's not real clear, like on a bank's surveillance camera, what do y'all do?"

"They'd send it to the crime lab in Jackson and try to enhance it. It's amazing how they enlarge parts, change the lighting, even pick up sounds nobody can hear. They got all kinds of tricks."

"So they might be able to see someone in a tape that wasn't visible on the TV?"

"They arrested a suspect that held up an ATM that way," Otis said. "I'm scared to ask why you want to know."

"Maybe I'd better not say."

"Mary Alice, I heard about somebody putting a dead vulture in your bed."

"Dining room. They wired it to my chandelier."

"What'd the sheriff say?" he asked.

"Don't live alone; find a man. He has no clues," she said. "Otis, I need to go. Thanks for the information. Don't worry. I'm fine."

He let her hang up after three more warnings. She felt the adrenaline buzz. The tape meant something, even if it only turned out to be hope.

It was almost four in the afternoon when she remembered the autopsy report Irene Bardwell had given her. The videotape had completely preoccupied her. She pushed aside a pile of paper football food decorations and laid out the crime scene photos. There were seven 8 x 10 glossies. Mary Alice assumed there were more photos, and that Irene Bardwell had selected representative shots.

Three pictures established the position of the body on the bed in the room and four focused on the body itself. Scott Bridges, naked, appeared to be sleeping. One photo was a close up of an injection site on his hip. The pictures disturbed her because he looked so young. Even if Scott Bridges had been awful to Sheree, he hadn't deserved to lose his life.

The examiner's report detailed in medical language how Scott Bridges had died from a myocardial infarction stimulated by an overdose of triptan. It estimated he had been dead six hours when the body was found. Hollis Tubbs, apartment manager, had discovered it.

Mary Alice wondered what Hollis Tubbs had been doing in Sheree's apartment. The body wouldn't have smelled bad yet. She returned to the photos. The haematoma where the needle entered his hip looked like a tiny Rorschach ink blot.

Couldn't they see that? Sheree wouldn't have jabbed him that hard. Mary Alice suspected they didn't want to see. But they wouldn't be able to ignore the videotape.

But of course she knew they could ignore the tape. There was only Sheree's word about when it was filmed. But still, if someone on the tape could be identified—

She tried to phone Sheree again, and again no one answered.

When she looked at her watch, it was time to find Tom Jaworski.

While dressing, she considered her choices as though they were theatre costumes. Jaworski was a cop, likely hostile to her, but Jaworski was also a man. She pulled out a low-cut, black tank top with a built in bra which she put on over a short black skirt. Her only jewelry was gold earrings. As she turned out the closet light, she grabbed a short sleeved jacket that she didn't plan to wear.

TJ's, WHICH OPENED IN THE sixties, looked like the architects were copying an English pub when suddenly they dropped acid. Shiny black tables and chairs rode uneasily on a tartan plaid carpet. A dart game lane was stuffed with pinball machines, only two of which worked. The charming fake windows whose opaque panes once glowed with lamplight, now framed tattered posters advertising long over Rolling Stones,

Cream and Moody Blues concerts. Georgia had described Tom Jaworski to Mary Alice, and she recognized him easily. He sat alone in a booth near the bar watching ESPN.

Jaworski looked tall and like he worked out regularly. His hair was dark and thick and he wore it longer than the popular cop buzz cut. His square jaw had a five o'clock shadow. He was handsome in an unconventional way. Rough hewn, but sensual.

"Mr. Jaworski? Could I talk to you a minute?" she said, not wanting to give him any reason to reject her yet. She felt his cool gaze down her front all the way to her ankles. The hair on her arms rose to attention.

He set down his draft beer and rose. "Do I know you?" He towered over her.

"I don't want to bother you. I won't take much of your time."

"What's this about?" He sat down, but didn't indicate that she should join him.

She slid into the seat opposite. "Scott Bridges." She looked directly into his face, forcing contact and saw that his soft eyes betrayed the stern jaw and lip. They were cornflower blue, liquid and vulnerable. She bet he wore sunglasses on duty most of the time.

"You a reporter? PI?" He sipped his beer.

"No, I'm not. I think Scott Bridges was working on something important." She hoped her voice conveyed a mix of seriousness and distress. "Something that'll get buried with him unless somebody does something." She saw him weighing the decision to talk to her or not.

She rushed on. "He knew about substantial drug shipments coming through Cotashona County and being warehoused here. He believed top city officials were protecting the shipments and profiting from them. He planned to blow the whistle, but was murdered before he could." She wondered why Georgia hadn't told her Jaworski was so good looking.

Jaworski maintained a poker face, but Mary Alice saw his pupils flare slightly. "How do you know all this?"

"Did you know what Scott Bridges was working on?" she asked, evading his question.

"He was always lining up a bust," he said. "That was his job."

She liked the timbre of his voice, husky and strong. She wanted to make him talk in longer sentences so she could feel the vibrations.

"Whoever killed him is going to go free, millions of dollars worth of illegal drugs will flood our schools and streets and elected officials will get rich on it."

"This is about Sheree Delio." Jaworski leaned back and pushed his beer away. "I know who you are."

He didn't need to say anything more. His body language said, Sheree's guilty and you're leaving.

Mary Alice rose. "I can imagine how you feel, Mr. Jaworski, but there's some new evidence. There's a videotape that was secretly made in Sheree's apartment the night Scott Bridges was killed."

"Then you don't need me. Go talk to her fancy lawyer."

"I will, but the tape might not be conclusive. Think about it, if Sheree's not guilty, somebody else is." She leaned in. "I thought you might know something. Maybe Scott told you something he didn't tell the others. It's too late for Scott, but you might could do something." She was almost squeaking in her panic to conclude before he threw her out.

"This conversation is over, ma'am." He returned his attention to the TV screen.

"Here's my name and number if you change your mind." She tossed the card on the table and walked away. She didn't look back, but was sure he watched her leave.

Driving to Sheree's, Mary Alice ate two Twinkies. Although the meeting with Jaworski hadn't produced the result she'd hoped for, she couldn't dispel the feeling he elicited. Her skin tingled; she felt swollen and breathless. She wondered if he had felt anything.

The sugar high from the Twinkies eventually brought her out of her sensual fantasy adventure. In real life Sheree Delio was about to cop a plea.

Mary Alice hoped that when Sheree saw the end of the videotape, she would maintain her innocence and her not-guilty plea. But whoever was on the tape didn't necessarily kill Scott Bridges. Or maybe they did and Sheree knew.

Mary Alice took her foot off the accelerator. It was the first time she had considered that Sheree killed or helped kill Scott Bridges. The car slowed. The truck behind honked, and she pressed the gas pedal. Sheree could be an accessory. Maybe she was helping the drug runners.

Mary Alice believed that Sheree wouldn't willingly be involved in a murder. Maybe she'd been lied to and used. The sweetness in Sheree that Mary Alice loved, unfortunately also made Sheree vulnerable. Still, Sheree was an adult with adult choices and consequences.

Gods, I just want to go to a football game.

But by the time she turned into Sheree's driveway, she knew that most of all she wanted Sheree Delio to be proven innocent.

If anybody ever needed to be rescued, Sheree did. And wasn't that true of many people sometime during their lives?

Even strong people sometimes needed extraordinary help. It was no shame to be desperate.

And it's not wrong to help someone—to be a rescuer.

She thought of the videotape and the double humiliation it represented to Sheree—first, to essentially be raped and second, to have it filmed so others could see the degradation. Mary Alice could think of nothing comparable in her experience. Watching the tape had cinched it for her. The tape formed her crucible. She knew she'd help Sheree no matter what. She remembered the first time she ever saw an animal being abused—a cat, four boys, firecrackers and matches. She'd rescued the almost tailless creature, who'd then lived for eighteen years.

CHAPTER 19

S HEREE AND MARY ALICE WATCHED the suspicious images on the videotape three times.

"It's not for sure it's a person," Sheree said, squinting at the TV screen.

"Otis says they can do things to a tape to make images clearer, like they do with voice tapes. I'm positive Zach didn't watch all of it. I wouldn't have if I hadn't left it running while I fed Boon."

"Even if it is a man," Sheree said, "how will anybody know he was there the night of the murder?" She sounded like she wanted to be hopeful, but was afraid.

"It could be a woman," Mary Alice said.

They sat side by side on the less saggy of the two sofas. Sheree nodded.

"It's not conclusive, but look, the painter found it with Mama as a witness. She gave it to the DA. It's clearly you and Scott and probably somebody else. That brings up new questions. And if we can identify the person on the tape, they can be questioned. It doesn't set you free, but Irene Bardwell can use it to break open other clues."

"She says if I plea guilty to manslaughter, I'll only have to do three years."

"Are you guilty of manslaughter?" Mary Alice asked.

Sheree looked up quickly. "You think I am?"

Mary Alice looked at Sheree's face: the smudged mascara on the alabaster cheeks, the thick blond hair with a mind of its own and her pretty mouth, like a Renaissance angel's. Her vulnerability, now underscored with fear, was unbearable.

"You think I had something to do with it?" Sheree's voice, sapped by disbelief, was no more than a whimper. "Like they call it, uh, accomplice."

"No. But I did wonder for a minute if maybe you knew— Forget it. No Sheree, I know you couldn't kill him. But when I watch the beginning of this tape, I wonder why not. He degraded you, humiliated you over and over and made you think you deserved it. You are not guilty. I want you to plea not guilty, but I know the justice system. It could go against you. You gamble either way. But don't tell yourself three years in jail is nothing."

"I can probably do three years," Sheree said.

"You think about it." Mary Alice felt like someone had tossed her into the lake wearing cement shoes. How could three years in jail seem doable?

"It's all I think about." Sheree stood up. "But I don't have options, like you do. You don't need to tell me that three years in prison sucks. I've been in jail, rehab, foster care. I under-stand institutionalization." Her breath came in rapid jerks.

"But twenty years is way worse. Irene says I need to be realistic when I decide how to plea. Shit happens."

Mary Alice sat very still, counting her breaths. Sheree was right, but she was operating out of fear and the best decisions rarely came from that place.

"It's not just the jail time," Mary Alice said. "You'll be a felon, a convicted murderer for the rest of your life."

Sheree ducked her head and frowned at the floor.

"I have to go in a few minutes, and I have to return the video to Zach. I don't want anything to happen to it," Mary Alice said. "Before I go, I want you to watch the first part. You need to see it all."

"Why? I was there."

"You'll know when you see." She pressed the play button.

Sheree sat stiffly on the sofa waiting for her picture.

Mary Alice wanted Sheree to see how Scott Bridges had used her and frightened her. She hoped that if Sheree saw what happened from the camera's perspective, she might find some righteous outrage to fuel not only a not guilty plea but a fight for her life.

The screen showed Sheree taking off her blouse. The lighting made her skin appear sallow and her hair, the color of old celery. Fumbling with the buttons, she seemed to grow smaller and more miserable as each was freed.

Sheree watched without showing emotion. If seeds of rage were being sown, germination wasn't assured. When it ended, Sheree got up and went to the bathroom. When Mary Alice heard the shower running, she turned off the VCR and TV and quietly left.

The BMW's engine refused to catch. She paused between tries, scared to flood it.

As darkness settled around her she felt cold fury in her core. She wondered how much humiliation Sheree could take, how much injustice. To Mary Alice it seemed like Sheree had come through a horrible illness. She'd not only survived, she'd triumphed. Now, a new equally insidious disease had taken root, an infection composed of fear, powerlessness, humiliation and hopelessness. And the disease was beginning to infect Mary Alice, too. She shook herself and turned the key again. The motor caught, and she gunned it.

Mary Alice telephoned Zach from her car.

"Where are you, honey?" Zach asked.

"In the car. Where are you?"

"Office. Lord, is it almost seven?"

"Zach, I watched the videotape you gave me."

"Kinda of rough, wasn't it?"

"Zach, did you watch it all the way though to the very end?"

"Until the pictures stopped, and it went grainy."

"I want you to watch it all the way through. I'll be there in ten minutes." She hung up before he could protest.

She eased through the Friday evening traffic. A sign in a store window on the square read: Go Rebs, Beat Bama. Pedestrians jammed the sidewalks and cross walks. Cana always filled up with visitors on Ole Miss football weekends. Jazz flowed from a restaurant that opened onto the street. She cruised the block north of the square for a parking space and waited for a Corvette to leave to take its place.

When she arrived at the court house, Zach met her at the side door. He locked it behind them.

"What you got?" he asked as she handed him the tape. "You sounded so urgent."

"You have to see it."

"Let's do it right now," he said and led her down the hall.

Mary Alice relaxed. Zach was competent and ethical. When he took charge, it was a blessing.

At the door at the far end, he fumbled with his keys. The third key finally worked, and he pushed open the door. When he flipped on the fluorescent lights, she saw a combination work room—conference room. The oatmeal floor and puke green walls conspired to produce an unhealthy looking space. Half-completed projects were strewn over the work tables and counters. She could imagine droid bureaucrats slogging away for days doing work that didn't need to be done. Across the room a television and VCR were set up. If the Cana Department had new digital equipment, she didn't see it. Zach dragged two folding chairs over to the monitor. He turned on the equipment and inserted the tape.

"Fast forward to the dark gray part," Mary Alice said. "Then you'll have to start checking. What I want you to see is just a few minutes from the end." She hoped he'd see what she had, but she wanted him to describe the shadowy image without her prompting.

He waited patiently through the sea of darkness on the screen while Mary Alice sat forward in her chair as though she were waiting for the starting gun at the dog track.

"There," she said. "Stop it and rewind a little."

The shoulder and head—if that's what they were—passed by the camera's lens followed by the blurry images—possibly a struggle on the bed. Zach watched it three times.

"What do you see?" she asked.

"I have no idea," he said. "What does it look like to you?"

"Watch again," she said.

The dark gray distortion followed the vague outline of a head and shoulder, but the last bit, instead of being solid, was wiggly. Something else was going on.

"Maybe something passed the camera," Zach said.

"And if it's a person?"

"If it is, why is that significant?" he asked.

"Zach, I see where you're going, but there's the possibility it's the killer or someone who knows something." Mary Alice tried not to screech.

"Calm down. Who knows when this happened, when this tape or this part of it was made? The camera could have been stopped and started any number of times or taped over. You're making huge assumptions."

"This tape was made the night Scott Bridges was killed. Sheree identified the action, the clothes, everything. Whatever is on the end of the tape, happened the night Scott was murdered."

Sheree and Scott's sexual relationship, which Mary Alice had told Zach about, was now vividly confirmed. She wanted to ask Zach what else he knew about Scott and Sheree, a relationship he had sanctioned by allowing her to become a drug informant. But she wanted even more to keep the focus on the figure in the tape.

"Hold on. I don't know this was made the night of the murder. All you have is Sheree's word."

Frustration made her want to shake him, but she knew he was right. No one but Sheree and the dead cop knew when the tape was made. And Sheree was hardly a credible source.

"But what if it were? That image could be the killer. I know the FBI has equipment that might show him up plain as day. Maybe there's something else in the tape we can't see or hear."

"You've been watching too much TV." He sounded paternal but not condescending. "First, it's not a federal case, so the FBI won't be interested. Second, that isn't much of an image, Mary Alice." He removed the videotape from the VCR and turned off the machine.

"Then some other lab. Isn't there a state crime lab in Jackson?"

"Yes."

"You'll check, won't you?"

"Absolutely. I didn't mean to imply I wouldn't. I just don't want you to get your hopes up too high."

"If you could identify someone, you could question them." She felt ridiculous leading the district attorney through criminal investigation procedure, but she also felt desperate. The DA wasn't going to be easily convinced.

"If we can find him or her."

"That's all I ask. Thanks."

"Mary Alice, you don't have to thank me. I want to apprehend Scott Bridges' murderer as much as anyone. The evidence suggests Sheree Delio had opportunity, means and motive." Zach sounded irritated, like a parent who'd had enough foolishness from a stubborn child.

"But Scott's work made him a target," she said.

"I said I'd get it looked at."

"How long will it take?" she asked. "The analysis?"

"This case won't be the lab's number one priority. Take a while."

"And Sheree's lawyer will get a copy?" Mary Alice asked.

"The defense is entitled to everything," Zach said, slipping the videotape into its case. "This material is sensitive so I won't make a copy, but Ms. Bardwell will be welcome to view it. I assume you told her about it."

"No, not yet. I wanted to see it first. After I saw the stuff at the end, I wanted you to see it again."

"There's no rush. It's Friday night."

"I'll be glad when this is all over," Mary Alice said. She felt relief that things were in his capable hands. Maybe the image on the tape would turn out to be nothing, but at the moment it was a possibility that offered hope. She rose and picked up her purse.

"I'll be glad too," he said. "And now we're not going to talk about it any more. We have a great day planned for tomorrow. Ole Miss just might pull off an upset this year." He hugged her closely to him.

She was dying to ask about Sheree's plea bargain, but forced herself to keep quiet. Irene Bardwell would know the details. It was complicated enough that Mary Alice was involved in a reevaluation of the videotape.

"I have a little less than an hour's work here. You want to get a steak after I finish?" he asked.

"I'm dead. I want to go home." Watching the tape with Zach had made Mary Alice feel uncomfortable. It wasn't that the tape exposed Sheree because the tape also offered a potential clue. The difficulty lay in the fact that she was poised to fall in love with the man who was prosecuting her friend. And maybe she wished she weren't poised to fall in love at all. At least right now.

"Hard day. I know," he said. "Well Missy, you go home and get you some beauty sleep because you're going to be the prettiest girl in the Grove come eleven o'clock tomorrow." He put on a heavy Colonel Rebel accent.

As he walked her to her car, Zach gave Mary Alice another lecture on being careful. He seemed more spooked by the dead buzzard incident than she did. He left when her doors were locked and the engine and the lights running. She watched him head back toward the court house. A car stopped to let him cross. He waved at the driver and jogged across.

She had a hard time evaluating Zach's feelings about the tape. He seemed so skeptical it felt to Mary Alice like he didn't want new information. But Zach was a professional without emotional attachments to the case. She realized that the tape would show something or it wouldn't. Zach couldn't refute a crime lab's report if it identified a suspect. He'd have to go after them. And Irene Bardwell would look even harder for clues on the tape. Mary Alice wished she'd asked Zach how and when Irene would get to see the tape. Mary Alice didn't relish telling Irene about this new evidence.

It's not my fault. I couldn't steal it from Zach and give it to her.

She pulled out onto the street and prayed that the image would show up in some lab technician's machine. It'd be a tall man, a killer who knew about Sheree's migraine medicine and how to use it to frame her. Mary Alice imagined him in black clothes, leather gloves and silent shoes. He'd be strong, armed and completely ruthless. Mary Alice remembered her close encounter with the intruder in Sheree's apartment and shivered.

Then she imagined a woman also in dark clothes. She wouldn't need to be strong, only ruthless. What woman wouldn't feel like killing her husband if she found him in bed with another woman?

As Mary Alice drove home she thought about the food decorations she still needed to finish. She could picture the morbid tableau of the crime scene photos waiting on the table surrounded by the tiny red and blue pom poms and Ole Miss pennants she'd made to decorate Latrice's special layered sandwiches. One man was murdered and another man went to a football game. Maybe the murderer would go to the Alabama game.

It didn't seem right.

Then she thought about one of her favorite literary detectives who liked to write down the facts of a case on index cards and then juxtapose the cards in endless combinations in hopes of seeing some unnoticed clue. But Mary Alice had used most of her index cards to make sandwich decorations.

CHAPTER 20

I T WAS NEARLY 10 A.M. by the time Mary Alice and Zach headed to Oxford and the Ole Miss campus. In the back of Zach's black Suburban were three dozen of Latrice Latcherie's special football shaped sandwiches. Layered inside fresh foccacia were two kinds of imported cheese, olive salad, smoked turkey, Virginia ham and Latrice's special sauce. Each was pierced with pom-pommed and pennanted toothpicks. They tasted like a cross between a Muffuletta and a Club Sandwich. Mary Alice felt like a farm wife going to enter baked goods at the state fair.

"Where are we going to park?" Mary Alice asked, thinking of the boxed sandwiches and her high-heeled feet.

"Will Corley isn't using his private spot," he said. "We'll only be a few yards from the Wooten tents." He exited the highway and headed for Jackson Avenue. Traffic thickened as they approached campus. Home game attendance often exceeded sixty thousand if the Rebels were winning. The pre-game energy buzzed.

"What do they pay for those VIP parking places?" Red and blue decorations covered everything: store windows, cars, and most of all, the fans.

"Two thousand, I think." He negotiated the traffic carefully; the party mood was evident everywhere.

Mary Alice did the math; a few hours of parking near the Grove cost the Corleys over $300 each home game. Of course, there were even more expensive parking places next to Vaught-Hemmingway Stadium.

They found the private space marked with a cross bearing the Corley name, unloaded and headed for the Wooten's tent located in a prestigious spot next to the Walk of Champions in the Grove.

"Look at all these party dresses," Mary Alice said. Hundreds of pretty co-eds paraded by in different variations of the same dressy dress—strapless bodice, slightly flared skirt—great for showing tanned cleavage and legs. She worried that her Lilly D'Argent dress and jacket looked matronly.

"I don't know when the cocktail look started," Zach said. "But I'm not complaining." His eyes followed a trio of tall blonde co-eds who tossed their manes and smiled, revealing perfect teeth.

Mary Alice smiled too, but felt old.

They wended their way through the ten acre party-tent city filled with 30,000 revelers. Every square foot not taken up with a massive magnolia, oak, dogwood or gum was paved with white, red or blue pop-up tents and every kind of portable party gear. Alcohol, though technically illegal on campus, was the oil that greased conversations throughout the Grove. On the way, they were stopped by friends of Zach's who all held tall tomato juices with celery stalk garnishes and pepper toppings.

"There they are," hooted Ce Ce Wooten. "I'm so glad y'all could come." She stood in the middle of the two connected Wooten tents that shaded five tables laden with food, drink and floral centerpieces. Already, Mary Alice could see that her sandwiches would win first prize if prizes were awarded. Red and blue cloths festooned each table and from a battery powered chandelier hung a sign of cut metal letters that read, GO REBELS. They made their way through the collapsible canvas chairs that ringed a battery powered television. The Georgia game was just about to begin in Athens. Ce Ce hugged Mary Alice and Zach and proceeded to introduce them to everyone in the Wooten group. Mary Alice already knew most of them.

"Rudy is Jimmy Fox's cousin from Yazoo City," Ce Ce explained.

"I'm so glad to meet you," Mary Alice said, pumping Rudy Joiner's plump hand. In his other fist he clutched a red plastic cup filled with what smelled like bourbon. Her mother had taught Mary Alice the trick of remembering names through associations. She'd said, "Remembering people's names makes them feel special, even when they're not." Rudolph-the-red-nosed-reindeer worked; Rudy's nose was pink and getting pinker.

Finally free from introductions, Mary Alice set out the decorated football-shaped sandwiches. Zach pressed a Bloody Mary into her hand and then joined a throng of male lawyers who welcomed him with what Mary Alice called the Good Ole Boys Shuck and Jive. Rife with sarcasm, put downs, teasing, back slapping and even some arm punching, the men conveyed their affection and acceptance. Zach, fast with witty come backs, had them laughing in seconds. He looked over his shoulder at Mary Alice and winked. She felt herself glow like the sweetheart of

Sigma Chi, Maid of Cotton, and a June bride all rolled into one.

On the other side of the Grove, the Ole Miss marching band, called the Pride of the South, struck up "Dixie" in preparation for the Walk of Champions, the parade of the players and coaches smack through the center of the Grove. Over the din Mary Alice heard her name called. She turned to see two over-groomed women about her age who were waving and bouncing on their tiptoes.

"Bitsy Biddy! Dianne McMillian!" Mary Alice screamed. There were no friends like old ones.

"Let me hug your neck," Bitsy said, lunging for her.

The three women hugged, kissed and caught up fast. Kick off was at one; only two hours and a lot of ground to cover.

"I don't even remember Alexandra Seale," Mary Alice said.

"Her picture's in the back of her book, on the dust jacket," Bitsy said. "I just know you'll remember her. She was here at Ole Miss with us." Bitsy slipped a foot out of her high-heeled shoe and pressed her toes to the cool plastic tarp floor.

"It's a picture book of butts?" Mary Alice asked again.

"Rear ends, derrières, tushes," Dianne said.

"Buns, butts and buttocks," Bitsy said.

They laughed.

"The title's *Bottoms*," Dianne added. "The book store on the square here has it. You've got to see it."

"Everybody's claiming they know who's who," Bitsy said.

"And they're naked?" Mary Alice asked.

"Some are," Dianne said. "Bless her heart, I hear Alexandra didn't have any trouble getting her subjects to bare all."

"I'm not sure I'd want to snap butts," Dianne said.

"There are some very important Mississippi bottoms in it," Bitsy said.

"Well, bottoms up," Dianne said, as she drained her Bloody Mary.

Mary Alice laughed thinking that one day Governor Zach Towree could be asked to have his fanny photographed for a coffee table book. Maybe the First Lady too.

"Do you suppose if this one's successful, she'll do a *Tops* book?" Mary Alice asked. It felt unbelievably good to hear familiar feminine laughter.

At eleven the entire Ole Miss football team and coaching staff, dressed in coats and ties, filed by thousands of adoring fans. Zach stood beside Mary Alice, his arm around her and cheered the boys down the Walk of Champions. She leaned into his warmth and felt as though the parade were especially for her.

Across the walk, Mary Alice saw more friends, families who had known her father. She waved and called to them. Hey. Hello. How y'all?

This is why I live here. All these dear people who I know so well. I could never duplicate this.

The emotion that welled up surprised her. An older gentleman holding forth on the skills of the team's star tight end spoke in a deep, cultured Mississippi accent. His voice was like a gentle wave, cresting and rolling over itself as prolonged diphthongs stretched between softened consonants more like music than speech.

She joined the group across the sidewalk and answered questions about her mother and asked about their children. Before it was time to walk across campus to the stadium, she'd been given a new red beans and rice recipe, a source for pass-along canna, asters and verbena, and an invitation to a barbeque.

The Ole Miss Rebels managed to beat Alabama by a field goal, making the after-game festivities in the Grove even more frenetic. At five, Mary Alice and Zach ducked out in order to make Judge Weeds' party back in Cana. Zach had to stop by his office, so they agreed to rendezvous at the party at eight.

Back at the lake house as she changed clothes, she refused to think about Sheree or the danger both of them might be in. When the thought of the videotape intruded, she dismissed it. It was Saturday; Zach would send it to Jackson on Monday. He'd said Irene Bardwell could see it. Mary Alice felt light, almost drugged from the afternoon. Everyone loved her and had been so glad to see her. Approval felt like heaven. She danced into her dress and sang to Boon, "Rock-a my soul in the bosom of Abraham, Oh rock-a my soul."

THE WEEDS' ESTATE COVERED EIGHTEEN acres nestled in a lazy bend of the Cotashona River just outside the Cana city limits. Minerva Weeds, a romance writer whose pseudonym was Flossie Beauchamp, had added on to the main house no less than six times. Minerva and Judge Weeds' parties were renowned.

The curving drive ended at a grandiose, marble fountain which Mary Alice thought was new. The Weeds, resplendent in formal attire, greeted their guests with hugs and hearty welcomes. Mary Alice's mama had told her that Minerva Shimp had been a silly, mousey little nobody in high school, and Elizabeth said it in a way that made Mary Alice think that her mama believed somebody better should have snagged Judge

Weeds. But Minerva wasn't mousey any more. She appeared to be in the process of turning into one of the romance heroines she created for her novels. Standing beside the judge and just in front of a marble column topped by an effulgent flower arrangement in an urn, she looked like a goddess. From Mary Alice's position in the doorway, the ferns and blooms of the arrangement seemed to be sprouting from Minerva's head.

Mary Alice entered the towering foyer that looked more like a resort hotel than a private home and greeted her host and hostess.

"Zach said to tell you he's here and to find him," Minerva said. She patted Mary Alice's shoulder in an approving, maternal way.

Weaving among the guests, Mary Alice found Zach talking to a lawyer and his young son. She waited until he broke away and caught up with him.

"Hey," she said, "You been here long?" She could feel him looking her over like he might judge a prize heifer. She had changed to simple navy cocktail dress, one of the last extravagant purchases paid for by Dr. Maudlin. The appeal of the dress came from the bias cut which made it move like a summer breeze. The hem fluttered above her well-shaped calves. Sexy didn't do enough to describe it.

"Just got here," he said. "My, don't you look pretty."

"Thanks. You tell all the girls that?"

"Absolutely. Let's get a drink." Zach took her arm and steered her through the crowd.

They joined a large group, many of them lawyers, where dozens of bottles of wine were being tasted and compared. Zach selected a bottle, poured two glasses and handed her one.

"Now this one is really nice," Zach said. He poked his nose deeply into the glass of Pinot Noir, pulled back, swirled the wine and inserted his nose again.

"Hell, it ought to be. It cost well over a hundred dollars a bottle," the man beside him said.

Zach sipped his wine, holding it in his mouth a few seconds with eyes closed.

"Really?" Zach asked sounding one shade less than pompous. "This one has a strong oaky edge." He sipped again. "Lovely strawberry and raspberry essences and a beautiful silken finish. You won't find a Cabernet at this price with this evolution of flavors."

It was as though Zach had lit a match to kerosene-soaked rags. Wine talk flared hot.

Mary Alice's father had said the people who knew too much about wine rarely knew very much about people. She decided that it would be a good time for a tour of the Weeds' house. She excused herself and handed her wine to a passing waiter. She found the strong oaky edge to be rough.

One beautifully furnished room led into another reminding her of Edgar Alan Poe's, *The Mask of the Red Death*. Minerva liked big and bold with exotic touches. A mammoth Chinese coromandel screen of cranes covered one wall of a sitting room which led to a guest bedroom done all in light gray and white. A white fur bedspread swathed the king size bed and spilled onto the white marble floor. Mary Alice wanted to throw herself on the fluffy bed the way she imagined Minerva's romance heroines did. Outside the guest room, a long hallway with an arched ceiling led to a glass atrium overflowing with exotic plants, most of which Mary Alice didn't recognize.

Beyond the magnificent windows, landscaped grounds with lighted trees, shrubs and flower beds complemented the interiors. In the distance she could see row upon row of Encore azaleas dripping with fall blooms.

In the library, dwarfed by a globe of the old world, stood a bent and shriveled man. How many times had Mary Alice seen him in her Daddy's fishing boat? She approached.

"Dr. Benton. It's Mary Alice Tate. How are you?"

"Hello, Mary Alice. I'm fine." They gave each other a gentle hug. "Just hiding out. I'm not much for big parties any more."

Dr. Benton looked deathly pale.

"You found a great place."

"I heard you were living out at your Daddy's lake house."

"I am. Please come out any time. Daddy would like that."

"Your Daddy and I used to tell a lot of lies out there," he said. His eyes closed briefly. "I still miss James. What is it, four years now?"

"Five. Me too."

They let the silence marinate a moment. He broke it. "So are you working, going to law school, what?"

"I'm working with Georgia Horn."

"The battered women," he said. "Well, good for you. I practiced medicine in Cana for forty years. That center's been needed for a long time."

"You heard about Sheree Delio, Dr. Benton?"

"The one they say murdered the policeman?" He sat carefully on the leather sofa, perching on the edge as though he might slide into its depths and never get out.

"I've been helping her, or trying to," Mary Alice said. "Through the Women's Center. I don't believe for a minute that she murdered that policeman."

"I see," he said. "Won't you sit?"

"Yes, thanks." She sat beside him, took a look at the aged doctor hiding from a party in the library and took a chance. "Dr. Benton, have you ever been asked to look at crime scene photographs? You know, for a medical opinion?"

"You mean dead bodies?"

She nodded.

"A small town physician does everything." He perked up. "Why? Do you have some crime scene photographs?"

"I do. I'm not sure of what to look for," she said.

"You have the medical examiner's report too?"

"Yes sir, but—" She turned to face him.

"It leaves some things unanswered?" he asked. Some of the color returned to his face.

"Maybe."

"Where are the photographs?"

"In my car."

He looked surprised, but pleased. "Well?"

"Will you wait here a minute?" she asked.

Mary Alice practically ran through the house out to the parking lot. She saw Zach in the den going on about Merlots, which he detested. He never saw her. She returned by another route, snagging a bourbon and branch for both her and the doctor. If he didn't drink bourbon, she'd have two.

"Thank you, child," he said, taking the glass. "How lovely." He sipped deeply.

Mary Alice spread the photos on the leather top mahogany desk. "He died from a heart attack caused by an overdose of a drug, triptan. He had heart disease."

Dr. Benton nodded. "Migraine remedy."

"Look at this one." She pushed a photo toward him.

"Looks like a bruise around a puncture."

Mary Alice noticed that the doctor didn't assume the bruise surrounded a needle mark or really that the mark was a bruise.

He looked at the picture a long time and then shuffled through the other six, selecting another full body shot of Scott Bridges lying on the bed. He held it under the desk lamp.

"What's your question?" He took another drink of the bourbon and savored it. "I'm not supposed to drink," he whispered.

"Oh no. I had no idea," Mary Alice said. "Let me get you a coke."

"One drink won't hurt. Judge Weeds' bourbon is the best in five counties."

She smiled and felt a tiny catch in her throat. It was the kind of remark her Daddy would have made, and he drank more than a little bourbon, too.

"What would it take to make a bruise like that?" she asked.

"Would depend partly on how easily the subject bruises," he said. "Surely you've experienced bruising after an injection or blood test."

"Yes, but I can't figure it. Sheree's tiny, not very strong. If she was going to kill him by injecting him with her migraine medicine—well, she had him in her bed passed out. Those needles are so skinny, he'd never feel it."

"You're sure of the cause of death?" the doctor asked.

"The report says so."

Dr. Benton paged through the medical examiner's report and read the paragraphs pertaining to the assay of the drug.

"It probably doesn't matter, but triptans also come in a tablet, a nasal spray and single dose vials," he said. "Perhaps even in a suppository."

"Why does that matter?" Mary Alice asked. "He had sufficient amounts in his blood to cause a heart attack."

"They'd test for triptan and do a standard radioligand. But often you find what you're looking for. Triptan was there but maybe something else was, too."

"So maybe the bruise was caused by another injection?"

"Or a bigger dose of the drug given by a needle. Even a lethal dose could take awhile to kill a man," Dr. Benton said. "Other conditions or medications could have influenced its effect, but the killer couldn't be sure his victim would die or die quickly enough."

"So he'd use a bigger syringe; get more in faster," Mary Alice said.

Dr. Benton nodded.

"And he had drunk a lot of alcohol—whiskey," she said.

"That could be why the drug was fatal. Every human body is different." The doctor took a long draw on his bourbon. "If your friend uses a particular medicine and the same drug is found in the victim and at the crime scene, then she looks guilty. But what if another drug was also administered? Or what if somebody has triptan nasal spray? See?"

Mary Alice felt confused, but in a way encouraged. She had been accepting the picture of the death scene as presented by the forces that wanted to convict Sheree. Maybe another perspective was possible.

"What also interests me is the other photo," he said, turning the photograph toward her. "Look at the mark on his thigh. Does the report mention it?"

"Yes, but it makes no guess as to how it got there. He had other older bruises and marks, too. He was a cop."

"It's surely possible there was a struggle," he said. "With somebody."

Mary Alice looked at the autopsy report. "The medical examiner wouldn't lie, would he?" asked Mary Alice.

"I doubt it, but if there's a pile up of homicides in Jackson, each case might not get the careful observation it deserves. One of the assistants might have done the autopsy." He looked at the photo again. "The examiner looks the report over and signs off. Somebody down there knows who did the autopsy. You can find out. Who's the girl's lawyer?"

"Irene Bardwell."

Dr. Benton squeezed one eye shut and tilted his head.

"You don't know her. She's with a Birmingham firm that takes cases like Sheree's."

"I see." He said it as if he approved.

Mary Alice put the photos back into the envelope. "Dr. Benton, thanks. I'll get Sheree's lawyer to check with the examiner's office. We don't have much, but there are lots of loose ends like this."

"Twist them together, and you'll have a thread," he said, circling the ice in his glass.

"Please come out to the lake," she said. "Go fishing. Daddy's boat is still there."

"Why thank you, Mary Alice," he said. "I just might do that."

She hugged him gently as though his bones might crunch under her touch.

As Mary Alice returned the envelope and examiner's report to her car and went in search of Zach, she wondered if she'd ever see Dr. Benton alive again. His comments about there possibly being another needle or another drug had opened a whole new territory in her thinking. If Scott Bridges' murder was premeditated, the killer may have intended to kill him some other way. The migraine drug presented him with an alternative with the added benefit of implicating Sheree Delio. The question for Mary Alice was what did this new perspective mean to the investigation? A missing syringe with the killer's fingerprints and Scott Bridges' cells? A second hard-to-detect drug? Whatever it meant, Mary Alice realized that the killer was smart, inventive and flexible. And hard to catch.

She heard Zach's laughter in the sun room and followed the sound. In top form, Zach entertained a group with a mix of football stories and district attorney lore. She hated to disturb him and watched him bask in the glow of the chosen.

As another man told a lawyer joke, Mary Alice approached. She knew everyone in the circle and nodded to Leonard Bass, president of Cana's biggest bank and Mickey Bartel, its biggest insurance agent.

"So the tiger in front, turns around and says, 'Don't lick my butt again.' The second tiger says, 'Sorry, I just ate a lawyer and am trying to get the taste out of my mouth.'" They laughed louder than the joke warranted. Zach slid his arm around Mary Alice.

"You haven't been with another man, have you?" he kidded, sounding a little drunk.

"I have, but he's my Daddy's age. You want to get something to eat?"

"You bet."

They eased away from the group and made their way down a hall with a carved, vaulted ceiling.

As soon as they entered the Weeds' huge dining room, Zach was accosted by an obese man barely five feet tall named Shorty, who in spite of his considerable weight was so impeccably dressed that his fat seemed merely the mark of prosperity. Mary Alice smiled knowing she wouldn't want to see Shorty in Alexandra Seale's book of back sides, but done up in a tailored suit, he looked like a senator. He smelled wonderful, like jasmine.

"You remember that new BMW-Z4 you saw me in last Wednesday? I had to take it back to the dealer," Shorty said, blocking their path with his girth.

"Did you?" Zach said.

Mary Alice could feel Zach trying to break away from Shorty.

"Mary Alice, Zach and I were pumping gas last week at the Chevron. After I filled the damn thing up and then found out I'd left my wallet at home. Zach bailed me out." Shorty produced his wallet and began pealing off tens.

"Glad I could help," Zach said taking the money. "We were fixing to get something to eat—"

Shorty plunged ahead. "I've been wanting this BMW convertible roadster for months. My partner has one. I don't work on Wednesdays so I got my wife to drive me to Memphis to pick up the darn thing. Brand new and she'll hardly run."

Last Wednesday, Mary Alice thought. She searched Zach's face. He looked down at the Aubusson carpet.

Shorty rambled on about the new BMW, but all Mary Alice could think was that Wednesday night had been the night a dead buzzard showed up in her dining room. Zach was supposed to have been in Jackson. He had called her the next day saying he'd just gotten back, but now he was acting like a preacher caught in a whore house. Instinctively, she crossed her arms. It wasn't chilly, but something disturbing had blown in.

When Shorty finally ran out of steam and padded away toward the dessert table, Zach took Mary Alice's arm.

"Come out on the terrace with me," he said. He sounded like a doctor telling a patient that their treatment might be painful, but that they'd survive. "Let me explain." He squeezed through a throng of noisy, hungry guests. She followed.

Outside the night had turned cool with a breeze that promised fall. They were alone, cushioned by the muffled voices of guests inside.

She stood quietly waiting for him to explain why he'd been back from Jackson on Wednesday night and had lied about it. She looked up at him.

"I'm so sorry. Once I realized how it was going to look, I couldn't tell you I'd come back early."

She didn't say anything which seemed to unnerve him.

"When Sheriff Gelly called me, I panicked. I left Jackson and drove ninety all the way back. I had to know you were okay. And I wanted to find out who'd done that to you. Put a dead animal in the house. But by the time I got back, it was all over. You were at your mama's, and I started feeling like—"

"What?"

"I wasn't a hero. I couldn't even help."

"But—"

"My ego took over. I guess it couldn't stand being superfluous. I'm sorry."

"Did you try to call me?"

"Yes. Your cell phone didn't answer, and I didn't want to wake Elizabeth at midnight to get you out of bed. Mary Alice, I'm so sorry. By the morning I realized what an idiot I'd been, and it seemed better to not say anything. I should have been there for you. Please let me make this up to you."

"Zach, I—" She had turned off her cell phone, but not until late. She was about to ask him what time he'd called and how often.

"I love you, Mary Alice. I've wanted to tell you that, but I know it's too soon. That's why I raced back after Gelly called. I'm in love with you."

Tears glistened in his eyes.

"Zach." She didn't know what to say so repeating his name seemed to work. It could convey lots of things depending on her tone. The third repetition must have sounded like "men are such idiots, come here you silly boy."

He took her in his arms. "I do love you. I don't expect anything. I'm in no rush. Please give me a chance."

Mary Alice felt comforted and relieved she wasn't expected to say she loved him. Of course she cared for him and had fantasized about marrying the next governor, but the timing was wrong on three counts: it was too soon after an acrimonious divorce, she was too involved with Sheree Delio to focus on Zach who was prosecuting Sheree, and there was the merest chance that her ex-husband's baby was growing in her womb. And in any case, she'd imagined a courtship that would last at least until Christmas before the L-word was uttered. But Mary Alice had no doubt that she'd passed the audition for governor's wife. The wind gusted, and she shivered in his arms.

"Let's go in," he said. "I'm sure you must have lost your appetite."

"No, I—"

"You still want something to eat?"

"Actually I do," she said.

He squeezed her shoulders in a way that she understood meant he not only approved of her, but admired her fortitude.

They walked back inside. Zach held her close to him as though she were a Ming vase. But inside, the heat, noise and smell of food made Mary Alice queasy. Across the room she saw Shorty poking an éclair into his mouth much as a heron swallows a fish. Her appetite vanished.

She was gratified that Zach had come back to save her, but the delicious feeling of the afternoon had left on the terrace breeze. She helped herself to kalamata olives, a wedge of Brie and a piece of fresh focaccia.

Zach had said he loved her. That changed everything, didn't it? She could coast on in now. Maybe there was still time to have children. Her mother would be ecstatic, other women envious. One had to take life as it came. Right?

Mary Alice bit an olive in half. It'd been quite a day.

CHAPTER 21

Early Monday, Mary Alice called Irene Bardwell in Birmingham to report what Dr. Benton had said. Mary Alice sat at the big desk in the study with a fresh pad of paper and a new gel pen. In swooping letters she wrote *needle marks, bruise,* and *videotape.*

"He thought the bruise on his thigh looked, I don't know, curious," Mary Alice said.

"We're evaluating the entire post-mortem," Irene Bardwell said.

"And something else," Mary Alice said. "We know Scott Bridges died of a heart attack, but something's not right," Mary Alice said. "I mean, even assuming the killer knew about Scott and Sheree's relationship and that she had migraines and used triptan, would he come to her apartment certain he could kill Scott with her medicine?"

"Maybe he, assuming it is a he, came with a different plan, but her medicine was available and convenient," Bardwell said.

Mary Alice could hear her shuffling papers. "That's what I thought, but he still had to administer a huge dose."

"And?"

"He'd have to zap a bunch of those single dose cartridges. That would take time and possibly wake Scott up."

"Unless he brought his own larger hypodermic," Bardwell said. "But there's no evidence of that."

"I know but—"

"Where are you going with this, Mary Alice?"

"I'm not sure. Something's not right."

"There's no forensic evidence that another needle was used on him," Bardwell said. "And what you're suggesting might bring up in the prosecutor's mind that Sheree had time to slowly give him a dozen injections. She could slip in that tiny needle all night long."

Mary Alice didn't want to think about scenarios in which Sheree was guilty. "Don't you have a medical expert to consult?"

"Yes and so does the Cana DA."

"But—"

"Mary Alice, I have to be in court in an hour. I understand what you're thinking, but it's possible the killer just got lucky. Maybe he didn't know exactly what constituted an overdose. But he could have known that Bridges was susceptible to any migraine drug because of his heart condition. The facts are that Bridges died of a heart attack, and he'd been given a drug overdose. He died in Sheree's bed; she admits she was with him; she had a sufficient supply of triptan. Further, she appears to have had a less-than-harmonious relationship with the cop. Motive, opportunity and means. That's what the prosecution will focus on."

"I know but—"

"I really have to go," Irene Bardwell said. "But I want to let you know that Sheree's sticking to her not-guilty plea."

"She is?" Mary Alice doodled Sheree's face on the pad.

"And I think she's doing it because you believe in her innocence."

"No, I believe in *her*," Mary Alice said. It felt good to believe she was helping Sheree. The persistent anxiety static that filled Mary Alice's head faded.

"I think it's foolish," Irene said. "A cop's dead. A Mississippi judge facing reelection in a couple of years will throw the book at her."

"There's something else," Mary Alice said. She was proud to have still more information. "A videotape." She worked to keep the superiority out of her voice. "It's of Sheree Delio and Scott Bridges. It was found in her apartment."

A long pause followed. Mary Alice didn't like it.

"A videotape?" Irene said. She enunciated the four syllables in videotape.

"My mama owns the apartment complex where Sheree was living. After she moved out, mama was having it painted and the painter found a hidden camera with a tape inside." Mary Alice repeated the story of what was on the tape and how it had bounced around and now was back with the DA, or on its way to the crime lab in Jackson. She knew she was chattering and couldn't stop.

"You're telling me that evidence, possibly a film of the night of the murder, has been discovered and no one has bothered to tell me until now?"

Mary Alice didn't like Irene's tone of voice. It reminded of her of her mother's tone prior to pointing out Mary Alice's inadequacies or those of her father. She'd expected this news to win the lawyer's approval.

"It all happened Friday," Mary Alice said. "Just two days ago," she added. "And besides, the DA doesn't plan to use it in his case. He told me he didn't need it, and that it'd just embarrass Scott's family."

"He did, did he?" Irene said. Sarcasm oozed over the phone.

"Yes, that's what he said. "Mary Alice realized she sounded like a child. She'd almost said *yes, ma'am*.

Where's the tape now?"

"Zach sent it to Jackson to the forensic lab," Mary Alice said. "The flicker thing at the end might be a person, and it's possible that—"

"A person?" she snorted. "And it never occurred to you to call me about this? Are you crazy?"

"It did occur to me. I just called you," Mary Alice said. She realized her defense sounded weak. If the DA hadn't been her boyfriend, she would have acted differently. "I just found out about it Friday. Today is Monday."

Just two days. It was the weekend. What were you going to do with the information on Sunday?

But she knew she'd screwed up.

"I have to go," Irene Bardwell said. "I want a copy of that tape right now."

"Zach—the District Attorney said you could see it," Mary Alice said, trying to prove she'd acted responsibly after all.

"Mary Alice, your thinking on this stinks. The DA's job is to win a conviction, not to play fair. We don't have a lot of time to build a case, and any videotape of the defendant and the murder victim—" She broke off.

"I'm sorry, Irene. I told you as soon as—I didn't think it mattered—"

"Because you don't know how to think about crimes and legal procedure. Believe me; the DA knew damn well I'd be screaming to see that tape. He's delaying. Next thing you know, the tape will have disappeared."

"I'm sorry. I was just trying to help."

"You didn't make a copy by chance?"

"No."

"But it was a tape, not digital."

"A tape. I saw it."

"I told you to keep me informed. Immediately. I have to go. I'm calling him right now, and I want to be very clear to you. You may offer Sheree Delio moral support and junk food. Get her a suit for the trial, but stay out of the investigation." Irene Bardwell hung up.

Mary Alice hung up, crumpled the piece of note paper and tossed it in the trash can. Irene didn't understand that Zach hadn't known what was on the end of the tape. He'd willingly given it to Mary Alice. He didn't have to do that. Mary Alice tried to call Georgia, but got no answer. She felt like when she was eight years old and had broken a porcelain vase while helping her mother dust shelves. All her good work dashed by one tiny mistake. Irene would get to see the tape. Big f'ing deal.

For two days Mary Alice sulked, hoping Irene Bardwell would call. She didn't. Mary Alice cleaned the house, swam the lake and drove herself nuts. Then an idea occurred to her.

Irene Bardwell can't order me around. Without me, she wouldn't ever have known about the videotape. Sheree's my friend, and she needs me. That's what matters.

The next day, Wednesday, Mary Alice called on the apartment manager, Hollis Tubbs. She wore black slacks with an off-white blazer that she hoped said official, but friendly. She knew she was defying Irene's warning, but Hollis had managed the Magnolia Arms apartments since her mother bought them seventeen years ago. If he opened up to Mary Alice, Irene would be glad to have the information.

"Miss Mary Alice, so nice to see you again," Tubbs said standing in the door of his apartment, three doors down from the one Sheree had occupied. He swiped his hand over his bald head. His fingers were tobacco stained, his nails chipped and a little dirty. He had always reminded Mary Alice of Ichabod Crane.

"How are you, Mr. Tubbs?" Dutifully, she shook hands. Hollis Tubbs smelled like an old funeral home.

"Since I had my gall bladder out, I'm fine. I guess your mama told you about that." He pawed at bits of dried egg on his sweater vest.

"I think she did mention it," she lied. "I'm so glad you're recovering. Say, Mr. Tubbs, could I ask you a few questions about what happened here September first?" She curtailed additional pleasantries, knowing a description of the gall bladder removal was next if he wasn't quickly distracted.

"You mean the murder?" he asked. "You working for the police?" He pronounced it po-lease.

"No." On the spot she decided to alter her job description. "I'm working with the defense attorney, Irene Bardwell. She may want to talk to you, too, but I have a few general questions." It wasn't a total lie.

"I been waiting for the police to come back," he said. "They said they might."

"They haven't talked to you since the night of the murder?"

"That's right. You want to come inside?"

"That'd be nice," she said and entered Hollis Tubbs' musty burrow. Mary Alice felt odd interviewing Hollis Tubbs. He seemed much older and yet he clearly deferred to her. And it wasn't just that she was a Tate and the daughter of his boss.

She wished he would stop being so solicitous. It occurred to her that digging up personal information was a dirty business that elicited a variety of responses. She thought of Marshall the meth-man's offer to buy her a drink.

"Could I offer you a glass of ice tea?" he asked, ushering her to the kitchenette. "I'm sorry I'm out of co-cola." He hastily pushed aside the piles of papers and magazines that littered the kitchen table. Several papers and a gun catalog fluttered to the floor. She could smell the last ounce of coffee burning in the bottom of a pot.

"No thanks, Mr. Tubbs. I just finished lunch." They sat, and Mary Alice retrieved a pad and pen from her bag.

He sat up straight as though he were on Court TV waiting for his first question.

"Mr. Tubbs, did you know Sheree Delio very well?"

"Naw. Your mama called and told me the girl was moving in and how much her rent would be. She was only there a few months. But she seemed real sweet. Pretty, too."

"Did she have much company?" Mary Alice took down phrases of the conversation.

"The cop, the one that's dead, you, of course and that black woman, uh—"

"Georgia Horn?"

"I believe so. She helped her move in, and I saw her here a couple of other times, too."

"Did Detective Bridges come by often?"

"No. Let's see. I saw him the night he died. Maybe another time or two." Tubbs watched her write on the pad.

Sheree had told Mary Alice that Scott Bridges dropped by frequently. Hollis wasn't making a lot of sense. Did Bridges come by a lot or not? She pressed on.

"Is it easy for you to be aware of comings and goings of the residents?"

"We had some vandalism a while back; you can ask your mother," he said. "So I keep a sharp eye out."

"And the night of the murder?" She shaped the examination the way fictional detectives did by asking general background questions to get the witness into the pattern of answering.

"I was sound asleep that night. Phone woke me up." He blew his nose on a wrinkled handkerchief and examined the contents. "Wasn't late, but I dozed off watching TV."

Mary Alice felt frustrated. She was getting nowhere and the smell of the apartment had brought on a headache. Her bladder was clamoring for attention, but if Hollis' kitchen looked bad, she could imagine what the bathroom might be like. She pictured a giant, soap-scummed pitcher plant waiting behind the toilet. "So you went into the apartment that night?"

"I opened her apartment for the police. Didn't want them to break down the door."

"But you went in; you saw the body?"

"I sure did." He leaned forward on the table and assumed an expression of wisdom. "I saw him."

"Did you notice anything unusual?"

"It was all unusual to me. They's a dead man in her bed." He pawed his paunch.

She wrote: nothing unusual. "Is Sheree's old apartment rented yet?"

"No. Your mama's redoing it, but folks don't like moving into a place where somebody was kilt. I told her I'd move in, and she could rent out this one, but she said no."

Mary Alice could easily imagine her mother doing almost anything to avoid entering Hollis Tubbs' apartment. She stood to leave. Her head was pounding, and Hollis, who'd slept through the murder wasn't breaking any new ground. "Mr. Tubbs, if you think of anything else, would you mind giving me a call? Sometimes things pop up in your head that you don't think could matter, but are a piece of the puzzle."

"I sure will, Miss Mary Alice. I will do it. I surely will."

Mary Alice got through the door and inhaled down to her toes. "Thanks for your time. It was good to see you, Mr. Tubbs."

"Oh, same here."

She paused on the stairs. "Mr. Tubbs, I just thought of another question. What time did the police wake you to open Sheree's apartment?"

"They didn't wake me up. I got a phone call. That's what woke me up. She said they was trouble in 1-B and then she hung up."

"Who said?" She returned to him standing in the open doorway. How could she have missed this detail, nearly left without asking this vital question?

"Didn't say. Didn't sound like Miss Delio."

"What did you do?"

"I liked to never got dressed, but I got over there fast as I could. I thought somebody might be hurting Miss Delio. I went down to 1-B and knocked on the door, but they was no answer. I used my pass key and went in. I didn't expect to find a dead man. Boy-howdy, I can tell you."

"You went in alone?"

"Yes Ma'am. Then I come back and called the police. I waited on the stoop for them. Didn't take two minutes. Then I let them in and told them what I knew which wasn't much."

Confusion fueled her headache. She had to get away to think. "You call me if you think of anything. Okay?" She stumbled down the stairs and took the short cut to her car though the dense magnolias.

"Miss Mary Alice?" Hollis called down.

She retraced her steps through the heavy branches, knocking off berry-filled pods. "Yes?"

"Maybe I do recall seeing that policeman here another time. Or two. And there was another man, too. I remember seeing him and Miss Delio leave together. That wasn't very long ago. Maybe three weeks. She looked real nice, and I remember thinking a pretty little girl like her ought to be able to get dressed up and have a fella take her out."

"You remember what he looked like?"

"Light hair, I think. Medium height. Medium build. Medium kinda guy. Drove a SUV kinda car. Dark color. Don't know the make."

"Did you see the license?"

"No, but it wasn't a Mississippi plate."

She waited to see what else Hollis might turn up as he mined the tailing's pile in his brain.

He smiled and blinked in the sunlight.

"Thank you again, Mr. Tubbs. You call anytime." She fought her way back through the dense magnolias.

Sitting in the heat of the closed-up car, she wondered if Hollis Tubbs was the shadow-man on the videotape. Had he blundered in and gotten filmed? If so, the tape wasn't going to be useful to Sheree's case. But who had Sheree gone out with? Sheree had never told her about a boyfriend. Mary Alice didn't want to think about the implications of Sheree having a boyfriend who might have found out what Scott Bridges was doing to his girlfriend, Sheree. And she didn't want to think that Sheree would lie or withhold information. What else was Sheree not saying? And how reliable a source was Hollis Tubbs, whose memory seemed selective if not inventive.

Mary Alice felt a twinge in her stomach, a pain she associated with cramps. She couldn't decide if she was about to start her period or if her body was reacting to the idea of being betrayed by Sheree on whom she'd lavished her time, energy and love. The dull ache pulsed, matching her throbbing head.

Driving with all the windows down, she dialed Irene Bardwell in Birmingham. "This is the voice mail of Irene Bardwell. Please leave a message, and I will call you back."

"Irene, it's Mary Alice. I know you told me not to mess with Sheree's case, but I just talked to Hollis Tubbs, who manages mother's apartments where Sheree lived. I've known him forever. Anyway, he told me that a woman called him the night of the murder and told him to come down to Sheree's apartment, that there was trouble. Hollis was the first one in the apartment. He's a little scattered and may not have told the police everything. He seemed to think they'd come back to interview him, but they haven't. Can you get phone records and see who called Hollis Tubbs?" She spelled the name. "I'm on my way to get my hair cut right now, but I'll be home later."

She chose not to mention Sheree's mystery visitor until she'd talked to Sheree about him. Mary Alice wanted to ask if Irene had talked to Zach about the videotape. She wanted Irene Bardwell to tell her everything was all right and that she, Mary Alice, was reinstated, back on the case.

MARY ALICE WALKED INTO THE Cut and Curl Beauty Den, waved at the owner, Arlene Bird and ducked into the tiny rest room. She relieved her bladder, and saw that her silk and lycra panties were clean, no spotting, no period. In the waiting area, she sat down and picked up the first magazine on the stack. The cover of *Parents* asked "Is forty too old to become a mother?"

A photo of a woman who looked thirtyish graced the cover. She held a perfect blond baby in an expensive periwinkle fleece blanket. Mary Alice slid *Parents* back into the pile and picked up *People*, whose cover exposed the bulging pregnant bellies of four young celebrities. Not a calcium deficiency among them, they glittered perfect teeth for eager cameras.

I wonder if they got pregnant for the publicity. People joined *Parents* and she selected a safe *National Geographic* with two different stories on the effects of global warming. Yes, she thought, forty was too old. Thirty-five, her age, maybe not. But then, if the ice caps were melting, was having a baby really a good idea at all?

Arlene called to her from the back of the salon. "Meet me at the shampoo bowl."

Arlene took her time washing Mary Alice's hair. The massage relieved her headache, and she noticed the crampy pain receding.

"You have great hair, honey. I bet even when it goes gray it'll be that pretty platinum," Arlene said.

"When's that going to happen?"

"Not 'til you're well over forty. Maybe later." She squeezed the water from Mary Alice's hair and wrapped her head in a pink towel. Arlene led her to her station, holding the towel in place.

"I'm going to get my new scissors. Wait a sec."

Mary Alice sat down, pulled the towel away from her ears and heard the woman in the next cubicle talking to a woman next to her. Cut and Curl was still a beauty parlor, not a hair salon and the workers were proud to be beauticians, not stylists. Men were neither employed nor served.

"All I wanted to do was to get rid of those awful, faded curtains in the Sunday school room," the woman said. "I told

Reverend Taylor I'd buy the fabric and sew them myself. He told me, Mrs. Magee, you go right ahead." The woman lowered her voice. "I made the mistake of telling Linda Ann Martin what I was doing and you would have thought I was trying to drape the sanctuary in day-glow Jamaican prints. Linda Ann said we had to honor the ladies who had made the cotton curtains years ago when the building was first opened. We couldn't make changes without asking them."

"Lord, I smell a committee coming," the other woman said.

"Of course then she told everybody I was tearing down the curtains in the Sunday school. I got ten calls about it."

Mary Alice couldn't hear what the other woman said.

"And to top it off, these ladies who I'm supposed to honor? They're all dead," Mrs. Magee said.

Mary Alice knew Linda Ann Martin and Mrs. Magee and imagined how their mutual officiousness had ignited the saboteur in one and the victim in the other. She suspected that later, they'd trade roles.

Behind her, overlapping the church ladies, Mary Alice heard two other voices. "She spoils him rotten," the lady in the chair said.

Mary Alice could hear the stream of hair spray being applied.

"My daughter does too," the beautician said. "She even told me she said she has to pick her battles. Can you imagine choosing what you're going to let a three year old get away with?"

The client continued. "She told me little David wanted to cut a hole in the bed sheet. He was sick in bed that day and bored and refused to color or watch his DVD's."

"Cut a hole in the sheet?"

"She told him twelve times he could not cut a hole in the bed sheet, but he kept after her until she told him okay, but just a small one."

"Just a small one?" The beautician laughed, and Mary Alice did too.

Arlene returned with new shears in their suede scabbard.

By the time Arlene finished Mary Alice's hair cut and blow dry, the shop was empty except for two ladies dozing under dryers. Arlene snatched the nylon drape from Mary Alice's shoulders, and put a hand on her arm.

"Mary Alice, now you got to take this with a grain of salt. I do run a beauty parlor, after all."

Mary Alice looked at her fresh haircut. She knew what was coming. It wasn't the first time Arlene had let her in on gossip that normally would not have reached her ears.

"What?"

"There's a certain curiosity about why you're helping that Delio girl and working against your own boyfriend."

Mary Alice talked to Arlene's reflection in the big mirror. "Arlene, she didn't kill that cop."

"Well who did?"

"I don't know, but there's some weird stuff going on. Things that I can't tie together, like how come Scott Bridges' wife didn't come to the funeral and hasn't been seen in Cana since the murder and how come there were bruises on the body and why won't the cops look for another suspect?" As soon as she'd spoken, she wished she hadn't mouthed-off. Detectives needed to be circumspect.

Arlene looked around the shop and stepped closer to Mary Alice. "I've done Katherine Bridges' hair for years. The day after Scott got killed, she called to cancel her appointment. I haven't heard from her since." She raised her perfectly-tweezed eyebrows.

"Zach said she'd left town," Mary Alice said. "I guess when your husband is found dead in another woman's bed you don't feel like having your roots touched up."

"If your husband just turned up dead, would you even think about a hair appointment?" She straightened the jumbo-sized bottles of hair products.

"No." Katherine Bridges was sounding more interesting.

"But that's not all," Arlene said. "She didn't sound bereaved. She wasn't crying. I've done her hair for a long enough to know intimate details of her life. I mean in-ti-mate. She wanted to tell me something." She slipped two combs into their Barbicide bath.

"But she didn't?"

"Not really. But I can't get over how she sounded when she called." Arlene checked for eavesdroppers. "She was frightened. I'd swear it on a stack of Bibles." Arlene worked the scissors in her hand in a random series of rapid air snips.

"How could she sound any way but upset that morning?"

"That's what I'm trying to tell you," Arlene said. "Katherine wasn't one to blather or whine. She was a firecracker. She would have gone to that funeral wearing red. I never could see why she married Scott Bridges, but that's another story. She sounded scared and like she was trying to tell me something besides that she wouldn't be in for a cut and color."

Mary Alice considered that Katherine Bridges hoped Arlene would read between the lines. Mary Alice filed Arlene's perspective of Katherine Bridges in her mental file of myriad clues that led nowhere. She had read about cold cases where clues continued to pile up like a serial wreck on a freeway. More and more facts which solved nothing. At the present rate she thought Sheree could serve three years in jail and parole before the real murderer was caught. If he ever was.

"I wish I could talk to her. Where you think she might have gone?"

"She's got people up here, Tupelo or Corinth," Arlene said.

"People usually tell somebody what's troubling them," Mary Alice said. "What was her maiden name?"

"Scholles." She spelled it out. "You sound like a detective. Mary Alice, now you be careful. What if you're right and there is a killer on the loose? He ain't going to like you poking the coals."

She wanted to tell Arlene about the buzzard, but apparently that wasn't common gossip yet.

Mary Alice took out her wallet. "I've been warned by Mama and Zach. I'll be careful. What do I owe you?"

Arlene took her money. "So are you and Zach getting serious?"

"Am I being recorded?" Mary Alice asked.

"When have I ever needed a wire to spread gossip?"

"I guess we are, Arlene. To tell you the truth, it scares me. I'm barely divorced. I planned on having a little time to—"

"Find yourself again?" Arlene asked. "There's a good article on that in this month's *Oprah* magazine."

Mary Alice gave her a weak smile and imagined a self-inventory in which she could rate her readiness to reconnect. *1. How often do you have nightmares about your ex? A. Monthly? B. Weekly? C. Daily? 2. If your ex shows up, do you A. Ignore him? B. Say hello and walk away? C. Take shots at him with your .45?*

"Opportunity knocks but once, my mama used to say," Arlene said. She had a stock of homilies, aphorisms and axioms and wasn't stingy using them. She walked Mary Alice to the front door of the shop. "You and Zach do seem well-suited, if you don't mind my saying so."

"Ah ha. So that's the gossip. We're well-suited, and they like us together, so I should just behave and quit getting in the way."

"That'd pretty much cover it," Arlene said.

Driving the BMW home and ignoring a funny clicking-clunking sound in the engine, Mary Alice quit worrying about Cana's opinion of her and Zach and tried to imagine what Katherine Scholles Bridges' disappearance meant. What if Katherine Bridges had found out that her husband was with Sheree and called Hollis Tubbs? Did that mean Katherine could have killed him and set Sheree up? But why call Hollis? Maybe what sounded like fear to Arlene was worry. And why hadn't the police thought of this and located Katherine? Maybe it all had nothing to do with Scott Bridges' bust of local kingpins.

Or maybe it did. What if Scott Bridges had told his wife about the drug depot he was about to bust? He liked to brag, be a big shot. If she thought her husband was murdered because of a huge drug bust, maybe she imagined the killers would kill her, too. Arlene Bird implied Katherine Bridges was frightened and had run from something.

She rubbed her forehead. Mrs. Magee's permanent wave lotion had ratcheted up her headache two notches and the pain at the bottom of her abdomen had returned.

She considered telling Zach what Arlene had said about Katherine Bridges' phone call the day after the murder, but decided against it. She'd keep quiet for awhile. Zach didn't tell her much. She'd already decided she wouldn't tell Zach about the "medium" guy who Hollis said took Sheree out. But she'd tell Irene about him after she talked to Sheree. Irene was right. Mary Alice needed to think like a lawyer.

She drove past a long line of perfectly matched Bartlett pear trees. An encroaching field of kudzu vine had been sprayed with herbicide to protect the trees, but Mary Alice wasn't fooled. In the end, the kudzu always won.

The kudzu made her think of Hollis Tubbs. Why would someone call Hollis and try to get him to come to Sheree's apartment? The killer wouldn't have been in any hurry to have the murder discovered. But somebody setting up Sheree would want her found ASAP. Or maybe a tenant saw or heard something suspicious and called the manager. She made a mental note to check on the other residents of the apartment complex.

When she pulled into the driveway, she saw Boon racing toward her.

She pulled up beside the house, killed the engine and opened the door. "Come here, Boon. How'd you get out?"

The dog ran around the car and jumped up on her. She hugged him and felt something scrape her wrist.

"What's this?" She caught his collar and in so doing, gouged her hand on a sharp barb. "Be still, Boon. Stay." The dog obeyed and posed beside car as she examined the thing that had cut her. Barbed wire.

Someone had fastened a wicked collar of braided barbed wire around the dog's neck. It looked like a crown of thorns. A sluggish sick feeling crept up from her guts into her throat where it lodged, squeezing off her scream. Boon licked her face. He wasn't hurt.

Her first impulse was to grab her cell phone and punch 911, but some fuzzy intuition told her to stop and think.

If she called the sheriff, she'd get a lecture on living alone, and maybe he'd find a way to make her move back to town. And what if Gelly was involved? How could the sheriff not be if Scott Bridges was right about illegal drugs being stored in Cana. If investigating Katherine Bridges was hard, checking out the county sheriff was next to impossible.

She carefully unwound the barbed wire from the dog's neck.

If she called Zach, she'd get another lecture. And if she did nothing? Whoever had attacked her dog wanted her to panic. And she wasn't going to panic.

She scanned the yard, deck and the lake. "You chicken shit," she yelled. Hot anger flared behind her eyes. The headache was gone. "Buzzards? Barbed wire? Halloween shit. You sneaky little coward. I'm not scared of you."

A breeze tinkled a wind chime on the far side of the house.

After inspecting the house with the shotgun firmly in her grasp and finding nothing else unusual, Mary Alice put the barbed wire collar in a plastic bag and stuck it in the desk drawer. She felt spooked, but knew that was just what the "they" wanted.

Buzzards eat the dead. And a crown of wire thorns? Martyrs wore them.

She changed into her old black bathing suit. With the security alarm activated and Boon patrolling the water's edge, she walked out onto the deck. Far across the lake, evergreens mixed with oak, willow, chinquapin, elm, maple and myrtle. Still green in September, they'd soon put on their autumn dresses of shimmering gold, red and orange. The thought occurred to her that she was being watched, and she was glad to see Boon nearby. She dove in, sending ripples like the rings on a target.

After a long pull across the lake, Mary Alice rolled on her back to float. "Daddy, somebody's messing with my head." She said it aloud as if her father would appear alongside her.

She could hear him again give her his lecture on fear. It was the one he had given her when bullies had mistreated her on the playground.

"Darlin', whatever they might do to you is probably not as bad as what you're doing to yourself, getting all worked up like this. If you don't stand up to them, they'll bully you all year. See them for the sad, little, mean people they've become and send them some love. Try to imagine them healed from whatever makes them so mean. You're strong, Mary Alice. You don't have to be a victim."

Elizabeth Tate had told her husband his advice about the bullies was foolish crap. She called the principal who called parents. Two boys were expelled for a week. Mary Alice never again felt safe when they were around.

She dove down deep and skimmed above the soft bottom for over a minute. When her lungs hurt she kicked hard and shot to the surface. She swam back to the house, feeling stronger. As she typed in the security code, Boon shook his wet fur. They went inside; Mary Alice locked the door.

On the kitchen counter, she saw the message light blinking. She pressed the button: one from Chase Minor, one from Irene Bardwell and another from her mother. She saved them for later. She headed upstairs for a hot shower, the .45 in hand.

CHAPTER 22

A DAY LATER, FRIDAY MORNING, WHILE driving to her mother's house, Mary Alice dialed Chase Minor. The cell phone peeped seven times. She felt tired; for two nights she'd had nightmares about Christian martyrs and wondered if the person who was harassing her was sophisticated enough to be into symbolism. Was he telling her not to be a martyr for Sheree? That didn't sound like Sheriff Gelly. But the crampy feeling in her stomach was gone—good news, bad news.

"Chase here," the voice barked.

"Chase, this is Mary Alice calling you back. I tried yesterday, but didn't get any answer or any machine." A shiny new Mercedes paused to let her change lanes.

"Turned it all off. I'm blocking act two of *Foxes*."

"How have you been?"

"Wretched." His voice caught. "I have the cast from hell. They've turned into the characters they play. If Garth Howorth threatens to quit one more time, I'm going to let him and play the damn part myself."

"I'm so sorry. I've been meaning to call Sara Beth Maxey to see if she needs any help with props."

"Sara Beth is just moving her own house onto the little theatre's stage," he drawled. "Props are tip top."

She waited to hear the reason for his call. Rushing was rude; he'd get around to it.

"What I really called about is a cast party," he said. "We need one in the worst way."

"Great. When?"

"Tonight after we run act one. I know it's no notice a'tall."

"What do you need me to do?"

"Set up the bar and pump up the egos."

"Shall I come by rehearsal and pick up a key to your house?" Mary Alice turned into Linnley's wide driveway and parked behind the house.

"Yes. Thank you, precious lamb," he said. "We need a good blow out."

"I'll see you tonight, Chase."

"We'll talk then. I have to get back to work before I forget where I was."

"Go."

"*Ciao*, sweetie."

She heard three kisses in the phone.

Mary Alice got out of the car and walked to the back door smoothing the creases in the simple gold sheath. It hugged her curves, yet had elegance. A ropy tangle of beads filled the neckline. The dress had been chosen to please Elizabeth—no simple task.

Elizabeth Tate sat ensconced behind her formidable desk when Mary Alice entered. The office had been Mary Alice's father's before he moved out to the lake house and in spite of Elizabeth's decorating, it still looked like a man's space.

"Reporting for duty as requested, ma'am," Mary Alice said. She unsuccessfully tried to assess her mother's mood.

Her mother eyed her. "I shouldn't think visiting your own mama was a duty," she said. She touched a solid brass globe that weighted a corner of the desk.

Briskness tempered her victim tone and confused Mary Alice.

"A duty and a pleasure," Mary Alice said. "Is that coffee?"

"It's probably cold. I'll get Maria to make us a fresh pot."

Mary Alice popped open the lid on the vacuum pot and felt the warm vapor rise. "It's fine." The smell made her long for a donut. Her Daddy would have had a whole box of Shipley's. Fresh and warm, they were so good you'd suck your fingers after the last bite. But Mama had no donuts.

Elizabeth picked up the phone and pressed an intercom button. "Maria, would you make a fresh pot of coffee and serve it in my office? And a few of those low-carb muffins." She didn't wait for an answer.

Mary Alice put the vacuum pot back on its tray and sat in the antique Chippendale chair in front of the desk. Fresh coffee would be okay, too. She wasn't going to get upset by her mother's high-handedness.

"Is everything okay, Mama?"

"I'm going to fire Georgia Horn as director of the Cana Women's Center, and I thought I should tell you first."

"You can't be serious."

"As serious as a stroke."

"Why?" Mary Alice felt as if she'd been tossed a bowling ball and was going down on the slick lane and into the gutter.

"I thought there were better candidates for the position when we hired her. My opinion has not altered."

Mary Alice winced. Her mother's formal speech was always a sign she was intractable.

"We held a board meeting yesterday and—"

"I'm on the board," Mary Alice said. "I didn't know about a meeting." She sounded petulant and fought to slow and lower her voice.

"It was an executive session with Ms. Horn and the officers. She requested permission to keep a percentage of money she raises from some grants, and we wanted to discuss the implications. But we also discussed her client, Sheree Delio. The executive committee felt too many of the resources of the center and too much of Ms. Horn's time was being absorbed by one person, Sheree Delio."

"Mama, Georgia has transformed that center. She's raises about half of the budget; she's broken racial barriers; she practically lives there. No one leaves the Cana Women's Center empty handed. How could y'all possibly think of replacing her?"

"That is one perspective, but not ours. If I may finish?"

Mary Alice tried to take a deep breath, but felt like she was back at the bottom of the lake and her air had run out. Aside from the disrespect and insult, Georgia's dismissal would have negative repercussions for Sheree. Georgia was the glue that held Sheree's hopes together. Mary Alice's, too. Mary Alice wanted to catapult herself over the wide desk, grab her mother and shake her hard.

"She verified in our meeting that she completely supports your efforts to help the girl," Elizabeth said. "She said your attitude and willingness to help had inspired her to get that Birmingham law firm involved."

"She said that?" Mary Alice felt unexpectedly gratified to hear herself praised by Georgia.

"Georgia Horn is directly responsible for your irresponsible and capricious behavior with regard to this case. Because of her, an untrained, unlicensed, private citizen is in jeopardy. You. Someone has broken into your house, threatened you. Hollis Tubbs said you told him you were working for Sheree's lawyer. And I know for a fact Zach thinks all the poking around you're doing is patently dangerous. The Women's Center is the organization that sanctions your behavior, and she is its director."

It was all Mary Alice could do to stay seated when she really wanted to hoist the brass globe or a jade Foo dog at her mother.

"That is eloquent garbage. Georgia couldn't have stopped me. I didn't even know she approved, but I feel better knowing she does."

"You were talking to a known drug user in a laundromat," Elizabeth said. She gripped a sterling letter opener. "Mary Alice, are you blind or stupid?"

"Who told you that?" She eyed the sharp opener. One slip of the silver blade.

"It's true, isn't it?" Elizabeth's voice rose and filled the room like a dead buzzard's smell.

Mary Alice saw Maria appear briefly at the door with a tray of coffee, cups, saucers and muffins and then, like a hiccup, retreat.

"Who do you want to get at more, Georgia or Sheree?" Mary Alice asked, shifting from defense to offence.

"They are incidental. I am scared to death about what will happen to you if you don't stop this lunacy." She pressed the letter opener's tip against her thumb.

"Firing Georgia won't stop me," Mary Alice said. "And another thing, I'm on the board for a two year term."

"I can take care of that, too." Elizabeth smiled like the Cheshire Cat.

Mary Alice glanced at the heavy gold dolphin paper weight on the desk. It seemed that only brute force could stop Elizabeth Tate.

Elizabeth continued. "Did you know Georgia Horn is being investigated by the IRS for tax evasion?"

"No. How do you know?"

"It came to the attention of Leonard Bass at the bank. The Internal Revenue Service contacted him."

Mary Alice waited for more.

"Leonard is the president of the bank and a major supporter of the center. He's concerned."

Mary Alice figured that Leonard Bass was concerned exactly to the degree that Elizabeth Tate required of him.

"So you'd dump her just because there may be a problem with her taxes?"

"Such scrutiny would bring her credentials into question," Elizabeth said. "I expect we'll have to audit the Center's books."

"That is so unfair." She scowled.

"You refuse to see the truth—"

"What do I have to do to keep her in that job?" Mary Alice interrupted.

"It's out of my hands now. She'll be evaluated and a recommendation made at next month's meeting. She'll have an opportunity to rebut."

Mary Alice knew what she had to do and that the ends would justify the means. She had to lie. It was her best shot.

"What do you want, Mama?" She forced herself not to grip the arms of the antique chair.

Mary Alice watched her mother study her. Elizabeth never liked to cut to the chase quickly, because that would prematurely end the drama.

"Let the lawyers handle the Delio case," Elizabeth said. "You stay away from her, her lawyer and her problems and stop playing private eye."

"Okay." Mary Alice paused. She knew she'd never abandon Sheree. "You win." She held her mother's gaze.

Mary Alice had no intention of obeying her mother, but she vowed to cover her tracks better and maintain a lower profile. She wondered how her mother seemed to know everything Mary Alice was doing.

Elizabeth made a show of looking at her watch. "Ye gods, it's late. I have a massage scheduled in an hour." She rose and swept out of the room. Her goodbye trailed down the hall like an automatic telephone message.

Mary Alice was glad of the opportunity to escape.

Back in her car, she took a deep breath and looked at her list of things to do. She knew Irene would get the phone records of calls made to Hollis Tubbs on the night of the murder. Irene had said that the police report noted that none of Sheree's neighbors saw or heard anything. Mary Alice still wanted to talk to them. Maybe the right questions weren't asked. Next on the list was Tom Jaworski. She hadn't given up on him and was still hoping he'd do some checking on whatever Scott Bridges had been working on. Maybe he'd call. She remembered his voice, the way she'd felt in TJ's Bar, and wondered if he were married.

Also she couldn't forget what Arlene said about Katherine Scholles Bridges sounding frightened. Maybe there were some Scholles in the phone book. And Georgia was on the list. Mary Alice didn't know how long her mother would delay firing Georgia, but she knew she had to talk to Georgia about it. And what about the blond guy Hollis said visited Sheree? On the end of the list she wrote, Star Liquor, Key to Chase's, Rehearsal.

WHEN MARY ALICE KNOCKED ON the door of the Women's Center's refuge house, it took Sheree a long time to answer.

"Were you still in bed?" Mary Alice asked. It was close to noon.

Sheree shrugged. "I wasn't feeling too good." She wore a red oversized night shirt with a teddy bear on the chest. With tousled, flattened hair and no makeup, she looked ethereal like a teenaged fairy.

"You need a doctor?" She looked at Sheree as if flu or meningitis might be written on her forehead.

"No." She sounded apologetic. "Had a migraine. It's okay now."

"Can we talk a minute?" Mary Alice saw Sheree stiffen. "Let's fix some coffee." They moved into the kitchen.

While the Mr. Coffee pumped hot water over grounds, Mary Alice told Sheree what Hollis Tubbs had said about getting a call the night of the murder.

"I sure as hell didn't phone him," Sheree said. "I left as fast as I could and come to your house. You think I called Mr. Tubbs?"

"No. I assume you'd be the last person to alert the police once you'd decided to leave, but somebody called. You got any idea?" They sat in their usual places at the kitchen table.

"The person who did kill Scott?" She answered as if she were a fresh "Let's Make A Deal" contestant.

"Bingo," Mary Alice said. "He said the voice was a woman's."

"Maybe the killer was a woman or had one helping him."

Mary Alice again thought of Katherine Bridges finding Scott and Sheree together. "Do you think Katherine Bridges could kill her husband and then call Hollis to make sure you were blamed?"

"I don't know her," Sheree said, running her hands through her hair.

"Irene's checking Hollis Tubbs' phone records," Mary Alice said.

"You think she'd be dumb enough to call from a number that could be traced?" Sheree asked.

Mary Alice shook her head. "Who knows?"

Mr. Coffee made orgasmic noises followed by burps, and Mary Alice poured coffee into two ugly mugs bearing advertising slogans for Porky's Plumbing and Dixie Termite Control. She thought that later, when all of this was over, she'd buy the shelter house a new set of dishes.

"Hollis said something else." Mary Alice paused, wishing they had some sweet rolls to go with the coffee. "He said you got all dolled up and went out with some blond guy a couple of weeks back." She set Sheree's coffee in front of her and sat at the table.

Sheree looked away.

She waited. "Want to tell me about that?" Mary Alice heard mistrust creep into her voice.

"Doug. He come by once."

"And who is Doug?"

"I knew him in Texas. I didn't say nothing because it didn't matter. I told him to go on, and I'd call him when I was through the informing deal. I didn't know Scott was going to get killed." She sipped the hot coffee, burning her lips.

"Why didn't you ever tell me about him? I mean a long time ago when we were sharing our life stories and secrets. You don't leave a significant boyfriend out of that." Mary Alice wondered if the omission irritated her because she had been left out on a secret when she had thought they were baring their souls to one another.

"I did tell you." Sheree turned her cup around and around on the table.

"You did?"

"I said his name was Travis and he was from Georgia."

"Doug is Travis? He was here?" Mary Alice felt a little like she had when her mother told her Cod Liver Oil tasted good. She'd heard an earful about Travis. "Why didn't he take you away with him?"

"He's in trouble hisself, and then I'd probably be a fugitive if I just ran off and—"

"You told me you were in love with Travis, I mean Doug," Mary Alice said. Sheree's story sounded plausible, but she would have had plenty of time to invent one. "Were you ever going to tell me he'd come by?"

"No, 'cause you were seeing the DA, and I could see you liked him a lot and I thought it might be hard for you not to tell him. I didn't want the law to know where Doug was. Maybe I didn't think it through very clear, but it didn't matter. It was nothing. Doug ain't part of this."

Mary Alice tried to look like she understood and agreed, but she was putting together a different scenario.

Sheree's lover, Doug, appeared, bidden or by chance, and came to understand his girlfriend was being abused by a cop—threatened with jail if she didn't have sex with the cop. Doug, who wasn't overly fond of cops anyway, decided to help. Maybe they decided together to get rid of the cop. But something went wrong, and she got caught. Mary Alice had to consider that she was being duped, that Sheree did it.

"Sheree, don't say anything now, but I want you to think over everything again. Have you not told me something else? Don't try to decide if it'll help or if it matters. Let me decide."

"I'll try," Sheree said. "But you can see how I mess up everything."

"Stop. Just stop." Mary Alice wanted to tell her that yes, she screwed up a lot. But given her history, how else could it be? How could Sheree have learned about love and trust when everyone who counted abused and abandoned her? "I have to go now, but you keep thinking. I'll call you."

As she drove to the Women's Center to find Georgia, Mary Alice tried to piece together a scenario in which somebody was harassing her with dead birds and barbed wire and also in which Sheree was involved in Scott Bridges' murder. Nothing fit.

But what if Scott Bridges' drug depot is all a lie, a diversion, and Sheree and Doug killed Scott Bridges?

Doug split and Sheree came to Mary Alice's. Was Sheree protecting Doug? A cop was dead. The cops would believe that Sheree was guilty. It made no sense.

But what did make sense was that the same cops didn't want Mary Alice to get Sheree off on some technicality. Maybe bringing in Irene Bardwell, who had already found out about the screwy informant deal had made them nervous. But would a cop put a buzzard in her house and barbed wire on her dog?

She swerved to avoid a chunk of concrete in the road. Maybe word had leaked about the videotape, and the cops thought it might help Sheree's case. Mary Alice passed a cotton field with an old barn pinning down the far corner. Or maybe that barn was chock full of cocaine and the mayor, chief of police and dog catcher were all keeping it a secret.

She wanted to believe Sheree's story and felt bad she'd questioned her innocence. But the appearance of Doug created a new picture Mary Alice couldn't ignore.

Heck, maybe Mama hung the buzzard and collared Boon in barbed wire. She has opportunity and her motive would be to scare me so that I don't scare her. Maybe she paid someone.

She hit a pothole and jerked the car back into the lane. The next car she passed was a Cana Police Department vehicle. As she passed, she locked eyes with the driver, Kenny Bates. She glared at him.

CHAPTER 23

THE FRIDAY AFTERNOON RUSH HEATED up as Mary Alice waited behind a line of cars at a red light two blocks from the Women's Center. The digital Time & Temp on the bank at the corner alternately flashed 6:16 and 87. It had taken most of the afternoon to make a drop off at the dry cleaners, unsnarl a snafu at the bank and get the car's oil changed. The mechanic tried to get her to opt for a tune up. She'd declined.

Only a week ago she'd been preparing to go to the Ole Miss football game. A week ago the judge had set Sheree's trial date. A week ago she'd talked to Tom Jaworski, who hadn't called, and probably wouldn't.

Jaworski's masculine intensity coupled with his liquid blue eyes had been hard to forget. She was fairly sure he had felt the pull of animal magnetism too. She suspected that if the cop called her, his baser instincts would be the motivation.

The light changed to green, but she didn't make it through the intersection before it turned red again. A glance to the side revealed two older ladies in a Ford Taurus. Their hair frizzed about their heads in identical caps of steel wool. Both wore metal framed glasses. The one on the right was struggling to open a package that Mary Alice recognized as Little Debbie Pecan Spinwheels. The driver kept reaching for the pack which her companion refused to release. Mary Alice saw their lips moving simultaneously. The driver jerked the package, tearing it. Like a Fourth of July fireworks finale, the wheels flew about the car. The women's eyes narrowed and their lips moved faster, but Mary Alice couldn't hear their attacks or defenses. The light changed to green.

The Women's Center parking lot held only Georgia's car and a boat-sized, older model Mercury. Mary Alice found the waiting room empty. The last light of day slanted through the blinds, painting long stripes across the floor, angling onto the furniture. The room looked tired, as if it were waiting until 6:30 to exhale the week's troubles.

"Georgia," Mary Alice called. She heard two voices saying goodbyes in Georgia's office.

A minute later the door opened.

"Come in here," Georgia said.

"You working late?" Mary Alice asked. She entered Georgia's office. The lights were off, and Georgia snapped closed the blinds, plunging the room into shadows. A dozen neat stacks of papers covered the desk. Mary Alice knew hundreds of other requests, evaluations and applications waited for Georgia's attention in the three mismatched file cabinets behind the desk.

"Closing up now. Had to help Louise Jefferson with her car payment. Without the car Louise can't work. Her son, Leon can't either. That is if he bothers." Georgia sounded bone tired.

Mary Alice heard a car cranking in the parking lot. "And that's cheaper than making her house payment," Mary Alice said. She sat on the fake leather chair still warm from Louise Jefferson's bottom.

"You're catching on." Georgia snapped on the desk lamp and looked at Mary Alice carefully. "What happened? Somebody die?" She leaned back and the desk chair creaked.

"No, but sometimes I wish my Mama had died instead of my Daddy."

"I saw her yesterday." Georgia shrugged. "She wants to get rid of me; doesn't she?" Georgia restacked a pile of papers.

"That's her plan," Mary Alice said. "It's nuts, but she might be able to convince the other board members. Half of them don't care one way or the other and would love a chance to suck up to Mama."

"Stay out of it, Mary Alice. You'll only make it worse." She laced her fingers together. "I might just resign."

"Georgia, I won't let her push you out."

Georgia looked past Mary Alice at the brown paneled wall. "You in charge?"

"I'm on the board too," Mary Alice said. She released her grip on the chair's arms.

Georgia made a half laugh, half snort. "No disrespect intended but—"

"Your record here speaks for itself," Mary Alice said. She tried to catch Georgia's eye.

"Your mama thinks your involvement with Sheree is my fault, and I can't say she's wrong," Georgia said, neatening an already neat stack of papers.

"If I'm in danger, I put myself there, not you," Mary Alice said.

"Mary Alice, that won't matter in the end."

"It might. She says she'll reconsider if I back off helping Sheree."

"And you'd do that?" Georgia asked.

"I've probably done all I can do," Mary Alice said. "As far as Irene Bardwell's concerned, I'm off the case. Anyway, when I do find out something, it goes nowhere or confuses things more." Mary Alice recognized that her efforts hadn't amounted to much so far, and that Irene Bardwell had cause to be mad at her. However, by no means did Mary Alice believe she had done all she could do. She hoped she could finesse things, skillfully help Sheree and keep her mother in the dark about it. She didn't need to let Georgia in on her plan.

"What's going nowhere?" Georgia tapped the tips of the pencils standing like missiles in a red leather cup.

"Sheree confirmed what Hollis said about an old boyfriend coming by. A couple of weeks before Scott was killed, this Doug, comes out of nowhere and takes her out. She never told me, and it bothers me."

"Because?"

"She might have told Doug that Scott Bridges was coercing sex and ole Doug might have decided to do something about it. If that happened, Doug's the killer, and Sheree might be involved in the murder."

"Might, might, might. What about the motive connected to drugs being stored around here? Doug part of that?" She pulled a pencil from the cup and inserted it in a battery powered sharpener. The noise was like a mini lawn mower.

Mary Alice waited for quiet. "I doubt it. She told me about Doug a long time ago, but she called him Travis, and she said it was over."

Georgia looked at the ceiling and shook her head. "So Sheree's not completely reliable? Selectively truthful?"

"She's scared."

"Is it possible there are two separate things going on?" Georgia asked. "Doug happens to kill Scott and Scott is about to bust a drug ring."

"Coincidence? I don't know," Mary Alice said. "I missed that class in detective school."

"I assume you got nowhere with Tom Jaworski," Georgia said.

Mary Alice nodded. "But the point is because I'm getting nowhere anyway, I can retreat from the investigation. Irene's checking on the videotape, on Katherine Bridges and on Hollis' phone records. Irene's on top of it."

"You don't really think Sheree's involved, do you?"

"I don't know. She could be involved, but in her mind she doesn't see it that way. She didn't mean for Scott Bridges to end up dead."

"Mary Alice, I know you, and I know you aren't going to let go of this case. You'll do something, the Sheriff will tell your mama and it'll be over like recess."

Mary Alice refused to confirm or deny Georgia's suspicion. "Georgia, you can't resign."

"Yes, I can. Right now I can. In another month, they'll fire me."

"Georgia—"

"It's not just the Sheree Delio mess."

"The IRS?"

"She told you about that too?" She slapped the desktop, sending a sheaf of papers to the floor. Both women went for them.

"They can't fire you for suspicion of tax evasion. You could sue them," Mary Alice said, kneeling beside Georgia.

Georgia laughed. "Where do you think I'd get the money to sue? It'd end up in a deal, and I'd be just as gone as if I was guilty." She sorted the papers.

"What's the IRS saying?"

"They're threatening to attach my pay for unpaid back taxes. News of other charges and penalties to follow soon."

"Is it true?"

"No, but they're the goddamn IRS. You ever talk to them? You never get the same agent or the same story twice. I get a different threatening letter every week. They're aggressive and scary, and they have the power to ruin your life." She rose, put the papers on the desk and sat.

"But quitting your job will just make it worse," Mary Alice said, getting up from the floor.

"It's occurred to me that, like you, I'm being harassed. You get vultures, and I get the IRS. Not so different really."

Mary Alice started to dismiss Georgia's comparison, but then she stopped. Maybe someone was out to get Georgia for the same reason they were out to get Mary Alice—to make sure Sheree was convicted.

"It's not hard to get someone investigated for tax fraud," Georgia said. "I knew a man who used a pay phone to call the IRS and tell them that he had been cheating on his taxes for years and wanted to come clean. He gave them his social security number. Only thing was, it wasn't his number. It belonged to a former boss who had fired him. The IRS contacted the boss. Eventually the boss was cleared, but it took a bunch of money and a heap of aggravation."

"Who'd want to get the IRS to investigate you?"

"Your mama comes to mind. But maybe it's the same person who put the dead bird in your house. Or maybe my number just came up and some IRS agent looked at my tax return wrong and flagged me. I'm tired and caring less and less. I struggle and work to help folks who need it, and people like your mama act like I owe it to them, like I'm having fun doing this work." Georgia put her head down on the desk.

"Georgia, let me think about this. I know a lot of people. Somebody will help." She crossed to Georgia and put her hands on her slumped shoulders. "Don't give up. There won't be a Cana Women's Center without you. Some incompetent bureaucrat will take over and alienate the clients and then the board can say, 'we tried to help those folks, but they just wouldn't help themselves. You can lead a horse to water.'"

Georgia didn't respond.

"Come get some dinner with me," Mary Alice said. "We have some time to think about all this."

Georgia sat up and pushed away from her desk. "I ate lunch late." She said it as if she wasn't planning to ever eat again.

Mary Alice turned Georgia's chair and leaned close to her face. "Now you listen. I've heard you talk to women in here who couldn't see because their eyes were swollen shut from a beating. They had no more hope than a cricket in October. But you kept at them, and I saw a teeny tiny spark of something light up. Anger or hope. I'm not as good as you are, but I'm not going to let you give up." She took hold of Georgia's shoulders and gave them a little shake. "You told me not to give up. Remember your case in Atlanta? What you did?"

"Maybe my gut feeling says it's time to move on."

Mary Alice checked her watch. "I promised Chase Minor I'd help him tonight, but this discussion isn't finished. You call me. No, I'll call you."

"Yes," Georgia said. "I'll just go on home now."

"Georgia—"

"Yeah, yeah. Go on. I'm all right." She turned off the lamp.

Together they locked up the center, turned on the security alarm and walked to separate cars. The parking lot light glare seemed to intensify the heat, pulling it from the asphalt.

"You sure you don't want something to eat?" Mary Alice asked. "I'm going to get some Bailey's chicken. Your cholesterol will be so high you won't care what the IRS does because you'll be dead."

Georgia gave a half-hearted laugh. She waved and got into her car.

Mary Alice watched her drive out of the parking lot. She hadn't seen that teeny tiny spark of hope in Georgia's eyes. Driving toward Bailey's she wondered if she had enough strength to be strong for Sheree and for Georgia. Waiting at the red light, Mary Alice remembered something Georgia had said about how she got the IRS and Mary Alice got vultures.

Mary Alice's connection to Sheree and her case was through the Women's Center and Georgia. So if they, whoever they were, got rid of Georgia, maybe they'd get rid of Mary Alice, too. Sheree could plead manslaughter and do three years. Case solved.

She pulled into the lane marked Bailey's Drive-Thru Orders. "I'll have a Big Chick with fries, slaw and beans. Large Dr. Pepper. Skip the Texas toast," she said to the squawk box. "Wait a minute. I changed my mind. I'm going to dine in." There was no hurry to get to the theatre, and she wanted time to think.

The voice told her to come to the counter to pick up her order.

She paid the pimply teenage boy at the counter, got her order and found a seat in the corner by a window. She ripped open ten ketchup packets and lay out the French fries on a sheaf of Bailey's napkins. Each napkin featured a drawing of a smiling chicken under the Bailey's name and the phrase, "We ain't afraid of grease!" She munched the hot, ketchup-dipped fries and the greasy chicken tenders. Spicy beans and tangy slaw went down in tiny plastic forkfuls.

She thought about Zach, and wished the two of them could go away to Florida as he had suggested. She'd talked to him on the phone but hadn't seen him since last Saturday night when he'd confessed he loved her. He was in Atlanta and wouldn't return until Saturday. He'd asked her to accompany him to a dinner party Saturday night—a political gathering that might not be much fun. Mary Alice realized it was another stage of the audition for the future Mrs. Towree. She wasn't worried. She'd been bred to light up dinner parties.

By the time she stuffed the last tender into her mouth and considered dessert, it was after eight. Bailey's cheesecake looked gelatinous, and the teenaged boy at the counter told her they were out of puddin'. A large pack of M & M's and a package of chocolate chip cookies waited in the glove box. Some of each. Life was short.

She drove through the town square heading for the theatre, slurping the last of the Dr. Pepper. Nearly deserted, the square looked like a movie set. Narrow store fronts, appearing much as they had when they were built in the 1840's, stood side by side, their darkened windows now glassy eyed. She ate the M & M's one at a time. The clock on the cupola of the courthouse in the center of the square said twelve. Nobody remembered if it had stopped at noon or at midnight.

Three blocks off the square, the darkness was pierced by the occasional street light and dull gleam from parlor windows. When she turned onto Third Street, she felt the lights of a car behind her. In the rear view mirror it looked like a big SUV. Irritated by the bright headlights, she flipped the rear view mirror into its alternate position and turned right to get away from the glare. The SUV turned too.

Was someone following? Images of an off-duty Kenny Bates crowded in. Her eyes darted to the mirror every two seconds.

She slowed.

The SUV matched her speed. As it passed beneath the only light on the street, she could see the vehicle was dark, probably black, maybe a Chevy Tahoe. Only a driver was silhouetted. She turned onto Lee Drive and the SUV turned too, staying a half a block back. As a test, she turned again quickly on Jefferson Davis Drive, passing a deserted elementary school yard. The dark SUV followed.

The gas gauge read less than a quarter full. She'd not seen another moving car since she turned off the square. Where was everybody?

Shit. I'm going to have to drive to the sheriff's office and run inside. Sheriff Gelly will love that. I might as well go to Mama's. Where else can I go?

Afraid not to stop at the approaching four way stop, she braked and rolled to a halt. Her eyes flitted to the approaching SUV which was bearing down on her fast.

"Jesus, he's going to hit me," she said aloud. She stomped the gas pedal and saw the BMW's speedometer shoot to thirty before she felt the impact against her rear bumper. Her head fell forward and then slammed back against the head rest as M & M's sprayed the front seat and dash. Her sudden speed had lessened the blow, but there was no doubt that the SUV had intentionally rammed her.

She tried to remember what her father had told her about evasive action. Something about lots of turns and keeping a cool head. The SUV slowed. Her speedometer read fifty. She hit the brake and skidded around a corner. The street, darker than the one she'd just left, didn't look familiar. The lights from behind were on her again before she could think what to do. She'd hoped for a well-lighted yard, maybe with a father pitching a ball to his son. She could pull in the driveway and get help. A faded billboard on the right caught her attention: Southgate—one mile.

She knew where she was. The road, put in by a developer who had gone bust, led to Southgate, a ghost town development of empty streets and saplings. She couldn't remember the layout, but was pretty sure the only way out of Southgate was the way in. Beyond the failed development was the county garbage dump. She thought the road went through to another county road, but wasn't sure. It'd been ten years since she driven this way.

God, why didn't I just drive to the police station?

The next glance in the rear view mirror showed the SUV coming up for another strike. Mary Alice waited until he got closer, and then floored the accclerator. She felt a bump, harder than the first one, as the cars raced past the entrance to Southgate. She remembered that Southgate had failed because a bunch of sink holes had opened up. A whimper turning into a growl vibrated in her throat. Ahead the road snaked up a hill.

As the panic thickened, she thought of her father and glanced at the passenger seat half expecting to see him. The seat was empty, but Mary Alice heard his voice.

"You'll lose him on the hill. You're lots faster. Make the curve, kill your lights and do a one-eighty. Head back the way you came and go straight to the police station. Don't even try to see who it is when you pass by him."

The road curved to the left at the top of the hill. Mary Alice stomped the brake and killed the lights. The BMW slid into a spin. She heard gravel hitting the sides and windows of the car as she fought the wheel, forcing the car out of the spin. The car stopped. The darkness seemed to tilt, and she didn't know which direction she faced. She could hear the SUV laboring up the hill, coming fast. She turned on the parking lights and saw a rock face a foot from her front bumper. She killed the lights, backed up and hit the gas just as the dark SUV rounded the curve.

Mary Alice drove back into Cana doing seventy. The SUV didn't appear in her rear view mirror, but she didn't trust her pursuer wouldn't find a way to head her off before she made town. She screeched into a Police Parking Only space, killed the engine and ran inside the police station.

The desk sergeant dropped the phone and his jaw when Mary Alice ran in. Her face was white, and she could hardly speak.

"I'll call you back," he said into the phone and hung up. "Ma'am, are you hurt?"

She could feel her mouth working, trying to form words, but getting out "someone tried to run me off the road" was impossible. She saw him pick up the phone and press a button. She couldn't understand what he said. She felt her whole body shake uncontrollably and half realized that she'd have to stop shaking if she was going to get help. What if they didn't believe her? What if they told her to go home?

"Help." She heard herself say the word. It sounded like a kitten's mew. "Help," she tried again, this time stronger. Then like a child who has learned a new word and wants to practice, she chirped a string of helps until she felt a strong hand on her shoulder.

"Ms. Tate?" the voice said.

She turned and looked into the blue eyes of Tom Jaworski. She turned away. He'd dismissed her from TJ's. He was no friend.

"Ms. Tate, you've got to calm down a little and tell me what happened," Jaworski said. He turned her to face him. He sounded kind, not as he had at the bar.

Mary Alice looked at his eyes. At the bar she'd thought they looked vulnerable, but now she thought they looked pained, like some terrible loss had etched itself in his eyes. She examined his thick dark lashes as though she had been asked to count them and report the number. She saw him say something to the desk sergeant.

"Ms. Tate?" Jaworski said. "I'm going to all an ambulance. I think you're in shock."

"No," she yelled. She had a vision of being in a hospital room, and the man from the SUV coming in when she was sedated. He'd press a pillow over her face. "Someone followed me. He tried to kill me."

Jaworski gently took her arm and led her down an ugly yellow hall to a tiny conference room. He helped her into a ripped green plastic chair. She pressed her finders over the rip and pulled the edges together in an effort to mend it.

"Officer Donovan and I are the only ones here right now, but I can call a female officer or your lawyer, if you want," he said.

"Am I under arrest?" she asked. She looked up at him, dazed.

Just a hint of a smile touched his lips. "No Ma'am. You came to us. Someone followed you in your car, you said."

"I was at Bailey's and on my way to the Cana Theatre. Someone followed me."

More or less accurately, she described her route, the first ram at the four-way and the second before the hill up to the landfill. Her shaking was replaced by fatigue. Her arms and legs felt like Jell-O. "I think it was a black Chevy Tahoe."

"You're shook up," he said. "It's okay. You're safe here."

"I'm not safe. I was lucky Daddy's old car is so fast. Whoever it was will come back." She felt salty tears on her face.

"Not tonight," he said. "Would you like a Coke or something? Might make you feel better. All that adrenalin whacks you out."

"No, thanks." She put her head down on the plastic table top.

He pushed a bottle of water toward her.

She ignored it.

He let her cry for a few minutes. "Ms. Tate, why don't you let me drive you home?"

She didn't want to move. With her index finger she petted a deep gouge in the table.

"Or maybe to a friend's house," he said.

She quieted but didn't move. Even her Mama's house sounded like a good idea.

"Okay," she said.

He led her down the same yellow hall, outside and to his car which was parked at the side of the station.

"You can get your car tomorrow. It'll be safe here," he said.

She felt a little more composed in his car. "I'm sorry I lost it in there. I was so scared."

"You did the right thing. Someone attacked you, but you're all right now." He talked, soothing her.

Mary Alice breathed in his words. She needed to believe them.

"I apologize for being rude to you the other day in TJ's."

She nodded and then tucked her head like a bird.

"I thought about what you said, you know, about Scott Bridges and the case he was working on. I did a little checking."

Her head came up. "You believe me?" she asked.

He turned toward her. "I knew Scott thought there was a drug warehouse near here and that some officials were protecting it. He was one to brag, but not to lie. And I found out something else interesting, I can't tell you about right now. I'd like to talk to Sheree Delio. Unofficially."

"She didn't kill him. I know she didn't."

"I want to talk to her, and I need you to be there. She might know more than she thinks she does, but I'll need her trust. I don't have time to build that, and she's not one who'd trust cops anyway," he said.

"I'll ask her."

"No. That won't work. Time will run out or it'll leak. She'll tell somebody or you will. Hell, maybe I will. We gotta just go for it, if you're willing. If Scott was even partly right—think about it. Some of Cana's most important citizens arrested. It's dangerous."

Mary Alice heard "dangerous" overshadow his proposal. If it was dangerous for a cop, imagine the danger for her. Being chased and rammed had brought the message home. She wondered if she'd ever feel at ease again.

"What do you want to do?" she asked.

"Let's go to Sheree's right now," he said.

She nodded.

"We'll have to go in your car. I'll leave my car behind at TJ's. I'll follow you there and then go with you."

"Yes."

He opened the door, got out and came around to help her. "You okay?"

Her legs felt like rubber, like the first time she auditioned for a play in elementary school. She took his arm, and it felt like steel. She let him help her into her car, absorbing his essence through touch.

"What if I hadn't come tonight?" she asked. "Were you going to call me?"

"Yes."

As she watched him walk back to his car, Mary Alice reasoned that she'd be with a cop, a good cop. Safer than alone. Jaworski knew about Scott Bridges' work. He'd help her find the killer and free Sheree.

The car started after three tries. She scanned the lot looking for a dark vehicle, a waiting predator. Jaworski pulled in behind her, but still she monitored the side and rear mirrors. He, whoever he was, was out there. He'd probably killed Scott Bridges and would have no trouble doing the same to her.

CHAPTER 24

MARY ALICE PICKED UP JAWORSKI in the back lot behind TJ's. He slid in the front and buckled his seat belt.

"Take old Highway 3 to the Chickasaw Cut," he said. "Less chance anybody will spot us. If whoever followed you shows up, I'll tell you what to do then."

"Do you think my being followed is connected to helping Sheree?" Mary Alice asked, pulling onto the street.

"Can't be sure. It's safer to assume so. Unless somebody else might want to put you out of commission." He looked over at her.

She drove extra carefully as if she were taking her driver's test. However, once out on the deserted highway, paying attention to driving competed with trying not to pay attention to Jaworski. He smelled like cedar and orange zest wrapped in fresh straw. Even with the window down, his scent danced over the dashboard and under the steering wheel toward her like a charmed cobra. She wanted to pull over and bury her face in his neck.

"Are you feeling all right?" he asked.

"Yes. Am I driving too fast?" They passed the defunct Rainbow Garden Center that had died when Wal-Mart opened on the big highway.

"No," he said. "I thought you might be having second thoughts."

"No. This is a good idea," she said. But tiny doubts were squeezing in. She was alone in a car on a deserted road with a man she hardly knew who might be connected to Scott Bridges' murder. She turned to look at him half expecting him to turn into a serial killer.

"Whoa, watch the road," he said.

She pulled the car back just before taking out the tall weeds on the shoulder.

They rode in silence until they approached Sheree's house.

"Let me off up there a ways," he said. "The house might be watched. I'll come in the back. Don't tell Sheree anything until I get there."

"What if she doesn't want to talk to you?" she asked.

"I'm betting she doesn't have enough options to pass up this chance. But if not, we'll reverse the ride and think of something else." He got out of the car and closed the door quietly.

She drove away leaving him in the dark. His scent lingered; she inhaled and felt herself relax. Tom Jaworski exuded confidence and competence. Mary Alice wasn't sure if the raw animal pheromones he stimulated were a plus or a minus considering the situation. Here was a man she could lean on. But she knew she always thought the men to whom she was attracted could be leaned on. She'd been wrong more often than right.

A minute later she pulled into Sheree's driveway. She could see the flashing glare of a television behind the closed curtains. She knocked on the front door.

"Sheree, it's me, Mary Alice." She heard the security chain click into place.

Sheree opened the door and peeked out. "I didn't know you were coming over."

"Me either."

Minutes later, Mary Alice let Jaworski in the back door. Without a word, he did a quick walk though and then turned up the volume of the TV.

Sheree looked frightened, ready to bolt. Mary Alice took her hand.

"The house could be bugged; don't talk loud," he said.

Bugged? Mary Alice tried to recall what she and Sheree had said that anybody could use against Sheree.

My God, are they powerful enough to use hidden surveillance?

Bugs seemed a big step up from buzzards.

He pointed to a sofa, and they huddled together, Jaworski in the middle.

At first, Sheree didn't want to talk to Jaworski. But he had been right; in the end she conceded because her few options were running out.

"Tell me everything that happened," he told Sheree. "Don't leave out anything. Go slow. Back up when you remember something. Pretend I don't know anything."

"Why do you want to know?" Sheree asked. She twisted a tuft of hair into a corkscrew.

Jaworski turned to her and looked directly into her eyes. Mary Alice saw Sheree register his gaze. "You don't know what you know that's important. Tell me everything that happened. Even little details. Start when you first met Bridges."

Sheree talked non-stop for fifteen minutes. Occasionally Jaworski asked a question. Mary Alice had to strain to hear over the TV as Sheree told how the relationship had started and soured. He asked her to repeat exactly what Scott Bridges had said about drugs being stashed and protected.

Repeatedly he asked, "Were those his exact words?" He kept his voice calm and steady like a psychiatrist.

"Mr. Jaworski, it's been a long time," Sheree said. "Most of the time I was trying not to pay attention to Scott."

"Okay. Take it slow. It's all in your head. You heard it. You've forgotten, but it's there. Did he ever say anything about the location of the hiding place?"

"He liked to call it a depot, like a train depot. I had the idea trucks were bringing it in from all directions, but once he said it was from Mexico."

"What were his words about Mexico?" Jaworski asked.

"Goddamned grease-balls," Sheree said. "He hated drugs. It was bad somebody here was importing them, but he really hated that Mexicans were bringing them in."

"Did he say Mexicans were transporting them or did he just think so?"

"I don't remember. He hated Mexicans even if they were legally here, so I don't know." She pushed her hair away from her face.

Sheree was looking tired and more and more anguished. She seemed to sense her answers weren't helping much. Mary Alice put her hand on Sheree's knee and patted.

"Okay, skip that for now. He told you that fat cats, Cana people were protecting the drugs. What were his words? Tell me any you recall."

"He said over and over, heads of the high and mighty were going to roll, like they were chopped off. He loved the idea that big shots were going to be humiliated and go to jail."

"Try for specific words."

Sheree closed her eyes and seemed to be visiting an ugly scene from her past. "I can't think." She chewed the side of her mouth.

"How many of them? How many heads?" Jaworski pressed.

"Maybe eight or ten. I thought the sheriff must be in on it and the police chief. The way he talked, it seemed like they were. The police chief cut the number of men on the drug team so Scott was suspicious of him. And something else. Scott didn't get promoted last go round. He said, 'I'm a fucking one-man drug enforcement unit bringing in more arrests and dope than anybody in history, and I don't get fucking pro-fucking-moted.' Or something like that."

"Good. You're doing good," Jaworski said. "How come you think it was eight or ten covering up the operation? Why not five or fifteen?"

"The people in that rhyme he used to say. It don't make no sense."

"Rhyme?" Jaworski repeated.

"Went like rich man, poor man something man, something chief. Maybe that's why I thought it was the police chief. I didn't think he meant a Choctaw chief. There were some others. Rich man, poor man—"

"Beggar man, thief, doctor, lawyer, merchant, chief," Mary Alice said. "Was that the rhyme?"

299

"Yes, that's it exactly," Sheree said. She sounded awestruck by the revelation.

Mary Alice looked at Jaworski.

"Say that again," he said.

Rich man, poor man, beggar man, thief, doctor, lawyer, merchant, chief," Mary Alice said. "It's a children's rhyme. There are some more, tinker, tailor, soldier, sailor."

"Scott stopped with the chief," Sheree said. "I don't know anything else about that. I swear. But he said the rhyme over and over and said they were all going to jail."

"You know more. Try to think," Jaworski said.

"No, I—"

"You do," he insisted.

Mary Alice could see tears well in Sheree's eyes.

"Tom, she's exhausted," Mary Alice said.

He looked reluctant to stop. "Okay. Keep thinking like this. Anything you think of, you tell Mary Alice. Tell her right away. But don't write anything down."

Sheree nodded.

"You thought of this; there's more," he said. He looked like he was going to pat Sheree's arm, but then decided not to. Jaworski rose. "I'm going out the back. Pick me up near the same spot in ten minutes." He slipped out the back door and was gone.

"You did good, Sheree. It's progress," Mary Alice said. She looked at the doubt on Sheree's face. "I had to take a chance on him."

"He's a cop," Sheree said. She turned down the TV's volume.

"I know."

Mary Alice gave her a hug at the door and then drove away into the pitch dark.

She looked at the green glow of the dash board lights. What if Jaworski were the enemy? Georgia believed he was straight, but Georgia could be wrong. Maybe he just wanted to find out what Sheree knew. Maybe she had put Sheree in even more danger. Mary Alice wondered if she trusted Jaworski because he was such a turn on. But the thought of sex with Jaworski when she could possibly be pregnant with her ex-husband's baby coupled with her developing romance with Zach brought on an anxiety attack. She rolled down the window and concentrated on breathing the moist Mississippi air.

I am in way too deep.

She didn't see Jaworski until she had almost passed him. He stepped from the shadows, and she slid to a halt. He got in the car.

"You think somebody's watching us, don't you?" she said. She could hear the anxiety in her voice but wasn't clear about its cause: terror of whoever followed her or doubts about Jaworski.

He hit the door lock button and clicked his seat belt. "No, not right now. But you can't be selectively careful."

"What do you make of the rhyme?" she asked. She had her own list of suspects.

"I think Sheree's right," he said. The chief is the police chief. I can't tell you how sick that makes me. Scott told me the chief was interfering with his investigation. I think he was trying to tell me a lot more, but I didn't listen. I didn't want to believe him."

"Who's your rich man?" she asked. She liked that he confided in her.

"Who's yours?"

"Leonard Bass," Mary Alice said. "He a bank president; he can launder money, and I think he's having Georgia Horn harassed by the IRS."

"And the doctor?" he asked.

"It's your turn."

"Medical doctors seem too well off to risk something like this," he said. "Maybe a university professor. Or a retired one." As they neared town, she saw him monitor the cars ahead and behind.

"What about Doc Hodges?" she said. "He's not doctor; he's just called that. He ran for something awhile back, and my Daddy said he had his finger in every shady deal, kick back and payoff ever hatched in North Mississippi."

"Good." Jaworski pulled his ball cap down low on his brow. "I have an idea about the beggar," he said.

"Who?"

"A cop. He's always asking for a few bucks, a loan, wants to borrow your car. He begs. Beggar is one of his nicknames."

"Who else?" She repeated the rhyme.

"Don't know yet. Let's switch cars, and I'll drive you home."

"I'm okay. I'll drive straight to my mama's."

He checked the mirrors again.

She turned the corner. "What can I do to help?" She felt that Jaworski had a few guesses about the identities of the others.

"You have to stay out of this for your own safety. I'm a cop. I'm going to do some checking and—"

"I've been in this since the night of the murder, and I'm not getting out. If we work together, we can help each other."

She pulled over to the curb at the darkest place on the block.

"You can talk to me, but I don't want you—"

"I'm not your snitch," she said. "This is my business. Someone tried to kill me. I'm in it."

"Shhhhhh." He looked at her, taking his time. "Don't talk to anyone but me. I'm going to check the financial records for the people we named—most of them. If they're involved, a lot of money that can't be explained could be moving though their accounts. With time, I can check all the doctors, merchants and lawyers. I don't have to find them all. If I find even one that's sure, he'll turn on the others. But I have to go slow and be careful."

"How can you check their accounts?"

Jaworski gave her a "don't be naive" look. "I have a friend."

"A friend who can get into people's financial records?" Mary Alice had the sensation she was in a John Grisham thriller.

Jaworski looked at her. "I hope so."

"I can't help?"

"Don't do anything unusual. Whoever followed you tonight is trying to scare you. Scare you bad. He'll do more if he thinks it's necessary."

"So act scared?"

"Try it."

"It won't be hard," she said.

"Another thing. When you met me at TJ's you said there was a videotape."

"It was made in Sheree's apartment the night Scott Bridges was killed. I can't prove that but—"

"Where is it now?" he asked. His voice, low in pitch and volume, sounded like a late night radio announcer's.

"The DA has it." Mary Alice described the videotape's bizarre travels from her mother to Zach to her, to Sheree and back to Zach and the suspicious images at the end of the tape. "He's sending it to a crime lab. Today's Friday. He'll probably send it Monday."

"Never mind. Sheree's probably the best resource. I'd like her to work with a hypnotist. I got a feeling there's more stuff in her head."

"Like Doug."

"Who?"

"An old boyfriend, Doug, visited her a couple of weeks before Scott Bridges was killed. She didn't tell me about it until I found out from the apartment manager," Mary Alice said.

"I want to know more about him."

"He's probably breaking parole," she said.

"That'll make it easier. Get his last name."

"You'll call me?" she asked.

"Yes. You got a cell phone?"

She dug in her purse and found it. "I never thought to use it when I was being followed."

"Next time you will. I'm programming in my number. It'll say 019 on your screen. Call me if you need to."

"Promise you'll let me know what's going on?" she asked. She felt his gaze rake her body. The gold dress she'd put on to please her mother had slid up and now revealed half her thighs. She didn't pull it down. "Promise me."

"As much as I can. You sure you're okay driving home?" he asked.

"Yes."

"Don't talk to anyone about this. Don't tell anyone you talked to me," he said.

"I got it."

He twisted to open his door and for a second paused.

She knew what he felt. The initial attraction, now compounded by danger with more risk to come charged the bond between them. She wanted him to kiss her. She imagined the kind of desperate, forceful kiss it would be. She touched his arm. He turned back to her, took her hand and held it. His touch felt like fire. Then he turned fast and got out of the car. After he was gone down the dark street, she pressed the back of her hand to her neck.

Mary Alice felt light years away from the warmth of football games and society parties. Those people and comforts were a distant memory. She, Tom Jaworski, Sheree and a few other players were racing toward their destiny, and it was hard not to think there would be a collision on the way and a lot of pain.

Mary Alice looked at the cell phone in her lap. She wanted to press the button that would make Tom Jaworski's phone ring. She wanted to tell him to come back. She looked again at the tiny lighted phone screen and saw Zach's name below Jaworski's 019 code and felt as she had when she rode the Tilt-A-Whirl at the Neshoba County Fair.

It felt crazy—a vanilla courtship with the DA and a hot fudge pursuit of a cop.

She took a sip of the melted ice in the Dr. Pepper cup. Thinking straight eluded her. What if Jaworski had tricked her? What if he was in on the deal and wanted to know how much Sheree knew to set her up again. Cinch her conviction. She breathed deeply, trying to get a grip. No. Jaworski was okay. She made a choice to believe that. She suspected the passion she felt was a result of the danger. She knew more now, and it was worse than she thought, but it was still exciting, close to the edge.

Now I can back off, act scared and let Tom Jaworski solve the crime.

She pulled the car back into the street, turned on the lights and headed for home.

"I'll go to Mama's. I'll stay in the carriage house for a while," she told the rear view mirror. "Whoever followed me will find out and think I'm terrified." She checked again to make sure no one was following her. Her hands trembled on the wheel, but she felt relief that finally she had some real help. A third feeling mixed with fear and relief, emptiness.

Why didn't she respond to Zach the way she did to Tom Jaworski?

She ran her hand inside the neckline of her dress beneath the chunky necklace.

She imagined meeting Jaworski at a seedy Pontotoc motel. She shook her head and jerked her hand away. When all this was over, the feeling would go away. She cared for Zach. They were building a real relationship, not some cheap emotional high that wouldn't last. Everything with Zach would work out for the best.

To her list of things to do she added, find out if you are pregnant and put an end to that craziness.

CHAPTER 25

MARY ALICE SPENT FRIDAY NIGHT at the carriage house, but returned to the lake house early Saturday morning to get her things. By noon on Saturday, she was back at Linnley unloading her car at the carriage house. She'd called Chase and lied about why she never showed up at the theatre. Car trouble. Her mother's house keeper, Maria came out to help.

"Mrs. Tate didn't say you were coming," Maria said. She sounded wary about any change to Mrs. Tate's plans. Mary Alice couldn't imagine Maria cared for her boss, but she wasn't friendly to Mary Alice either.

"Where is she?" asked Mary Alice. "Boon, get out of the way."

They struggled up the stairs with bags and boxes enough for a month's stay.

"She drove to Atlanta with three of her lady friends," Maria said. "Left early this morning. The hotel's name is on her desk."

"Thanks. I'll call her later. When's she due back?"

"Monday night," Maria said. She stood in the door as though she were waiting for further instructions.

"Thanks for your help, Maria."

Maria closed the door and quiet as a ghost, disappeared.

She is so odd, even creepy.

Mary Alice patted Boon. "This is too good. Mama gone for three days."

Boon thumped his tail hard against an antique Chinese wedding box.

Mary Alice went into the bathroom and opened the medicine cabinet, pulled out a bottle of aspirin and downed three pills, hoping they'd be enough to calm the soft throb of a toothache somewhere in the lower left quadrant of her mouth. She'd read that fifteen percent of Americans were dentophobic, afraid of dentists, and she numbered herself among them.

She dug in her purse and exhumed the pregnancy detection kit she'd bought that morning at the Wal-Mart. She'd grabbed the cheapest of four brands and had been relieved to see that she didn't know the Wal-Mart checker, who might gossip or call for a price check. Even so, she had considered telling the checker that the kit was for her niece's science project.

But now, examining the stick-looking thing, she felt anxious. She knew she wanted it both ways: pregnant to have the child she craved and not pregnant because having this child would be complicated. She went into the bathroom.

"Here goes." She inserted the stick's tip into a stream of urine, trying not to get it all over the stick and her hand. The kit directions said to wait five minutes. Two rosy lines meant yes and one meant no. She left it in the bathroom on the rim of the white porcelain sink and busied herself unpacking so she wouldn't have to think about how a funny swab-thing was lining up her future.

She hung up her clothes in the antique armoire, glancing toward the bathroom door every few seconds as if a plump nurse in starched whites were going to emerge with the results wrapped in a pastel blanket.

Boon paced beside her. Exactly five minutes later, she picked up the stick to read her fate. Instead of two or even one rosy band, there was a watery pink line waving though the field. She tore thought the trash to find the kit's directions.

"You're either pregnant or you're not."

Boon woofed.

The fine print revealed that occasionally, sometimes, a kit went wrong and delivered inconclusive results. There was a toll free number to call, but Mary Alice knew that ultimately the voice on the phone wasn't going to know if she was or was not going to have a baby.

After all that worry and denial, not to mention purchasing the test kit and she had to start all over. She tossed the stick in the trash and wondered if there was any hidden meaning in that she'd purchased the cheap kit.

Lying on the bed, she stared up at the canopy. The late night before with Tom Jaworski, the move to the carriage house, the toothache and the fact that the BMW had taken an hour to get started had worn her out. She needed to take the old Beemer in for repairs, but knew even something simple would cost more than she wanted to spend at the moment.

Boon jumped up on the gold silk sofa, stretched out and rested his chin on a matching tufted and pleated cushion.

Mary Alice closed her eyes and found Tom Jaworski behind them. He looked like he could be on the cover of some earthy men's magazine that promoted sweat over cologne. Except for the startling blue eyes, he looked tough, capable and entirely sexy. But Mary Alice knew Tom Jaworski was smart, too. He'd coaxed from Sheree the identities of the Cana drug cartel. Almost. Jaworski's image was replaced by a line up of faceless men in dark suits. Who were these rich men-poor men?

She imagined the thief would be the hardest to identify. He probably wasn't literally a thief, and she'd never know why Scott Bridges viewed him as one. She had thought Leonard Bass was the rich man because he was rich and was connected to the IRS's investigation of Georgia, but Cana had lots of rich, ambitious men. It was Saturday and unlikely that Jaworski's contact could produce anything before Monday. Searching computers could take a long time.

"Rich man, poor man, beggar man, thief, doctor, lawyer, merchant, chief."

Cana had dozens of lawyers and merchants, but only two chiefs—fire and police. And who would Scott Bridges consider poor? Mary Alice tried to think of anyone who had lost a lot of money in the last few years.

It was frustrating to her not to be able to ask Zach. She couldn't even tell him about the black SUV that had tried to run her off the road. She and Jaworski agreed she would tell no one about that. She'd made no police report. The day-dream shifted again, and she and Jaworski were sailing in the Caribbean wearing little more than sun block.

"I have to stop this," she told Boon. In spite of the incon-clusive test results, Mary Alice felt more confident that she wasn't pregnant. And if she wasn't, then fantasizing about Tom Jaworski was problematical in light of her relationship with Zach, but it wasn't crazy. Jaworski had all the characteristics of the forbidden and thus was extremely desirable. But she knew she'd flip flop and start to worry soon enough. For once she was glad that Wal-Mart never closed.

Mary Alice left the carriage house and wandered around Linnley's ground floor, ending up in her mother's bedroom. Immense and lavishly decorated, the room had been copied from pictures of bedrooms belonging to famous film stars of the forties. Mary Alice felt she was walking on glass. When Mary Alice was a child, her mother had used one of the bedrooms upstairs; her father slept in a small room off the study. As a child, Mary Alice had never minded the arrangement. It was just what was.

Mary Alice examined the collection of cut glass bottles on the moiré-skirted dressing table. She knew that some were worth thousands of dollars. The glass sparkled in the light, winking at her, perhaps smirking—Mama loves us more than she loves you. She moved away.

On a book shelf she noticed a green marker sticking out of a book she recognized, Alexandra Seale's *Bottoms*. The marked place revealed a photo of the backs of three older women sitting quite close on a bench. Three naked backs and butts. Mary Alice wondered who they were. Her mother knew. Mary Alice returned *Bottoms* to its shelf.

On impulse, she opened the closet and was buffeted by her mother's scent—not unpleasant, but not comforting. She regarded the neatly spaced and color-grouped hanging dresses, blouses, slacks and skirts. Touching a long velvet dress, she thought of drama queens and avatars. She had to fight off the sadness she felt that there had been so little closeness, no dressing up together, and no sharing jewelry, not even an argument over who had borrowed what and when. She closed the closet and left the room.

In the study, she found the note in her mother's crimped, precise handwriting describing her mother's trip and hotel arrangements. Mary Alice sat in her mother's ergonomically designed chair that had replaced her father's comfy, old leather one. She dialed Georgia's home phone.

"How's the Belle of Cana Detective Agency?" asked Georgia. The TV played in the background.

"Peachy," Mary Alice said. "I talked to Tom Jaworski again." Mary Alice wanted to keep Georgia up on everything, but she knew Tom was right about how word got around. She couldn't tell Georgia about the SUV chase or the rich man, poor man rhyme, but she could tell her that Jaworski was helping them.

"And?"

"Maybe I'd better tell you in person."

"Enough mysteries, Mary Alice. Why did you call me?"

"To tell you I'm staying in town at Mama's for a little while."

"Did something else happen at the lake?" Georgia asked.

"No. I just want you to know where to reach me," Mary Alice said.

"Wait a sec. You are at your Mama's house so that she won't fire me. Right?"

"Yes," Mary Alice said. Already she regretted calling.

"Good."

"Good?"

"Yes."

"Last time we talked, a mere twenty-four hours ago, you'd all but resigned."

"And last night, I got a bunch of new clients—five kids, and I'm all that is between them and a very tough time. For now, it's important to me to keep this job."

"I don't trust Mama, but if I'm here, she'll feel like she won and will probably just hope the IRS ruins you and she won't have to."

"Come by the Women's Center Monday morning and take a walk with me," Georgia said. "Wear walking shoes. Bye." Georgia's phone clicked off.

Mary Alice hung up the phone, relieved that she didn't have to worry about Georgia leaving at a critical moment preceding Sheree's trial. It was bad enough that Georgia might leave at all. But maybe some unseen force was at work and in time a tipping point would be reached and things would start going Sheree's way. Right would be rewarded. Maybe things had already started to tip. She thought of Tom Jaworski again. With him on her side, how could the dark forces win? Then she thought about the pregnancy test kit and Zach and the whole town of Cana. Hester Prynne of *The Scarlet Letter* had been forced to wear the letter A for adultery on her dress. She had refused to reveal the name of the father of her illegitimate child. Mary Alice similarly would be disinclined to reveal that her ex-husband was her baby's father. If there was a baby.

Poor Hester. It's all so unfair.

Determined to take her mind off babies, Mary Alice set a crisp sheet of paper in front of her on the desk and made quick sketches of every person involved in Sheree's case. The drawings ringed the page: Katherine Bridges, Otis Turner, Sheriff Gelly, Kenny Bates, Georgia, Hollis Tubbs, Doug, Leonard Bass, Zach, Tom Jaworski, and Sheree. Tom Jaworski looked like a muscled construction worker with a badge. Beside Otis she drew a camera, Hollis held a phone, and Katherine Bridges, a suitcase. Below the doodles of people, she drew a button that looked like an M & M.

Otis Turner's picture pulled her attention. She knew he had to be loyal to the police, but she sensed he wanted to help her because he liked her. He always had, even in grade school. She pulled the slim Cana phone directory from the desk drawer and scanned the T's for his number. She punched in the seven digits. He answered immediately.

"Otis, hello. It's Mary Alice Tate."

"Mary Alice," he repeated, sounding like he'd just won a prize at the Neshoba County Fair.

"Otis, I want to thank you again for the information you gave me about videotapes," she said. "It helped so much."

"You're welcome. So there is a videotape?" he asked.

"Zach—the DA has it. He's sent it on down to Jackson for analysis, just like you said."

"Probably he told you this, but if forensics has the video camera that took the film, it can tell a whole lot more stuff."

"Like what?" Mary Alice asked. Zach hadn't mentioned the camera and as far as she knew, her mother still had it.

"It's called detect editing," Otis said. "I studied it at the academy. If they have the camera, they can tell how that particular camera records images. See, the camera is putting all kinds of information on a videotape you never see. For example, it shows if a tape was taped-over or edited."

"So they could use the camera and make another tape for comparison." Mary Alice said.

"Exactly. How'd you know?"

"Wild guess."

Otis described a dizzying array of things videographers could do. Mary Alice listened, finally working around to Sheree's case and anything Otis might have heard. But on that, he was tight lipped.

After she hung up, she searched the study for the video camera Scott Bridges had used. She felt sure her mother wouldn't have thrown it away, and the study was the only place she'd store it. It seemed unlikely that Zach had it. He'd said nothing about the camera. She had to find it.

Starting at one corner of the study, she moved through the room, canvassing each drawer, shelf, nook and cranny. As she dug beneath boxes of check stubs in the lower right drawer of the desk, her eye caught her name on what appeared to be a list. She carefully removed the sheet, marking its location in the stack of papers.

An inventory of her comings and goings in Cana filled the page. Someone had been spying on her. There was no parallel structure to the notations. One said visit with S. Delio Wed. 9/14; another read, met with Marshall Dugan at Laundromat for an hour. M. is on parole for drug convictions. She read on: called about dead bird in house, visited apartment of Hollis Tubbs. She reread it three times, each time feeling more like a poisoned insect. By the third time she could hardly move.

This is what Sheree felt when she looked at herself on the videotape.

Closer examination of the list showed that some visits to Sheree had not been logged and that the September 3 visit to the crime scene at Sheree's apartment wasn't mentioned nor was the one to the Pegues' farm. The list stopped on September 15, Thursday. She wondered if last night's trip to Sheree's with Tom Jaworski would show up on the next report.

Two reasons for the list's existence occurred to Mary Alice. Her mother really was frightened for her daughter's safety and had hired a private investigator to follow her and perhaps protect her. Or her mother was involved in the sale of illegal drugs. Maybe it was rich woman instead of rich man.

Mary Alice thought about confronting her mother with the log, but knew Elizabeth would swear that her fear for her daughter made her hire a PI. Mary Alice would then look like a snoop and her mother would look responsible, even caring. Mary Alice imagined her mother connected to a lie detector machine that doled out jolts of electricity for answers to questions Mary Alice didn't like such as, "Why did you give the videotape of Sheree to Zach?" Answer "I certainly couldn't give it to my irresponsible daughter who would use it to help that little tramp." Zap. Mary Alice could almost smell the sizzling hair and lashes.

Before Mary Alice could think through any further meanings of the log noting her activities, Maria knocked once on the study door and opened it. Mary Alice jerked, sending a cinnabar box of paper clips to the floor. She slid the log back in its place in the drawer.

"I'm going out," Maria said. She eyed the paper clips, but made no move to collect them.

"Have a good evening," Mary Alice said. She smiled and wondered if Maria had spotted the log and how much Maria knew.

An hour later Mary Alice was getting dressed for her date with Zach when the phone rang. She answered. Hollis Tubbs was calling Elizabeth Tate with a list of repairs at the apartments.

"I'll call your mama back Tuesday," he said.

"I'll let her know you called, Mr. Tubbs," Mary Alice said. She continued painting her toenails red to match the strappy sandals she planned to wear.

"But say, while I have you on the phone, maybe I ought to tell you something I saw a couple of days ago," he said.

"What?" She felt the urge to put on a robe.

"Let's see. I saw you on Wednesday, and it's Saturday so it must have been Thursday night he come by."

"Who?"

"The blond-haired fella. You told me to call you if I thought of something. Well, I didn't think of it, but I saw it."

"What?" She didn't bother to point out that Hollis had called her mother, not her. It was merest chance that he was speaking to Mary Alice.

"That same young man who visited the Delio girl was back here looking for her. I heard him ask her neighbor, well the woman who used to be her neighbor, where Sheree had gone to. Of course, Norma didn't know much to tell him."

Doug was back. Had he found Sheree? Mary Alice looked at her toes. She'd slopped nail polish on the cuticle and would have to start over.

"Mr. Tubbs, thanks for letting me know. If you see him again, would you mind giving me a call?"

"Not a'tall. And it was an out of state plate on his SUV."

"What state?"

"Not sure, but not Mississippi," he said.

"What kind of SUV was it?" she asked.

"Big ole Chevy, black as a hearse."

Could Doug, whoever he really was, have been the one trying to run her off the road? It made no sense if he cared about Sheree. Mary Alice was helping Sheree. But what if he didn't? What if Doug had been paid to kill Scott Bridges and now wanted Sheree to take the blame?

She thanked Hollis Tubbs again and hung up the phone.

It occurred to Mary Alice that perhaps Hollis Tubbs was spying on her for her mother. He had been quick to let Elizabeth know that Mary Alice had visited him. He had likely told Elizabeth everything he told Mary Alice. She didn't know what to do with the information about Doug. Should she tell Irene Bardwell? Irene had been so furious about the videotape. Yes, she'd tell her. But Mary Alice also wanted to talk to Sheree about Doug. She didn't have a good feeling about his return to Cana.

Mary Alice rubbed her right big toe with polish remover until the rosy red color disappeared. Zach would be there to pick her up in twenty minutes. Boring, obsequious dinner parties must populate the life of a successful political candidate. It was a wonder anyone wanted to run.

She sat on the edge of the bathroom sink and began again to paint her toes the color of blood.

CHAPTER 26

MARY ALICE FELT SLIGHTLY NAUSEATED riding home from the dinner party. It was almost midnight. Zach hardly spoke, and Mary Alice knew why.

"Are you mad at me?" she asked.

"Why would I be mad?"

"Because I drank too much." She couldn't quite bring herself to admit that drinking four glasses of wine in as many hours had made her accost Leonard Bass. "If I was obnoxious, I'm sorry."

"Everybody has one too many now and then," Zach said. He turned the car into Linnley's driveway and parked beside the carriage house steps.

It was like Zach to be forgiving, but if the party had been a test of her skills as the wife of a governor, she'd scored a D plus at best. "Did Leonard Bass say anything to you about me?" she asked. "I saw y'all whispering on the porch."

"What? No. Leonard's still afraid the Jews are taking over the country club."

"Nothing about me?"

"Not to me. What did you say to him?"

"I badgered him about Southgate."

Zach turned to face her. "You lost money in the Southgate deal?"

"No. I asked him how come it failed; how come they didn't know about the sink holes."

"I assure you, Leonard wishes he'd known about the sink holes."

They sat in the car looking straight ahead. The air-conditioned air slowly dissipated and the edges of the windows started to fog.

"How much did he lose?" she asked.

"You didn't ask him?"

"He wouldn't say."

"And it matters to you because?"

"It doesn't. I was trying to make conversation with somebody at the strangest dinner party I've ever been to, and I've been to some real loo-loos."

"I'm sorry you were bored."

"I was trying not to be bored by talking to Leonard. But I have to tell you that I think he's my mama's toady, and he's probably sicked the IRS on Georgia. Unfairly, I might add. I got carried away when he got defensive about Southgate." Mary Alice, even in her mildly intoxicated state, realized she needed to shut up. Both Irene Bardwell and Tom Jaworski had warned her not to share information with the DA even if he was her boyfriend, or especially because he was. She couldn't tell Zach about her theory on Leonard Bass' involvement in the drug deal. And lying, as she was doing, wasn't a good idea with Zach. An excellent lawyer, he was famous for tripping up untruthful witnesses on the stand.

"I figure he lost a bundle," Zach said. "They all did. Who'd imagine a dozen sink holes were going to swallow up a development in Cotashona County?"

"I was in Dallas when Southgate went under, but I remember reading in the Cana paper about it. Somebody accused the developers of something—paying off the county commissioners—I can't remember."

"There's not a building project that somebody doesn't complain about." Zach opened the car door and walked around to Mary Alice's door. He opened it.

When she stood up, she felt dizzy. Her body sagged against Zach, and he caught her.

"Let's get you to bed," he said.

She didn't resist, and he guided her up the steps, unlocked the door and flipped on the light. He remained outside on the landing.

"You're not coming in?" she asked. "Mama's not due home till tomorrow night. She won't catch us."

"You need to sleep. I'm sorry you didn't have a nice time. I should have realized."

"Did you have a good time?"

"Mary Alice, I thought you understood it was a business dinner." Zach gripped the door jamb. "Those men and women have power in the election process. I can't run for governor without them."

Zach's patronizing tone and the alcohol made Mary Alice want to lash out. Hadn't she just endured, for him, the most boring four and a half hours of her life? Nobody but Leonard

Bass had even known she was there. And why was Zach taking sides with that arrogant ass?

"You didn't hear what Leonard said or how he said it," Mary Alice said. She stuck out her chin and narrowed her eyes.

"Mary Alice, I'm glad you've come to your senses and are staying with your mama. The Delio case has made you crazy. You need to stay out of it."

"Is that an order?"

"In future, I will not discuss any part of the case with you. Is that clear?"

"Because I got Sheree to plea not guilty? Does that make things hard for the prosecution?"

She knew she was taunting him, but she couldn't stop. How could he dismiss what was most important to her as merely "the Delio case?"

"How could Sheree resist, what do y'all call it—ten, seven and three?"

"You may not have done Sheree a favor," he said. "I'm going. You're tipsy. We'll forget all about this tomorrow. Good night." He closed the door.

She wanted to throw one of her mother's precious porcelain cache boxes at him.

She listened to his descending footsteps and to his car drive away and then opened the door to let Boon out. The dog scrambled down the steep steps to the yard. She watched him sniffing and thought about how Leonard Bass had sounded when she asked him about the demise of Southgate. He had become as defensive as Bernie Ebbers during the WorldCom trial.

Bass had been the principle investor in the Southgate project. After the sink holes, the entire area had been condemned, and he couldn't even sell the acreage. This knowledge had made

Mary Alice shift Leonard Bass from the rich man position in the rhyme to the poor man spot. As a banker he was in a perfect position to launder drug money, and after Southgate, it seemed he needed to.

"Boon, come on, boy," she called and the dog returned. As she got ready for bed, Mary Alice regretted the scene with Zach. He believed Sheree was guilty; it was that simple. He wasn't obligated to see her point of view which was hardly indefensible in any case. But she knew unflappable Zach had depth of character and resilience. He wasn't going to stop seeing the woman he'd said he loved over something as trivial as this.

Lying naked under 500 threads per square inch cotton sheets in the luxurious canopied bed, Mary Alice asked aloud, "If Bass is the poor man, who's the rich man?"

She pressed the button on her cell phone, the one that said Zach. She listened to a recorded message.

"Zach, I'm sorry I was rude to you. I hope I didn't embarrass you tonight. I don't usually drink very much. I don't know what happened tonight. Anyway I'm sorry." She hung up and looked at the other numbers on the contact page of the phone. Tom Jaworski's numerical code, 019, stared back at her.

It was only a little after twelve on a Saturday night. She pressed the tiny button.

"It's me. What's up?" Tom Jaworski said.

She realized he knew who was calling him. It was like a James Bond movie, all codes and secrecy. She loved James Bond.

"I have some things to share with you," she said, trying to match his secret agent tone.

"Tomorrow at TJ's at noon." He clicked off.

Mary Alice rolled over in the bed and wrapped her arms around one of four down pillows. The mix of danger and attraction was intoxicating, and she felt as if she'd just downed another eight ounces of Chateauneuf du Pape. She did have a lot to report to Jaworski, and she wanted to know if he was making any progress with the financial records of their suspects, but she also thought about what she was going to wear to TJ's.

She fell into an alcohol-laced dream in which she was swimming in the lake trying to get Tom Jaworski to follow her. However, he couldn't hear her, and then she couldn't find him.

A mild hangover induced Mary Alice to sleep until almost ten. Boon seemed to need the extra sleep too as he didn't whine. The phone awoke her.

"Wake up, sleepy head," Zach said.

"What time is it?"

"Time to rise and shine," he said.

"Zach, did you get my message?" she asked.

"I did and as I told you last night, we're going to forget all about last night. It never happened," he said. "I called to see if you'd let me cook dinner for you Wednesday evening. I have to go to Atlanta, but I'll be back by Wednesday afternoon."

"Yes, I'd love it. And thanks for being so understanding."

"It takes two Mary Alice," he said. "I was there, and I knew you were miserable. You were my guest. I should have gotten us out of there lots sooner."

Mary Alice felt a rush of sentiment. Zach Towree was thoroughly decent and forgiving. How could you not fall in love with him? She vowed to behave herself with Tom Jaworski at TJ's. It would be strictly business to help Sheree's case.

"Can I help with dinner?"

"No ma'am. I have something special planned. I'll call when I'm back in Cana."

After they hung up, Mary Alice put on a swim suit and took Boon outside. He wandered around the pool while she swam laps. The exercise felt good, but she hated the chemical-laden water. She could feel the lithium hypochlorite etching her skin. When she pulled herself out of the pool, she noticed a face at an upstairs window. It pulled back quickly when it saw that Mary Alice had spotted it.

Is Maria spying on me too?

In spite of her earlier promise to herself, she chose her outfit with attention to what she thought Tom Jaworski would like. She hardly knew him, but he was a man. She finally settled on a black just-above-the-knee straight skirt and a clingy coral knit top. Real coral earrings and necklace and her Jimmy Choo bronze leather shoes—the ones with the skinny heels and pointy toes that made her walk like a beauty pageant contestant—completed the ensemble. She hoped she looked good, but thought that probably Tom Jaworski wasn't going to look at her clothes too much anyway.

At a quarter to twelve, Mary Alice drove to TJ's and parked near the street. There were only a few cars. TJ's opened at eleven on Sunday for a special brunch. The sale of alcohol was illegal on Sunday, so TJ's adapted and became a restaurant popular with the after-church crowd.

Inside, as her eyes adjusted to the dark, she saw Tom Jaworski drinking coffee at the bar. As she approached, he got off his barstool and walked toward the restrooms. Instinctively she followed, unsure of what she'd do if he went in the men's room.

The restrooms, with "Does" and "Bucks" written on the doors, were down a short dark hall. Jaworski waited at the end. Without a look back, he dropped a TJ's bar napkin on the floor. He went in the door marked "Bucks." Mary Alice picked up the napkin and saw something written on it. She went in the ladies room, read the directions and then went back out into the bar. Jaworski was gone.

She had a pretty good idea of where she was going when she left the parking lot. Apparently Jaworski didn't feel safe talking to her in TJ's. She felt the adrenalin pump and took a deep breath as though she were dragging on a filterless Camel.

Thirty minutes later, near the Cotashona County line, she turned off on to another county road and then immediately onto a dirt road which meandered through tall pines and ended at what looked like a hunting cabin. She supposed most North Mississippi men owned a hunting cabin and a duck blind. Killing was ingrained in them, and frequently photos of young boys doused in the blood of their first kill appeared in the Cana newspaper.

There were no other cars. If Jaworski was there, he was waiting to be sure she hadn't been followed. She looked behind her. No one. She got out of the car and felt the heavy dust that her car had kicked up creep up over her delicate shoes and calves. A million humming insects droned their mantra. Then behind her she heard his voice.

"Go inside."

She stepped up on the narrow porch and opened the door. As she closed it, he opened a back door and entered. He wore a cammy tee shirt and dark pants with boots. He'd probably hiked in from another road. He looked more virile than any man she'd ever seen, even in her dreams. She had to stifle a whimper.

"What have you got?" he said.

"Huh?"

"You called me. What?"

"Three things." She tried to sound business-like to calm her pulse. How did he do this to her by merely showing up? But she knew. Jaworski was forbidden fruit like the caves, like Darnel the banker, like all the thrills. An adrenalin junkie's wet dream. "Hollis Tubbs said he spotted Doug, Sheree's boyfriend. He was at the apartment looking for her Thursday. And get this, Hollis says he drives a big black Chevy SUV."

"Like the one that followed you."

"Yes. Like it. Maybe it."

Jaworski didn't take time to review what this information could mean. It was obvious, and it couldn't be proved.

"We need his last name," he said. "If we find his car, we might find out if it was the one that hit you. What else?"

"I found a log of my recent activities—who I've met, talked to—in my mother's desk drawer," she said. "It goes through last Thursday. The next installment may report our meeting at Sheree's."

"Any chance your mother is involved with the rich men-poor men?" Cat like, Jaworski moved about the cabin, touching nothing. He looked out the windows and seemed to be listening to Mary Alice with part of his hearing and for other sounds with the rest of his attention.

"Unless she's in some financial trouble I don't know about, I doubt it. She'd think it was tacky."

"You said three things." He moved closer to her, and she could smell the odor of clean sweat.

"I was at a dinner party with Leonard Bass last night." She described her evening. "I think he's the poor man, not the rich man. He lost everything in the Southgate debacle."

"I'm having him checked on next. I think I got the beggar. Bass will know how to be careful, how to hide infusions of cash, but the beggar is an idiot."

"You're already working on the—I thought. I don't know what I thought."

"We don't have much time," he said. "If they get suspicious someone's on to them, they'll move the drugs. The person who's helping me is a computer expert, not a mole."

He was standing very close to her. The warm air felt as if it were pushing them together. She closed her eyes. But behind her eyes she saw the rosy wavy lines of the failed pregnancy test. What if she got a positive reading on the next test? She stepped away and broke the tension. She was sure he was a half second from grabbing her, and it didn't take much to imagine them naked and entwined on the rough bed in the corner. "That's it. I better go," she said. She felt perspiration pearl at her hairline and between her breasts.

"Drive normal. If anybody asks, you got lost," he said as though he were giving directions at the tourist center. "If you need to talk to me again, call me and say the number two. Nothing else. I'll get in touch and tell you where to go."

"This is like a John LeCarre novel."

"Is it?"

"Codes, secret meetings," she said.

"One man's dead. If Scott was right, there's a lot at stake. It's no story book thriller. Be careful." He looked at her in a way that was the opposite of paternal. He reached out and touched her shoulder so lightly she wasn't sure he'd actually made contact.

She held her breath.

"I will. You, too," she said. With those words, Mary Alice felt she and Tom Jaworski had sealed a contract of unexpressed intimacy and undetermined content. She felt connected and was certain he did, too.

As she drove away, the sexual tension dissolved and was replaced by fear. The empty road felt ominous. She wouldn't want to run into Kenny Bates out here.

On the way back to Cana, Mary Alice decided to swing by the lake house. She missed her home, her daily swims across the lake and thought that just being there for an hour or so would restore some balance. And in any case, her mother, the whole reason she was staying at Linnley and pretending to distance herself from Sheree, wasn't even in Mississippi.

As she drove in she saw Clay's truck in the driveway.

"Hey, Clay. What you doing?" she asked, walking toward him. He was on the deck near the water.

He jumped up, surprised. "You scared me. Boat got loose. I's just tying her up again."

"Oh. Well thanks."

"You still staying at your Mama's?"

"Yes. I came by to pick up a few things." She didn't like the way Clay was acting even though she couldn't exactly say how he was acting. He seemed different. Weird.

"Sheriff came by yesterday," he said, looking at the ground.

"You talked to him?" she asked.

"No, just saw him," he said. "Maybe he was making sure nobody was out here,"

"Yes, that'd be like him. Making sure I'm not here."

"You want me to pull the boat out of the water?" he asked.

"No. I'll be back out here soon. Just leave it for now."

"I checked the first aid kit. It's good. Fastened it under the bow."

"Never know when you'll need first aid," she said.

He nodded, pulled his Ace Hardware baseball cap down and walked back to his truck without another word.

She felt glad he'd gone. She doubted Clay was one of the major players in a drug deal, but then he'd be perfect to report on her comings and goings from the lake house. Clay knew when boats pulled loose from their moorings, when sheriffs visited. And Clay knew the backwoods of Mississippi like she knew designer shoes. He could supply a dozen unused barns and hidden sheds in which to store mountains of cocaine. Clay would be very useful to an illicit drug operation.

When he was gone, Mary Alice went in the house. It wasn't until she started looking for Boon's rope-toy that she sensed it. *Someone's been in here.*

She thought about Clay as she slipped into the utility room and took hold of the shotgun. What did she really know about Clay? She'd blithely assumed that because her Daddy had hired Clay years ago, he was an okay guy—a loyal hand. But enormous sums of money from drugs could change anyone.

She went to the study to confirm her suspicion. She leaned the gun against the side of the desk. Everything looked normal, but when she searched the desk, she saw that her address book had been moved to the back of the drawer and her note pad was gone. Then she remembered tossing the doodle of Sheree in the trash can. She'd drawn it when she'd talked to Irene Bardwell a week ago. The trash hadn't been emptied. In the can she found only a Milky Way wrapper.

She skipped through the house looking for missing valuables, but by the time she reached her Daddy's gun collection, she realized that whoever had come in wasn't after household loot. She felt a chill like a breeze on wet skin. The intruder had wanted to know more about her and what she was doing.

Shit. He went though my trash. She remembered a movie in which the killer went through the garbage cans of his victims.

Clay had said Sheriff Gelly had been there, and Sheree suspected Gelly was involved with the drug deal.

She wanted to call Tom Jaworski, but didn't want to act like a— What? Hysterical woman? And what could he do? He already knew someone was watching her. She remembered how Jaworski had assumed Sheree's house might be bugged. Her gaze tracked over the draperies to the light fixture and down the Chinese chest.

The fear she was supposed to fake became real and surged in almost suffocating her. They had more power than she did. She picked up a photo of her father taken only a year before he died.

"Daddy, I remember how you always say that we create the fear we feel," she whispered to the picture. "We write the story and churn up the emotion. But—" As she struggled to keep from crying, she heard his voice inside her.

Darlin', whatever you're afraid of is in the future. You're inventing how it will be when you don't really know. Get out of the future and decide if a plan would do you any good. Not a plan made in fear. Just decide if there is any precaution you need to take. Don't imagine being swept away in the flood. You're not in a flood. But if the radio says a storm's coming, you can calmly decide to move to higher ground and you don't have to be scared about it first.

Mary Alice sought to negate her terror by washing it away. She pulled out the glass shelves of the refrigerator and scrubbed them in hot soapy water, straightened drawers and cupboards, dusted the blades of the ceiling fans, wiped baseboards, Windexed windows and scoured the tile floor and its grout. Then wet with wash water and sweat, she removed her jewelry and shoes and jumped into the lake with all her clothes on.

Sitting on the deck, drying in the late afternoon sun, she realized that the centering calm she'd hope to find at the house wasn't going to make an appearance, and all the scrubbing hadn't removed the intruder's stink. Even her father's remembered words felt hollow. A storm was coming, but moving to higher ground wasn't an option. She wouldn't abandon Sheree. It seemed to be a race against time. Would Irene find something incriminating on the videotape; would Tom Jaworski find criminal activity in the financial records of some of Cana's leading citizens, or find a barn full of drugs? And who all might pay the price if nothing was found?

Mary Alice collected her shoes, purse, Boon's toys and the photo of her father and locked the house. Glancing back at the house in the rear view mirror, the two dormer windows looked like eyes—anxious, wary ones.

CHAPTER 27

MONDAY MORNING SIMMERED IN A haze that promised a drizzle, but that didn't deter Georgia from her early morning exercise march through town. Mary Alice struggled to keep up. Just south of the square, Georgia dropped the bomb.

"I talked to Irene Bardwell this morning," Georgia said. "She says the videotape is missing."

"Sheree's videotape?" Mary Alice's mouth went dry.

"That's the only one we got. But it looks like we don't got it," Georgia said. She jogged across the street. Mary Alice, wild-eyed, followed.

"It can't have disappeared. Zach and I watched it together. He sent it to Jackson." She grabbed Irene's arm to slow her down.

"What showed up in Jackson, according to Irene, was a blank tape. So far, no one can find the real one."

"What does the DA's office say?" Mary Alice's mind leapt ahead to questioning Zach and the unpleasant scene that would follow.

"The DA says that he didn't personally send the tape; obviously, the wrong one got sent; they'll find the real one, and the trial is a month away so Ms. Bardwell should chill out," Georgia said. "Only he said it in that superior white male lawyer tone of his."

"But the stuff at the end of the tape. If it's the killer or even a person, it's important to find them. That'll take time." Mary Alice found Georgia's apparent ease with the situation exasperating.

"That's exactly what Irene said to the DA," Georgia said. "You want to ask ole Zachary about it?"

"He won't talk to me about the case. I don't think Irene will either. I can't believe this. I have to sit down, or I'm going to puke."

The both sat on a bench in front of a store with a sign that bragged it only sold products made in Mississippi. The town square slowly awakened.

"The tape might have been critical to Sheree's defense," Mary Alice said. She looked at her green sandals that matched her Capri pants outfit.

"You didn't think to make a copy of it, did you?" Georgia asked. It was a rhetorical question.

"I asked Zach about it," Mary Alice said. "He said that due to the sensitive nature of the contents he wouldn't make a copy. He said he'd inform Sheree's lawyer that she could look at it and the results of the crime lab's analysis. Shit." She propped her elbows on her knees and hung her head.

Mary Alice tried to digest this setback and to put it into perspective with what Tom Jaworski was working on. If the Cana eight, as she'd started thinking of them, were found out, the videotape was less important. But the clock was ticking. Sheree's trial date was coming up fast.

"One good thing from this," Georgia said, "is that Irene thinks she can get the trial delayed." Georgia tightened the lace of her running shoe. "And who knows, the tape may show up. It's only been officially missing a few hours. Actually it's not even officially missing."

Mary Alice tried to think of who would steal the tape? Who had access to it? Zach had said he didn't plan to use it to prosecute the case; that it would only embarrass Scott Bridges' family. But Irene Bardwell might have found a use for it. Someone protecting Scott's reputation, a cop perhaps, might take it. A cop might steal it for Katherine Bridges. But such a cop would only know about the sexual nature of the tape, not its mysterious end.

"I can't believe it."

"The tape will probably resurface."

"I'm going to call Irene," Mary Alice said.

"I thought you said she'd shut you out."

"Hollis Tubbs told me Sheree's boyfriend, Doug-somebody was back in town last week looking for her. He visited her before Scott Bridges was murdered.

"You still think he might have killed Bridges because of what he was doing to Sheree?" Georgia asked.

"If I were him, I'd be tempted." Mary Alice wanted to tell Georgia about Doug's black SUV and the similar one that tried to run her off the road, but she didn't.

"What about Detective Jaworski?" Georgia asked.

"What about him?" Mary Alice asked sounding defensive.

Georgia raised her arched eyebrows and waited.

Mary Alice was dying to catch Georgia up on Jaworski, especially the way he'd gotten Sheree to remember the rich man, poor man rhyme and all it implied, but she'd promised him she wouldn't talk to anyone about their meeting and their suspicions. Jaworski was right. Talking could get them killed. "Nothing to tell. Yet."

"I have to get to the center." Georgia stood and easily bent to touch her toes. She apparently decided to skip quizzing Mary Alice about Officer Jaworski.

"How are the children you rescued?" Mary Alice asked.

"Foster care, but good folks. I know the families."

"Split up?"

"Three ways. I gotta go. You gotta call Irene. Keep me posted." Georgia stood, stretched her calves and was off striding across the street toward the Women's Center.

Mary Alice pulled her cell phone from her purse and dialed Irene Bardwell's number. She listened to the purrs of the phone rings and gazed around the square at the Indian summer foliage. The merest hint of the coming fall was written on the leaves, the huge magnolia cones and the wisteria that was trying to choke a hundred year old oak tree. *Thirty days hath September, April, June and November.* It was September 26th. Even if Sheree's trial date were moved forward, by November 26th it would all be over.

Mary Alice was surprised to get though to Irene immediately.

"Georgia told me about the videotape," Mary Alice said. "That's it's been misplaced."

"No point in wasting energy on what we don't have," Irene said. "It's not your fault the tape is missing."

"Thanks for saying that. I called because I found out from Hollis Tubbs that one of Sheree's old boyfriends showed up a few days ago looking for her." Mary Alice repeated what Hollis said and her own scenario in which Doug murdered Scott Bridges. She could hear Irene Bardwell writing notes.

For an instant Mary Alice felt lost in a sea of incomplete clues known to some but not to others. Did Irene know about the barbed wire on Boon's neck? Had she been told about the video camera that might still be in Elizabeth's house? Did Irene have a suspect she hadn't told Mary Alice about? Did it matter? Mary Alice deflected her confusion with a question.

"Did you find out anything about who called Hollis the night of the murder?"

"Downtown pay phone," Irene said. "One of the few left. Probably no one noticed, and I don't have the staff to check it out. But I got something on the medical examiner's report."

"What?"

"Turns out the state examiner was on vacation when Scott Bridges' body was autopsied. And the substitute examiner was working with another doctor who's sort of a coroner-on-call, but the sub examiner didn't know that and signed off without further examination."

"Is that illegal?" Mary Alice asked.

"No, only irregular. Its value is that it raises questions."

"What about the photos?" Mary Alice asked.

"Under the circumstances, I can argue that vital evidence was overlooked and possibly misinterpreted."

"More doubt," Mary Alice said.

"Yes. There are questions about the bruise on the thigh. Mysterious, undocumented bruises cast doubt. Of course, Sheree could have caused them, but she's not physically powerful. Anyway, doubt is good and a delay in the trial would be even better."

"Will you get it?"

"Fifty-fifty chance and I won't know for awhile because the judge may want to wait to see if the tape shows up," Irene said.

Mary Alice's head felt like a gyroscope close to the end of its ride. She wondered if she should tell Irene that somebody had been snooping at the lake house. She decided no, she'd only tell Tom Jaworski. Irene already thought Mary Alice was mucking up the investigation. "You know I'm staying at my mother's house in town until the trial?"

"Yes," Irene said. "It's a good idea. I'm sure it feels confining, but we don't need to worry about Sheree and about you."

Mary Alice wondered if Irene knew that Elizabeth had threatened to fire Georgia. But the threat was now on hold and in any case, Georgia should be the one to tell her.

"I'm going to visit Sheree after lunch and ask her if she's seen Doug," Mary Alice said.

"Will she tell you if she has?" Irene said.

"I hope so. But then I don't know what to do with the information."

"Call me. I need to know everything. I cannot manage the big picture if I don't know details."

"Right." Mary Alice suspected she should tell Irene that Tom Jaworski was looking for eight people identified by a rhyme Scott Bridges had repeated to Sheree. However, she'd promised Jaworski not to talk about his involvement to anyone. If

Jaworski was right, whoever killed the cop would have no compunctions about killing another cop. Of course Irene would have to know ultimately, but later on, when Jaworski wasn't so vulnerable. And anyway, lawyers always thought they needed to know everything. Maybe they did and maybe they didn't.

After she hung up, Mary Alice sat on the bench a moment longer watching the action on the square heat up. A group of lawyers in handsome dark suits got into cars and drove away, the UPS driver delivered a full hand truck of boxes to the candy store and Paula Dubose in her McDonald's uniform went in the bank. It was a scene from a Joni Mitchell song: *and watch the morning on parade in morning Morgantown.* It was beautiful. How could there be a murder and a drug ring in her Morgantown?

Mary Alice walked to her car thinking about the photos of Scott Bridges' body. Now there was suspicion about their meaning or about the substitute coroner who wrote the report. There seemed to be suspicion about many things, but everything dead-ended. She remembered her plan to write all her clues on index cards the way her favorite fictional PI character did. Kinsey Millhone filled dozens of index cards. *I'll start with the button I found in Sheree's bathroom.*

On the way back to Linnley, Mary Alice stopped at Wal-Mart and purchased a pack of plain note cards, a big box of Banana Moon Pies and four pregnancy kits. The checker looked worn-out and would have rung up hand grenades without comment. When Mary Alice pulled into the driveway, she could tell her mama had returned. She straightened her clothes and reapplied lipstick.

Leaving the kits, cards and pies in the car, she went in search of her mother, who was lunching on the side porch. The fussy glassed-in porch, done completely in white, looked as if it might crack.

"Maria, bring another plate for Mary Alice. Hello dear. The tuna is delicious," Elizabeth sang out as though there had been no fight, no acrimonious words, no mother-daughter power play. Elizabeth looked svelte in a navy blue pants outfit with a silk red checked blouse and a long white silk scarf that resembled a lithe snake.

Mary Alice suspected her mother's ability to "move on," as she called it, accounted for her resilience and youthful appearance. She knew it was also a sick denial of reality and a form of control. What was real, what had happened or had not happened, was what Elizabeth decided had happened or had not happened. But Mary Alice was on a peace mission. Her goal was to keep Georgia's job and to appear to be subdued, even frightened.

"Thanks, Mama. How was your trip? Buy anything?" Through the pan-seared fresh tuna with pear, spinach and avocado salad and heavily sweetened iced tea, Mary Alice listened attentively to a litany of who bought what where and how much they paid. The ladies, all old friends, had had a ball in Atlanta.

"Of course, Anna Patton buys everything a size too small." Elizabeth snapped a chunk of pear in half. "Bless her heart; she hasn't been a size twelve since we were debutants together."

Anna Patton was one of Elizabeth Tate's best friends.

Mary Alice imagined her mother on trial for cruelty and vicious gossip. Anna Patton would be foreman of the jury.

"Maria says you've taken up residence in the carriage house," Elizabeth said.

"Until Sheree's trial is over," Mary Alice said, trying to eat a bite of the half-raw fish she detested.

"You're doing as I asked? Backing off as it were?" Elizabeth turned her profile as though she were in a soap opera anticipating a close-up.

"Yes. I plan to help Sheree buy clothes for the trial, things like that, but I won't be involved her defense." She thought of the log of her activities in her mother's desk drawer and had to dig her fingernails into her palm to ward off a confrontation.

Elizabeth rose from her place at the wrought iron table and walked around to Mary Alice. "It's for the best, dear." She put her hand on Mary Alice's shoulder in an imitation of care or comfort.

Mary Alice hated being called "dear" by anyone, especially by her mother. She imagined the heavy iron table falling over, pinning Elizabeth under it or crushing her well-turned ankles. Elizabeth would call "Dear, dear, help," but Mary Alice would turn a deaf ear.

"We'll have fun while you're here," Elizabeth said as if they were going to host a pajama party. "But don't worry. I won't intrude on your life or monitor your guests."

Mary Alice inferred that her mother meant it was okay for Zach to sleep over. What a hypocrite. Elizabeth had shredded friends whose daughters brought home boyfriends and were allowed to sleep with them. It was such poor taste, so déclassé. The sex didn't matter, the appearance did.

"Yes, Mama. Maybe later you can show me some of the clothes you bought."

Elizabeth's eyes lighted up like a Coney Island bally.

As they left the delicate white porch, Mary Alice asked, "Mama, do you still have the video camera you found in Sheree's apartment?"

Elizabeth stopped dead still. "Why?"

"Forensics can use it to make more sense of the videotape," Mary Alice said. She didn't add that the tape was at least temporarily missing.

"You're doing it. You're still doing it. On the case, fanning flames, putting yourself in danger. How can you be so stupid?"

"No, I'm not," Mary Alice said. "It's just that I'm the only one who can ask you for the camera without the police getting involved. I know you wouldn't want the Cana Police to search the house for it, and Sheree's lawyer might get a judge to order that. They'd rifle through everything." Mary Alice was amazed at her facility at lying. She hadn't even prepared.

"Let them ask. You stay out of it." Elizabeth narrowed her eyes and glared at Mary Alice. "I'm not easily fooled, Mary Alice, and you're not very good at concealing your feelings. If you help that Delio woman, I'll get rid of Georgia Horn. It's that simple."

"I understand," Mary Alice said. She wanted to scream, "If you get rid of Georgia, you'll never see me again and supposedly, the whole reason for protecting me is so that you can see me."

Elizabeth turned to go to her room. "I'm tired from the long drive. Think I'll take a nap."

Mary Alice made a violent gesture to her mother's back only to become aware of Maria silently watching her from down the hall.

Mary Alice strode out to the carriage house to get Boon. She imagined Elizabeth falling down the stairs a la Scarlet O'Hara. Her long white scarf would wind around her neck as she rolled and at the bottom she'd be as done-in as Isadora Duncan.

Mary Alice drove to Sheree's and found her in the scrubby back yard sitting in a saggy lawn chair. Mary Alice made a note to get some lawn furniture for the house. Home Depot had some on sale. Boon lay down in the shade of a 200 year old catalpa tree.

"Hey," Sheree said. She had been reading a Barbara Kingsolver novel that Mary Alice had given her.

"Hey yourself," Mary Alice said. She felt tense from the wrangle with her mother and didn't waste time getting to the point. "Sheree, Hollis Tubbs says that Doug was back in town looking for you."

Sheree's eyes flared.

"I have two questions. Did you see him and what the hell is his last name?"

"No, I ain't. Does he know where I am?" Sheree asked. She sounded like she wanted to see him if she hadn't.

"I don't know. But if you've seen him, I'd like to know."

"I told you no. And his last name's Quarles." She spelled it.

Sheree sounded if not irritated, at least less controllable or pliable. Maybe some of the gumption Mary Alice had been telling her she needed to find was finally surfacing.

"Doug Quarles is a suspect as far as I'm concerned."

"And if I talk to him, I am too?"

"I didn't say that."

"Right. I am anyway." Sheree closed the book.

"Ah, shit. Look, there isn't much to go on and now the damn videotape is missing." Mary Alice sat on the back door's stoop.

"Ms. Bardwell told me. Maybe there wasn't anything on the end anyway." Her tone softened.

"And maybe there was. She tell you about the photos of the bruises?"

"Yes. Think they'll exhume the body?"

"Exhume? Where'd you hear that?"

"*Law and Order*. It's pretty common," Sheree said.

Mary Alice wished she smoked. If she did, she'd be lighting up. She realized she didn't want to talk to Sheree about the case. Mary Alice was afraid she'd reveal something she wasn't supposed to repeat, and she knew that there was the slightest possibility that Sheree would repeat it to Doug Quarles who would repeat it to God knew who.

"Look, one other thing," Mary Alice said. "Tom Jaworski says it'd help if you were hypnotized to see what else you might recall about Scott. Would you be willing?"

"No. Absolutely not," Sheree got up knocking over the flimsy chair. "I don't want nobody in my head."

"It's not like that. A hypnotist cannot make you do anything you don't want to do," Mary Alice said, hearing her patronizing tone. "Skip it."

"I don't know why you trust him. He's a cop," Sheree said. "Another species. Your wanting to fool around with him shouldn't be part of your thinking on this."

"Me? You think I want to sleep with him?" Mary Alice played aghast to buy time. How had Sheree spotted it?

"Hell, I want to. If he wasn't a cop," Sheree said.

Mary Alice recognized just in time that this was a moment in which she could connect with Sheree. She dropped her defense. "He is pretty hot, isn't he?"

They laughed loud and their giggles eased the tension.

"Think anybody else would be able to tell I was interested?" Mary Alice asked.

Sheree laughed again, a deep, free sound.

Mary Alice hung out with Sheree for an hour. They ate Little Debbie Fancy Cakes washed down with Crystal Light Peach Tea. Again, Mary Alice remembered why it was impossible for her to abandon Sheree. She loved Sheree like a sister. Sheree touched some deep part of her psyche or soul. More mystical than rational, Mary Alice felt Sheree was some sort of cosmic test. Mary Alice couldn't save every stray, runaway or orphan, but she could save one, and if one could be saved, redemption for all was possible.

After she left, she drove around Cotashona County. She hoped Sheree wasn't lying to her, but wondered what she'd do if she found out Sheree had seen Doug. If their positions were reversed, wouldn't Mary Alice want to see an old boyfriend? Wouldn't she lie about it if she thought it had nothing to do with her murder trial? Probably so.

The rain had never materialized, but the temperature dropped. Fall was definitely gaining ground on summer. She passed an automobile graveyard where a hundred rusted cars sat like dead cicadas filling a shallow valley. Her father's favorite saying, *this too will pass*, floated through her head. But a lot of shit could happen in the meantime.

She smiled, thinking again how transparent she'd been about Tom Jaworski. In no time Sheree had understood Mary Alice's clothing and body language.

Tom Jaworski.

She fished her cell phone from her purse and without agonizing, pressed 019. She needed to tell him Doug's last name, to tell him somebody had been in the lake house. When Jaworski answered she said, "two" and hung up. Before she reached one of the six Cotashona River bridges, he called back.

"Tomorrow, same cabin, two p.m."

She clicked off without a word.

Mary Alice could feel her pulse race, yet she felt in control. The alluring Mr. Jaworski wasn't going to get her in the sack because first, she had a boyfriend, second, she didn't have a negative result on the pregnancy test, and third, because she suspected she liked the idea of a steamy tryst more than the fact of it. She didn't want to see Jaworski's mismatched socks, wipe up his dribbled mouthwash or pick up the coins that escaped his pockets into her sofa cushions.

She glanced in the back seat at the plastic Wal-Mart bag that contained the test kits. Boon's head rested on the bag.

I'll do it tonight. I'll do all four of them.

CHAPTER 28

B UT MARY ALICE DIDN'T USE even one of the pregnancy kits that Monday night. She was flat on her back in bed with food poisoning. Her mother had it too. They concurred it was the under-cooked tuna. Pregnancy testing would have to wait.

By late morning Tuesday, she felt well enough to eat crackers and drink herb tea. She intended to keep her two o'clock appointment with Jaworski no matter what. She took another slug of Pepto Bismol.

Bored, but too sick to do much, she unwrapped the pack of index cards. Sitting at the triple-draped table beside the window that overlooked the pool, she wrote down clues. On the second card she started adding sketches. One image per card: the person in the bathroom, the button, Katherine Bridges' absence, Katherine Bridges sounded scared to Arlene, bruises on Scott Bridges' body, migraine drug, buzzard in house, female called H. Tubbs— "There's trouble in 1-B."

Shadowy image at end of videotape, Boon barbed-wired, Scott Bridges' autopsy report-not usual coroner, Doug Quarles appearance before murder, Doug Quarles second appearance, did Sheree know about second appearance? Lost/stolen videotape and log of her activities in Elizabeth's desk.

The cards covered the table. She made one each for the rich man, poor man, beggar man, thief, doctor, lawyer, merchant and chief. She thought her sketch of Leonard Bass, poor man, was quite a good likeness.

She tried to arrange them up in some meaningful order, but found there were at least two orders—chronological time and the time in which she discovered the clues. Then she remembered Kinsey Millhone and that what mattered to the index card system was moving the cards around so that unusual juxtapositions occurred. The cards functioned to stimulate the creative, less logical parts of the brain. She put Hollis Tubbs' mysterious voice in 1-B card next to Katherine Bridges' card. Mary Alice had not tried to locate any of Katherine's relatives in Corinth. She made a note to contact Patsilu English, who practically ran the historical society in Corinth. Patsilu knew everybody living and most of the dead. Mary Alice considered calling her, but decided a surprise visit would be better. Maybe Thursday. She had to meet Tom Jaworski this afternoon, and Zach had invited her to dinner Wednesday night.

By noon, Mary Alice felt well enough to wiggle into her tightest jeans. She topped it with a fitted white shirt with long tails. She wore heels because she liked the contrast between jeans and heels and thought all men liked high-heeled shoes on women. A hundred women's magazines made it clear that heels made legs look longer and slimmer, an asset in attracting a mate. Her Daddy believed men favored them because women couldn't run in heels.

She wasn't out of the driveway before her cell phone rang. It was her mother.

"Where are you going? You're sick," Elizabeth said. She sounded like she wanted Mary Alice to be as ill as she was.

"How are you feeling, Mama?" Mary Alice said. She sped up.

"Terrible. I asked you a question."

"Just out for some air. I'm feeling better." Mary Alice knew she felt better because she had only eaten a few bites of the fish. The rest, she'd scraped into a wad of Kleenexes and deposited, first in her purse and later in the toilet.

"Dr. Mason called in a prescription for me at Walgreen's. Can you pick it up?"

"I'll try, Mama. Don't they deliver?"

"Yes, but if you're just out getting air, can't you pick it up?"

"Air is in the country, not in the shopping center."

"Fine. I'll wait for the delivery. Maybe it'll get here by tomorrow." She hung up.

Mary Alice had a vision of Elizabeth, dehydrated and pale, on a huge canopied bed like the one King Louis slept in at Versailles. Mary Alice would show her mother index cards on which were printed all of Elizabeth's shortcomings and sins. Mary Alice would read each aloud and flip it onto the bed until Elizabeth was buried under a snowy paper blanket.

Mary Alice drove carefully to the cabin in the woods. She changed her route and watched for anyone following. There was no one. She felt her heart rev.

However, although the door was unlocked, there was no one in the cabin. She was sure she'd gotten the time right. She'd said the code word two, and he'd said two p.m., same cabin. She wandered around the single room resisting the urge to dust and tidy up. A male domain, it still showed the detritus of the last hunting expedition, cigarette ashes, mud and poorly washed dishes. She sat on the bed feeling dizzy. She'd forgotten to bring water and didn't trust that the water from the sink faucet was potable.

A red wasp outside tapped at the window. Slowly a creepy feeling crawled up her back. Tom Jaworski hadn't come because something was wrong, something had happened. He couldn't risk leading someone to her at the cabin. He couldn't even risk calling. She knew she had to get out and fast.

She tried to remember what she'd touched. Everything. No use in wiping fingerprints. But it wasn't against the law for her to meet Tom Jaworski at a remote hunting cabin. It might be called tacky, but never illegal. She grabbed her purse and ran to the car. The people who cared about her secret meeting with Jaworski weren't interested in the tacky aspects.

Please start. Please start.

The BMW sputtered. She cranked again and again, risking running down the battery. *Start damnit.* The engine caught.

She turned around and raced down the dirt drive kicking up a tornado of dust in her wake. She didn't care. She had a bad feeling that wouldn't go away.

Safe, five miles away and on the main highway, she called Georgia at the Women's Center.

"Where are you?" Georgia asked. "I can barely hear you."

"In the car."

"Tom Jaworski is in the hospital. His car ran off the road and rolled."

Mary Alice thought her heart had stopped. She slowed to twenty miles per hour. "How bad is he?"

"Not conscious. He's in the ICU."

"When?" In her head Mary Alice repeated *Oh my god* over and over.

"Late last night, early this morning. I just heard about it," Georgia said.

"What do the police say?"

"Car wreck, no alcohol involved, who knows."

It was no accident.

Mary Alice looked in her rear view mirror. She wanted to go to the hospital to see for herself, but knew that was stupid because it would expose their relationship and because the hospital wouldn't let her see him anyway. "Lord," Mary Alice said.

"Anything you want to tell me?" Georgia asked.

Mary Alice realized Georgia suspected that Mary Alice had finally gotten Tom Jaworski's help, and that if he were involved in finishing what Scott Bridges had started, the probability existed that his accident was no accident.

"No," Mary Alice said. She had to think things through before she talked.

He's identified one of them. They know.

Who else could help her? Tom could tell her who to go to, but he wasn't saying anything for the moment.

"Georgia, I can't hear you. You're breaking up."

"Call me later," Georgia said.

When Mary Alice got home she read the short piece in the newspaper about Tom Jaworski's accident. It had occurred on a deserted road that she knew was a few miles from the hunting cabin. The paper called it an accident. The article was brief because it must have been reported just before the paper went to press. Wednesday's paper would feature a photo of the smashed car and an official picture of Officer Jaworski. Unless he was dead by then.

Please don't die. I got you into this. I'm sorry. Tom, please don't die.

CHAPTER 29

B Y Wednesday morning Mary Alice had fully recovered from food poisoning. Her mother, not so fortunate, sent Maria with a message.

"Mrs. Tate is still very ill," Maria said, inferring that it was somehow Mary Alice's fault. "She's resting and doesn't want to be disturbed." She looked straight at Mary Alice without expression.

"I wouldn't dream of it," Mary Alice said. She couldn't judge where Maria really stood with regard to Elizabeth Tate. Maybe Maria was only protecting her job, but she seemed to Mary Alice to be protective of her dragon-lady boss. When Maria left Mary Alice's carriage house retreat, she resisted checking that Maria wasn't outside the door, eavesdropping.

When Zach called that afternoon, Mary Alice told him about the tainted tuna.

"Want to cancel tonight?" he asked.

"I'll be fine. What are we having?"

"Not tuna. It's a surprise. Shall I pick you up?"

"Why don't I just drive over?" she said.

"Come about seven, and you can watch me cook," he said. "And I'm making a sinful Mississippi Mud dessert."

She hung up and wished she could tell Zach that a really good dessert for her would involve Kraft's marshmallow cream, coffee ice cream and hot fudge sauce.

Mary Alice pawed through her closet for something appropriate to wear. It didn't escape her attention that she chose differently for Zach than for Jaworski. She found a pretty cream colored pants outfit that was sophisticated and would suit the cooler evening temperature. It looked like something a governor's wife might wear.

Through informal channels—the wife of the chief surgeon at the hospital—Mary Alice had found out that Tom Jaworski was in critical but stable condition. There was nothing Mary Alice could do until he could talk to her. The best plan was to act as they had agreed. To that she added praying for him.

When she arrived at Zach's house, Mary Alice was greeted with a warm hug, the kind you get after you've been away a long time.

"I missed you," he murmured in her ear.

"You've forgiven me for harassing Leonard Bass?"

"Who's Leonard Bass?"

Mary Alice relaxed. With her ex-husband, last night's incident would have been a two week confrontation of blame and guilt. Zach had a big heart. She was beginning to believe that qualities like steady and caring might outrank gutsy and chancy.

"What'd you like to drink? Vodka tonic?"

"Great. Make it light. I don't want my stomach to rebel."

"A congressman gave me this Russian vodka. Says it's the best in the world." He mixed two drinks.

Soft jazz filled the living room; music that offended no one but inspired no one. The house looked exactly the same as the last time she had visited. She could see the dining room table set for two with heavy silver flatware, starched linen napkins and candles. A masculine version of her mother's house.

"How was your trip to Atlanta?" she asked.

"Huh? Oh. Atlanta. Fine. Got a lot of work done," he said, handing her a tall vodka tonic. "Cheers. To health."

"To health."

"Were you working on a case or on the election?" she asked.

"Both," he said. "Let's sit a minute before I start cooking."

They sat on the sofa and turned to face one another.

"What'd you do while I was away?" he asked, reaching for her hand.

"Besides getting sick from raw fish, not much," she said and took a sip of her drink.

Mary Alice figured Zach knew about Tom Jaworski's accident, but she didn't trust herself to discuss him. She didn't even want to think about Jaworski when she was with Zach.

They discussed cars, the crime rate in Atlanta and the weather, which had shifted to early fall. He told a blond joke that involved a blonde who expected alligator shoes to be found on the feet of alligators.

Mary Alice laughed.

"I'd better launch into the final phases of our dinner," he said. "Want to watch?"

"That won't ruin the surprise?"

"Okay, smarty pants. You stay out here and put on some music you like." Zach rose. "Can I freshen up your drink first?"

She shook her head. "One is my limit." She could already feel the vodka pleasantly snaking through her bloodstream to her brain.

Zach went into his huge kitchen that was more like a laboratory. She heard drawers open and close and utensils bang.

Mary Alice looked at Zach's extensive collection of CD's all arranged by type and by the last name of the artist. She looked through the classical stuff, but the mood she wanted wasn't Vivaldi or Bach. She heard the brief gunning of a mixer in the kitchen. She had to pick something.

She spotted Frank Sinatra's Capitol Years CD, grabbed it and turned off the mindless jazz. She heard Zach open and close the refrigerator and then, just before Sinatra's intro began, she heard something else. Whistling.

She barely heard the low and breathy sounds, and she probably would have paid no attention except that the hairs on the back of her neck stood on end. Kinesthetic memory. Quietly she moved toward the kitchen door. She could see him sorting through a drawer filled with kitchen implements. He was whistling a tune she'd heard before. She didn't know its name, but it was the same tune the man in Shcree's apartment had whistled as he searched for something he didn't want anyone else to find. He pulled a garlic press from the drawer.

Mary Alice's mouth went dry. She told herself that it was impossible. Zach was the DA. He was the law. In a hideous spiral her thoughts raced down the path of events she'd missed. Zach needed money for the gubernatorial election and the Cana drug depot was supplying it. Then Scott Bridges became a threat. Zach knew Sheree had migraines and about the relationship between Sheree and Scott. Zach had killed the cop and framed Sheree for the murder. Zach was the shadowy image on the end of the now-missing videotape which of course he had destroyed. She couldn't move. *God. And I was telling him everything I knew.*

"You okay?" Zach called.

Mary Alice couldn't speak. Her mind screamed at her that she must say, yes I'm fine. Is the music okay? She must act normal. But she stood frozen by the kitchen door. She could see him, but he couldn't see her. She saw him look up and then turn to put a Pyrex dish in the oven. She knew he'd come to check on her next. Frank Sinatra sang a chilling counterpoint: *Put your dreams away for another day.*

Bathroom. On tiptoe she streaked down the hall, disappearing inside the bathroom just as Zach came out of the kitchen.

"Mary Alice?" he called and called again.

She flushed the toilet in answer.

She heard him walk away, maybe back into the kitchen. The bathroom had one very high stained glass window. She couldn't stay forever. She pressed her mouth to the faucet, gulped and tried out her voice. It shook. She glanced in the mirror over the sink and nearly fell down. She was chalk white.

She opened the bathroom door and walked down the hall toward the kitchen and living room. She saw her purse on the sofa. Zach was busy in the kitchen again, and he was whistling. Mary Alice knew her mother was right that it was impossible for Mary Alice to hide her feelings. She'd never make it through dinner with a murderer. She heard her Daddy's voice inside tell her to get the hell out.

When Zach's back was turned toward the oven, she darted past the door to the sofa. She grabbed her purse and on tiptoe slipped to the foyer. She could see the BMW in the driveway. She heard something in the kitchen clatter and took the opportunity to pull open the front door. She didn't bother to close it. She ran to the car, jumped in and locked the door. Her hands shook so badly she couldn't get the key out of her purse and when she finally did, she couldn't insert it in the ignition.

Have to hurry. He'll notice. He'll come.

She was panting loudly, struggling with the key. It slipped into the slot. She turned it. Nothing. Not even the usual *rhum-a-rhum-a-rhum* noise. She could see the front door gaping open and light pouring out into the dark. She tried again and again and heard the car strain. Rhum-a-rhum-a-rhum.

"Come on. Come on."

It wasn't going to crank. There was only one thing to do. Run.

She unlocked the door, opened it and screamed. Zach stood by the car door.

"Where you going, baby?" he asked.

"I don't feel well, Zach." She sounded like Minnie Mouse.

"You don't look well either. Think maybe the food poisoning came back?"

He pulled her out of the car.

"Yes. I do. I think it did." She knew she sounded distraught and hoped it would pass for sick. She thought about just running for it. Maybe a car would pass before he caught her.

"Come on back inside, honey. I have something for a queasy stomach," Zach said.

She turned away from him, but had taken only one step before he caught her arm and with his other hand turned her face toward his.

"You know, don't you? Somehow you know," he said. He said it quietly with no emotion just as he might have said, please pass the barbeque sauce.

"You killed him. The drugs. Money to run for governor," she said, knowing lying was futile. Her eyes bugged with terror and her whole body announced that she knew she was in great danger.

"Mary Alice, you've gone and ruined everything now," he said in the same even tone.

She felt her lips moving, but no sound came out. It was like in a nightmare when you can't scream even though the monster is about to clamp its sharp teeth through your head.

He gripped her face, and she watched the thoughts turn in his mind as he came to a decision about what he had to do. It didn't take long.

"Zach," she chirped.

In a quick move he forced her arm behind her. Pain shot though her shoulder; she screamed and felt his hand on her throat choking off both sound and air. Then she felt a blow to the side of her head and everything went black

When she woke up she was aware that she was in a moving car. She tried to swallow and wondered if she'd ever be able to talk normally again. She lifted her head and realized her wrists were taped together. They rested in her lap, useless.

"I'm sorry about all this, Mary Alice," Zach said. "Really. I had you picked to be Mississippi's First Lady. But you only have yourself to blame."

Mary Alice tried to say his name but it came out as a squawk. Her head throbbed.

"I warned you to back off, stay out. It makes me mad—that little tramp you just had to save. And for what? But I must say I underestimated you. You just kept digging. And when you and Jaworski teamed up, I knew things weren't going to work out. Did you fuck him in that hunting cabin?"

Mary Alice struggled to relieve the burning in her throat. The noise that came out of her mouth sounded like a protest. They were barreling down a dark road in what she realized was her car. For him it had started.

"No matter. Going through bank records, he would have found out something pretty quick. We had to do something. Would you like a little music?" He snapped on the radio and clicked through stations with baseball, advertising and preaching. He turned it off. "Aren't you going to ask who 'we' is? Well, you already think Leonard Bass is in on it, but would you guess that the chief of police is helping. Another cop too and Mickey Bartel, the biggest insurance agent in North Mississippi. A big help moving the money around. Doc Hodges is hiding the goods in his tobacco warehouse. Nobody here ever grew tobacco. Wonder why he called it that." He slowed the car. "So, did you fuck him?"

By the time Zach turned on the county road that led to the lake house, Mary Alice had no doubt that he was going to kill her. She considered she had two options. She could go insane with fear until she was dead, or she could look for an opportunity to escape.

He wants to make it look like an accident or like somebody else did it.

Then she remembered Georgia asking, "what would I do if fear wasn't controlling me and all my decisions? When I stopped being so scared, lots of ideas popped up." Georgia had been about to lose her job; Mary Alice was about to lose her life.

She struggled to calm her breathing by focusing on the air as it entered and left her body. Breath in, breath out. Her Daddy had told her that when she focused on her breath, she wasn't in her mind, her thoughts. In the space of no-thought, God could speak to her. She only vaguely heard Zach behind her breath.

"I am sorry about the buzzard in your nice dining room and about the barbed wire on Boon. I was careful not to hurt him. I was just trying to scare you off so that exactly this wouldn't happen." He looked over at her, smiled, and shrugged.

She was certain now that he was headed for the lake. Maybe she could somehow hit the panic button on the burglar alarm.

"I want to thank you for pointing out to me that I had showed up at the end of that videotape," he said. "You're right. With modern technology, it's possible that I'd be identified. But when you gave me back the videotape I thought everything was going to be okay. I buried it. I even stole the camera from your mama just in case."

Mary Alice continued breathing and could feel herself calming. Saliva returned to her mouth and throat.

Zach pounded the steering wheel. "Shit. Katherine Bridges ran away. Why couldn't you have just backed off? A conviction and three years wouldn't be anything to that little Delio bitch. Didn't it get your attention when I practically ran you off the road? I could have killed you, you know. But I didn't want to kill you." He tapped the steering wheel. "But I wanted to kill that fucking cop Jaworski. Watching his car flip and roll was a pleasure." His mouth hardened into a tight line.

From the look on his face, Mary Alice thought that in Zach's mind, another man had taken his woman. He'd been scorned, humiliated. Maybe killing her would be a pleasure, too.

He turned onto the gravel driveway that led to the lake house.

Mary Alice tried to anticipate what he might do. She tested the duct tape around her wrists; nothing moved. All she could do was be alert. But she noticed that Zach's running commentary seemed to be disjointed. Maybe that was common to murderers preparing to murder again. His justifications sounded more and more juvenile.

"Your mother was even helping me keep track of you. But you wouldn't stop. Naturally, Elizabeth didn't know what she was doing. She thought we were protecting you." He chuckled.

Mary Alice worked her tongue in her mouth so that when she had the chance to speak, she'd be ready.

Zach stopped the car in the driveway close to the house. He got out and came around to her side of the car.

Mary Alice thought of trying to lock him out, but with her hands taped together she knew she'd never get both doors locked. Then she heard the keys jingle as they slid into his pocket.

He opened her door, reached in and jerked her by the hair to a standing position.

She stifled a scream. She needed to be conscious if she was going to talk him out of killing her.

He pushed her ahead of him toward the huge deck that ran down to the water. She stumbled on the slope, but he held her fast, tearing her hair.

Clay. Clay is always around. Maybe he'll see or hear. Unless he's one of them.

Mary Alice made as much noise as possible clomping over the wood deck. Zach didn't seem to mind as long as she kept moving. Then she heard herself speaking.

"Are you the one who called Hollis Tubbs?" She realized that Zach wanted to talk about the case, the murder, all of it. And the longer she talked, the longer she lived.

He said in a falsetto. "Trouble in 1-B. Pretty good, don't you think? Of course that old sot Tubbs can't hear for shit. Almost a waste of acting talent."

They stood at the dock's edge next to the boat. He kept his hand on her in a tangle of clothing and hair.

"Pretty smart how you framed Sheree," she said. "Genius really. To use her migraine medicine."

"I must admit it was pretty sweet." He smiled. "Very helpful to have access to records on both of them."

"But, of course, there was the one screw up," she said. An idea, born of desperation, percolated. She might have a chance to unnerve him just enough to get away. It could backfire; nothing was sure, but she had nothing to lose by laying the groundwork.

"What screw up?" He tightened his hold.

"The button you left in the bathroom. The one you came back for." *Keep him talking.* She felt his grip on her hair tighten. "I was there, Zach. Inches away, behind the shower curtain."

His grip shifted again, and he mumbled, "Whaa?"

"What's that tune you whistle under your breath?" she asked.

"That's how you knew. Goddamn. I could have taken care of Jaworski without you ever knowing. Don't you see? You have fucked this up." His grip tightened. "We could have had a wonderful life. This is all your goddamned fault."

She could feel the hair at the base of her skull ripping out.

"But what were you going to do if Sheree didn't have enough of her medicine?" she asked. His grip relaxed. "Did you bring extra?"

"Providence provided. When I got to the apartment, the door was unlocked, and they were both passed out. I brought some of the drug, but then I found Sheree's supply in the bathroom. Ten little cartridges with, as it turned out, her fingerprints on most of them. I planned to shoot him if I had to. The bitch, too. A murder-suicide."

"But Scott Bridges woke up?"

"The drug worked fast. And the alcohol he'd drunk helped too. I knew it would. The internet is a powerful source of information. There was an online video about the dangers of combining drugs. Did you know all migraine drugs are contraindicated for heart patients? Contraindicated. Don't you love jargon?"

He seemed to be reliving the scene. "I popped in a monster dose, must have hit a blood vessel. Then I used her little single-dose vials. I think the heart attack woke him up. I had to kneel on him to hold him down. Your little drunk friend never even turned over. See, everything but you was conspiring to help me."

"But you left a coat button?"

"You can understand; I wanted to get away. But again providence helped. I realized that night at your party it had fallen off, but the police never found it."

"No, I found it." Mary Alice felt sick thinking how Zach had come to her party shortly after killing a man.

"I assumed as much. Where is it?"

"I gave it to Tom Jaworski," she lied. "Ask him. Your fingerprints must be on it." She intended to make Zach think he might not get away with two murders, but then she realized that if Zach killed her, Tom, helpless in the ICU, would be the third. The DA wouldn't have any trouble getting a private interview, after which Jaworski would stop breathing.

Mary Alice took another slow deep breath.

"Fuck it. The button doesn't matter. You took it; it's not evidence any more." He released her neck and reached out for her bathing suit which she had left on the deck railing to dry. "Put it on." He shoved it into her hands.

She heard the shift in his voice. He was finished recapping the crime. She took the swim suit. With her wrists taped, getting it on wouldn't be easy.

"Put it on." he said again.

She unzipped the slacks and let them fall to the deck. If they were going in the water, a bathing suit was a plus. With difficulty, she tugged the suit up over her hips and stood clutching the top part of it.

He watched. In the dim light, her skin looked pearlescent.

"So beautiful," he murmured. "What a fucking waste."

"I can't get my top off with my hands taped together," she said.

Zach looked puzzled. He hadn't counted on this. "Fuck it. Leave it on. I'll take care of it later." He spun her around. "Get in the boat," he said. Holding onto her, he forced her to step into the center of the boat. He jumped in behind, and they both sat as the boat lurched. He released the mooring and paddled away from the dock. "We're going to take a little boat ride now. Too bad the moon's so pitiful tonight."

She sat in front of him in easy reach. "Zach, if you kill me, they'll find out." She heard the fear that coated her voice. There was nothing in the boat she could grab to hit him with. All she could do was keep talking, wait and watch.

"They might. That's why you're going to have an accident. You've been upset about Sheree's trial and Georgia losing her job, which by the way she is going to lose. And you weren't thinking too clearly so you came over to the house, put on your bathing suit and went for a swim. You've swum at night before. But this time you got a cramp, got some water in your lungs and were too far from shore. I'll be distraught. Grief-stricken over the loss of my bride-to-be."

The boat was making rapid progress across the lake. Mary Alice guessed that he meant to drown her in the shallow waters of the far shore where he'd have complete control. There wasn't much time before he would make his move.

"They'll find out because of the videotape," she said, her voice steady, belying the pounding in her chest. She had to seed doubt and cloud his thinking.

"No, that's gone. It's toast."

"Not the copy."

There was not a sound on the lake. Even the boat as it cut through the water was noiseless.

"You're lying."

"Are you sure?"

More dead quiet.

"Where is it?" He wrenched her around to face him. Even in the dark, she could see his crazed face. His mouth was twisted as though his last words were still on his lips. "Where is it?" He clamped his hand on her throat, but she could see that he believed there was a copy of the tape that could put him on death row.

She struggled. "It's here," she said. She couldn't risk being choked. There wasn't time. She needed to be able to breathe. She first had thought of telling him the tape was back at the house, hoping he'd make her take him to it. That would buy her more time. But then another idea nudged her panicked brain.

"Where?" His fingers dug into her neck.

"In the first aid kit under the bow."

As he moved toward the bow, the boat pitched in the water. The white first aid kit shone in the dark. As he passed her, Mary

Alice pushed her full weight against him, sending both of them flying into the cold water. The small boat rocked back, and Mary Alice heard a dull whap. She kicked hard to surface and to get a breath. With her hands duct taped together she had only her legs to power her. As she broke through to the surface, Zach did, too.

"You bitch," he yelled, thrashing toward her.

Her plan had worked. In the deep water, she had a better chance than anywhere. She shoved him, but he grabbed her tight and pushed her head under the water. She elbowed him in the ribs, heard him grunt and felt him release her. She snatched a deep breath before he was on her again.

And then she sank, using her taped hands to hasten the trip toward the bottom.

He sank with her, at first pushing on her head and then just holding onto her.

She knew she had at least a minute of air, and bet that she could outlast him. Thirty seconds later, Zach let go and kicked to the surface. She had to decide whether to use her remaining seconds under water to chew the duct tape from her wrists or to swim away. She kicked hard, holding her hands in close and keeping her head straight in front to cut resistance. She figured she'd make maybe thirty yards before she had to surface and that when she did, he'd know where she was.

When she broke through, she heard him beating the water. Something wet slapped the side of the boat. He was taking off his clothes. She knew that she would have had little chance if she were being weighed down by her slacks. The sleeveless top she still wore was bad enough. She sucked in several breaths and sank. Maybe he hadn't heard her. She went to work on the tape and as she chewed she heard, Oh God, Oh God, Oh God in her head. She felt a rip at the edge of one strip of tape, but she couldn't free herself before she needed air.

When she surfaced, in the darkness she saw his white face next to the boat. He was holding on to it. "You goddamn bitch." He pushed away and swam toward her in a sure, strong crawl.

She surface dove and kicked hard, trying to put distance between them. Without her arms to help her swim, the water felt like cold honey. She sensed him closing in, and she was running out of air. She surfaced again.

This time he was only a few yards away, but he was turned toward the boat scanning the lake for her. She could see how far they'd come, and that they weren't too far from the shoreline. She dove into the black again and headed for the cliffs.

She was a stronger swimmer than Zach, and she knew he was tiring. And Mary Alice had another advantage. She knew the lake. She frog-kicked hard toward the rocky precipice she had jumped off as a kid. It was deep, and there were sharp rocks on the bottom. By touch alone she found one and worked the tape against it, but had to give up when her air ran low. At the surface, she saw him. He was panting and growling, and he was coming straight for her. He rose out of the water like a dolphin and landed square on top of her. She felt his hands on the duct tape band, yanking her up to the surface.

"I'll kill you. I'll smash your skull, you fucking bitch," he said between pants and chokes.

Mary Alice could hardly speak. She kicked hard in the water, rising up and looked over Zach's head toward the shore. "Clay," she yelled. "I'm over here. Help."

Zach took the bait and turned. Mary Alice jerked her hands down hard and was surprised to feel them separate as the duct tape gave way. By the time Zach was certain there was no Clay, Mary Alice had slipped out of sight into the dark water.

With her hands freed, she swam easily underwater toward the rock wall. When she came up for air again, she heard Zach swear and saw him alter course to swim toward her. She looked up and made out the lightning shaped mark on the cliff above. A quick surface dive led her to the depths beside the submerged wall of stone.

Zach followed.

Like a blind fish, she felt for the opening that she knew existed directly beneath the zigzagged stain on the wall above. She pretended she was swimming into the secret cave for the first time. Her Daddy had shown it to her, because he didn't want her to mistake it for a safe cave. It was actually a series of caves in which her father had warned one could become lost forever.

She knew the plan wasn't infallible, but that inside the caves she'd have the advantage of knowing the terrain. She could hide or better, lead him into a trap.

When her hands found the opening, she looked behind her and was shocked to see Zach right behind her. In the dark, he looked like a hungry great white shark. She swam inside the cave.

The cave, about thirty yards across was pitch dark. When she'd first seen it as a girl, her father had shone a light on its damp gray walls. They'd played with the echoes, and he'd shown her another smaller, connected cavern.

The water inside felt cooler. Not trusting luck, she swam straight for the second submerged opening. She heard Zach surface for air. She stayed under. As soon as she was through the smaller ragged opening of the second cave, she pulled her body above the hole and held onto the rocks and roots. She tried to slip off her top, but the wet cloth gripped the buttons.

Slowly, she poked her head above the surface and sucked desperate breaths. Then she felt the currents as Zach swam through the opening beneath her. He'd found the second cave. She ducked below the water's surface as he broke through it, but she could hear her name echoing on the walls. He called to her in water-logged, furious bursts, "Mary-yal-ish." He gasped for air. "Mary-yal-ish?"

Warily, she reversed her path and noiselessly swam underwater passing by the entrance into the third cave. With tiny flutter kicks, she swam back into the first cave. Being quiet was critical as any sound, even a ripple, would reverberate and reveal her whereabouts. Her lungs were about to burst, but she couldn't risk snatching a breath. If he heard her now, he'd follow her out. She kicked hard and thought of all the swim meets and races she'd won. Her Daddy had always said she won because she didn't give up.

She felt the rocky edge of the cave opening and shot through to the surface. Exhausted, she grabbed a crevice in the shear rock cliff and held on by her fingertips, gasping.

She had no idea how long it would take Zach to find his way out. She had no time to lose. Keeping close to the shoreline, she swam until the cliff sloped down to a rocky coast. She crawled ashore and started running like a crazy woman.

It was impossible to see or hear Zach pursuing her. She knew he was still on her trail and that on land he was stronger and faster. Rocks tore her bare feet. Her shoulder and her head throbbed like alternating drum beats, but she ran on, the unfastened top of her bathing suit flapping against her thighs.

Stumbling in the dark, she ran headlong into a thicket of briars which tore at her bare skin.

Don't panic. Think. Think. You know this land. You grew up playing here.

She tried to slow her breathing when a sound from near the water's edge startled her. Frantically, she charged along the path of least resistance trying to put distance between her and the noise. Then she heard them—footsteps behind her. Running fast.

He grabbed her from behind, saying her name. She felt his hand on her breast. A scream exploded from her, and she twisted to break the hold. Believing death was imminent, she turned and tore at his face. He could kill her, but she wasn't going down without a fight. Her death wouldn't look accidental.

"Mary Alice." He held her roughly at arms length.

When he changed his grip, she struck. Her fist connected with his jaw followed by a terrible pain in her wrist. She hit the dirt face down. Then a blinding light doused everything. Another man was there. Zach? Then she heard Sheriff Gelly's unmistakable redneck accent command her to freeze. Someone pinned her arms while someone else held her legs. She had no reserves. It was over.

So Gelly was in on it. Too late to tell, too late to warn Sheree.

They talked in whispers, and she guessed they were trying to decide how to finish her and dispose of the body. She felt like telling them that if they put her back in the cave she'd just been in, nobody would ever find her. In fact, she knew that there were a series of a dozen linked caves, each smaller than the one before it. Her Daddy had said that there was methane gas trapped in some that would kill a person foolish enough to go inside.

"Mary Alice, Mary Alice," Sheriff Gelly repeated as he turned her over.

She squinted in the glare of the flashlight, and he aimed it away from her face.

"She's hurt pretty bad," the other man said. His voice was flat, emotionless. "There's blood all over her."

Mary Alice couldn't make sense of much, but the word blood registered. Had she somehow hurt herself running in the dark? Had Zach cut her and in the cold water and ensuing panic, she'd not felt it? Were they going to let her bleed to death, saving themselves the trouble of murdering her? She tried to sit up, but was immediately restrained.

"You bastards," she said. After that there was only a fuzzy blackness.

CHAPTER 30

MARY ALICE FELT HERSELF MOVING. Bright lights appeared to flash as she moved. Was this the light after death she was supposed to follow? She couldn't open her eyes.

I'm still alive.

Everything hurt so much that she imagined a quart of morphine wouldn't be sufficient to alter the pain. She tried to put her hand on her burning abdomen, but a needle in her arm twisted and pricked so she gave up.

When the moving stopped, she forced her eyes open. The lights stung her retinas. She closed her eyes. Her wrist and shoulder hurt unbearably, and her guts felt like she'd swallowed some of Marshall's Red Devil Lye. She slipped back into the darkness and found her Daddy.

"Darlin', you rest. I'm here. It's gonna be okey-dokey," she heard him say.

Oh. This must be the end. Daddy's helping me cross over.

WHEN SHE OPENED HER EYES again a sea of faces surrounded her. She recognized her Mama, Georgia and Sheriff Gelly. Some medical-looking people stood on the periphery.

"Mary Alice, my baby," Elizabeth wailed when she saw her daughter's eyes flutter.

Mary Alice heard Georgia sigh.

"Can I ask her a few questions?" Sheriff Gelly asked a large woman clothed in white.

"Make it quick. Don't wear her out."

"Mary Alice, did Zach Towree tell you anything about the drug trafficking he's involved in? It's important we move fast if we're going to catch them."

"Is Sheree okay?" She was aware she was speaking very slowly as though in an underwater dream.

"Sheree's fine," Gelly said. "Try to focus. Did Zach tell you anything about where the drugs are stored or who else is involved?"

"Zach killed Scott. Made y'all think Sheree did it. And he destroyed the videotape." Slowly, bit by bit, Mary Alice repeated what Zach had told her about Leonard Bass, the Chief of Police, Mickey Bartel and Doc Hodges' tobacco warehouse. "But Tom already had some of the bad guys figured out," she said.

Tom Jaworski. He wasn't safe. He was in a coma in the hospital. She had to get to him to warn him. She tore the covers aside and sat up.

"Whoa," the doctor said, running to the bedside. "Where you going?"

"Tom Jaworski. I have to warn him. Zach—"

"Officer Jaworski's safe," the doctor said. "He's conscious. He's the one who told the sheriff about—It's all over, Mary Alice."

She sank back on the clean smooth sheets and felt the soft pillow under her cheek. The bad people were going to be caught, Sheree was free, and Georgia would keep her job. Tom was okay. What about Zach?

"Where's Zach?" she asked. The sheriff was no longer in the room nor was her mother. Georgia moved in close.

"No one knows yet."

"He tried to drown me." Mary Alice felt tears come. "He followed me into a cave." She remembered the terror of the ordeal: Zach's maniacal face in the dashboard light, him ripping her hair and the feel of his hands pushing her under water.

"Take it easy," Georgia said. "Don't think about him now. There'll be time later."

Mary Alice stopped crying. Any movement hurt; salty tears burned the deep scratches on her face.

"There's manhunt on for him," Georgia said. "He's not the kind who can hide too easily," Georgia said.

"Am I hurt bad? Tell me the truth. I can't feel much right now." She glanced at the IV suspended above the bed.

"Broken wrist from hitting the sheriff, dislocated shoulder, scrapes, contusions and a concussion. You'll be out of here in a day."

"What about the blood?"

"Blood?"

"Was I cut?" Mary Alice asked. "I wasn't shot. I'd know if I'd been shot. They said 'blood' and I had blood all down my front. Everywhere."

"Menstrual blood," Georgia said. "Wouldn't you know you'd get your period just when you're running for your life?"

Mary Alice ran a hand under the covers and felt the sanitary napkin between her legs. She wasn't pregnant. She had four pregnancy detection kits and no use for them. Tears gushed down her face. Tears of relief and of sadness.

Georgia said nothing.

"Where's Mama?" Mary Alice asked. She wiped her face on the pillow slip.

"She's in the hall recovering. You know your mama. She's making this whole deal all about her. The doctor had to prescribe some Xanax for her. Want me to call her in?"

"Not right now," Mary Alice said. "Thanks, Georgia. I'm glad you're here. I need a friend."

"So do I." Georgia took Mary Alice's hand and held it gently.

Mary Alice could feel waves of sleep coming for her. She felt gauzy white fluff raking over her, stealing her will to stay awake. She tried to ask Georgia to bring her a Twinkie or a Snowball, but she couldn't form the words.

"You saved Sheree," Georgia whispered. "You're a hero."

Mary Alice shook her head, no.

"Yes. You stuck by Sheree," Georgia said. "You never gave up. That's what made the difference. If you hadn't, they would have gotten away with it all."

Mary Alice struggled to stay awake. She wanted to hear what Georgia was saying. Maybe her sleuthing hadn't been perfect, but she'd had obstinacy, grit and tenacity. She'd prevailed. She saw Georgia's lips moving but the sound was distorted.

"And I think this is a perfect time for the Women's Center to have a huge fundraiser," Georgia said.

Mary Alice closed her eyes and remembered a party with an ocean of champagne punch drenching the kitchen floor. It seemed ages ago.

The End

ABOUT THE
AUTHOR

DINAH LEAVITT SWAN, A NATIVE of the Gulf Coast of Mississippi, is the author of *Cana Rising* and *Now Playing in Cana*, the first two books in the Mary Alice Tate Southern Mystery Series.

She's also written eighteen plays—all produced, five national award winners—and the women's lit novels, *Romantic Fever* and *Hacienda Blues*. She lives in Colorado with her husband and dog.

An excerpt from the second book in the series,
**NOW PLAYING IN CANA:
A MARY ALICE TATE SOUTHERN MYSTERY**
by Dinah Swan

Chapter One

February 26, Monday

The lights of the town appeared. The foggy sleet had kept most of Cana, Mississippi's 15,000 residents at home, and the yellow lab named Boon seemed puzzled by this midnight run.

"We're almost there," Mary Alice told the dog, who eyed the wipers fighting a losing battle.

She'd explained to him about leaving her cell phone at the theatre, but now questioned the urgency.

When the car slipped into a fog bank thick as dough, she hit the brake. The old BMW fishtailed and spun a one-eighty sending the car into the opposite lane. The centrifugal force slammed her head against the window and sent Boon to the floor. Pelting ice was the only sound. Frantically, Mary Alice tried to crank the dead motor. There was no traffic, but any minute someone headed home from Mickey's or another local watering hole could barrel around the curve. Her fingers fumbled the key.

She heard her father's voice telling her exactly how to start the temperamental car he'd loved so much. The engine sputtered then caught. She drove to the next road to turn around. Pausing, she petted the dog that had crawled back into the seat.

He seemed fine, but she was shaking. "A few more miles. Might as well go on, huh?"

The dog didn't look convinced.

She switched on a Memphis radio station, Roy Orbison cry-i-i-i-ing over somebody.

Going twenty, the car crept through the empty town square and eased to a stop in front of the theatre's door. With the engine quiet, the sleet ticked like nervous fingernails on the car.

Housed in a converted cotton gin, the Cana Little Theatre stood as a testament to what wealthy patrons could do for the arts. Wrapped in rosy hues, the jewel box boasted 200 seats, a fly loft, a trapped stage floor and a state-of-the-art lighting system.

"Come on Boon. Run for it."

The lab followed Mary Alice out of the car and after a quick detour through the largest puddle in the parking lot, skittered under the theatre's front overhang. He pressed his soggy fur against the glass while she found her key and unlocked the door.

A desk lamp in the box office glowed. Theatres didn't have light switches by the doors because sooner or later someone would accidentally flip on the lights during a performance and engulf Shakespeare's dark witches in hot white watts.

By the gleam of the night light, Mary Alice made her way past photos of long-ago productions: Annie Oakley astride her horse, Blanche Dubois repeating that she had always depended on the kindness of strangers, and a photo from ten years ago of Mary Alice playing a woman who had shot her husband.

She pulled aside the heavy velour drapes that covered one of the auditorium entrance doors and stepped into the dark. A stark ghost lamp, one bright incandescent bulb in a shadeless floor lamp, stood center stage. Without the amber stage lights, the auditorium felt foreign, making her a trespasser. Still shaken by the spin-out on the highway, images from *Phantom of the Opera* crowded in. A dank subterranean grotto inhabited by a scarred madman.

If her mother hadn't bitched incessantly about her inability to reach her daughter, Mary Alice would have been home watching Claudette Colbert and Joel McCrea in *The Palm Beach Story*. She felt a "Do-Mama-In" fantasy setting up. A cherished childhood ritual, the mental movies had finished off her mother, Elizabeth Tate, in dozens of satisfying ways: an avalanche of Austrian cut glass, a fall from one of the balconies of the ancestral home, a choke on cheese grits.

This time she pulled from the 1940's film. Joel McCrea was kissing Claudette Colbert. Then Claudette turned into Mother and Joel was suffocating her. His mouth clamped over hers like a Tupperware lid. Elizabeth struggled, flopped about and then lay still. Wind on the theatre glass rattled the fantasy loose.

She heard her dead father, *Honey, don't let your mama get to you. You know she means well.*

Only five months ago Mary Alice had almost been murdered, drowned in the lake. Since then Elizabeth Tate called constantly. She heard her Daddy, *the past, which can't be changed, loves to be relived in endless repetitions. If you let yourself become a victim, and most, including your mama will be happy for you to do that, you'll be as dead as if you'd been drowned.*

She straightened her back and marched forward into the gothic cavern.

Beside the seat on the aisle where she'd sat during rehearsal, she felt the floor for the missing phone. Her fingers grazed an unidentifiable gummy substance but no phone. Boon headed down the aisle toward the stage as Mary Alice returned to the box office telephone. She dialed her cell number and heard the tinny notes of Beethoven's *Ode to Joy*. Back in the auditorium she easily found the phone wedged between two seats.

"Hello?" she answered her own call. "Hello? Look if you're a prank caller you better start panting, or I'm hanging up." She closed the phone. Levity hadn't made the theatre any friendlier.

"Boon?" She heard him but couldn't see him.

The *chiaroscuro* shapes created by the scenery made her pause at the back of the theatre. Flats defined the walls, but they hadn't been painted yet, and the furniture pieces were mostly temporary. A heavy desk anchored stage left, and in a nook down right sat a daybed. Even unfinished, the set was already doing its job: forming an apparition where every night the characters' problems were analyzed and then, in some manner, solved. In the theatre King Lear and Willy Loman died, but balance was restored to the community. Here, life worked out. Always.

She saw Boon in the shadows, nudging the bed.

"No, Boon. Come on, let's get out of here."

Boon whined.

"No, no, no," she called, her voice echoing in the empty space.

In a dozen strides she was down front and up on the stage. The ankles at the foot of the bed stopped her. As she drew closer and her vision overcame the deeper darkness, she saw legs, torso, arms and head. The playwright, Jamie O'Malley, slept soundly on the rumpled bed.

Mary Alice laughed. Her friend, Kate, hadn't managed to entice the sexy guest artist after all.

"Jamie," she whispered. "Jamie?" she said louder.

He didn't move.

Before she saw it, she felt a sensation like a wash of low voltage electricity—sickeningly painful, but not incapacitating. And there was a smell, compelling because she couldn't identify it. She moved in, touched his shoulder and then saw

384

that the blue bedspread was soaked black. Dull eyes looked at her without seeing.

Her brain rejected what she saw, but a primordial response unlocked her frozen legs and forced her to back away from the bed. She barely missed stepping on the gun that rested center stage.

"Boon, come," she croaked.

The dog whined, but followed, making damp tracks across the stage.

If she left immediately, someone else could find the body. She had to get out. Her breath came fast. But what if someone has seen her car parked out front? Jamie had been shot. The police would ask why she hadn't called. How could she explain?

She edged to the front of the stage and sat down on the apron. Her arm stayed tight around her dog. Roy Orbison sang on in her head: "I was all right for a while; I could smile for a while." She felt the cell phone in her hand and pressed a pro-grammed number. Like the freezing rain that was coating the roads and power lines, fear stole over her, immobilizing her.

"Dear God in heaven, please answer." Her breath now came in sips.

Boon cranked his head around to look at the body.

"Hello." Police Detective Tom Jaworski didn't sound as if he'd been asleep. The cell phone screen said it was just after midnight.

"Tom, I need help," she whispered...